THE CRIMSON FOLD

With stories by
Teri Adkins
Susanne Saville

Paranormal Romance

New Concepts   Georgia

Be sure to check out our website for the very best in fiction at fantastic prices!

When you visit our webpage, you can:
* Read excerpts of currently available books
* View cover art of upcoming books and current releases
* Find out more about the talented artists who capture the magic of the writer's imagination on the covers
* Order books from our backlist
* Find out the latest NCP and author news--including any upcoming book signings by your favorite NCP author
* Read author bios and reviews of our books
* Get NCP submission guidelines
* And so much more!

We offer a 20% discount on all new Trade Paperback releases ordered from our website!

Be sure to visit our webpage to find the best deals in e-books and paperbacks! To find out about our new releases as soon as they are available, please be sure to sign up for our newsletter (http://www.newconceptspublishing.com/newsletter.htm) or join our reader group (http://groups.yahoo.com/group/new_concepts_pub/join)!

The newsletter is available by double opt in only and our customer information is *never* shared!

Visit our webpage at:
www.newconceptspublishing.com

The Crimson Fold is an original publication of NCP. This work has never before appeared in book form. This work is a novel. Any similarity to actual persons or events is purely coincidental.

New Concepts Publishing, Inc.
5202 Humphreys Rd.
Lake Park, GA 31636

ISBN 1-58608-841-6
© 2006 Teri Adkins & Susanne Saville
Cover art (c) copyright 2006 Eliza Black and Dan Skinner

All rights reserved, which includes the right to reproduce this book or portions thereof in any form whatsoever except as provided by the U.S. Copyright Law.

If you purchased this book without a cover you should be aware this book is stolen property.

NCP books are available at special quantity discounts for bulk purchases for sales promotions, premiums, fund raising, or educational use. For details, write, email, or phone New Concepts Publishing, Inc., 5202 Humphreys Rd., Lake Park, GA 31636; Ph. 229-257-0367, Fax 229-219-1097; orders@newconceptspublishing.com.

First NCP Trade Paperback Printing: September 2006

CRAVINGS
Teri Adkins

For my parents, for teaching me love;
My brother for teaching me laughter;
And my two sons, for teaching me true joy.
But most of all, my husband, for giving them all to me.

Chapter One

Happiness in life is not free. You pay for every minute of it. And believe me, it doesn't come cheap.

Payment comes due the instant awareness sets in. At least it did for me. I woke up one day, took a look around and thought, *Hey, life is good.*

That very night, I made my first payment.

The good news is I won't be making another. That one took care of my happiness problem. No happiness, no payment. See how well things work out?

I live in Memphis. That's Tennessee, not Egypt, although we share more than a name with our counterpart across the ocean. We have a modern day Pyramid and our own life-sustaining river. And six years ago, we discovered the West Nile Virus had arrived.

A year later, I teamed up with two doctors to study this virus and discovered more than anyone wanted to know.

Something else had arrived with the infected mosquito. Or maybe the vampires had been here all along, and we'd just never known about them.

Either way, they changed my life. That was five years ago.

My name is Lindy Campbell and I'm a vampire. Sometimes. Other times I'm human, with warm blood flowing through my veins. Makes life confusing, but there you are. Officially, I'm considered a *Vamp-hum*. Not very original but since I'm one of a

THE CRIMSON FOLD

kind they didn't know what else to call me. Mostly, I consider myself a big mess.

Since it is most inconvenient to go dead when you're least prepared for it, I've learned to always be prepared. Unprepared will get you permanently dead.

There was a time when I was completely human. When I belonged among the living. The littlest things will get you kicked out of that club. Like growing fangs. Now I live among the undead. It's not that I'm totally accepted there either. They're just a bit more forgiving of the strange and unusual.

I owe it all to Malcolm Montay. He's the bat boy who bit me.

I was down in New Orleans doing research on the Vampire community last year. My momma always told me if you go looking for trouble….

Luckily, one of the doctors from St. Frances I was working with at the time knew what to do. Doc started a blood transfusion immediately and got me to the hospital quickly. Would have worked too, if Malcolm hadn't been so old and powerful.

It cost me my job at the hospital. Can't have a vampire, even one half human, around all of the bloody patients, of course. So, I work in the Vamp community now.

The Memphis Vampire community is small time, a sort of test case for the larger cities who still deny they have any citizens who could drink their neighbors dry. The community welcomed my help. Sort of.

I was a nurse in my other life, but there wasn't much use for one among those who never die. Talk about your wasted college years. So the mayor decided--after pressure from the government--to name me the Director of the Bureau of Vampire Affairs.

We have one employee. Me. I had a choice between a dingy office in North Memphis or an office in my nineteenth century home in Midtown. It wasn't like I was ever going to use my dining room again anyway.

Basically, I do what needs to be done. I mean, not all cities cater to our undead citizens who live by the night and sleep in the day. Makes it hard to conduct business during regular working hours.

There are also the security issues to be dealt with. If you want to kill a vampire, what better time than when the sun is high?

Lately, I've been mediating between the societies. It's amazing how much the vampires and humans hate each other. I've learned from experience the hate is bred by fear. I can understand it. At times, I fear them both myself.

I haven't turned in almost a week. I know its coming and the wait is getting to me.

Usually, I look normal. Okay, a little better than normal. My hair grows quickly, I can't keep my nails trimmed, and I've never been in better shape. Must be the extra iron.

All the result of turning. Even then, I'm not the traditional vamp. Sunlight doesn't faze me. I'm a mixture of human and vampire at all times. Just like in life, I can't seem to commit.

Vampires don't kill their meals anymore. Much. Its illegal and bad publicity. Instead, we have nightly deliveries of blood, much like the milkman. They even have these nifty containers that keep it fresh and at body temperature. You'd be amazed at what humans are willing to sell for the right price, lucky for us. And blood is at a premium. The mayor also reminds his citizens on a regular basis that if the blood supply runs low, the vampires will go out searching for their own meals. Gives a whole new spin on blood drives.

Downtown Memphis belongs to the vampires. Being on the Mississippi River, humans couldn't tolerate the mosquitoes since the big invasion, so they gladly turned it over. And it is good for mosquito control. One bite of a vamp and the pesky little things drop dead. Humans couldn't be happier.

Few security measures are needed in the undead community. Vamps are vulnerable and the humans could easily slay them. What prevents it? The living sleep at night and vamps believe in revenge. You tell me, who's scarier?

Which brings me to my newest problem. Someone killed a vampire last week while he rested. Now a human has disappeared in apparent retaliation. Talk about my worst nightmare.

Everyone is putting pressure on me. The mayor suddenly remembers that I'm half human, and the vamp community now acknowledges I'm one of them.

My first course of action would normally be to meet with the head vampire. The Master. Problem is, he's the one found staked out at dawn. The city has run amuck every since. Even the undead need leadership. I have rogue vigilante groups forming on both sides and the only thing standing between them is me.

I could talk to Joe Andrews, the MPD detective heading the case, but we're kind of not speaking at the moment.

We were dating when I became *one of them*. Believe me, it's never a good idea to date your food. Joe was the appetizer, entrée and dessert all rolled into one. Not that I ever had the chance to indulge.

Funny, *'I love you no matter what'* doesn't include turning into a vampire during sex. And *'adrenaline made me do it'* doesn't help.

Joe tried, I guess. But when I couldn't promise it would never happen again, our trouble began. Then he refused to move in with me on my side of town, and I couldn't move in with him on his, so we reached a stalemate. Talk about irreconcilable differences. Geez, it wasn't as if I bit him or anything.

So that leaves me with Malcolm. As the oldest vampire left in the city, he's next in line as the head boss. Lucky me.

I'll have to talk to Joe eventually, but given a choice between the man who tried to kill me or the man who dumped me because of it, I'll take the biter any day. At least Malcolm could claim hunger. Which explains why I was on my way to see the scariest man in town.

I turned on Central Avenue and parked my car at the Castle. It had stood for over a hundred years. Built by an eccentric in the eighteen hundreds, at one time it had housed a bar, restaurant and now the master of the vampires.

It was a beautiful place--an accurate replica of a mid-size castle that could be found in Scotland. I had heard rumors the stones had been shipped from there, taken from an old keep that had fallen to ruin.

Matching round turrets stood on each end, connected by a balcony on the second floor. There was an otherworldly feel to the place, as if centuries of souls had soaked into the stone and were standing guard, protecting all who entered. Oddly enough, it was a comforting feeling.

I had dressed carefully for this meeting. It was illegal to bite a human against her will, but I wasn't sure I completely qualified. And some men broke the rules. Just in case, I took the time to cover all of the tempting points.

Black leather boots covered the ankles and stopped at my knees. Custom made 4" bracelets covered both wrists and came with a matching necklace made of platinum. It was a fashion statement all its own. Starting at the top of my neck, the tiny spider web weave spanned to the top of my shoulders. I had had it made after the reprimand from Doc when he patched me up after Malcolm bit me. Someone whose dark blue veins stood out under pale, translucent skin should not walk around looking so tempting. There are plenty of other places on a body blood could be taken, but since complete body armor was gaudy and rude, I ruled against it. No sense insulting the man I had come to question.

I walked up the stone steps and reached down deep for my courage. I don't have much, and I keep having to replenish my supply. I hoped I had enough to get me through this meeting.

The style of a vampire varies, depending on his age. I have to admit, I prefer the older ones. The tight britches, tall boots, and flowing white shirts with lace at the cuffs remind me of the historical romance novels I sometimes read. Okay--not good for my tough woman image, but I'm a romantic at heart. Not that it's doing me any good.

As my eyes gawked at the man who led me through the halls, I wondered if becoming a vampire made everyone beautiful, or if there was a rule against biting someone ugly. Of course, if you were going to be shackled to someone for eternity, which would you choose?

He smiled when he caught me staring, but for the life of me, I had never seen a red haired vampire. Curling naturally, his thick mane reached his mid back and framed his pale face. I could see him in a plaid kilt, standing formidable on a mountain looking down over the valley. He was Scottish, I just knew it. Good thing he hadn't spoken a word to me, since it would be quite embarrassing to start fawning all over the enemy. It was the accent that did it to me every time.

After leaving me alone in a room, he made his exit quietly. I knew the building had electricity, but for some reason it wasn't in use. Candelabras were strategically placed around the room and were the only source of light. It reminded me of old black and white Dracula movies. Colorizing them had ruined the eerie effect, but they still showed some of the originals. How ironic was it that I had always loved them?

The room had been decorated true to its history. Rich fabric in red and gold brocade covered the windows and settee, as well as the chairs. The antique pieces were mahogany wood and were in pristine condition. It was as if I had stepped back in time. I had to remind myself there was a room full of coffins somewhere in this place to keep the romantic in me at bay.

"Ms. Campbell, how daring of you to visit."

I hadn't heard him enter. Not very smart of me, to go off daydreaming when I'm about to meet with my worst nightmare.

I turned and faced him. I didn't flinch or run, score one for me. In truth, Malcolm was a handsome man. His face was aristocratic and caused the observer to wonder at his origins. Had he been the son of a noble in his other life? His eyes were blue and fringed with dark lashes. His hair was dark and flowed down over his shoulders. Again, the romantic in me tried to surface, but I beat her back. I may not require much in the men I date, but a heartbeat was definitely high on the list.

"Not really. I think the risks are minimal." Unless you counted the risk of heart failure from my racing heart or the increasing possibility of turning with so much adrenaline flowing through me. Turning in the presence of the vamp who bit you couldn't be a good thing, could it? Talk about losing the upper hand.

"How so?" He moved across the room to the side table.

"Well, it is illegal to bite me for starters. Not to mention that the case I'm working is high profile, making me a hot commodity. Someone would certainly miss me if I were to disappear. And you need me Malcolm, whether you're willing to admit it or not." I didn't add that no one had a clue that I was

THE CRIMSON FOLD

even here, and were I to disappear, the path would not lead to Malcolm's door. I'd make certain the next time it did.

"Ah, interesting. So you feel you are safe with me?" He filled a silver goblet with deep red liquid, held it up in a silent offer. I shook my head. It wasn't wine he was offering.

He reminded me of a cat playing with his food. I wasn't sure if he thought of me as the main course or dessert. "You won't kill me, so don't toy with me Malcolm. Two men have already been killed."

"You could be right. I will not kill you, as you say." He sipped his drink, savoring it. "However, not for the reason you think. There has been only one death. Surgis. The human that was taken still lives."

My body silently did a little thank you dance, but outwardly, I was the epitome of calm. It would seem callous of me to gloat. Still, it would make my life so much easier if the vamps hadn't killed yet.

"How do you know?"

His raised brow told me clearly he found the question amusing. Glad I could oblige.

"The human taken is not worthy. Surgis was master among us. He had lived for centuries and was an honorable man. The human that was taken is beneath him." Could there be such a thing as an honorable vampire? I doubted it but didn't bother to argue the point. Maybe his ideas and mine were different.

"Okay. So why take him?" He raised the goblet to his lips slowly. I wished he would just drink it and be done with it. It was beginning to look a little too good to me.

"I said they have not killed him. I did not say they would not."

"Where is he, and how do I get him back?"

"It is not so easy."

Nothing ever is. "Look, the last thing any of us want right now is a war. We need to work together to stop this thing before someone else is harmed. And we have to figure out how to protect everyone until we end this."

"I agree we need to take precautions to ensure the safety of our own. I am not concerned with providing the same to the humans."

Okay, that made sense. But what I was about to suggest didn't. "Protecting them is protecting us."

"Us? Are you one of us, Lucinda?"

Since I still haven't figured out what I am, I ignored the question.

"Guarding against a daytime attack will be complicated, if not impossible. We can't stand guard during the day. And the humans will need to stand guard at night. Inconvenient, but possible. I have a plan that will benefit all."

"Continue." Finished with his nightly snack, he crossed to the chair in front of me. No man should move that gracefully. I preferred him at a much larger distance. Vampires move at breakneck speed, so the distance would only be an illusion of safety. I'd take what I could get.

"Well, it's simple really. We have the humans protect us during the day, and we protect them during the night."

"You would have our enemies guard us while we sleep?" The humor in his voice told me clearly what he thought of my plan.

"We're not all your enemies. Some of us have honor as well. There are those among us who can be trusted, just as there are those among you." I was not going to get into a debate about trust with someone who didn't bother asking permission before draining you dry.

"So, you stand with the humans once again. You jump sides easily, Lucinda."

"I have no side, Malcolm. You saw to that." Probably not a good idea to bring up unpleasantness when I wanted something from him. Nor to remind him of his failure in turning me.

"I would have welcomed you as one of us. You chose against it. I am not responsible for the dilemma you face." He steepled his long fingers in front of his face, bracing his elbows on the arms of the chair.

"Aren't you? I didn't ask to become a vampire."

"If I am responsible for your unhappiness, I can certainly rectify it. I can turn you Lucinda, you've only to ask. I will give you a side in this battle." His eyes took on that glassy hue of shadows and fog. The look that hid centuries of secrets, lifetimes of things seen and done so horrible that most humans would never believe them. I wasn't one of them. I had seen some of those nightmares first hand.

"No thanks." I moved to the edge of the seat, ready to bolt if the need showed itself.

"Very well. I will not force you." His eyes cleared and my stance relaxed.

"Why?" I know, I should just be grateful. But I don't trust unexpected gifts. Given the opportunity, Malcolm would force his will on anyone to get his way. "You said earlier you would not kill me for your own reasons. What are they?"

"Why would I remove from the world something I enjoy? Until I cease to enjoy your existence, you are safe."

Oh, yeah. "You tried to change me once. How can I believe you won't try again?"

"You are a worthy adversary. It is rare in a woman. You have been offered a gift--to be part of two worlds. I find that interesting and possibly beneficial to me at some point. We have a connection that can only be broken through death. I will not deny that I want you by my side. However, you have earned the right to choose. That is why I will not turn you completely against your will. You will come to me, but of your own accord."

Wanna bet? A vampire is a dangerous creature. But that creature was once a man. And this man came from an era when honor meant everything. I trusted him not to kill me. At least not yet. How stupid is that? What was even scarier, I felt something intriguing about his words. His body called to mine. Whether it was the adrenaline or his blood in my veins I didn't know. But I knew I would turn soon, and I didn't want to be anywhere near him when it happened.

I crave two things when I go dead. Blood and sex. I'm not picky, any order will do. Give me a quart of blood, a good vibrator, and locked inside my apartment I can calm the beast enough to survive. It was like eating fat-free cookies instead of Oreos. It satisfied the hunger but not the craving. Instinctively, I knew if Malcolm was around me there would be no taming, no settling of the beast. I'd want the damn Oreo.

"Give some thought to my words, Malcolm. I'll speak with the living"--I needed that distinction to remind myself that giving in to lust would get me undead--"and let you know of their decision."

I left on that note. Got out of there as quickly as I could without actually running.

On my way home, I made my weekly stop by Doc's house for my contribution to science. I'm the perfect specimen. Doc would love to dissect me, but we compromise and I give him blood instead.

He's trying to define the cause for my cell regeneration. If he can do this, it would be a real breakthrough. Cancer could be eradicated. Many illnesses would be a thing of the past. It's worth a needle prick to me.

Lately my life seems to revolve around blood. Pulling it out or pouring it in. I made my donation and left quickly. I was not in the mood for questions, and Doc always had plenty.

I decided to skip my talk with Joe for the night. I didn't need the stress, and the threat of turning was enough of a scare to have me postponing until tomorrow. I went home and dropped into bed. Working both the night and day shift is rough. I try to make it to bed by two a.m. and rise by ten.

Ten o'clock comes early when you've had little sleep. I slapped the alarm, then showered and dressed carefully. Unlike last night with Malcolm, I wanted to attract attention today. My ego demanded it with Joe.

I wanted to look good. Shoot, I wanted to look better than good. I wanted to give him a few sleepless nights, thinking about what he had given up. Pathetic, I know, and probably it would never happen.

I had just the little black skirt to do it. I even wore heels to showcase my long legs. What was the risk of a turned ankle when compared to making an ex regretful? Joe had always had a thing for my legs. I added a white blouse and short jacket then glanced in the mirror. I looked like a sexy businesswoman. He would never know he was being set up.

Chapter Two

I had gotten to know the men at his precinct while Joe and I were dating and most of them still treated me the same. Guess they had seen bigger monsters than me. I stopped at a few of their desks, making small talk and just catching up. I was stalling, working up the nerve before I walked into Joe's office.

I didn't bother to call first. I didn't want to give Joe the chance to refuse to see me. So when I walked into his office unannounced, his surprise was genuine.

"Hello, Joe." My voice was low, seductive, but he didn't know it was from nerves.

"Lindy." He stood. "I wasn't expecting you."

"I'm sure." He looked good, damn it. It wasn't fair that he should look so good to me after he'd broken my heart. All of the time I had spent cursing his soul to hell should have done something, if only in my mind.

"You're looking good, Lindy." He walked around his desk, stopped at the corner while I crossed to him.

"Yeah, dying agreed with me." Low blow, I know. Maybe I still had just a little resentment going on. The way he was filling out those jeans wasn't making it go away. His hair was dark chocolate and a little longer than he usually wore it. I could tell his fingers had made several trips through it already. That little habit of his had always given him that just out of bed look. Unfortunately, it had always been one of my favorite looks. Getting it that way had always appealed to me even more.

His hand on my shoulder guided me to the visitor's chair. Even through the layers of cloth, I could feel the heat, the strength of those fingers. Joe wasn't a stranger to hard work, and all of that manual labor had built up calluses on his hands. Those rough patches of skin had burned a trail across my body on too many occasions.

"Have a seat. Can I get you anything?"

Oh, yes. A quick round of sex, please. Joe still had a body that sent me on red alert. And it had been a while for me. Okay, a long while. Like, since Joe. I needed sex in the worst way. For someone who craved it as much as I did, I sure wasn't getting any.

THE CRIMSON FOLD

"I'm here about Surgis and the man who has gone missing." Pull your mind from the gutter and back on business, I chided myself. There were better times to lust over Joe's body. Like when I was alone in my bedroom, the last place he'd be.

"Larry Brown. Do you know where he is?"

"No." I knew wherever he was, it was likely a vampire was holding him there. Maybe more than one. Memphis might be a big city, but it had a small town feel about it. And gossip ran wild in small towns. Word on the streets was we had the makings of an all out race war.

Joe moved back around to his own seat, and I sat down. I could feel my skirt riding up an inch or two. When his eyes lowered and watched the movement, I bit back a grin. Maybe I wasn't the only one feeling the heat here. Not that it was going to do either of us any good. Getting all worked up with no way to relieve it was pointless.

"Stay out of it, Lindy. It's a police matter." His eyes were back on mine and all cop. I have a thing for those stormy, gray eyes of his. When he's fully aroused, those eyes darken like the sky before the rain. Long, dark lashes frame them to perfection. Laugh lines fanned out from them, but the recent addition of lines on his forehead gave me the impression he was doing a lot more frowning these days. I didn't want that to be true. My Joe-- the old Joe--had always had laughter lurking just below the surface. He broke eye contact first.

"You know I can't do that."

"Can't or won't?" he asked.

"The mayor has already contacted me. Can't."

"That's right, you've got yourself a big job these days, taking care of the dregs of the city. How's that working out for you?"

I wouldn't let his words hurt me. Not again. I could be as flippant as him. "You know, the job opportunities for someone like me are endless, but this one is working out great. At least I know where I stand with everyone I deal with. And look how important I am. The mayor calls me daily." Usually when he needed a good ass to chew on, but hey, at least he knows my number.

I could feel Joe's eyes drilling into me as if he were trying to solve some great puzzle. Most likely, wondering what he ever saw in me.

"Fine. Tell me what you know." Guess he had found his answers. I leaned back, ready to play the game. But I wasn't going to be the only one offering up information. I was going to get as good as I gave.

"We'll play show me yours and I'll show you mine." My face burned as the meaning sunk in. Flirting with Joe was not only stupid, it was nonproductive. Sort of like getting all dressed up for a date, only to end up watching the late show alone. Too late to take it back.

"We've already played that game, Lindy." His deep southern drawl dug up memories I'd rather forget. That same voice had whispered words of love and magic as he had slid into me, as I had closed tightly around him. Words he hadn't meant.

"We share information. Tell me what you have and I'll do the same."

He leaned back in his chair, those gray eyes studying me a little too deeply. "Have dinner with me."

Okay, that caught me off guard, since an invitation was the last thing I had been expecting from him. I also wasn't expecting the way my heart skipped, then doubled its beat. My body was such a traitor. Look how quickly it just forgot all of those long nights shoveling in chocolate chip ice cream with crushed Oreo's on top and the exhausting exercise regiment we'd suffered through to pay for it. All in the guise of getting over Joe. It had finally worked too.

"What you mean is sex." I kept my voice level.

He shrugged casually as if it were my call. "If you'd prefer."

Oh yes, I would definitely prefer. He grinned that sexy little grin that was half boy, half man. And all charm. Damn him, I wanted to say yes.

"You know it wouldn't go anywhere. There's too much standing between us." An entire race, to be exact.

"I miss you, Lindy. Its just dinner." His face sobered just enough to cause me doubt. We both knew it would end in bed. But unlike Joe, I also knew that since I was overdue turning, my dinner could consist of a warm glass of O positive. I didn't think he would sit across from me, calmly eating his steak, while I drank it down.

"I'm sorry, Joe." More sorry for me than him. After all, this split had been his idea. I'd simply been living in my own fantasy world. The one where love really did conquer all.

"So am I. Where does that leave us?" He leaned back in his chair, and ran his hands through his hair.

"Working together on this case. I believe this Larry Brown may still be alive." I would start giving information first if it meant changing the subject. I'd do just about anything at this point to change the subject. I just couldn't start thinking about Joe in a good light. Not yet. I was still too vulnerable to him. My heart just couldn't take another pounding from him.

"You know that's unlikely." He raised his brow. Only one. Just like Rhett Butler. Why was that so sexy? And why was my mind locked on sex when I had real problems, life and death problems, to contend with? I swore I'd pull double duty with the vibrator tonight if I could just get my mind back to murder.

"What do you know about him?"

"Average, middle-aged guy. Works as a security guard, struggles to pay the mortgage and smokes two packs a day. The guy next door."

"Not prime material as a blood bank."

"No. I would imagine most bloodsuckers would prefer a healthier snack."

"I spoke to Malcolm Montay. He has just taken over as the Master." Let's see how he liked that little bomb.

"You two are friends." He shook his head and snorted. "Why does that not surprise me?"

I ignored the statement. Why was it that everyone assumed that just because they shared the same parasites, all vampires were friends? Most vamps were loners, truth be told. But fighting with Joe would get us nowhere. The only place I wanted to be right now was away from him. I'd had enough walks down memory lane.

"Malcolm said Brown was unworthy of Surgis' death."

That got his attention. Joe the cop was back. I could deal with him much better than Joe the man, Joe the stormy eyed ex-lover.

"Where would they keep him?" He leaned over his desk, braced his arms on it.

"I don't know, and Malcolm swears he doesn't either."

"We need to find him if we're going to prevent all-out war."

"I know. I've suggested to Malcolm extra security be added to both sides."

"Couldn't hurt." He nodded.

"Glad you agree. The problem is daylight guards are hard to find in the vampire community. I suggested both sides work together to protect each other."

Normally I love Joe's laugh. Deep and warm, straight up from the chest. Not today. Today it set my nerves on end.

"And what did old Malcolm think of that idea?" He rocked back in his chair again.

"Same as you, apparently. It could work, damn it. If we used men we could trust, we could end this thing before it goes too far."

He sobered. "What happens when someone gets through the guards and kills one of them? Do you honestly believe they wouldn't swear that we had allowed the breach on purpose?"

Okay, so the idea had a few kinks. Nothing that couldn't be worked out.

"Each side would have to trust the other." I knew it could work. If everyone would stop being stubborn about it and gave it a chance, I knew it would be the perfect solution. Either way, it was the only one I could come up with.

"Poor Lindy. Still trying to make us all one big happy family?"

I stiffened. I don't do pity well. Giving or receiving. "If you have a better idea, then let's hear it."

Joe hated vampires. One had killed his partner before the no biting law had been passed. Joe blamed himself. Not because it was his fault, but because Tom had had a wife, kids. Joe had been single. He should have been the one to go down, hear him tell. Survivor's guilt. Joe had it in gallons.

Joe had killed the one responsible but his hate had lived on. And I had become one of them. He had every right to be bitter. Then, so did I. If I could deal with it, then I felt he should too. Maybe I'm asking too much, but I didn't think so.

"We can guard ourselves, so why do we need the vampires? We don't combust under the sun," Joe added sarcastically.

"Yes, but they can't protect themselves sufficiently without human intervention. Where else are they going to find men who won't hesitate to let them get killed? You're policemen, sworn to protect all citizens. The only way they're going to agree is if both sides are vulnerable to each other." I waited. "You know it could work."

"Or it could blow up in our faces. Did Malcolm agree?"

I shifted in the chair. I had been expecting the question and would have liked to say yes, but Joe would know if I was not straight with him. "Not yet, but he will. He's smart enough to know there aren't any better options."

"Let me check out a few things, give it some thought. Set up a meeting with Malcolm for me. If I decide to do this, I want to meet with the man--creature--face to face."

Joe calling Malcolm a creature didn't offend me. After all, I had called him much worse since the night I'd met him, standing in an alley a few streets from Bourbon. And I didn't relate the monster calling to me. I might be one now, but I still feel like me so it's hard to relate.

I nodded and got to my feet. The quicker I escaped the office the better off we would both be.

He walked around his desk, crossed the room and caught me just before I twisted the knob. He was too close. The scent of fresh air, of Joe, filled my senses. I had always loved the way he smelled, the way he took over a room. I had felt safe tucked beside his six three frame, with his hand on the small of my back. But he hadn't been able to protect me from my own stupidity--walking into danger and being bitten. He hadn't been able to shield me from the worst hurt of all. His rejection.

I felt his arms around me, drawing me into the safe net again. I closed my eyes and for a moment let it surround me. How long had it been since I had felt so cherished? The answer came quickly, the last time Joe had held me.

His lips found mine, allowing all of the pent-up frustrations to flow from his lips. I met it with my own. I could say yes and spend the night in his arms. Feel him drive into me, joining our souls. I had never wanted anything more in my life. But

THE CRIMSON FOLD

tomorrow he wouldn't be able to stay. When I turned--and I would--he'd say goodbye again. Just as he had done the last time he had held me. I couldn't go through that again. I pushed against his chest. The light pressure stopped him. My strength could have pushed him across the room and we both knew it. But it would never be needed with Joe.

He released me and I walked out of the room. Out of the building. Out of Joe's life.

I walked down Front Street feeling sorry for myself. I wasn't proud of it, but at least I could admit it. I had always hated it when people whined over the roads their lives had taken. As if they had no control over it. Turn off, I used to say with such arrogance. And here I was, doing that very thing. But for the life of me, I couldn't find anywhere to turn.

My life wasn't what I'd dreamed it would be. Okay. Whose was? How bad was it? I was a vampire. Well, only half. Better than 100%. See, I could be positive. I missed Joe. There was the real problem. Couldn't do anything about that one.

I love the sunshine. I wasn't banished to night yet, but it didn't seem to matter. Joe and I used to spend hours riding through the hills behind his house. His horses now shied away from me. I didn't want to be different. I wanted my life back.

It was dark by the time I reached my apartment. I'd regrouped by shopping. I had sexy underwear, a sleek black dress, and new heels. My problems weren't solved but I felt better equipped to deal with them.

Until I found Malcolm standing in my living room.

"Fantastic view." He didn't turn from the picture window that overlooked the garden.

"Glad you're enjoying it. I thought you guys had to be invited in before you could enter." I slammed the door, since holding it open wasn't going to get him to leave any quicker. We both knew he wasn't going anywhere until he was ready.

"But you forget you are mine." His voice danced over my skin, and I reminded myself it was not real.

"Half." And that was half too much. It galled me to have to admit to even that much. But had he turned me completely, he would have been my master. Half was definitely better than that option.

"Enough to gain my entrance."

Was that a smirk on his face? Did vampires smirk?

"Figures." Wasn't my luck improving? Just what I wanted, the head vamp coming and going as he pleased.

"Try it on."

"What?" I stiffened. He turned to smile at me.

"The black dress in the bag." He nodded to the bag I was holding.

"Don't do that, it creeps me out." The shudder down my spine proved it. It wasn't that he was reading my mind. Truthfully, I didn't know what it was. He was ancient, and the older vampires just seemed to have the power to know things.

"As you wish. I'll wait while you change."

Did he know I hadn't turned in a week? Could he smell the need on my skin? No, he'd been talking about the dress. Get a grip, girl. "I'll pass. What is it you want Malcolm?"

"Business, of course." He strolled across my living room as if he belonged there. But he didn't. He had taken enough from me. I wasn't about to give him more.

"Joe Andrews, the detective in charge, wants to meet with you." I dropped the sacks on the table and moved into the room. I didn't have a lot of choice, since it was my place.

"Did he find the idea amusing?" His eyes were on me, staring too deeply. What other allowances did our shared blood bring? There should be a manual somewhere. Maybe I'd write one. Secrets to vampirism.

"Will you meet him?" I asked.

"He is your lover, is he not?" Malcolm slid gracefully onto the couch and motioned me over. Spider to the fly.

"Ex. And that's none of your business." I leaned against the back of the chair.

"Everything that concerns you is my business, Lucinda."

"How do you know about me and Joe?" I didn't really want to know, but if I planned to sleep at all tonight, I needed the answer.

"I shared your memories when I drank from you. Your blood, your very essence is such sweet nectar. There will be a time when I drink my fill. You can deny what is between us, but that will not change it."

"The only thing between us is a small percentage of blood cells." I said it as if it was nothing, as if it didn't creep me out. Just thinking about part of him inside me was more than I could take. Best not to dwell on it. The straight jackets came in my size.

"The strongest bond there is."

No, love was. But I didn't argue the details. Even love, I'd learned, had breaking points.

"Will you meet with Joe or not?" My patience was growing thin. I was the victim of a robbery, still facing the thief who had stolen my blood, my memories, and Joe. That last one really made me cranky.

"Yes. You'll wear the black dress. As well as the feminine under-things in the bag," he added with a grin that seemed to say he had won and he knew it.

"Like hell I will." I jerked upright.

"Your choice, as in all things." His smile didn't fool me.

"I'll call Joe, see if he can arrange to meet tonight." I moved toward the phone.

"As my choice is to not meet with your ex-lover without you by my side."

"I'll be there." I had to. This was my little red wagon, after all.

"Wearing appropriate attire as befits my escort. The dress."

"Men are bastards, dead or alive," I muttered, and then cursed when he laughed.

* * * *

The meeting was set for midnight at the castle. Malcolm was flamboyant but no one could argue his style.

I wore the black dress and had to admit I looked good in it. I liked to think it was my own idea, but I knew better. Easier to have Malcolm on my good side, if such a thing is possible.

Joe arrived ten minutes early. Always on time, that's my Joe. Just having him in the room made me feel better. Which is crazy, since I would do better in a fight here than he would.

I felt his eyes scan me slowly and wondered what was behind his scowl. I had brushed my black hair until it shined, then pulled it up. The ringlets of curls that brushed my shoulders were a romantic whim.

I had had Joe in mind when I had picked out the dress and wondered if he approved. The material of the full skirt danced around my ankles, the sleeves of lace ended in a V at my wrists. The front was form fitting, showing my figure without losing modesty. I had applied my makeup to complement my midnight eyes. I looked good, damn it, and resented the lack of appreciation from Joe. It never dawned on me his scowl might be for the cozy setting he'd walked into.

Refreshments were offered, but Joe accepted only coffee. My stomach was too jumpy for anything. The crystal decanter with its thick burgundy liquid was starting to look too tempting to me, and I figured I would turn before the dawn broke. Great. I just wanted to get away from this place before it happened.

I had spent too much time in Malcolm's company. His blood called to mine--or rather to that part of me I had gained from him. It was too strong to fight.

It seemed to grow worse with nearness, so I stood and moved to the fireplace, putting distance between us. I felt my blood began to warm again.

Since this was my idea, I assumed it was my show.

"We're here to discuss details of a joint security task force."

"I didn't realize all parties had agreed," Joe said, turning his eyes to Malcolm in question.

"Everyone is here. I assume that to mean we are all in accord," Malcolm replied.

"I'm not convinced this is a good idea," Joe said, and I fought the urge to strangle him.

"Nor am I," Malcolm agreed.

"Then we're wasting our time. I'll let myself out." I was tired of their game. It was like having two bulldogs fighting over the same bitch in heat. And I so did not like *that* analogy.

"Are you always the impatient one?" Malcolm stood to block my exit. I walked around his tall form.

"Yes." Joe tried to hide his smile behind his cup, but Malcolm didn't miss a thing.

"That's right, you two are...were intimately acquainted." Malcolm knew where to throw the darts.

Joe's smile fell. I wanted to tell him I hadn't divulged that information, but I didn't. I could see it didn't matter.

"That business has no place here. If you want to talk about security, I'm listening." Joe slid his cup onto the small table.

"I assume you would be in charge of the living's security over us," Malcolm started.

Joe nodded.

"And I would be over yours?"

"Seems fair." Joe's eyes never left Malcolm. If these two were going to be in charge, the plan was doomed. The lack of trust between them was too obvious.

"Then Lucinda would coordinate the operation."

"I don't want her anywhere near this." Joe was still ignoring the fact that I was even in the room. Talk about childish.

"I work security all of the time, Joe."

"Not this time," he snapped. Improvement. He might not see me, but at least he was hearing me.

"My agreement is based on Lucinda's involvement. I trust her. I do not, however, trust you." My biggest enemy in the world was defending me to Joe.

"The Memphis Police department will provide the security for everyone. I don't need your involvement."

"No. One side cannot control this. There must be a level of vulnerability. Why would we put ourselves at your mercy?" Malcolm added angrily.

"Look children. It needs to be coordinated through my office, and you both know it. I'm the impartial party. And I'm the one who can speak for everyone without daylight restrictions."

"Choose your men. I want to have a meeting with all involved. I don't want any misunderstandings." Joe stood. "I'll take you home." Oh, sure, *now* he decided to look directly at me.

"I will see to Lucinda's return."

"I said I would take her home. I want to make sure she reaches it safely." Joe was holding his temper, but I could tell the hold was precarious.

"Do you doubt my ability to protect her? If so, how do you expect me to protect you?" Malcolm's voice was condescending.

"Let's get one thing straight." I walked in between them. "I don't need anyone protecting me." I turned to Malcolm. "Especially you."

I had had enough. I picked up my purse and made it to the door before either of them noticed. They weren't trying to protect me, but their own egos.

"Where in the hell do you think you're going?" Joe's demand didn't slow me, much.

"Home. The same way I got here, in my own car. I don't need two oversized egos fighting over who gets to protect the little woman." I heard Joe's curses as he followed me out.

"I'll follow you home."

"Suit yourself." I watched his eyes fall back to the castle.

"So you're with him now." Was that regret in his voice? I almost wished it was. I might even have cared if he hadn't just insulted me. How could a man who knew everything about me, a man I had slept beside every night for two years, actually think I would get involved with Malcolm? If that didn't just tell me how hopeless a relationship between us was.

"No. I'm not with anybody. And it wouldn't be your concern if I was."

"There's something between you. I felt it. He wants you." I cared about Joe, always would. The weariness in his voice softened me. He had a tendency to throw himself into a case, even to the extent of forgetting to take proper care of himself. Was there someone to make sure he ate when he should, sleep when he needed it? I hoped he had that, yet couldn't stand the thought of another woman in his life--caring about him, being cared about by him.

"He wants my blood," I corrected. There was nothing to gain from discussing this tonight. Like Joe, I was bone tired.

"Its illegal to bite you." It was a statement only a cop would make. As if because it was law, it was as good as done.

"Didn't stop him before." I made it to my car, but his hand on my arm stopped me. I turned back to look at him. Moonlight couldn't soften the tightness around his mouth.

"He's the one?" The anger in his voice stopped any smart remark I might have made. He really didn't know. And how could he? I had never told him.

"Who turned me? Yeah." I sighed, and rubbed at the ache forming behind my temples. You would think since I was capable of self-healing, I would not have to deal with headaches anymore. The problem was, in my human form I wasn't able to heal even the smallest of injuries. And pain relievers had little effect on me. "What you feel between us is my intense dislike for him and his frustration over failing to turn me." I didn't want to use the word hate. If Joe and Malcolm were going to work together, I didn't need to create more animosity between them.

But it was only fair that Joe know the score. Or at least all of the players.

"He wanted to kill you." He grabbed my other arm, turned me to him. His hands bit into my arms, not painfully, but forcefully enough.

"No. He wanted to turn me. And he considers the job unfinished."

"He's dangerous. I want you to stay away from him." He pulled me close, too close. His scent filled my head, went straight to my need for him. There is nothing like the smell of Joe. Woodsy, fresh and all male.

"He can't take the risk of biting me again."

"If he touches you, I'll kill him. I might kill him anyway for what he has already done." His hold tightened, but with my newfound strength, I could handle it. Even if I did have bruises tomorrow to show for it.

"It would be murder. He's not worth it. We can't undo what he's done. And I can protect myself from him." I hoped. "He can't finish the job unless I agree." I was reasonably sure of that.

"How in the hell do you expect me to work with him, knowing he's the one who did this to you?" He leaned his forehead against mine. His breath was hot on my skin. "God, Lindy, how can you stand to let him near you?"

I tried to pull away, but he held tightly. I pulled my head back.

"I can separate personal from business. I don't have a choice. People are dying. More will, if we don't stop this."

"It's my job, let me handle it."

"That's just it, it's my job too."

"Tracking down killers is for the police. You are a liaison for the vampires, not their damn personal police force."

"I'm not chasing down killers. I'm standing on the fence, trying like hell to help both sides find the answers we all need."

Joe reached out and tucked a stray curl behind my ear. Goosebumps ran up my arm when I saw his eyes soften. There had been a time when I would have given anything to have Joe look at me with those eyes. But not anymore. I was smarter than that. And if I could convince myself it was the truth, maybe I could finally get over the man.

"Would you allow him to touch you?"

"I've got enough vamp in me as it is. I don't want more."

"But his blood flows in you. There's a connection between you two, even if it's one you would rather deny." I didn't understand the anger that filled his voice. If he could even ask such a thing, it only explained why our relationship was done and over. If anyone should be angry, it was me.

"Yeah, there's a connection. It doesn't mean anything. After all, we had one once." I waited for him to speak, but no words came. "Goodnight, Joe." I pulled away and he let me go.

I saw his headlights drive away after I pulled into my drive. It would have been easy to invite him in and fall into his arms. I wanted him, more than I cared to admit. I had always felt lovable in those strong arms, had believed they would be there to hold me forever. I should have known from experience that love never lasted.

I never knew my father. And I hadn't been enough to keep my mother clean and sober. She died when I was twelve and the state sent me to live at St. Peter's orphanage. I had thought the only place they existed were in old movies until that day. But the nuns had been good to me, and I had eventually made some friends.

But I had never felt loved until Joe. That he could throw something so special away so easily had torn me apart. Sure, I still loved him. Enough to invite him in to stay. Even if I wasn't afraid he'd refuse, I wouldn't. It was over for Joe and me. It had died with the other half of me that night in the Big Easy.

I washed my face, pulled on my worn flannel gown, and crawled into bed.

Chapter Three

I opened my eyes and knew the moment Malcolm's blood flowing in me had won the fight against my own. My body felt cool, sensitive. His blood brought a chill to mine, even on the warmest of nights. The air from the ceiling fan brought a tingle to my skin. No matter how many times I turn, it always amazes me that my own body can feel so alive. As if all the nerve endings are exposed. The slightest brush of wind, the faintest scent comes alive.

Which explains my obsession with sex at times like this. The dream I'd been having about Joe had brought about my turning, but my turning wanted to make that dream a reality. I could get myself in real trouble.

I was restored, rested after only two hours of sleep, but the night called to me like a long-lost lover. Like Joe. I sauntered from my bed, stripped off my gown, and stepped into the shower. I loved the feel of water cascading down my body. Each cool drop pulsated against my skin, tingling energy. I pulled the black dress I had left draped over the foot of my bed over my head and reveled in the caress it gave my body as it slid into place. I wanted the feel of the cloth against my skin, a sensual caress with each movement.

I brushed my hair into a shimmer of night and applied mascara to eyes that glowed a hint of red back at me in the mirror.

I didn't have a destination in mind, but it mattered little. The vampire in me needed the night surrounding me as desperately as my human side needed air.

Doc says everything has a scientific explanation. A virus creates vampires. The virus is passed one of two ways. Drinking their blood is a surefire way. But that seems to be asking for all kinds of trouble anyway.

The second way is a bit more complicated. When vampires bite, they immediately deaden the bite with a chemical, a natural painkiller of sorts. This is pumped into the victim through a cavity in the fang. Makes the experience more pleasant for the victim, and the fight a lot less.

Once the area is numb, the vamp can drink his fill. Unfortunately, the fluid also contains the virus. Normally one bite does not provide enough of the virus to cause a change. Hence, the three bite rule. You must be bitten three times before you can turn. This provides enough of the virus in the blood stream to mutate the cells. Doesn't explain what happened to me. One bite--and I did not drink his blood. I would have remembered that.

Vampires don't hypnotize. Sure, they can blur the memory a bit and command with their voice, but it's not the same as hypnotizing. But then, they don't have to. Vampires are gorgeous. If you were going to spend an eternity looking at someone, wouldn't you pick perfection? Again, doesn't explain me, but who can?

As for the rest, it gets a little strange. Doc tries to come up with answers where sometimes there just aren't any.

Me? Well, I don't like the mystical, scary stuff that can't be explained, so I deny it.

Like the fact that my cravings are increasing. More often and more intense. The virus is growing. Simple. So why does it flare up when Malcolm is around? Blood can't really call to blood, can it?

I looked up and found myself standing in front of the only place open I'd be welcomed at this hour.

The Cave was more than a bar. Owned by vampires, it was the only place in town that catered to the desires of the undead. Blood was offered by type, fresh or aged. The problem with my unpredictable turning, it makes blood delivery nearly impossible. I can't predict when I might need it, and the waste of such a needed thing prevents me from having it delivered nightly. There is a shelf life. So, I have to find it when I turn. The Cave is an easy solution, and they know me there. How sad is that?

The music ranged from smoky blues to ear-popping rock. Tonight, luck was with me. Soul was on the menu. As I let the sound of Otis Redding ease through me, I made my way to the bar. The place was crowded.

What went on here was between consenting adults and stayed within the walls. There was a room for every fantasy. Though vamps could ease their hunger with readily available blood, nothing could quench their thirst for feeding. Sometimes fangs just need to sink into flesh.

Biting humans was legal if consenting, and this was the place to find them. It amazed me what kinky little oddities some humans leaned toward. There was also the option of other vampires. It was a rush between trusting vamps, sometimes exchanging powers in the process. And the blood from another vampire gave extra strength.

I guess the risk added to the fulfillment. A vamp could drain another dry, and until the blood was replenished, it was agony. Didn't sound like fun to me, but what did I know?

Heads turned my way as I drank my first glass. They could smell me. Going dead wasn't the same for me as it was for them. Doc had explained my body went into a sort of hibernation mode. My temperature dropped down to the forties and to a vamp that was warm. My heart and other organs just took a sort of rest, but didn't cease altogether. By human standards, I was dead. To vamps, I was alive. This made me not only a meal, but also a legal one. Not a safe place to be in a bar surrounded by hungry feeders, but I still had to consent. And they all knew that wasn't going to happen. It wasn't the first time I had stumbled in here after midnight trying to ease a craving I couldn't name.

I knew the moment Malcolm approached me that he was near. I turned and found my hand clasped in his. I followed him to his private table in back.

After the fate of the last master, Malcolm kept guards. I slid into the bench across from him without words.

He caressed the inside of my wrist, making my blood pump faster. I knew he noticed the veins at my neck. "Come upstairs with me, Lucinda. I can ease that pain."

He knew I had a need so deep it hurt. "No."

"It would be good between us." I felt my pulse race. It would be good, but the cost would be too high.

"I'm afraid." I found it odd that I had spoken the truth so easily. I mean, admitting your weakness to someone looking for one can't be a smart move.

"I would not harm you." No, I wouldn't feel a thing as he drained the life out of me.

"It's not the pain I fear." Not that pain was something I enjoyed. It just wasn't a big factor for me now that I knew it couldn't kill me.

"Then what keeps you from your greatest desire?"

"Devouring myself." I could easily give in to the burning need and follow Malcolm upstairs. He could assuage every desire I felt tonight. But tomorrow when I woke, who would I be? What my vampire needed was not what the woman in me needed. If I gave into it now, I was afraid the Lindy I knew would no longer exist.

"We were meant to be one." I just couldn't believe my fate could suck that badly.

"No." I shouldn't have come. The temptation was too great. It had been too long this time. And now that I wasn't with Joe, the need for sexual release was with me even when I was in human form. I would find someone for a one-night stand if I thought it would help, but I knew it wouldn't.

I didn't need the physical act half as much as I need the emotional one. And the only one I wanted was Joe.

I stood and fled like a frightened child who'd just found the monster under the cover. But I couldn't outrun this monster. It was in me.

I don't know how long I walked the city, fought the demons inside me. Nothing would ease the pain, the need. Defeated, I stood before the wooden door and knocked. When Joe answered, he wore nothing but his hastily adorned pants and that sleep-filled sexy look in his eyes. I couldn't have turned away if I'd wanted to. His chest was bare. I drank in the mound of muscle on his arms, across his massive chest. The cut of his waist disappeared inside well-worn jeans. The top two buttons were open. Good lord. Even his feet were bare.

The punch of need hit me hard, nearly knocked me to my knees. Not a bad position to be in, if I'm in front of Joe.

My eyes dropped to his crotch, and I knew two things from the bulge. He wanted me as much as I wanted him, and he hadn't bothered to put on his briefs. I licked my lips and my mouth watered.

"I need you," I whispered, defeated. All of the fight in me was gone. It had been too long between turnings, too much time spent in Malcolm's presence. And too long without Joe.

He didn't say a word. He knew instinctively what I needed. He picked me up and carried me to his bed. It was the bed we had once shared together.

Our clothes were shed in record time. I knew his need was as desperate as mine. Nothing mattered, not the wide expanse of the world that was keeping us apart, not the angry words spoken at the end. Nothing but his hands on my skin, my hands on his.

My skin tingled, the nerves beneath jumped as he trailed his hands over my breast. Tiny flames leapt when he lowered his head and swirled his tongue around my nipple. When he took it in his mouth, I cried out from the pain of needing him so deeply.

Even before I had turned vampire, Joe had been able to play my body with just the right stroke.

He bit the hard peak, then soothed the ache with his tongue. He started to suck, gently at first, then increasing the pull until I started to beg. He knew that was the one thing that drove me to madness. No one would ever understand my needs like him.

We danced as one, our steps perfected from practice together. His hand stroked my hip, ran up my spine.

My body begged, matched my words as I pleaded for him to end the torture. Joe entered me in one hard stroke. I needed that, the wild abandon. Like two primitive animals fighting for nature's way.

There was nothing slow and soft about our joining. I followed his pounding pace, as skin slapped against skin. The scent of our joining drifted to me. Primitive. Hot.

After so long apart, neither of us could stop the frantic pace. He leaned over me, his tongue lapping at my sweat-slicked body like a man dying of thirst.

I couldn't think, could do no more than feel as he continued his thrust inside me.

Joe filled me completely. Every inch of his hard erection slid against my inner walls, driving me beyond sanity. He shouldn't be able to last so long. His stamina had always amazed me.

I screamed his name when release finally came, and felt him follow me over as wave after wave of aftershocks rippled through me. I clenched around him tightly, milking every last drop.

We lay exhausted covered in sweat. No lights had been turned on and only the sound of our breathing filled the room.

"Thank you. It had been too long and I couldn't control it this time."

"I should be thanking you." His arms tightened around me as he rolled onto his back, bringing me to rest on that perfect spot on his chest. My hand automatically reached across his chest, rubbing the soft hair. I felt the tears sting my eyes as mascara bled, but fought them back before one could fall. "Let me turn on a light, and we'll talk."

"No." There was nothing to say that hadn't been said. Nothing that would change the bitter truth. "Look, we both know this doesn't change anything. It can't. I'm still the monster in your eyes."

"Lindy--"

"Let me finish. I need to say this. Tonight, well, I almost did something I couldn't have lived with." I thought about Malcolm and fear hit me hard. If I was going to make a gigantic mistake, it would be with Joe. Never with Malcolm. "You saved me from that. I love you, Joe. I think I always will. But we're not good for each other anymore. I can't change what I've become and you can't change that you hate the thing I am." I swallowed back the tears again, nearly choking on the lump that slid down my throat. "Give us tonight. Leave the lights off and hold me. Forget I'm what you despise, and let me forget."

"I could never despise you, Lindy. I--"

"No. Tomorrow will come soon enough, and you'll see me for what I am. Give me tonight, Joe."

"Okay, sweetheart."

Morning came soon enough, but Joe woke alone. Cursing myself as a coward, I snuck out in the hours before dawn. After a perfect night in his arms, I didn't want to see the knowledge in his eyes that he had made a mistake.

I refused to allow myself time during the day to wallow. Joe and I were consenting adults, and we had made a decision to enjoy each other for one night. I would stand by that decision and face the consequences.

* * * *

"Don't ever do that to me again." I knew Joe would be at the castle for the meeting, and I had tried to prepare myself for his anger. But the minute I had stepped from my car, he had been there ready to pounce. As if he had been waiting on me to arrive. I knew better. It was just my rotten luck.

"I'm sorry, Joe. I shouldn't have showed up last night. It was just... There's no excuse." What could I say, that I loved him, craved him? I pretty much said that last night. Yeah, it had been sex that I wanted, but sex with him was what I'd needed.

"That's not what I mean, and you know it. Don't ever sneak out on me before daybreak like somebody who just paid for sex."

"You're calling me cheap?" I stopped, daring him to admit it.

"No. I'm saying that's the way you made me feel this morning when I woke up alone. Like I had been used."

Shit, hadn't that been exactly what I had done? Used Joe, knowing I would walk away come daylight.

"That was the last thing I wanted. I just thought it would be easier." I stepped back to lean against my car, sliding my hands behind me. I had the nagging urge to wrap my arms around him, try to make up for the rotten way I'd made him feel. If it wouldn't just make him feel worse later, I'd probably give in.

"Easier on who?"

"Both of us. I know how you feel about me--" He stood in front of me, his hands fisted at his side. The anger rushing through him was so strong, I could almost feel the waves of energy from it.

"Don't tell me what I feel, Lindy." He turned his eyes from me, but I still saw the disgust directed my way. Well, that made two of us who were disgusted with me.

"Do you deny your hatred for--what did you call them?--the devils revenge? That's what I am now. A scourge sent by the devil."

"Damn it, Lindy, it's so easy for you." His anger caused his voice to rise.

"Easy? You couldn't even deal with me becoming part vampire. How in the hell do you think I live with it?" My voice rose, squealing as the blood raced through me. "You think this is easy for me? God, I don't even recognize my own life. For a year now, I've tried to start over. Do you know what that's like? The career I spent years preparing for vanished overnight. I was forced to leave my home by narrow-minded neighbors who didn't want my kind near their kids. My friends disappeared one by one, and the man that I cared about turned away from me in disgust."

"Sweetheart." He reached for me, and it almost did me in.

"Don't. I mean it, Joe. I don't want your pity. It does me no good. I have a life again, such as it is. If it disappoints you, get over it. I have.

"I have a business, a job that I'm good at. People might not like what I am, but they sure as hell call me when things go to shit. I learned a hard lesson, but I won't forget it. People don't stand beside you when you need them." I brushed past him, started to pace as his eyes followed me. "Well, I don't need anyone. I can take care of myself."

"I didn't walk out on you, Lindy. You did the walking." He said flatly.

"You were already gone, Joe. All I had was your shell."

"You're wrong. You had my heart. You just wouldn't fight for it. For us. Instead, you ran." He stuck his hands in the pockets of his well-worn jeans.

"You wouldn't have been able to stay with me." Had I been the one to run? That time in my life was a blur to me. A nightmare of broken dreams and constant cravings. I wasn't sure anymore if he had walked, or I had been the one to run.

"We'll never know, will we? Yes, I had a hard time accepting things, but you didn't give me time. You had little faith in me."

"You would have ended up hating me." Like I had hated myself at the time. I had seen the loathing on Joe's face every time vampires were mentioned. I had tried to hide all of the signs of my turning from him. It had worked for a while, until the night I had turned while making love to him. In shock, he had pushed me away.

"I've spent the last year hating you for leaving. I don't have any hate left." It hurt all over again to hear him admit it.

"So where does that leave us? We have to work together. Can't we at least be friends?" Could I be only friends with him? I would take whatever scrap of his life I could get. And wasn't that just depressing.

"Sure. We'll be friends. We'll speak on the street, send Christmas cards. Now there's a meeting we're late for."

He turned and left me standing on the drive. I watched him enter without me and had never felt so alone.

I needed a minute by myself to clear my head. Or rather, my eyes. I didn't want my emotions high when I walked into that room with other men's tension filling it. And I certainly didn't want wet eyes. Men always associated a woman's tears with weakness. It wasn't true. Crying washed away weakness, leaving strength behind.

I crossed to the porch and then dropped down on the stone steps. I wouldn't cry. I had never been promised the fairy-tale life, so how could this one be so disappointing? I had no expectations in life. It was hard work for little reward, but the only choice I had was to play the scenes until it was done.

I heard the pop and felt the pain in my chest. I hurt, Lord I hurt. The force knocked me flat on my back. I stayed there, looking up at the ceiling of the porch. There had been a scream on impact, but it never occurred to me it had come from me.

Joe was there. I don't know how, but I was looking into his beautiful gray eyes. Damn, but I loved his eyes. Last night it had been too dark to see those gorgeous eyes of his.

"Don't move."

My hand reached up to caress his jaw. He needed to shave, his five o'clock shadow prickling my fingers.

"Hurts." Talking hurt almost as much as breathing.

"I know, sweetheart." I could see fear in his eyes. Anger, concern. I lowered my hand to my chest and when it came away slick, I knew. I had been shot. Shit. This day was turning into a contender for the worst one yet.

"Call an ambulance!" Joe shouted.

"There is no time." Malcolm was there, standing over Joe. I couldn't see his features that were cast in shadows, but I knew the voice. "It's a chest wound, and it's not a hospital that she needs. She has lost too much blood to make the trip. There is only one way for her to survive."

"Do it," Joe demanded.

"I cannot. Only she can save herself. She must turn." Malcolm sighed, the words heavy.

"I can't." My words came out as a whisper.

"Damn it, Lindy, do whatever it takes to save your life."

"I can't," I repeated, louder this time though the effort hurt like hell.

"Only you can choose. You die tonight, or you stay to fight again." Malcolm made it sound so easy. Like what, I wouldn't turn into a freaking werewolf if that would stop the pain?

"I don't know how," I snapped, and it cost me to admit it. I had never changed at will, never had any control over it.

"You must control the beast, or it will control you." Malcolm told me, as if that made any sense. So far, it had done one heck of a job controlling me.

"How?" I managed to ask.

"Stop fighting it. Bring her inside."

Tender arms lifted me. Joe. I was too weak to put my arms around his neck. Turning my head to his chest, I inhaled the familiar scent.

They were all there. Humans and vampires standing side by side, watching me. Their eyes told me clearly that they didn't expect me to survive.

"We'll get them, Joe," someone said and murmurs of agreement filled the room. Great, they would avenge my death. It was something I guess, but at the moment, it was a lot less than what I needed. I needed major painkillers and Doc.

Joe carried me down dark stairs, placed me on a bed of red silk. My blood wouldn't leave stains.

"Look at me, Lucinda," Malcolm commanded, and I obeyed. "Feel the beast, let him free."

"I'm trying but..." I looked at Joe. I couldn't turn in front of him again, let him see the monster I was. It was stupid. I was dying, and Joe no longer loved me. But he was blocking me, preventing me from turning. "Go away, Joe."

"I'm not leaving you." He took my hand, and held tightly.

I looked back at Malcolm and let the truth show in my eyes.

"She cannot do this thing while you watch," Malcolm said as the truth dawned on him.

Joe dropped my hand and turned his back to me.

"There is little time. I can bite you, turn you--"

"No!" I saw Joe turn and take a step toward Malcolm.

"Then follow my words." Malcolm put my hand to his neck. I could feel the blood pumping. "Feel my blood, hear it call to you. Answer it, love. Come to me.

"Smell the blood, sweet, metallic. You can taste it. Warm, life sustaining. Come, my love."

I could feel my heart slowing, my body grow cool. Was I dying? I wanted to taste his blood. Wanted to feel it slide down my throat, warm, sweet. I reached for him.

I could feel the change coming over me, and instinct had me fighting it. I didn't want this, damn it. Never wanted the change to happen. My heart rate increased, pounding in my chest. My breathing doubled, tripled as I struggled for more air, the panic robbing me.

And then I felt my heart beat change. The signal it had begun. One beat so fierce, my body jerked with it. I waited for the next. I knew it wouldn't beat again for three minutes. I had timed it once. But subconsciously, I waited. Hoped this time it would be different. Prayed it would be. It was the longest three minutes of my life. I knew it would come. It always comes. Nevertheless, waiting for that lone beat terrified me.

The next one was softer, weaker. My fingertips and toes were cold. I felt it spread through me. I took another breath, my last one for who knew how long. Maybe forever. My lungs stopped. I closed my eyes and waited. I was so tired. Dying takes too much out of me. Yet, there is no peace that comes with mine. Five minutes after the last beat, I felt the faint beat. Also my last. Check my vitals now and I would have been all but dead.

It has always amazed me that my body can recover from such an ordeal. My skin began to tingle. I knew Malcolm's blood was awakening and flowing through my body. I no longer was tired but felt invigorated. I felt my fangs cut through my gums. A vampire's teeth do not grow. Contrary to today's myth, my fangs were separate and come from the front side of my gums. It hurts, that slicing of skin. But thanks to the vampire blood that was now filling me, I could handle the pain.

I felt the last of my body die, but no longer cared. The night was alive and calling to me. Nothing else mattered. My senses intensified. I could see clearly in the dark and knew I would be able to hear conversations thought to be private behind locked doors. I inhaled deeply. Not for the air, but for the smell of the night. Sweet, erotic. The wind across my skin would squeeze a moan from my lips, caressing, teasing my body until I burned for a touch. I would feel invincible, beautiful, and sexy. I would feel like the night.

But there was no night around me. The walls surrounding me kept it out.

The pain had eased until it was no more.

I felt my senses sharpen. My body come alive. Malcolm was there, offering his neck to me. I had not drank from his blood after he had bitten me, and was still paying a price anyway. I didn't care. I reached for him, but Joe was there. He pushed Malcolm back a step and lowered himself to the bed next to me.

I couldn't do it. I couldn't bite Joe. I pulled from him, shook my head.

"You need fresh blood, sweetheart, not the aged stuff. Let me give it to you." I saw no condemnation in his eyes.

"No." We both knew I couldn't turn him. I was only half vampire and didn't have enough of the bacteria in me to turn him if I bit him. Still, I couldn't do it.

He took the choice from me when he took out his pocketknife and sliced along his arm. The blood flowed, reached my senses. He held his arm to my mouth, and I drank greedily. I couldn't meet his eyes as his sweet essence ran down my throat. Nothing had ever quenched my thirst like the powerful taste of Joe.

Malcolm pulled Joe back before I drank too much. Wouldn't want to drain him. With one craving satisfied, I felt the second one hit me. Hard. I pulled back, looked into Joe's eyes. His were watching me, unreadable.

I knew my eyes glowed red, as my body glowed. I was undeniably beautiful. Weren't all vampires? I reached for him.

When he pulled back, it didn't deter me.

"No, Lindy. Not here, not now." His voice was rough.

"I need you, Joe." I crawled across the bed on all fours, after his retreating form. I pushed his chest until he was flat on his back. I straddled him, crawled the length of him letting my body drag against his strong, stiff form. I reached for his arm, licked the wound. The taste drove me closer to the edge before the trickle of blood stopped. But I was through with his blood. He had something else I wanted now.

"There's no time. The men are upstairs waiting." Did his voice sound thick? Yeah, I was sure I was getting to him.

"There's time." My fingers slid down the front of his shirt, popping buttons. I loved the sound. His chest was tan from years of sunlight, thick from years of labor. Just a dusting of pale hair circled each nipple and as I pealed his shirt back, my tongue circled each peak. I nipped, just a small bite without drawing blood before my hand slid lower.

I found the waistband of his jeans and popped the first two buttons, then slid my hand inside. He still wore cotton briefs. I could picture him in them, his hard erection straining to get out. I found what I was searching for and closed my hand around him.

I loved the smooth feel of the skin, the way it pulsed in my hand. Velvet soft, hard as steel. My mouth watered. I wanted to feel the head of it slide over my lips, swirl my tongue around slowly until my mouth was filled with him.

Another button on his fly popped before he grabbed my hand.

"Fuck." His deep raspy voice sent a shiver through me, increasing my need.

"I'm trying to."

"We can't." My hand was locked beneath his, still holding his erection tightly. Proving that we could.

"I've got to. I have to feel you inside me. I'll die Joe, I swear, if I can't slide your dick home and come apart around it."

"Shit, Lindy." He released my hands and pulled my shirt over my head. Yes. I had won. Finally. I could almost taste him. Sweat and sex, as his dick would slide in and out of my mouth.

"Good God." His hands slipped beneath my bra, circled my breast, squeezed just the way I liked it. Joe always knew just the way I liked it. Not soft, teasing caresses but full-blown fire.

"No need to be crude," Malcolm said.

I could have killed him. Pulled that artery right out of his freaking neck. One word, and Joe remembered we weren't alone. He jerked from me, rose from the bed.

"Joe." I'd beg. If I had too, I'd do it.

"This isn't the place, Lindy. Not the time."

"I am afraid Lucinda is correct. The time must be taken. She cannot enter a room full of men without satisfying this need. She will awaken the beast in every vampire and some of the men will not be as able as you are to control their blood lust.

"As sorry for it as I am, detective, someone must see to her needs. If you cannot, then I will take it upon myself."

Funny, Malcolm didn't look sorry about it at all to me.

"Like hell. Touch her and you're dead." Since he had been dead for centuries, it wasn't much of a threat.

When a woman entered carrying a small bundle, Malcolm spoke softly to her before turning back to me.

"Joe." My voice pleaded with him.

"Ah, so that is the way of it then. Very well. Tonight, I bow to you. But know this. There will be a night when she will come to me of her own will. She will be mine."

Malcolm crossed the room to the door. "I have taken the liberty of having a bath drawn and fresh clothes laid out"--he pointed to a door just as the woman came out--"there. Do not dally overlong. We will await you upstairs."

"I'm going to kill that bastard one of these days," Joe stated coldly as he pointed to the bathroom door, and like a good little girl, I obeyed. He knew better than to touch me until we were alone.

He locked the door and leaned against it while I pulled the blood-soaked clothes from me. I dropped them on the floor, sure it wasn't the first time Malcolm had had blood on his Italian marble. I rubbed my hand over my breast, amazed no hint of the wound remained. I had healed minor wounds before but nothing of this magnitude. I felt Joe's eyes follow my movements and felt the quickening between my thighs. Stepping into the tub, I soaped my hands, lingered on my breast, paying special attention to my nipples.

I had been afraid my turning would repulse Joe. But from the lust in those darkening gray eyes, he was far from it.

My hair had been spared the blood, so I concentrated on washing my body. Thoroughly, enticingly slow.

His eyes burned a trail across my skin, as they followed my every move. It only encouraged me more.

I stood, water cascading down my body. My hands followed the trail. Down across my breast, lower over my stomach, stopping at my thighs.

When I moved toward the one place I burned for a touch, I heard Joe's sharp intake of breath. My finger moved over my clit, slow and easy. I looked up, my eyes locking with his. His echoed with the same need.

When I stepped from the tub, Joe was there. But he didn't hand me a towel. Instead, he grabbed me, shoved me onto the cool marble vanity.

It wasn't my need that had him entering me with such force, but his own. I wrapped my legs around his waist, curled my fingers around the edge of the marble and met his demanding thrusts.

This was what I wanted, what I needed. This and only this. Joe. No one could make me feel more alive, more complete than this man.

The marble was cool beneath me, a soothing contrast to the heat of my skin. I lay back against it, Joe wrapping my legs around his neck. It forced him deeper inside me.

He leaned down over me, his hands on my shoulder, locking me against him as his punishing hips slapped against me. I wanted more of him, all of him. I wanted him buried so deep that he'd be lost inside me. Lost without me.

The grinding pace pushed me over much too quickly. His fingers dug into my legs as he followed me over.

Sex had never been our problem and wasn't our answer. But when he was buried deep within me, the questions no longer mattered.

Chapter Four

We entered the main room some time later. Joe's hand rested protectively against my lower back. Malcolm's fancy white shirt did little to hide my still aroused breasts, but my bra had been ruined. Bullet holes and blood will do that.

I had tied the blue swath of silk around my hips in a wrap-around skirt fashion. With each step, it caressed my legs.

We had cooled the beast but not driven it away completely. My eyes showed a hint of red, and my fangs had retracted to the size of my other teeth but remained dangerously sharp. It wouldn't take much to call the beast back, but it was tame enough to keep it from awakening the others.

As I entered the room, I bit my lip to stop the laughter that threatened to escape. No one was in the mood for humor. It shouldn't have been funny. And I definitely shouldn't have allowed that laugh to escape, if the dirty looks I received were an indication. The heads that snapped at my giggle confirmed that. But never had I seen such a contradiction in men.

Vamps were seated on the left, dressed in their finery. Cool silks, flowing lace, and plenty of leather. Vampires dress for flare. Cops were seated on the right of the table facing them, dressed in rough denim and wrinkled cotton. Flare was the last thing these men cared about. Both sides seemed braced for a fight. They sat staring, mistrusting, across a conference table that could have graced any large corporation boardroom.

Malcolm sat on the left with his men, next to the head of the table. Joe took the seat opposite him, to the right. This left only the head chair for me. Meant I was in charge. Was this my lucky day or what?

Ten sets of eyes followed my movements as I dropped gracefully into the chair.

I'm not the best speaker. I don't have time for niceties and figured these guys were in no mood to hear them. So, I dove right in.

"As you can tell, I'm not dead." Oops. Poor choice of words. "Or no more than usual. Before we begin, its only fair to point out that being on this task force is not going to be good for your health. Obviously word has gotten out, as proven by the hit on me earlier. I have enemies, but none have ever wanted me dead. So we must assume we all might become targets. And while some of us are harder to kill, we can all die."

"I disagree that we all are in danger. We are but soldiers. You are the force that brings us together. Remove you, they remove the alliance." Malcolm said.

"Okay. So I'm the only one they want dead," I snapped.

"Possibly," Malcolm said as he inclined his head to me.

"Great. My day just gets better. Lets assume, for my sanity, that they're pissed off at all of us and not just me. Everyone must choose to put their life in jeopardy--"

"There are no cowards here," one of the vampires said, as if I had just insulted the whole lot of them.

No cowards. Wanna bet? I knew of one standing before them right then. "Okay. So, we're all going to do this.

"You men at this table are on opposite sides. It is evident by the seating arrangement. I understand this. You've been enemies in the past. But if we are to beat this, it stops here. The man next to you, across from you is now your partner. Joe and Malcolm have hand picked each of you because you are up to the challenge. We will work together, side by side, or we will fail.

"As you know, we have a nut case out there. He killed Surgis, and as of this morning another has been staked out at dawn." From the collective gasp, most hadn't heard this news. Obviously, Malcolm had told Joe after his phone call to me this morning since he didn't appear to be one of the shocked ones.

"There is a human we need to find, a lunatic we need to kill, and retaliation we need to stop. Since this is Joe's area of expertise, I'll let him take over. He'll lay out the plan for added security.

"But before I do, let me say that I'm here to help both sides become one. Everyone knows where to find me if they need me. Malcolm and Joe will be in charge of the different shifts."

I turned to Joe as I took my seat and listened to him as he laid out the details. It took a bit of time to work them out with Malcolm and the men. Guarding the vampires would be fairly simple. Most stayed in groups, living in community housing

similar to the castle. A few strategically placed men would serve well.
The humans were not so convenient in their living arrangements. Spread out over the city as they were, night patrols were the best that could be offered.
But even with so little security, the humans' protection was almost guaranteed. One word from the Master and humans would be off limits. To go against Malcolm's command was a death wish. And they didn't die slowly.
Joe finished up, and then it was my floor again. I hated to approach the next subject, but someone had to do it. And I was the one in the head seat tonight.
"I'm not a detective, and I don't claim to be. I'll leave that up to you guys. But everyone here has contacts and can ask questions. The more asked, the better chance we have of getting the right answers."
I hesitated, gathering courage. There was a path my brain had been following all afternoon, and I wanted to hear their opinion. They weren't going to like it, but I wasn't here for a popularity contest. Besides, everyone knew I'd lose hands down.
"I'd like to run something by you guys, get your take on it. We're assuming a human staked Surgis. We have no proof and all of this is assumption. I'm not disputing this. I'm just playing the what-if game.
"What if it wasn't a human?"
"Are you suggesting Surgis was killed by one of his own? That is absurd." Rena was the only other female at this meeting, but it was easy to see why she had been chosen. Her body was lean, toned to deadly precision. And she had an attitude to match.
I had heard of her. She was the only other vampire in town, other than Malcolm, to pass the five hundred year mark. She had belonged to Surgis, though there was doubt as to who belonged to whom. Surgis might have been her master, but she was treated with respect due one her age. Or maybe she had just grown too strong to control. It explained what she was doing at the table.
Few had her powers. Had it been possible for a female to head the clan, she might even have been Master instead of Malcolm. I decided to give her a wide berth.
"Maybe. But hear me out. Surgis was starved when he was found. How? We know he'd eaten just after dusk. There were witnesses to this and means it wasn't lack of feeding that starved him. That would indicate blood loss."
"Someone cut him then," Detective Johnson offered.
I shook my head. "Surgis was not a rookie. He would have healed a single wound long before the blood loss would have starved him."
"Multiple wounds would bleed out quickly," the detective suggested.

"Yes, but would he stand by while someone cut him up?"

"No," Malcolm said. His agreement encouraged me to continue.

"Blood sharing. If he were drained, he would be starving and weak. It would be in line with the condition of the body when he was found. The autopsy report I received from Doc indicated the body was all but empty." My friend Doc performed all autopsies on the vampires. The mayor figured it would help him in his research, and lets face it, nobody else wanted the job. In the five years that Doc had played coroner to the dead, he had performed two. Shows how big of a job it was.

"There would be a great amount of trust for that to happen."

"Exactly. And another thing. Most people believe what they see in old movies. What does a stake through the heart do to a vampire?"

"Kills." This came from one of the cops.

"See? Most humans believe that. But it's not true. It immobilizes the victim until the stake is removed. Eventually, their blood supply would be used up trying to heal the wound."

"Could that have happened?"

"Doc doesn't think so. A young man maybe, but Surgis was powerful and his healing abilities extraordinary. He was strong. He could have removed the stake himself."

"Unless he was too weak," Joe said.

"Exactly. Same goes for binding him to stakes in the yard, waiting for sunrise."

"He would never have allowed it to happen had he been able to fight," Malcolm confirmed.

"Which means he was weak from the start, or trusted someone completely."

"So it was one of us," Malcolm said what everyone thought, but was afraid to say. I could hear defeat in his voice and something a lot more dangerous.

"I'm saying it could be. My point is we don't need to center this investigation on one certain type. We don't know what we're dealing with, and we need to keep an open mind. To go out searching for a certain race will limit our chances of success."

"There would be marks on his neck." Rena just couldn't let it go. I didn't blame her. No one wanted to believe their own was capable of such an act. I knew from experience everyone was.

"Doc says marks can be made from fangs or just made to look like fangs using thin hose. There was too much damage from the sun to find any. They wouldn't prove a thing. We need to look for motive. This could be a hate crime, but what else? Who had problems with Surgis, who stood to gain?"

"That would seem to be me," Malcolm replied.

"Great. Case solved. Where were you Tuesday night?"

"You can not be serious. I will not stand for your insults to the master."

Just what I wanted, a pissed-off vampire more powerful than ten combined.

"It is okay, Rena. Lucinda has a point; none of us are above suspicion. I was at the Cave, which can be verified."

"See how easy that was? We can mark one off our list, after we've checked it out. We need to check everyone. No one is above question, not even me.

"Another thing. Jackson was Surgis's man. Maybe he knew something, or maybe he was killed for the same reason. Either way, there is a connection."

We assigned tasks for everyone and agreed to meet in a few days to compare notes. The meeting ended with hardly a problem, unlike the beginning. Being shot seems a problem to me.

"I'll drive you home." Joe was close behind me as I readied to leave.

"Thanks, but I've got my car."

"You almost died tonight." There was no anger in his words this time, just resignation.

"She will be protected, as she is staying here. I can protect her better against the humans."

"In case you weren't listening in there, we don't know for sure it's a human we're after. What if it's one of you?"

"I can protect her against anyone. No one would dare harm her here under my protection."

"They didn't seem to mind shooting her on your porch, did they? She's coming home with me. Damned if she's staying here alone with you."

"Geez, no wonder I don't date. Listen to you two. You sound like a couple of high school hormones, fighting over the newest piece of ass. If you would like my opinion, I think it would make more sense for me to stay here." I felt Joe stiffen but had to ignore it. This was not personal, this was my job. "Whether a vamp is the one doing the killing or not, so far they are the only ones being killed. I need to stay close to it. This is where it's happening. I won't be any good to anyone tucked away in some cozy little house across town where nothing is going on."

"You're not staying here with him alone."

I gave Joe my best try-me glare but I could tell it had little effect on him. "Your men will be here on duty."

"Only during daylight hours. At night, you would be without other humans around."

I didn't have the heart to remind him I wasn't exactly human myself anymore.

"I'll stay as well." From his sigh, I knew he wasn't happy about it.

"Oh yeah. One big happy family," I mumbled. Okay, I'll admit there was a time in my life when I wanted to live with Joe. Sharing the third floor in the relic castle with vamps sleeping in the basement wasn't my idea of co-habitating.

The fact that all other residents were dead to the world half of the time made it a little too cozy for me, and a little too creepy. Good thing we both had jobs to do and a life.

Only thing was, our jobs and our life seemed to lead down the same path lately. So, we ended up partners, so to speak. Not my idea of avoiding the forbidden fruit.

* * * *

It only took a few days to settle into a routine. Joe and I beat the bushes in the day, and Malcolm joined us at night. By the end of the first week, we had nothing new. And another human had gone missing.

This one was certainly more worthy of Surgis. Tim Dunlund owned a large portion of Memphis, literally. His buildings housed some of the largest corporations in town. The mayor was unglued and screaming down my neck. It was one thing to kidnap a nobody, but Memphis' best-known millionaires couldn't start disappearing. We just don't have that many to spare even one. And this one was well known for his contributions to St. Jude Children's Hospital.

Anyone involved with St. Jude carries an elevated status in Memphis. Everyone's heart broke over the children in pain. Dunlund was on the board.

I knew it was likely retaliation for Jackson, the second vampire staked. He'd been Surgis' right hand man but was only a babe in vamp years. It would have been easy to get the upper hand on him. I wondered when the human bodies would start stacking up.

The weekly task force meeting brought little news, and I decided to stop by Doc's afterward, Joe in tow. I hadn't been able to shake him all week, and he was getting to me.

As usual, Doc seemed glad to see me. I knew it wasn't because of my weekly blood donation. Okay, not entirely anyway.

He was a lonely old man, though he never took time to notice. Buried in his work, he seemed oblivious to the way he was shunned by most of his own colleagues. Everyone knew his work was important and applauded his effort. But they didn't trust a man who'd made studying the makeup of vampires his lifelong career.

"Lindy, honey, come in. Come in. I see you brought that man of yours along. Good to see you, Joe." Doc pushed his bifocals up the bridge of his nose and looked around the room as a frown creased his brow.

"Nowhere to sit," he said.

That was an understatement. Papers, tubes and fast food boxes littered every space.

I hopped onto the counter and Joe leaned next to me. Satisfied his guests' needs were met, Doc continued.

"I've found it, Lindy." His eyes sparkled.

"The answer to cancer?"

"What? Oh, no."

"Isn't that what you've been working on? A way to fight cancer cells?"

"I am. Was. However, I've discovered something else quite by accident. I know how to rid your body of Malcolm's cells."

I slid from the counter slowly, my eyes locked on Doc's. I couldn't get my hopes up again, not until I heard the details.

"It's so simple, really. Course, there are risks. But I believe we can minimize those."

"From the beginning, please."

"Of course, sorry dear. You know the leukocytes outnumber the erythrocytes in the blood of a vampire. The basophile excretes a substance--"

"English, Doc," Joe pleaded.

Doc looked lost as he stared at Joe, as if English were unknown to him.

"The white blood cells outnumber the red in vampire blood," I translated.

"Yes. Yes. Actually, the red are near non-existent, since the vampire needs no oxygen. They have an increased level of lymphocytes."

"The part of our immune system that produces antibodies to fight viruses, bacteria, invading forces," I added.

"Our immune system cannot attack the cells of its own body in an autoimmune reaction or it damages the organism and leads to death."

"What does this have to do with Lindy?"

Doc waved his hand toward Joe. "I'm getting to that. When the bacteria entered Lindy's system, it increased her white blood cells. Normally, a high count would indicate infection. However, her count has remained high for a year, and still she remains healthy. This causes her ability to heal quickly.

"The transfusion I administered immediately after she was infected saved her red cells. As long as the body receives oxygen and can process it, it can live. She has only a small part of the bacteria in her. We need to kill the bacteria that attached itself to the blood she received from Malcolm.

"Usually blood cells clone to fight a virus. But Lindy's blood cells and Malcolm's have remained separate. This is good news. If we can destroy Malcolm's cells without destroying hers, she will be cured."

"When Lindy's cells are dominant, she remains unturned. When the bacteria rise, or flare up, Malcolm's cells are the dominant ones. She turns."

"Which explains my urges. I mimic Malcolm." Thank goodness, there was a reasonable explanation. A scientific one. That his blood calls to mine is just a little too creepy.

"Of course. His blood controls you at such times. Not your brain, of course, only your body's reaction to the blood reaching your organs, your brain. Your neurological system is taken over by the virus."

"So how do we kill Malcolm's cells without killing my own?"

"I have been studying the latest victims' cells. It is rare to be able to study a deceased vampire--they so rarely die. It seems a dying vampire's cells attack their own as part of the dying process. Highly unusual. They seem to turn against themselves. If we injected the cells into Lindy, they would attack Malcolm's cells, as they would recognize them as their own. Her own cells may even turn against these foreign cells then."

"Are you saying the blood cells you have would do it?" Joe asked.

Doc frowned. "No, they're already dead. And they don't match the cells you have. The match must be perfect."

"So only Malcolm's blood will do." Perfect. Somehow, I didn't think Malcolm was going to offer to kill himself just to give me blood before he died.

"Yes. And there is a narrow window of time, a fine line between the cells trying to heal and when they turn against their own. They kill quickly before all cells are dead."

"So Malcolm must die. Not a problem," Joe said.

I shuddered at the coldness in Joe's words. I'd thought it, but didn't say it aloud. Makes me the nicer person, huh?

"So we inject the killer cells from Malcolm into Lindy and they kill the bad cells."

Leave it to Joe to simply things.

"What prevents them from turning on Lindy after they've finished?"

"I don't think they will."

"But you can't be sure."

"No. Normally I would test my theory. Check for errors. However, this is a one-chance proposition. Once Malcolm's cells start to attack there will not be time for tests. And since there is no other like our Lindy, no preliminary tests can be performed."

"So she's a test case. Too risky. You need to remove the risk, or you'll have to keep looking for another way," Joe announced, as if it was his decision to make.

"Hold on one damn minute. It's my life, my risk and it's my decision. I say we go for it." Okay, I felt a little guilty. I'd just signed Malcolm's death warrant. There had been a time once when I would have killed him myself. But I felt differently about it, about all of the vampires. I understood them. Hell, I was them. "Is there a way to mimic death, instead of actually doing it?"

"You got a problem killing Malcolm?" Joe challenged.

"I've got a problem killing any person."

"You're in luck then. Malcolm's not a person."

I found it best to ignore that. Vampires were infected humans. Was it their need to feed, to preserve their own life that made them the monster? Did the level of red blood cells in my veins make me so different?

Living people hated the vampires because they feared becoming one. In fact, they were all just one parasite invasion from it.

"I honestly don't know, Lindy. Once the cells turn, there must be a way to stop them. Otherwise, vamps would be easier to kill."

"What's the best way to kill Malcolm and preserve the cells?" Joe skipped right to the heart of it.

"Sunlight burns them up too quickly. Starvation would do it, but it's a long process. Then the body goes into a dried hibernation mode. Fresh blood restores them."

"Could I starve, have my own cells turn on me, then add human blood to bring me back?"

"No. Damages the organs beyond repair. You are half human. You would kill the human in you. All that would remain would be Malcolm's blood.

"Scratch that idea. That's the side I'm not real fond of."

"You can only kill the cells once the death process has started. It would be easier to bring a vamp out of that than someone who is part human."

"Oh, so we're trying to save the vamp now?" Joe stepped away from me and started to pace.

"Don't be hateful."

"I just want to make sure I'm up on this." He stopped and turned to face me. "First, I get to kill him, and then I have to save him."

"We're doctors, we save lives."

"Lives?"

"Yes. No matter what form they are."

Chapter Five

It was just after dark when we walked into the castle. All the boys would be awake. Yippee.

I dropped onto the sofa, my feet aching after hours on them. Everyone in the room looked like they'd slept like the dead. Ha.

"A message was delivered for you. We have detained the messenger in case you have need to question him further."

Malcolm strolled into the room, looking as fresh as ever. Once, just once, I'd like to see the man rumpled and dirty.

I took the rolled parchment from his hands. Who uses this stuff anymore? I unrolled it and stared at the words.

"Is this written in blood?" I shrieked a little too loudly. Okay, the sight of blood probably shouldn't freak me out so much. But whose life is as centered around the stuff as mine was? Unless I was craving it, I just didn't want it to be so important in my life. When I was hungry, nothing looked more appealing.

Malcolm leaned over my shoulder and sniffed the paper. "It would appear so."

"Yuck." I fought the urge to throw it down. That would make me look like a sissy and while I'll admit to being a girl, I refuse to be a sissy.

Joe was suddenly beside me, all cop.

"Fingerprints, don't touch it."

"Your men have already dusted it. It lacked any evidence," Malcolm announced smoothly.

"Doc can tell us if it is human, animal, or vamp blood." I could have sworn Malcolm rolled his eyes. But it would have been beneath him, so I scratched the idea.

I passed the paper to his outstretched hand. His tongue flicked over the dried blood.

"Human. Male, between twenty and thirty years of age. Relatively healthy, light drinker."

"Well, that was attractive." My stomach rolled, and human or vampire, I swore off eating in the near future. Malcolm's brow rose, obviously amused.

I took back my little note to see what someone felt important enough to write in blood.

"You have been warned once, now twice. There will be no third." I looked up and tried to smile, but even I knew I failed miserably. "Goody. You think that means they're giving up?"

No one laughed. This was one hard crowd. I gave up all pretenses of being strong and sturdy, said my goodnights, and stomped off to my room. It was barely nine o'clock. Seemed late enough to me, and I'd had my fill for one day of murder, threats and blood.

* * * *

Joe was waiting for me when I stepped from my room the next morning. I had insisted on separate rooms, even though I knew we'd probably just end up sleeping in one bed.

But at least with separate rooms, I had a place to hide out.

His eyes moved slowly down my body, but I couldn't read whether he approved. I was dressed in a skirt for a meeting with the mayor. His office had called wanting an update. I had offered to email him one. He suggested that we compromise, meaning I did what he wanted.

Joe's eyes stopped at my feet, and I wondered if he liked my bright red toenail polish.

"You didn't wear"--Joe pointed to my feet--"those before."

"Fuck-me heels?" Crude, I know, but there just wasn't a better description for the four-inch heels with the thin straps. There had been a time when I hadn't owned anything above a two-inch heel, and those had only been worn on special occasions. The truth was, I'd developed an odd appreciation of shoes lately and had a closet full to prove it. Nothing made a woman feel more womanly than a pair of sleek heels.

I couldn't tell if Joe approved of my new style, but it had certainly grabbed his attention.

"Shit, your mouth, Lindy." He cringed, leaning against the doorframe to his room.

I raised my brows at the apparent irony of his words. "My language has always been gutter. But I've never heard words like that from you."

I started down the stairs and he fell in step beside me. "I never wore the heels because I was on my feet at the hospital. They weren't practical." I chose to answer the first question and ignore the second.

"Everything about you has changed."

Why did I get the feeling that wasn't a compliment? "Why? Because my clothes are different? Because my mouth's a little harsher?" I turned at the bottom of the stairs and went into the kitchen. It was the one place we were assured privacy. No one else in this house had probably even been in the room.

Joe and I had stopped at the market and stocked the place, mostly for the guys working shifts here. "Maybe I'm not the same. I was naïve once. I lived in my small, safe little world. And when that world crumbled, I metamorphosed. Change with the world or be crushed by it."

I found the coffee filters, added coffee and water to the pot, then waited on the one craving I had carried with me even after Malcolm took a bite out of me. I leaned against the counter, mimicking Joe's pose.

"I'm not locked into anyone's rules but my own. If I'm a little rougher now, not the sweet, gullible little girl I once was, then be proud. It means I just might survive in this world. It's a lot tougher than the glass house I lived in before." I tried to keep my voice light, since I didn't want to start my day fighting with him. But it was hard. "I won't mourn the loss of the little girl." I didn't need to. I had mourned her a year ago.

"I didn't say you should. Takes some getting used to, but I like who you've become," Joe said.

"I didn't ask for your approval." That I wanted it really pissed me off. There had been a time when his approval had meant too much to me. I wasn't ready to give him or anyone else that kind of power again.

"I noticed."

"What do you want from me?" I rubbed my eyes, tired and weary. I needed a few hours, a couple of days, by myself. Away from constant turmoil.

"There was a time getting you back into my bed meant back in my life."

"I can separate the two," I said.

"Can you? Pity, I can't. I want you, Lindy." How long had I waited to hear those words from him, to know he meant them? I couldn't trust that he meant them now.

I filled two mugs with coffee, passed one to him. We both took it black and strong. Another thing we had shared. The scene was a little too familiar for me. How many times had we shuffled into that rustic kitchen in Joe's ranch house, after making love all night long? I'd start the coffee, and we would pet around on each other while it brewed. Joe never could make a decent cup of coffee.

Those mornings had been some of my favorite times. When early morning sunlight shined through the picture window, warming the room while we warmed each other.

Had those times meant so little to him that he could just toss them away? Damn him and his prejudices.

"Check back with me tonight." It was a shitty thing to say, but I was feeling pretty shitty at the moment.

"Damn it, I'm not talking about just sex. I want you in my life. Completely." If only he did. It really pissed me off the way he reached for me one minute, then pushed me away in the next. I wasn't some damn toy to pick up and play with, then toss aside when he was finished playing.

"You can't have me, Joe. Not anymore. I won't accept a man who can't accept me as is. I deserve better."

"Yes. I guess you do." His eyes looked away.

"You want me now, but when the excitement wears off and we get back to everyday life, I'm still what you hate most."

"Doc's cure might come through." He didn't bother to deny it. I felt my heart break.

"Yes. But it won't help us." And he'd never get that. Love didn't attach addendums. I loved Joe no matter what, that he couldn't say the same said it all.

"I need to get to the precinct this morning, fill the captain in on what's going on." He was suddenly restless, as if he remembered that he needed to be somewhere else.

"Okay. I have some work at the office to take care of after I meet with the mayor. I'll see you back here later."

"I don't think so." Joe stepped through the door, scanned the living room. "St. John, you're with Lindy today."

"Yes, sir."

"I don't need a sitter." I followed him through the door.

"Oh, that's right. You don't need anyone. Just because some psycho is sending you threats written in blood, why should you change now?"

I watched him storm off, stop to talk to St. John before he walked out.

Detective St. John approached me carefully. "Looks like I caught a break in partners today."

"What did he say to you?" I took another sip from the mug, trying to ignore my stomach as it rolled. I hated bickering with Joe.

"Not much." I hadn't really expected him to tell me. Cops stood by each other, even when it came to women. Or maybe especially when it came to women.

"Huh. Why don't you hang with Erickson today? I'll be safely tucked inside my house." It was worth a shot, although I knew it wouldn't work. These guys obeyed Joe, no questions asked.

"Can't do. Joe said if you ditched me, I'd have a career as a crossing guard at the elementary school. Besides, I sent Erickson after Joe. His rule, remember? Can't go around alone."

I fought a smile and lost. "Good move."

"Thanks." He nodded.

"Did it ever occur to you that I should be protecting you? I can take a bullet, a knife, and beat you in a fight."

"Sure it did." His grin was schoolboy wicked. "So protect me, baby."

I laughed. St. John could always make me laugh.

"You know, none of us are invincible, Lindy. Not even you."

So much for laughter.

* * * *

I had almost made it through the day without incident when the call came in. I grabbed my purse and headed out. After dropping my partner for the day at the station, I headed toward Joe's office. For someone I had been able to avoid for almost a year, Joe was popping up much too often.

He was lost behind a mound of paperwork that looked dangerously close to falling to the floor.

"Peter Caldwell is missing," I said.

He looked up as I entered the room.

"Who's Peter Caldwell?" He stopped in mid motion, as if he could deal with me quickly and get back to what he was writing. Boy, was he wrong.

"An eighteen year old kid who thought being a vampire would solve his problems in life." I dropped into the chair.

"Stupid kid."

"Yeah." I blew at the loose strands of hair that fell across my face. "He's been missing two weeks." Joe didn't seem happy to hear that news. I could relate. I'd had about the same reaction when I'd heard. He didn't bother asking how I knew before he did, he being the cop. Vampires didn't report crimes to the police. Ever. They had a code to handle their own. Most of them didn't trust cops.

"And we're just now hearing about it?" He dropped the pencil on his desk, ran his fingers through his hair. My fingers itched to follow that same path.

"Had a fight with his girlfriend. She just realized he hadn't been ducking out on her but was really missing."

"His body should have shown up by now, if he's a victim."

"Yeah. We have no idea how long he's been missing, but it doesn't appear any humans have paid for his disappearance." So far, the missing vampires had turned up at first light. The humans still hadn't turned up at all.

"Maybe because his disappearance hasn't been made public or because he hasn't been murdered. Think he's our guy?" Joe asked.

"My gut tells me no, but none of this makes any sense."

"You know him?" He leaned back in his chair, crossed his ankles on the desk.

"He came in to talk to me before he made his decision to change."

"And you couldn't change his mind?" His eyes narrowed, as if he didn't believe me.

"I tried, damn it. His girlfriend had been bitten back in the day, and he thought he couldn't live without her."

Joe rolled his eyes. "Did you tell him women were everywhere? Damn, he could have just found a girlfriend that was actually breathing."

I blinked, and it felt like he'd just slapped me. I tried to recover before he caught on, but he knew he'd hurt me. Well, screw him. I was a big girl.

"Yes, actually I did. Though I hope I did it with a little more finesse. But he seemed to think love really mattered. Like you said, stupid kid."

Joe cursed as he dropped his feet to the floor. "Maybe he found out the truth after he'd ruined his life for her and he snapped. Or maybe she just dropped him cold, not believing in him enough to give him a chance." We both knew he was talking about us, not two kids he didn't know. "Shit, eighteen years old. Can't even buy beer, and he can consent to becoming a bloodsucker."

"He's grown, legal to vote." I didn't know why I was arguing with him, since I agreed with what he was saying.

"You're condoning his decision?"

"No, just accepting that it was his to make." I stood, and tucked another stray hair behind my ears. I had meant to pull it up this morning, but other things had interrupted. With the heat and humidity, it'd grow six inches before night fell.

"I'm on my way to see his girlfriend. Thought you might want to tag along. If you're too busy, I can give you an update later."

When he shook his head and followed me to the door, I called myself ten kinds of fool for making the offer.

Chapter Six

Angel Henson, Peter's girlfriend, worked on Beale Street. It had been a while since I'd been down there and the changes astounded me.

Beale was like a chameleon, ever changing on the outside but locked into itself on the inside. I could say the same for me.

I had seen the pictures of the many faces of Beale. In the late eighteen hundreds its casual atmosphere had been a mecca for freed slaves, with its muddy cobblestone streets, gamblers, prostitution and murder. I'd heard the stories about Little Ora, the best pickpocket in the south, and Mary the Wonder, who could offer her voodoo protections for a price. There had been the castle of missing men, the Monarch, where a man could walk in the front door and be carried out the back by the undertaker that shared the back alley.

Mosquitos had nearly destroyed the city back then. Cholera and yellow fever epidemics had killed or ran off over half the population, much as they had six years ago when they swooped in with the West Nile Virus. Guess we owed the vampires something for saving it.

It had survived a hundred years, to be reborn again. The rundown, desolate area had given birth to the blues. This was a time-weathered street that grew old--and not always gracefully.

However, no one could doubt its ability to survive. Humans hadn't given up the street just because the vampires had moved in. It was the one area of the city where all cultures, all races mingled. This street had seen enough segregation.

The atmosphere never changed--loose and free, with a mysterious magic that hung in the air. I could see why the vamps loved it. It felt ancient, other worldly, with secrets of its own.

Angel worked at Silky Sullivan's. Last time I'd been to Silky's it had been down on the square. Shows how much I get out these days.

Silky had moved the best with them. I made my way through the crowd and took a deep breath once I was on the terrace. It was hot, thick, humid southern air, just the way my lungs preferred it.

Angel was dressed in the usual uniform of short black shorts, white shirt, and black bow tie. Not unique, as it was the uniform just about everywhere around here. She was cute, in an eerie sort of way. It seemed strange for a waitress to have fangs, but the girl had to make a living. Turning didn't come with a pot of gold, as I'm proof of. I doubted she'd find one working at Silky's.

"Angel? Why don't you take a break? We have a few questions we'd like to ask you about Peter. Detective Andrews is with the MPD, and I work for Vampire Affairs."

"Have you found him?" I saw hope fill her eyes.

"Not yet. Let's grab a table under that tree. We've cleared it with your boss."

"Sure, okay. My feet could use a rest."

"Do you have any idea where Peter might be?" She shook her head, still clinging to that hope. I didn't want to be the lucky one who had to take it from her.

"We had a fight. You don't know how screwed up my life is. I'm a freakin' vampire."

"I'm Lindy Campbell. Ever heard of me?" It's not my ego talking. I'm somewhat of a legend around here. One of a kind, usually hated by both sides. Seems someone is always bitching about me. Makes you known.

"Sure, you're the Vamp-hum. So, you like know what I'm talking about. How do you keep it from driving you crazy?"

I didn't pretend to not understand the question.

"Sure, it sucks. Just remember to never lose sight of yourself. No matter what anyone has done to you, you're still you. You just have a different lifestyle."

Her smile was sad, her eyes showing weariness much too old for someone barely on the verge of life. "Peter said you were cool. You pissed him off, trying to talk him out of that lame idea of his."

"It didn't work," I said.

"No, but for what it's worth, I couldn't change his mind either. But I couldn't do it. Turn him I mean. He found someone else to bite him. Now we're both lost souls. How could he think that's what I wanted for him?" Her eyes glistened with unshed tears.

"He loves you," I said softly.

"And I love him. That's why I, like, freaked when he turned on purpose. I mean, we'll be together forever, and that's pretty cool." She rubbed her eyes before the tears could fall.

"He worked so hard to put himself through Med School," Angel added.

"Doctor?" I asked.

"Yeah. He's an intern at St. Jude's. Was, anyway. No way they're gonna let him work in the lab now."

I knew how much that sucked. "What did he do there?"

"Worked with cell regeneration, if you can believe it." Angel's eyes filled. "He just threw it all away. Can you believe it?"

I couldn't. I had lost the same life as Peter, but I'd had no choice. No way would I have given it up voluntarily.

"He made his choice, which is more than you had," Joe added.

"My moaning won't help Peter. What do you need from me?" She slipped off her heels, and I fought the urge to join her.

"Does he have any enemies, Miss Henson?" Joe asked.

"No. Everyone loves Peter."

"Had he been upset lately?" I asked.

"We've been fighting a lot lately, about his turning." She shrugged, as if at a loss.

"Other than that?" I asked.

"No. When he was upset, he would go down to the river, watch the barges. I shouldn't have waited two weeks. My pride wouldn't let me call him. I thought he was just trying to make me crazy, like only a man can. You know?"

My eyes drifted to Joe automatically. "Yeah, I know."

I thanked her for her help and promised to call her if we found out anything. The way it was looking, I wouldn't be making that call any time soon.

"That's the second time I've heard St. Jude mentioned in connection with this case. Think it's a coincidence?" We stepped out into the hot summer humidity, and I could feel the air growing heavy.

Joe shook his head. "I might, if Larry Brown hadn't worked security there."

I slid behind the wheel. "They do a lot of work with blood diseases. Could be they stumbled onto something, or maybe someone wanted to take a short cut on research."

It was late when we returned to the castle. I wanted a hot bath, wine, and food.

What I found instead was chaos, attitude, and Rena.

She was lounging on the settee, posing for the room in a sheer, floor-length negligee. All eyes followed her every move as she lifted the delicately detailed goblet to her mouth. That she was sipping blood didn't seem to matter to the humans in the room.

"Stop toying with them, Rena." I snapped. My feet hurt, I was developing a headache and I was feeling a little sorry for myself after my talk with Angel. Nothing like a big fat reminder of just how screwed up your life is to bring a girl down.

"I'm bored." Rena slid the empty goblet onto the table and rose. I saw her intent as she glided toward Joe, and every muscle I had tightened. I'd need that hot bath before this was over just to stand erect.

"I need something a little more appealing to play with." She stopped in front of Joe and ran long red nails through his hair. I was mad at him, I reminded myself. He had been a real shit in his office, and even though he hadn't meant to hurt me, he hadn't apologized.

Rena was beautiful. In a way that made men stupid and women crazy. Fortunately, I was neither stupid nor crazy.

"This one is not so easy to tame." She practically purred.

"He won't consent to being bitten." Wasn't my problem, but I thought I'd give her the facts.

"Biting is not what I had in mind."

Did Joe need protecting? Did I have the right to step in and slap this hussy straight? When her hands slid to his open collar, I didn't care if jealously led me. I'd follow. Follow her straight to hell if those fingers went any lower.

"He's not for you." I tried to keep my tone light, unconcerned.

"Is he for you?" She turned her eyes to me, studying me carefully.

"That doesn't concern you. All you need to know is he's off limits." I ignored Joe's raised brows. Let him gloat. I should just stay out of it. Let him get into the trouble he was asking for. He was pissing me off anyway, allowing her to rub herself against him. But you didn't go around playing with a vamp fatale. Not unless your intentions were to see it through.

"That makes it all the more exciting, don't you agree?" Her hand slid lower, heading straight for his button fly. Joe stood stock still, no expression on his face. But his eyes were locked on me.

"I won't tell you twice." I stepped forward into their private space.

"Should he not decide for himself?" Rena complained.

I could feel her power rising, though the smile never left those blood-red lips. I could force the issue and end up in a catfight over Joe.

I knew Malcolm wouldn't allow her to kill me. He wanted that pleasure for himself. And while any damage she could do to me might be uncomfortable, I would heal. For Joe, I'd do it.

I looked at Joe, waiting. My hand itched to slap the smile from his face when it appeared. He was finding this amusing, at my expense. I was actually willing to take physical pain for him, the jerk. Screw him.

"He's a big boy, knock yourself out." It felt good to watch his smile fall. I don't do the jealous little woman well. And it rubbed, that I was sleeping with him but still didn't have the right to be jealous. There had been a time once, when I would not have hesitated to slap any woman who had the nerve to rub herself against him in my presence. It was a matter of pride.

But that wasn't the case any longer. I had made it clear that sex was all that was between us. Besides, Joe didn't seem to be in a hurry to stop the woman and her roaming hands.

THE CRIMSON FOLD

I crossed to the bar and poured a vodka and cranberry. I needed something more substantial than wine tonight. As I added ice, Malcolm approached. His long graceful fingers slid down my arm, leaving little goose bumps behind. Great, maybe I would turn and we could get a foursome going. I turned up my glass and drained it.

"How was your meeting, love?" I hated when Malcolm called me that. I turned to tell him just that when I felt Rena's eyes burning into my back. Well, wasn't this interesting? Could it be our little vamp had a thing for the master?

"Fine." I made me another drink, this one to go. "I'm going upstairs, Malcolm." I'd had about all I could take for one night. If Joe wanted to hang out with the vamps, I sure as hell wasn't going to stop him.

"I'll walk with you." Malcolm purred.

"I know the way." But I didn't complain when he followed me toward the stairs on the far wall.

"You're tired. I'll have a bath drawn for you and food sent up."

I chuckled. "You're from another era, Malcolm."

"Yes." He stiffened. For some reason I couldn't explain, I didn't want to leave it as an insult, when I hadn't intended it as one.

"It was a good era. I often said I would have liked to live in that time." A time when men had cherished women. Even the staunchest feminist couldn't find any negative in that.

"You would have been most welcomed. It would be simple to live in future times, Lucinda. Maybe you could find one that is as equally pleasing."

He was escorting me up the stairs, his hand on my elbow.

"Not so simple, Malcolm. My time is here."

"Time is what you make of it, love."

"Don't call me that, please. You know we can never be more than friends." I wasn't completely convinced we could be even that, but at least I was trying.

"Can't we?" I felt his eyes on me.

"No." I couldn't help but wonder, had I met him in another time, under other circumstances, would things have been different?

"You are still in love with him," he said.

"Who?"

He eyed me with an amused tolerance. If I couldn't even fool him, how in the hell was I supposed to fool myself?

He bowed regally at my door and I smiled. "I'll see to my own bath Malcolm, but thanks for the conversation." Oddly enough, I meant it. He had taken my mind off Joe and for a moment, I had even been able to relax around him.

I took my drink into the bathroom and filled the water in the oversized tub to the top. Malcolm might have his flaws but taste wasn't one of them. The tub was the size of my bathroom at home and any girl's dream. I added lavender from the crystal bottle setting on the ledge.

As I soaked in the steamy water, my mind wandered to the room downstairs. Was Joe still there, with Rena?

I had had sex with Joe twice in two weeks. It was more than I'd had in a year. It should have been enough.

But I felt more starved than ever. I wanted him to hold me, utter those loving words while he made love to me. To the real me. Not because I needed to assuage some lust craving of Malcolm's, but because he wanted me.

He wouldn't turn me down if I needed him as a vampire. Would he turn me down if I needed him to make love to me? He could turn off his feelings long enough to have wild sex with me. But could he turn them off while making love to me? That was what I needed, the emotional connection.

I felt as if he were cheating on me with me. Am I losing it or what?

And then the man walked into the room, as if I had conjured him up just by wishing him there.

"Lost? Rena's room is down the hall." I picked up the sponge and squeezed water down my arms, ignoring him.

"Jealous?" He leaned against the wall, his stance anything but relaxed. His eyes followed the drops of water as they slid down my arms.

"Of course not. She's not your type. She's a vampire, a bloodsucker."

"Seems I'm not adverse to having sex with them."

I felt my face burn. "Them. You mean because you've been sleeping with me?"

"We haven't been sleeping, babe."

He was in a mood, as his sarcasm made evident. He had no reason to be hurt or angry as far as I was concerned. "Get out. I'm not here for your sexual urges. Go find Rena."

"No, I'm here for yours. We fuck only when you need me to assuage some lust craving brought on by Malcolm's blood, is that it?" He didn't raise his voice, but it vibrated with anger. As if he had reason to be mad at me, when he'd been the one to let another woman hang all over him.

"Let me bathe in peace. Go find your little slut downstairs. I don't need your charity fuck." I tossed the sponge into the water and slid lower until my head rested against the edge. Closing my eyes as if blocking him from sight would make him disappear.

"No, Malcolm will be happy to take care of that for you." He stepped toward the tub, his hands fisted at his side. My eyes opened, then widened.

"What'd you do, drop your sure thing to run up here and see if I was getting lucky?" I asked.

THE CRIMSON FOLD

Candlelight flickered around the room, casting shadows that faded quickly. As Joe took a step toward me, I saw the look on his face. Rage. "Back off, Joe. I mean it, don't make me hurt you." I stood, dripping water, just in case I needed to defend myself. Joe had never tried to hurt me before, but I had never seen him so angry with me.

"Too late for that." He reached for me. I could have fought him. Should have. But what was the point? We both knew I wanted it. I felt his anger die, the minute I was in his arms. He was lifting me, carrying me to the bed. How many times had he carried me to our bed over the years we had been together? No use dreaming about the past, when the present was pressing against my stomach.

As he pressed into the mattress beside me, his fingers trailed slowly down my face, my neck, stopping on my stomach. His mouth covered mine, but not with the strength of the other two times. This time Joe was slow, feather light. His thumb traced my jaw as his tongue slowly made love to my mouth. He moved lower, covering my breast as his tongue traced lazy circles around my nipple. Fire raced through me as my body came to life.

And then I realized what he was doing. He was making love to me, making me open my heart and feel. This wasn't what I needed. It might be exactly what I wanted, but want had no place here. I wanted it all with Joe. The fairytale. Kids, dogs, forever after. What I could have was sex.

I didn't want to taste slow, sensual love only to be denied when my heart fell for him again. Didn't want my heart involved at all. I wanted fast, hot sex. The kind where you couldn't think.

I reached for him, trying to drive him faster. "Hurry Joe." I was ready for him, more than ready.

"We've got all night." He murmured against my skin as his tongue continued on its slow meandering path. "Slow down just a bit."

His soft caresses stirred too much in me, too many memories. Of long nights making love while the rain beat against the window. Of Sunday mornings, staying in bed to make love until noon. Of laying on the couch, just kissing for hours. I didn't want to be reminded of those times. All they would do is make me need him again. Make me feel as if I would die without him. Make me feel, damn it. I couldn't fall for Joe again, because the next time I lost him, it would surely kill me.

I rolled him over, straddled him, and then slid over him in one quick move. I closed tightly around his hardness, savored the feeling of our bodies connected for only a heartbeat before I started moving at a frenzied pace.

I closed my eyes against the disappointment I saw in his eyes. The minute he gave himself up to the ecstasy of our bodies, he rolled me over and took control, driving us harder. It was over quickly. Exhausted, I closed my eyes and gave in to sleep.

The next morning, he was gone. It was probably not payback for the same stunt I'd pulled on him, but my mind couldn't keep from accusing him. When the entire day had passed without so much as a call from him, I knew that was exactly what it had been.

Joe was angry at me for having sex with him. He had wanted to make love, wanted more than the physical act. The hell of it was, I wanted more as well. I was just smart enough to know there was no more for us.

* * * *

By nightfall, I was irritable, lonely, and fighting the change once again. No wonder I was sitting in the main room, with Malcolm to keep me company.

"There will be a gathering here tonight of my people. Many belonged to Surgis and must now swear allegiance to me."

"No problem, I'll make myself scarce," I said.

"On the contrary, I would prefer that you make yourself abundantly available. It would be an excellent opportunity for questions, and we could possibly learn something beneficial to the investigation."

Every vamp in the city, probably in this county and the surrounding, was coming to the castle and Malcolm wanted me to be there. I so didn't want to.

Since the bureau had been formed, it was law for all vampires to register with me, to keep an accurate count. The city officials wanted to make sure the vamps didn't suddenly outnumber the humans. I didn't think that would be a problem. Since the no biting law, the number of newly turned vampires was surprisingly low.

I knew their numbers to be only around fifty, give or take, including the few new applications I had processed this year. Not many, in a city of hundreds of thousands. But one vampire was much scarier than a hundred, maybe even a thousand humans, so I figured they were a lot more evenly matched than anyone figured.

Malcolm was right. Tonight would be the perfect time to snoop around. It meant I needed to talk to Joe, and that was almost worse than facing the vamps tonight. I knew he was angry with me, and cowardly or not, I just wasn't ready to face him yet. Actually, maybe it was the perfect time. With so many of the bad guys around, he wouldn't have time to chew on me.

"Inform Joe, so he can have the team here." If the request surprised Malcolm, he didn't show it. Maybe he knew Joe and I were having our little spat.

"You know how pissed off the MPD would be if one of their finest got himself drained tonight, right?" I asked. A room full of vampires and human cops seemed like begging for trouble to me, but it wasn't my call.

"If one of the men, how did you put it, get themselves drained, it would likely be of his own doing."

"You know what I mean," I snapped.

"Yes. I can assure you my people would never feed on one of my guests without permission."

I waited, but he said nothing more. "And you won't give that permission, right?"

"It would be impolite," Malcolm said.

Why couldn't I ever get a solid answer from this guy?

"Impolite and illegal. Just see that none of them get carried away."

"You seem to conveniently forget, Lucinda, that you are a vampire."

"There's nothing convenient about my life, Malcolm." I left him and went back up to my room. If I was going to be on display tonight, I wanted a little down time to prepare myself.

I'm like the main attraction at a freak show. Humans and vamps alike both watch me intensely, just to see if I am more dead or alive. I get the impression both sides hope I'm not like them.

Neither care much for me. The humans figure any vampire blood is too much, and since I can grow fangs and suck them dry, I guess I agree. The problem with the vampires, well, I don't exactly hide the fact that I don't want to be one of them, and I guess my denial offends them most of the time.

The truth is that I find both sides equally annoying. I wouldn't admit this aloud, but the vampires are growing on me, and I actually like some of them. Doesn't mean I want to be one. I just understand their hard position. Most of them, like me, didn't ask to become what they are. They have spent years, sometimes decades, evolving into their lifestyle, and you have to admire them for that courage.

I took a long bath, in no hurry to join the party below. I would have to make my way down to the basement level before long, but Joe and the other cops had been off for a few hours, and I knew they would be downstairs already.

I pulled on my tightest black jeans, not for the attention they would draw but for the hardship they would present on removal. Closest thing to a modern day chastity belt, and since I could turn at any time, I needed the added security.

I slid into my black leather boots and a white peasant shirt. I loved the way the billowy sleeves caressed the tops of my hands--plus they would hide the bracelets. I added the necklace, but with the low neckline of the blouse, it was fashionable instead of a blatant insult. I brushed my hair until most of the curls had straightened, but I knew in the Memphis humidity they would bounce back before I descended the stairs. My slow, careful hand applying my makeup wasn't because I cared how it turned out, but because I was stalling. Once I realized the ploy, I finished quickly and forced myself out of my room.

The house was eerily quiet. If there was a party going on downstairs, it wasn't like any I'd ever attended. In the south, you could count on a running theme through all of the parties. Plenty of drunken rednecks and ear-busting music. Both seemed absent tonight.

I had been to the basement only once, and after being shot, I didn't remember much about it. The bedroom where I had been taken was the first door I passed, and I continued down the long dark hall, praying I would come across others soon.

Yes, I still pray. I gave up on church services last year, but not out of fear of burning to death on the threshold. Truthfully, most congregations don't want my kind inside their doors, and I can't stand a hypocrite. I still pray, and even wear a cross necklace on occasions. I figure I need God more these days than ever.

My heels clicked over the uneven stone flooring as I turned the corner of the torch-lit passageway. It opened into a large room, packed full of standing bodies. Some were even breathing. The silence was deafening. There seemed to be some kind of show down front, and something told me I didn't want to see it. As I made my way down, the crowd of bodies stepped back to let me pass. Joe appeared and fell in step beside me. He didn't speak, so I knew he was still mad, but at least he was there.

When I stepped through the crowd, I realized what had everyone's attention. Malcolm was seated in a chair large enough for a king. His black pants were tucked into boots that stopped just below his knees, and unlike mine, his looked as soft as baby's skin. His white shirt was unbuttoned down his chest, the lacing left open to show his muscle and tone. Vampires approached him, offering their wrists to him as they knelt at his feet. I watched as his fangs pierced skin, sank deep into the vein to draw out the very essence of the man. Then I realized that this was what it meant to swear allegiance to the new master.

Surgis had turned many of these present, and the only way to ensure they would follow the new master was to bind them through blood. Malcolm would have their memories, know if they lied to him, and he would be able to call to them if the need arrived.

I realized that the man kneeling to Malcolm was unknown to me, and as my eyes scanned the room, I realized many faces were unfamiliar. There were many more than fifty here, nearly twice that number. It seemed not everyone felt the need to obey the registration law. I hoped it was the only law they were breaking. After Malcolm had his price in blood, the man moved off and the next stepped up. At this rate, Malcolm wouldn't need to feed for a week.

Rena stood on Malcolm's right, Ian on his left. I stepped up beside Ian. "Can he feed from all of them?"

Ian chuckled at my question, but it didn't annoy me. Had anyone else done that, I would have been bristling, but Ian didn't make you feel as if he was laughing at you because of your ignorance, but rather that you had indeed amused him. I was glad to oblige.

"He does not feed, merely takes enough for the binding. Tis not a hardship. Most here are his own."

I knew the significance of Ian's position in the room, as it announced he was second only to Malcolm. What surprised me was that Rena stood in the third position. She had climbed the ranks in this new clan quickly.

"Did Malcolm bind Rena to him already?"

Ian looked shocked by my question.

"Rena is as old as Malcolm. She answered to Surgis, as master. Once that bond is broken, she will na be owned by another. She gives her alliance freely, ta demand blood is to suggest her disloyalty. Malcolm would ne'er dishonor her so."

I nodded and continued to watch the show. I should have been horrified, watching someone suck the blood from another. That it didn't, horrified me even more. Malcolm was right. I was becoming more like them every day. Would I wake up one day and not be able to feel the sunshine on my skin? Would I be forced to rely on the blood from a human as my only sustenance? I shuddered and fought the urge to cry. My eyes cut to Joe. His face was hard, the lines around his mouth tight. What was he thinking about this little performance? I was certain he wasn't standing there with his mouth watering, as mine had just started doing. How would he react if I were the one drinking from another's wrist instead of Malcolm? I was certain he would be mortified.

Chapter Seven

I felt, more than saw, Malcolm stiffen and instantly knew something was wrong. The man at his feet was also unknown to me, and I had no idea what had prompted Malcolm to rise to his feet.

Malcolm turned his mouth away from the wrist and then spit the mouth full of blood on the floor.

"Rise!" Malcolm demanded.

The vampire jumped to his feet and took a step back. My skin began to tingle as I felt the surge of power fill the room. Ian stepped forward, his chest nearly touching the man's back.

"How dare you offer me tainted blood? You present to me your wrist, when you should be presenting me with your carved heart. You have betrayed our kind and brought shame to our race."

"No, Master. I have done nothing wrong." The vampire's eyes looked left to right, wide with fear. Whatever he was accused of doing, the guilt was evident on his face.

"You, Trayvor, were made by Surgis not by my blood. My blood is the blood of the Memphis Triad. Ptah, the high God of Memphis, Sekhmet, mistress of war, sickness, battle and her child Nefertem. How dare you taint the blood of the Gods?"

"Please, have mercy on my line, Master." Whatever the man had done, he was terrified now that he had been found out.

"Bring forth your line so that I may see what you have born."

Trayvor motioned to a young woman, and she stepped forward. She was beautiful, with an intriguing allure of innocence rarely seen among a race that had seen more than most people could envision. Youth wasn't the reason for her innocence, though she couldn't have been more than eighteen at the time of her death.

She held a tight grip on the hand of a man twice her age but still handsome and strong. Though not matching in age, it was obvious they were matched in their feelings for each other. They both bowed to Malcolm.

"Stand," Malcolm demanded, and from his tone I could tell he had little patience left. "You are of Trayvor's line?"

"Yes, Master. I am Raymon, and this is Shayna. Please take what I offer." The man offered his wrist, but Malcolm only stared into eyes the color of creamy coffee. Whatever Malcolm had been looking for in their depths, he seemed satisfied that he had found it, as he took the offered wrist into his mouth. Raymon gave a slight jerk as Malcolm's sharp teeth tore into the flesh. The wound was ragged and punishing painful.

My stomach rolled as I stared at the gaping hole of flesh just as Malcolm covered it with his mouth. He took a minimal amount for a true exchange before shoving the hand away. When the woman presented her wrist, it was shaking. I couldn't blame her. It took a great deal of courage for her to offer it, after seeing what Malcolm had just done to the last one offered to him.

Malcolm didn't rip the flesh open this time, simply sank his sharp fangs into the creamy white skin. I had experienced the shot of pain fading to ecstasy that Shayna now felt.

Malcolm drank deeply, and for a moment, I thought he was going to drain her completely. I saw Raymon stiffen, but he wisely stood back while Malcolm made his own decision.

What was I supposed to do if he decided to drain her, right in front of all of us? It would not kill her, but it would be a painful agony until the blood was replaced. I was the one person the vampires were supposed to turn to for help and protection, but did I dare protect them from their own master? The rules were strict and failure to follow them could easily insult them all. I knew this was not an area I should intrude.

I didn't want to watch it. Just as I made the decision to turn away, Malcolm released Shayna's wrist. When she swayed on her feet, Raymon reached for her, holding her around her waist to steady her. Together, they stepped back.

"Mercy will be granted to your line, Trayvor. As of now, they are of my line. Step forward."

The man hesitated, finally realizing he had no other choice but to obey. Just as his feet moved him forward, Malcolm's hand shot out. Power rose higher, the pressure building inside my head as it built inside the room. Trayvor froze, locked in place as around him, people took several steps back. No one wanted to be connected in any way to what was about to happen.

"You have thrived on the adrenaline of those who fear you. You have used the strength granted you by the Gods to bring terror into those who have been entrusted into your care. It is against human law to drink from those unwilling, yet you have killed many in your thirst for power."

There was the problem with allowing a vampire to drink from your veins. They knew your darkest secrets. Had I had such things to hide, I would never have shown up tonight and offered my wrist to a man who wielded that kind of power.

Joe's head snapped to Malcolm at this news, and I knew he was about to do something really stupid like interfere. He couldn't help it. It was the cop in him.

I put my hand on Joe's elbow to stop him, knowing that this was to be handled by the master. To interfere was dangerous. Joe turned to look at me, understanding but debating on breaking that rule.

"You have walked a path of your own making, and you have chosen poorly." Malcolm's words caught Joe's attention and mine.

I watched in horror as the blood began pouring from the vampire's pores. "You are not worthy of this blood."

There was a gasp of shock, surprisingly from my own throat. My eyes stared at the form, trying to make sense of what I was seeing. The body was coated in red, soaked in the very thing that had led him to this pain. It poured to his feet, pooled there. Just when I thought it would cover the floor, Trayvor dropped to the floor, empty. No one moved. So much fresh blood, the good kind from a vampire, and not one vampire went for it. Then I found out why.

Power continued to build, and I felt my eyes watering from the pressure. My head throbbed as I stared at that blood.

Then the blood started to bubble, popped as it slowly began to take another shape. Each drop grew, began moving as it turned into a thousand roaches. It was a mound of moving legs, scattering from the light. I saw one run across my foot. I would have jumped and likely screamed, but I was locked in place with fear. How was it possible that such creepy things erupted from blood? Was Malcolm really that powerful? No way would Doc find a scientific reason for that trick.

Finding every crack and crevice, the nasty little things disappeared as if they had never been. The body was cleared from the room, all evidence of Trayvor's existence gone with the fleeing insects. I can't say I wasn't glad. But before I could even take a calming breath, my lungs grew tight. The power had not evaporated and was looking for a new target. As the closest, it found one in me.

Changing always hurt. Can't die without a little pain. But this was no slow transformation. The beast was pulled from, screaming. One minute I was alive, the next I was dead. The undead. I felt my heart stop, the breath ripped from my chest. My fangs, without the preparation, felt like knives pushing through my gums. I would have fallen to the floor had Joe not held me tightly.

I opened my eyes, looking up at him through red haze. "Welcome, my child." Malcolm's voice was deep, echoing in my head. "Come, swear alliance to your master."

I wanted to run from the room, deny it. Then the vision started. Egypt, in all its glory. The pyramid, the alabaster sphinx, the statue to Ptah. There were people entering a pyramid, loaded with baskets of silk, trays of food. Gifts to honor their Gods.

"Memphis was beautiful."

"Was?" Malcolm was looking at me strangely.

"It is a dead city now, isn't it? Shame." At his raised brow, I continued, "Deserted. I read it somewhere."

"You see what we want you to see. Because it is void of humans does not make it an empty city. Is not your Memphis void of humans?"

Good point. My Memphis had been turned over to the undead.

"Come to me, Lucinda." He held out his hands, and for a second I felt the need to reach out and touch them. But Joe's hold on me tightened, and the need passed. Slowly Joe moved us toward the door, then we were moving up the stairs. When we got to the main room, I dropped to the sofa while Joe poured himself bourbon. My head still ached, but it was a throbbing I could live with. Without the power rushing through me, I could think clearly again.

I heard the footsteps on the stairs, and now everyone was leaving quietly. Obviously, the party was over. I'd been to some wild parties in my life, woke up with some pretty bad headaches, but tomorrow would probably be the worst yet, and I hadn't drank a drop. I guess a power high was as bad as alcohol.

"We must retire now. Dawn approaches soon." Malcolm sauntered into the room like any normal man, instead of the monster I just learned him to be. As if he hadn't just drained a man and turned his blood into a thousand filthy roaches.

"I'm not sleeping in this house. Ever." I crossed my arms over my chest and played the sulky little girl really well.

"You insult the master if you leave," Rena said, as if I really cared. But then again, I had just watched what the master had done to the last guy who made him angry.

"Insult him? He filled this place with roaches. Thousands of them. Rude, if you ask me. And do you know where all of those roaches are now? No. You don't. And neither do I. I'm not closing my eyes and having them crawl all over me!"

"They will not harm you," Malcolm said, as if I would believe him.

"Wanna bet?"

"You fear no man, no vampire. Yet you are afraid of a insect a mere nothing to your size?"

Boy, did he have me pegged wrong. No fear? Most of the time, I was too damn scared to move. Let them think what they will. It was better that they didn't know that they terrified me. "I'm not afraid of them, they're just nasty. And those innocent little nothings will be here long after we're all dead and gone. They're harder to kill than you are."

"You cannot leave," Malcolm stated again, more firmly.

"They don't come out during the day, much," Joe added, as if that was helping any. "Should fit right in around here. We'll sleep after the sun rises.

Malcolm frowned. "I do not like your sleeping arrangements."

"Tough." Joe stood beside the fireplace, his arm braced on the mantle.

Sleeping in a coffin is worse than sleeping with roaches," I said. Wasn't it?

"I do not sleep in a coffin. I have a vault. Inside that vault, I have a bedroom with a bed. It is more like your large safe than a coffin. Fireproof, neither sunlight nor human can enter. Only I can open it."

"Makes sense." Couldn't he have shared that little news flash the first day?

"I'm glad you think so. Others who are not so fortunate make their own space. In basements, crawl spaces, whatever is convenient. And yes, some sleep in coffins. There is a large room downstairs made to the same specifications as mine. It holds many beds.

"My blood grows stronger in you, and you weaken during sunlight hours."

The denial was on my lips.

"Do not deny this. You cannot hide your restlessness, your weakness from me. You may join me to rest. You will benefit from being locked so deeply away from daylight."

"We'll pass, thanks. I'll take care of Lindy." Joe eyed Malcolm with a warning in his eyes.

"You begin to bore me, human."

"And you're about to piss me off. I've heard all I'm going to about Lindy from you. She's not yours, Bloodsucker. Get over it."

"And if I choose not to *get over it*, human?"

"Boys, stop it. Thanks for the offer, Malcolm, but we're fine. I'm only a little tired from lack of sleep."

"You haven't fed," he said, like I needed him to tell me that.

"I was getting around to it."

"Soon you will need fresh blood for your first bite. I will provide a willing partner."

"Nice try. I might follow the storybooks on most of this, but I know that deal. If I bite, I turn. Permanently."

"Not exactly. You will turn regardless. Having fresh blood only lessens the pain." As if turning dead permanently could hurt more than doing it weekly.

Just what I wanted to hear. I didn't want to think about that.

"I saw you with Rena earlier. Did anyone learn anything new tonight?" I wanted to change the subject, and blood and murder always worked with this group. Man, do I need some new friends.

"We have learned that a vampire does not have the humans."

"How do you know that?" My attention was on Malcolm now.

"I asked."

I snorted. Not very ladylike, but why break my image now? "You asked. Why didn't I think of that? Come on Joe, let's go knock on a few doors. If we run across the killer, I'm sure he'll confess immediately, saving ourselves tons of work."

"Sarcasm does not become you Lucinda," Malcolm said.

Says who? I think it totally becomes me.

"And they would not lie to me," Malcolm added.

"Sure, Malcolm."

"They are mine. The penalty is too steep, and I would know."

I tried to read the answer in his eyes but gave up. Did I really want to know? I knew he could read things from the ones he had taken blood from. And he had taken my blood. There was a pattern there I didn't want to exist. Closing your eyes against unpleasant things didn't make them disappear. I had learned that one quick enough. So, I asked the one thing I didn't really want to know. "How?"

"The same way I know when you are lying to me."

Not going there. Nope. No way. "Fine. If they don't have them, then who does? That leaves other humans and that just doesn't work for me. Why would they grab their own kind?"

"You tell me. What is to be gained by it?"

That one was easy. Only one place this was headed if we couldn't stop it. "War between the races. You saying it's a setup?"

"I do not know. I only know that if my people tell me they do not have the humans, then that only leaves other humans."

I plopped down next to Ian on the sofa. I liked Ian. I did not like this conversation. I had liked Ian the minute he had opened the door to me that first day. There was just something about him that attracted others.

"You are tired, lass."

"Yes." He put his arm around me, and I laid my head back. It felt good, resting on Ian's arm. "Talk to me, Ian."

"About?"

"Anything. The weather for all I care. Any words rolling off that tongue of yours soothe me." From his chuckle, I knew he didn't think I meant it. How could he not know how beautiful that musical lilt was?

"Ye remind me of me own dear sister. Headstrong and stubborn, that one."

"Thank you." I closed my eyes and let his words flow over me. Strange how much they soothed me.

He chuckled again, warm and deep. "Aye. She'd have mistaken it for a compliment as well."

I opened my eyes and grinned at him. "You need a woman, Ian."

"Is it an offer you're making me then?"

This time, I laughed. "I wish. I seem to have one man too many in my life as it is." I nodded toward the corner, where Malcolm and Joe had carried their conversation.

"Ah, but I can solve it for ye, just say the word."

"Do you like it, Ian? Being a vampire, I mean."

"I know what you mean. Aye. Malcolm is like me own brother."

"So he's the one who turned you?"

"Aye, that he'd be. And I whipped his arse good for it the first score of years."

I laughed again, as he'd meant for me to do.

"Then we became the best of friends."

I closed my eyes again and drifted on the melody of his words. I could sleep here. Ian would keep the bugs away, would watch over me while I rested my eyes for just a few minutes.

Chapter Eight

I awoke to the stream of sunlight across my face. I didn't remember going to bed. It was the fist time I hadn't needed sex after turning. First time I hadn't fed, for that matter. Maybe Ian was good to have around. I'd talk to Doc today about that. Maybe my cravings were getting better. I knew it wasn't true, but denial worked on rare occasions.

From the corner of my eye I saw Joe stirring across the room.

"Morning," he said.

I looked beside me, noticing that Joe's side of the bed hadn't been slept in. So he was still mad at me. I couldn't expect anything else. I had been a real bitch to him, but it was the only thing I could do for both of us. I didn't want sweet words from Joe. Couldn't let such things get to me. They were just words, cheap to give but expensive to receive. I'd be the one paying for them.

"Morning. Who put me in bed?"

"I did. You were out cold, and Ian's arm fell asleep. It was also time for his watch."

"Thanks."

"No problem. I was surprised you slept after the statement you made."

"Guess I figured Ian would keep me safe. Not much that isn't afraid of the big, bad vampire." I stretched like a cat.

"I don't make you feel safe, do I, Lindy?" He stopped strapping on his holster, staring at me. I knew this was a serious question, and I knew more was hanging on my answer than the question implied.

"You always have." I could sense he didn't believe me. How could I make him understand I couldn't let all of my guard down and trust him completely? Ian couldn't hurt me, because I didn't love him like I loved Joe.

My cell phone interrupted further comment, joined a second later by Joe's beeper. It was another victim. I knew it even before I heard the words in my ear. However, this time, the victim was not dead. And not a stranger.

* * * *

I stared down at Ian, bile rising in my throat. He had been staked on the cobblestones at the boat ramp at Tom Lee Park. The other members of the team who had beat us here had already cut him loose and moved his body into the back of a box truck. Odd, but an ambulance let in too much light and choices were limited on short notice.

I leaned over him, my tears dripping onto his face.

"Oh, Ian." It hurt, seeing him that way. Ian was my sanity in a world gone mad.

"None of that, lass."

I wiped them away. Tears would do him no good now. "Bite me, Ian. Drink from me and you'll be all right."

"Too late for that."

"No, it's not." I grabbed a box cutter that had been left in the truck and pricked my finger. I held it over his mouth, allowing the drops to fall. I knew he was right when he turned his face away.

"Human." He mumbled. "Too much power. Tis a wee man what brought me down. Look out for Malcolm, tis him they wish to harm." He closed his eyes. I shook him, tried to wake him, but his was an eternal sleep.

Sunlight doesn't turn a vampire to dust. Nothing so instantaneous. It burns, straight through skin, muscle and tissue. Once the veins are exposed, the blood dries up. No chance of recovery since the blood has nothing to travel through even if it is replaced. It is an excruciating death, a slow one. One Ian didn't deserve. One someone was going to pay for.

* * * *

I was unlucky enough to get the pleasure of telling Malcolm his best friend was dead, but it was something that would have to wait. I still had a few hours of daylight left and a dozen reports to complete. Joe's report to his superior was nothing compared to the dozen I had to complete every time one of the dead died. And the mayor was being his usual impossible self. I snagged the forms and agreed to complete them at Joe's office, while he did his own.

I wanted to be there when Doc did Ian's autopsy.

Officially, it couldn't be done until after the sun set. The law had passed last year prohibiting daytime autopsies for vampires. Right after one had been performed on a vamp down in New Orleans who hadn't actually been dead. Even a vamp can't recover from being dissected. It's a good law, actually. Since vampires have no vitals, mistakes are easily made. Joe and I argued over going. He didn't want me there, and I refused to budge. I understood he was trying to protect me from hurting more over Ian's death, but some things had to be faced.

He ended up staying with me, which still didn't make me happy. He was standing several feet from me, trying to ignore my tears as effectively as he was ignoring me.

I couldn't blame him. Most men didn't know what to do with a woman's tears. I hated them myself, but couldn't seem to stop them. Seeing Ian as he was hurt like hell.

"He was empty." Doc hadn't started the actual cutting, but preliminary tests wouldn't hurt Ian. Not that anything could anymore.

"He couldn't be, Doc. I saw him last night and he was healthy. No way was he starving. And Ian would never let another vampire drain him. Could the sunlight have dried it all up?" I couldn't think about the last time I had seen Ian. It would do him no good, and I needed to pay attention so I could get this bastard.

"It is possible, I suppose. But I do not think that is what happened. You said there was no blood at the scene. If the damage to his body caused him to bleed out, there would have been a large amount of blood once the sunlight opened up the veins. It appears he was completely drained. Not starving, not sun damaged, but drained."

"Ian said the man that did this was human." I moved away from Ian's body, leaning against the counter that was covered with surgical instruments. The room Doc used to perform autopsies was connected to his lab, but unlike the lab, this room was kept sterile.

"He also said with strong powers," Joe added.

So he was listening. He had moved across the room to join us but still kept his distance from me. It just proved how screwed up I really was that I wanted him standing closer. Close enough so that his scent filled my head, instead of the smell of Ian's death.

"What does that mean? How can a human have strong powers?"

"You do. You're stronger than any human even without the change." Joe looked my way, but it felt as if he wasn't really looking at me.

"Doc, there isn't another Vamp-hum, is there?" I asked.

"I've heard rumors. Not of another Vamp-hum, and I would have heard about that. I believe it is safe to say you are the only one in existence." Lucky me. I just love being one of a kind.

"There are stories of those who seek eternal life without the sacrifices that accompany it. It is said that they drink the blood of vampires, believe it gives them power without turning."

"Why haven't I heard these stories? Surely the vampires would know of such a group?" I asked.

"Maybe. This was many years ago, in the New Orleans community. Most believed the stories were merely tales for the benefit of the tourists. There were a few deaths for a brief period--unexplained, of course. Then suddenly they stopped."

"Maybe whoever was behind them left the area," Joe said.

"Or maybe they never existed, and the deaths were unconnected. New Orleans can be a rough town. You must understand that most of these tales are created solely for the mystic. Vampires thrive on the fear they bring to men," Doc said.

"How could it even be possible to drink their blood? Anyone who took a few sips would become infected."

THE CRIMSON FOLD

"Yes. Like I said, only tales. Stories to frighten us."

"But if someone believed it to be true, maybe they would try to accomplish it by drinking the blood," Joe said.

"It's common knowledge that's how the virus is transferred. They'd know the outcome. And that doesn't explain the humans that were taken. They have nothing to offer," I said.

"Quite right." Doc removed the soiled latex gloves from his hands and dropped them in the trash. "Except blood."

"It's about the blood. I can feel it."

"I would agree with you." Doc moved to the sink, washed and dried his hands.

"What gives me my strength, Doc?"

I could tell Doc was pondering the question before he gave his reply. "Malcolm's blood."

"Yes, but what exactly in his blood? Is it the virus?"

"His blood is the mutated cell from the virus."

"But what if we removed the virus? What would be left? Regular blood, right? What would then happen to Malcolm? Would he become human?"

"No, he can't. He is not alive, his organs are dead. There would be no way for him to breath air, no heartbeat."

"So he would die." Really die. Not just the mock death he did every morning at daybreak.

"Yes. However, if we were to take a living being, a human, and give him vampire blood, then accurately kill the virus--"

"He would have vamp power without turning vampire." I finished for him. That was the great thing about working with someone so closely for years; you could almost follow each other's train of thought.

"Exactly."

"But you are talking about the cure," Joe supplied.

"I know."

"How is that possible? There is no cure, you said so yourself."

"I don't know. Dying cells are the only things we've come up with. The question is, what is stronger than vamp blood?" Doc asked, his mind already working to find the answer.

"Did you run those samples for me?" I had asked Doc to run a few tests on my blood, pitted against the samples of vampire blood he had from the victims, just in case I decided to try his antidote. Provided of course, that Malcolm would ever conveniently die to give me the necessary blood. Not likely, I knew.

"Yes, just finished the test earlier."

"So tell me then, what is stronger than vampire blood?"

"You are. Your blood anyway, so it would seem."

"Sure it is, Doc. That's why Malcolm's can control me so easily, why I crave blood."

"But the fact that you don't crave it continuously proves my theory. Look here."

I followed him to the counter and then peered into the microscope.

"I was using your mutated cells. Half yours, half Malcolm's. I expected when I added another's pure vampire blood, yours would be gobbled up first since it is still half human.

"What I got was the opposite. The mutated cells attacked the new invader, which means--"

"My mutated cells are stronger than pure vampire blood. So another vampire could bite me and I wouldn't turn completely." Nice to know.

"Correct. Unless it is Malcolm. I still don't know how his blood would react with the mutated cells. We can assume if you ingest more of his mutated cells, they would succeed in killing your own cells this time, and you would truly become a vampire."

"And if my blood recognizes his as a component of my mutated cells, they would not attack. Then this supposed cure someone might have created would not work on me."

"True. But your blood can kill the blood of another. While it may not work against Malcolm's, I suspect it would work on any other vampire."

I would have to give that one some thought. It meant that my blood might actually be used in the cure for other Vamp-hums. If any existed, anyway. "Would it work on the newly bitten? Could I be the missing link in a cure for others?"

"Only for a short window. The problem is, the organs die quickly after someone is bitten. Once they have died, they can never return to living. Which means that the blood must be administered at the precise moment."

"So I could be the answer to the cure." It wouldn't help me any, but at least others could benefit from my being bitten. It was something, at least.

"Yes. But it will take more study to perfect it." Doc reached across the counter, his hand squeezing my arm. I knew it was his way of showing me he cared. "You need to be careful, Lindy. Whoever is behind this, may have already figured out you are not as you seem. Any human would have died from the shot you received. Yet you were walking around in the sunlight, which indicates you are not a vampire. And you are known. If there is someone out there playing this roulette, you would be his answer."

"I'll be careful."

Doc pulled on fresh latex gloves and added his cotton apron. Performing an autopsy on a vampire is risky. Since the blood carries the virus, one little slip of the knife and you could easily infect yourself.

THE CRIMSON FOLD

Ian's wasn't so dangerous, since there wasn't a drop of blood left, but still Doc took the proper precautions. He'd be a fool not to. Doc might live in his scientific world most of the time, oblivious to the real world around him, but he was no fool.

"It's dark outside." I looked toward the windows to confirm Doc's words. Sure enough, my own image stared back at me as the black turned the window to a mirror.

It wasn't a pretty sight. Dark circles under my eyes made me look as if I'd been in a fight and lost. My hair had turned into a nightmare of curls from the humidity. I normally didn't worry too much about my appearance unless I was trying to get to Joe, but this was even bad by my standards.

"We'll begin." Doc sounded much more excited than the rest of us as he approached the body. He saw this as a great scientific mystery to unfold. I saw it as the cutting up of a friend. I guess I wasn't cut out for the medical world anymore.

The scalpel was sharp, and I turned away before Doc made the first cut. These things didn't usually bother me. No way they could after working in a hospital in my other life. But this wasn't just anybody. This was Ian. I had a soft spot for Ian, and I couldn't watch him get cut up.

The metal door to the lab swung open with such force, it banged against the wall, startling the life from me. From the look on Joe and Doc's faces, they were just as surprised.

Chapter Nine

"Touch him, and you will die." Malcolm's voice wasn't what caused Doc to drop the scalpel immediately. It was the power surrounding Malcolm, the threat in his eyes.

"Malcolm." Since I recovered first, I crossed the room, stopping just out of reach. With Malcolm's strength and power, the same city wasn't far enough. He was on the edge tonight. I didn't blame him, but I didn't want to be the one trying to calm him down. As the only other person in the room anywhere close to his strength, I knew it was up to me.

"I'd hoped to tell you about Ian before anyone else had the chance. I'm sorry. We were just too late."

His eyes never left Ian's body as he glided toward the table. His feet were on the ground, but I swear he didn't use them.

Malcolm didn't answer me, didn't so much as acknowledge my presence in the room.

The pain in his eyes as he stared down at his oldest friend was more than I could take. I moved my gaze to the wall of books behind him and tried to read the names.

Anything to keep the damn tears away.

Doc's gasp brought my eyes back to the center of the room.

The palms of Malcolm's hands had been slashed open, and blood was quickly spilling over. Malcolm had laid both of his hands on Ian's face, the blood soaking into the dried flesh. I wanted to tell him it was too late, but as I watched Malcolm cover Ian's face in his blood, I wasn't so sure. I silently prayed that I was wrong.

Malcolm pumped his hands, kept the blood flowing freely as his hands moved lower, covering Ian's chest. I watched in horror as he literally gave Ian a blood bath.

And then I realized what he was doing. His blood, the ancient blood of the gods, was the most powerful. As Ian's master, his blood would flow in Ian's veins. By covering Ian's body, it was as if Ian's own blood was repairing himself.

Rebuilding each layer, beginning with the veins.

Malcolm swayed on his feet, his concentration so locked on his task I don't even think he noticed. He was draining himself in order to provide the massive amount of blood needed to cover Ian's body. I don't know if he wasn't aware of the risk, or if he just didn't care. Either way, I couldn't watch it happen.

My eyes met Joe's and I saw the fleeting thought cross his eyes. This could be our chance to try Doc's cure. If Malcolm killed himself in order to save Ian, we would have our blood necessary for the trial. Even as I read Joe's refusal of the idea in his eyes, I was stepping forward.

I knew what Malcolm needed. I didn't like it, but there was nothing that could be done about it. Aged blood would not be strong enough to sustain Malcolm's life. Weaker than fresh, the amount needed would be too great. And I doubted Doc kept that much on hand. He kept a small supply for me, just in case.

My blood was a delicacy. The human in me filled it with life, the vampire filled it with power--Malcolm's power, ancient and pure. And I was the only one in the room who could handle the large donation that was going to be needed. I knew the minute Joe figured out my plan.

"No, Lindy. I'll provide what he needs." The sacrifice of that didn't escape me. Joe providing for a vampire in order to save me from doing it was a huge sacrifice. He hated them, had for years.

"You can't take the loss. Let me try and if it becomes too great, I'll let you. Please, Joe, let me try. If you lose too much blood, we won't be able to replace it." We wouldn't even be able to do a transfusion, since the only human in the room was Doc and he'd be needed to perform it. "And I might need you to replenish me." I hated to say it, to remind him I was the same as the two vamps we were watching doing things too hideous to consider. I'd hate it even more if I had to drink from Joe again. While I loved the taste of him, I knew he hated it.

THE CRIMSON FOLD

His nod was hesitating, but I didn't wait for more affirmation, knowing I wasn't likely going to get any. As I joined Malcolm next to Ian's body, I realized Malcolm hadn't spoken since his first declaration when he had threatened Doc. Since I wasn't sure if it was a concentration thing, I remained silent as well.

I looked down at my wrist. Should I cut it open with the scalpel? The thought of Malcolm's fangs sinking into my flesh wasn't as creepy as it should have been and the stirring I felt in my loins caused me to take a step back. Not a good thing to be turned on by the enemy.

My movement caught Malcolm's eyes. He watched me through distant eyes, giving nothing away of his thoughts.

Doc provided the answer to my dilemma by handing me the scalpel. The slice from the blade burned against my skin, but nothing I couldn't handle. Hell, I'd handled bullets, so I'm not sure what would constitute too much to handle for me these days.

I held my wrist up to Malcolm's mouth in a silent offer, and the minute he scented the blood he latched on. Relief flooded me when I realized there was nothing sexual about this.

We were like a feeding assembly line. Doc gave me a bottle of the aged stuff since my loss was still minimal. I poured it in as Malcolm sucked it out. Ian's body was healing fast, and Malcolm closed the cut in his palm and offered his wrist to Ian's mouth. Ian didn't even puncture the skin.

Malcolm swore, the first we'd heard from him in what seemed like hours but was more like thirty minutes. He slashed his wrist with his nail, a nifty trick I knew I'd never try, and forced the blood into Ian's mouth.

Unlike when I had tried this morning, Ian's throat slowly began to swallow. Suddenly, both of Ian's hands gripped the offered wrist, and he drank greedily. For a moment, I thought he would suck the entire arm down his throat.

The sucking on my wrist increased to accommodate Malcolm's blood loss, and soon my head began to swim. Malcolm realized none of us would be able to drink our fill and pulled his wrist from Ian. He released mine almost simultaneously.

It was almost comical to see three powerful vampires as helpless as babes as Malcolm and I leaned heavily on the table beside Ian.

Slowly, Ian's eyes fluttered open. Standing closest to him, I was the first one he saw. His voice sounded hoarse, barely a whisper, but the silence in the room had carried the words.

"Ah, me very own angel come to save the devil." I took one look into those beautiful eyes of his and did the one thing that horrified everyone in the room. Myself included. I broke down and sobbed.

I don't have many friends. In fact, its safe to say Joe would be my only one, but since I'm sleeping with him, I guess ulterior motives exist there. Doc would count, but sometimes I wonder if I've only become a specimen to him lately. Malcolm, well, he's the last one I'd call a friend since he tried to kill me. And I'm sure the only reason he still puts up with me is that he's hoping to finish the job. But Ian, well Ian is the only one that doesn't want anything from me. The only one who is nice to me for apparently no reason. Having him back meant a great deal.

I wiped at my eyes, moving away from the table to retreat to a corner. It didn't take long for me to get it together.

* * * *

We took Ian home with us. Not a bad night, if I do sound like I'm bragging. Arrive for an autopsy, leave walking beside the body. When we arrived home, and I use that word even though it creeps me out, we settled around our cozy little living room. Almost sounds normal, huh? Only instead of coffee, some of us were drinking our O positive.

Ian looked better than Malcolm or me. Says a lot for the ancient blood. His mood, however, was much worse. Seems I'm not the only one getting killed pisses off.

"How can you not remember something as important as the man who attempted to kill you?" Malcolm didn't try to hide his disgust.

"I dinna forget the man, you fool, I ne'er saw him. I tell you, he snuck up behind me and laid me low."

"Then how did you know he was small? In the truck this morning, you said he was a wee man."

Ian softened his tone for me. "Not his size, but his stature. His…" Ian seemed to be searching his mind for the right word. I decided he'd been through a bad enough day, so I helped him out.

"Energy."

"Aye." Ian grinned his thank you. "He was no strong one what did me in, but a mere human."

"With vamp powers."

Ian turned his head, didn't meet my gaze. "I dinna see this to be sure, but no mere human could accomplish such an attack. I am no mere bairn."

"He could have been newly turned."

"I agree," Malcolm added.

"Why did you think he was after Malcolm?"

"Ach, I canna believe I was that close ta the bastard and dinna wring his neck." Ian paced the room, angry energy circling him. "It was Malcolm, ta be sure. He said me blood was preparation for the true test ta come. The most powerful blood. As Malcolm is master and ancient, twas him that he spoke of."

THE CRIMSON FOLD

"Wasn't Surgis older?" Joe was sitting next to me on the sofa, but there seemed to be miles separating us.

"Yes, by two hundred years."

"Then his blood should have been the key. Seems his would be more powerful than yours." I turned back to Ian. "Did he say powerful? Were those his exact words?"

Ian frowned, searching his memory. "Strong, but is that na the same?"

"Not necessarily. Malcolm's may be the most powerful, but depending on what you intend to do with it, his might not be the strongest."

Malcolm disagreed from the sound he made. Snorting really didn't sound natural coming from him. Should I tell him Doc's theory? About his attempted cure? Malcolm might be on my side today, but tomorrow, we could be enemies again. Especially if he decided to pursue killing me. But what could he do to prevent the discovery of the cure? I gave up and told him everything. Ian and Rena seemed more interested than Malcolm.

"What is needed for this cure of your doctor's?" Malcolm asked.

"Your blood," Joe supplied. Then followed that up with a statement he seemed a little too happy to make. "Withdrawn moments before your death."

Malcolm slid his eyes to me. "I can see the problem."

"This isn't about Doc's cure." There was no reason for me to feel guilty. I hadn't tried to kill Malcolm for his blood, while he had done exactly that to me. I met his eyes evenly. "This is about some crazy who may be stealing vamp blood. The reason I told you about Doc's theory was to help us catch this lunatic."

"And you believe this man is trying to create a cure?"

"Not exactly. I think he may be trying to extract all of the good from the vampire and none of the bad."

"Selfish prick. Does this na prove it then? The man is after Malcolm's blood. Ya said yourself that his is the key."

"The key to curing me, as it is his blood that infected me. But not the key to a general vaccine. Doc seems to think I am that key." I didn't meet their stares. I didn't want to be a key to anything, damn it. Like everyone wasn't already out to get me without adding extra incentive.

"Yes, that would appear to be the case," Malcolm said. "Then we can assume he will come for you when the time is right. When he does, we will have our killer."

"You think you're going to use Lindy as bait." Joes words were low, but no one could miss the threat, the anger. "Think again. This bastard won't get within miles of her."

"She will be protected."

"She sure as hell will. And not by some parasite that doesn't give a damn about her."

Joe might be mad at me, but he would protect me. Guess he didn't hate me after all. Not that I had really believed he ever had. But telling myself that sure made it easier to keep my distance from him.

"It's not like I'm fragile, guys. He'll come for me, whether I'm guarded or not, when he's ready for me. We can assume the timing is not perfect. He will need time to run his tests from Ian's blood. The virus takes two days to completely overtake the body. We should have at least that much time to come up with a plan.

We tried for two hours to come up with something, but in the end, we only came up with more arguments. I finally gave up and went to bed.

* * * *

I hate whiners, people who complain twenty-four-seven. So when for three days once a month I become one of them, it ain't pretty.

This is, of course, Malcolm's fault. Going dead wreaks havoc on a woman's monthly cycle and mine has ceased altogether. That's the good news.

Bad news, I still have PMS, only without relief. It worsens each month. I used to be scary once a month, now I'm downright psychotic. And I know this. Should make it better but the truth is, I just don't care. I have a right to go a little crazy every once in a while.

The only thing that has ever helped me through is chocolate. I've craved it since my periods began in junior high.

So naturally, it is one of the things my body can no longer tolerate. It makes me sick. Really, really sick. I know this because I have refused to believe it and tried to make my body learn to get over it.

Normally, I try to hide out in my house when I get this way. I hate taking it out on unsuspecting others. Innocents. But lucky for me, this month I have the culprit right downstairs.

I had waited all day to vent my frustrations, and the time had finally come. I wanted to be cruel, vindictive. A real bitch. I'd lost chocolate, for God's sake.

"You're looking a bit peeked tonight, Lucinda."

Malcolm's first words when I entered the room. Now, you tell me--who started it?

"This from a man who has been dead for more than five hundred years?" I snickered. Wasn't proud of it, but that's what I did.

"True. However, your coloring is usually more warm."

"Used to be even warmer before I met you." I slumped onto the sofa.

"Ah." Malcolm's lips curled. "A pity party."

"Screw you."

THE CRIMSON FOLD

"Your mood is rather annoying tonight." He was standing near the bar, drinking down his breakfast.

"You think?"

"I *think* I do not wish for the honor of your company in this present mood." He slid his empty glass onto the mahogany surface of the bar and turned his attention to me.

"You kicking me out, bat boy?"

"Bat boy? Amusing. I am simply telling you to improve your attitude or excuse yourself."

"Like hell." I jumped from the sofa. "You don't like my attitude, tough. You're the reason for it. You and every other crawler of your species." I wasn't singling out vampires, just men in general.

"Hello, sweetheart." I spun on my heels, stared at Joe's grin. He picked *now* to be nice to me?

"What is so damn amusing?" Hands on my hips, I was ready for him if he dared to draw any closer.

"Nothing at all. I'm just happy that for once in our relationship it's not me you're chewing up and spitting out. PMS, huh?"

That's the problem with keeping the same guy for any length of time. They think they learn you.

"Its doesn't take PMS to get fed up around here. And we don't have a relationship, in case you haven't noticed. We have--"

"Sex," Malcolm offered. I shot him dead with my eyes. Shame it didn't work.

"All of this is your fault. Your life is shit, so you have to make sure everybody else is miserable, is that it? Well congratulations, Malcolm. You succeeded. Now I hope you rot in hell."

It would have been a beautiful exit had it not been for the black cape draped over the ottoman, dragging the floor. And who wears a cape these days? I stumbled right over it, struggled to keep from falling down. Again, Malcolm's fault.

I fled the house. Wasn't very well done of me, but done anyway. I knew Joe, and probably Malcolm, would be mad at me for leaving alone. Hell, after what we'd discussed last night they'd probably be beyond mad. I also knew the risk was low, since it was too soon for the test on Ian's blood to be complete. Course, I could be wrong about the whole thing and the guy could make a grab for me tonight. With the current mood I was in, I almost wished it. Besides, a person could only hold in so much anger before they self-combusted.

I walked down Crump Boulevard toward the river. This part of town had once fallen to crime and decay, but it was coming to life again. I hated to admit it, but it was the vampires that had revived the area.

To the right, I heard horses whinny. I had missed the sound. Maybe if I snuck around quietly, I could get a glimpse of them without setting them off. Horses hated me now. Joe loved horses, owned several. See how deep our problems run?

I turned down Florida Street. There was a stable up on the overpass, where they kept the horses when they weren't pulling tourists in their fancy buggies around town.

It was still dark in this area with most of the streetlights busted, but vamps preferred it that way. I heard the voices in the shadows just as I stepped under the viaduct. My eyes adjusted to the dark.

He was no more than a kid, sixteen at best. And although I knew it couldn't be, he struck me as fresh, newly turned. Nobody got to turn in this town without consultation with me first. And I had never laid eyes on this kid.

Our eyes met, and I saw the fear, the confusion in them. The cross that was held in front of his face seemed to catch what little light existed, shooting out a prism of light in all directions. The teenagers, near his own age, blocked his path.

I stepped forward. The cross couldn't hurt me, couldn't hurt the kid either, but he didn't seem to know that. How could he not? That was one of the first things I had learned. We weren't the devil, made from the devil, or evil incarnate. God hadn't turned on us.

"What is going on here, boys?" I moved slowly, as if I didn't really care what they were up to.

"Nothing that concerns you, lady.

There is nothing worse than a hateful kid. "Well, now I guess I'll be the judge of that. Why don't you let him go on his way?"

The tallest boy laughed. Lord, I hate adolescence. When kids think they know it all and don't really know diddly.

"He's one of them." He nodded to the kid as if that would be enough to cause me to turn and run.

"I see. So what are you planning to do about that?" I positioned myself between them and the kid, just in case this got out of hand.

"We don't want his kind around here. Nobody around here would miss him. Hell, they'd thank us for driving his kind away."

Where had I heard that before? I stared at the kid, his skin the color of coffee, and replied. "There was once a time people said that about your kind. Don't you think this town has seen enough racism?"

He stepped back, shamed I hoped.

"What are you, some vamp-loving bitch?" This from the greasy head wearing the leather jacket. It was a warm night. The humidity in had already dampened my hair and this kid was decked out in leather. I hope he felt cool, cause he looked like an idiot.

"Director of Vampire Affairs, to be politically correct. Now you kids run on home before you get into some real trouble."

I saw the moment leather jacket made his decision. Damn, but I hate fighting kids. Where the hell were their parents anyway?

He stepped toward me, took a swing. I had expected it and dodged his fist easily. I never expected the other kid to throw one.

He caught me on the cheek, and my head popped back. It hurt like hell. When I didn't go down, he knew he had screwed up. I felt the change coming over me, and I knew he had, too.

When I opened my eyes a short time later, they had all wisely cleared out.

"You're a vampire," fresh face announced, as if he was telling me some great news.

"Took you long enough to figure that out, kid."

He shrugged.

"How old are you anyway?"

"Sixteen."

"By that, I hope you mean you've been undead for that long." The kid's hair looked to be caked with crud, his clothes dirty and torn.

"No. I'm sixteen, but I've been a vampire since yesterday."

I choked on air. No way was this kid leveling with me. It was illegal to bite anyone under eighteen, consenting or not. And even consenting, there were still rules.

"Where's your master?"

"Who?" He actually looked confused by the question.

"The vampire who bit you," I clarified, using the last of my short supply of patience.

"I don't know."

I shook my head in denial. "It's his duty to train you once he has turned you." That was a new law, and one of mine I'm proud to say. I wanted to ensure no one else was dumped alone and trying to figure out how to fill up the hunger pains.

"I don't know anything about that. I just remember getting bit and then waking up yesterday, uh, last night I guess."

"Where?" I searched the dark corners, hoping to spot some guilty vampire.

"I woke up in a warehouse a few streets from here."

"Where were you when you were bitten?" I spit out.

"Oh. Beale Street. I was walking to my car. I'd parked it behind Alfred's, cause they don't break into them as bad there. I was buzzing pretty good, so I don't remember much. Didn't see anybody, just felt those teeth."

"And you've been wandering around since last night? Great." I eyed him carefully and noticed the blood on his T-shirt. "You haven't fed, have you?"

He turned away, ignoring my question. Shit. I had my answer.

"Damn it, you have!" I stepped toward him, and he made a fast retreat.

"Wasn't my fault! I couldn't stop myself. I was so hungry, and the guy was just lying there, sleeping in the doorway. Man, I think I killed him. Shit. What am I gonna do now? I wanna go home. I'm going home. I don't wanna be no stinkin vampire."

I knew the feeling. Shame that didn't change a darn thing. "I know. You ever heard of the castle?"

He shook his head, wiped at the tears on his face. Shit, a kid. Just what I needed. "Never mind, I'm going that way." Or it looked like I was now. I wasn't ready to go back, to face Joe and Malcolm and listen to their recriminations.

Chapter Ten

"Malcolm, this is Billy. He's one of yours now." I'd met Malcolm and Joe standing in the front yard, getting ready to call out a full search for me. Joe was pissed, so I pulled a stunt he had pulled on me many times. I jumped on him first, threw him off balance while he tried to figure out what I was mad about and then ignored him. Works for him sometimes, so I thought I'd try it. How come it never works for women?

"Pardon?" Malcolm's manners could get on a persons nerve sometimes.

"He's yours. A rogue bit him yesterday. He needs guidance." And I needed a shower. Between the humidity and the sweat from my walk, I smelled rotten. As the kid stepped closer to me, I was relieved to realize the smell wasn't coming from me.

"Then we will find someone--"

"No. He's killed already. It'll take someone who can help him learn control over his bloodlust. As master of Memphis, it's your responsibility."

"He is just a mere child." Malcolm looked over the boy as they followed me into the house.

"Yeah. Life sucks, huh?"

"This is payback for biting you," Malcolm announced, and he actually sounded snippy.

I stopped, turned to look at him. Was I punishing him? No, not yet. But that didn't mean I wasn't enjoying the hell out of this. "No. Sticking you with a teenager is just an added bonus. You'll know when payback comes."

I showered, dressed, and stomped back downstairs. My problems were growing by truckloads. Everyone was still gathered in the main room, Joe on the phone. I waited while he ended his call.

"That was the chief. Tim Dunlund just surfaced." Joe dropped his cell back into his pocket.

"Alive?"

"Completely. He walked into the station. Seems his housekeeper fainted when he walked into his house this afternoon. When she recovered from her shock, she explained to him he was missing, presumably dead. He went downtown to clear things up quickly. Guess he didn't want the will read yet.

"According to him, the housekeeper was confused. Claims he's been out of the country, vacationing."

"And they believe him?" People as powerful as Dunlund didn't just disappear.

"I spoke to Hotchkins myself. He said Dunlund appeared a bit dazed but otherwise coherent. No marks on his neck, and since he was out and about in mid daylight, it doesn't appear he has turned vampire. If it was a lie, it was a convincing one. No one can seem to come up with a motive, either."

"I could find out if he is being completely truthful." I looked at Malcolm and shuddered. One taste of blood and Malcolm could tell you things about the guy even his mother wouldn't know.

"I don't think taking a bite out of a favored citizen is what the mayor has in mind here, Malcolm. Thanks for the offer."

Malcolm shrugged, as if he didn't care one way or another.

"Wherever he has been, it seems unconnected. I guess we need to concentrate on the current problems. We can worry about Dunlund later." I explained my meeting with Billy, and his lack of a master.

"It would seem we have a rogue." Malcolm's calm voice indicated it was a small thing, easily handled. I knew better.

"A rogue. Shit. I ain't got enough problems? Missing humans, dead vampires, and millionaires who disappear and reappear better than a magic act. Problems seem to find me at an alarming rate."

"You're not alone in this. We'll deal with this problem first, since it seems the most pressing." Joe was talking to me again, but I wasn't sure why. Yeah, I have a real problem with things coming too easy.

I glanced over at the kid just as he pulled the glass away from his mouth. He had a liquid mustache, but instead of milk, it was O positive. Christ, the kid wasn't going to last a day.

"I need to go to the warehouse where our kid over there woke up. The rogue just became priority."

"I agree. Let's go," Malcolm said as he stood to join Joe and me.

A cop and a ancient vampire. Could a girl feel more protected? Not in this city.

The building was on Front Street. I had passed it a dozen times and it always piqued my interest. Arched doorways and wrought iron railings that led to what once had been a cobblestone courtyard could be seen from the street. And lucky for us, the lock on the gate had been busted. We let ourselves in.

There is a smell that develops over time of rot and decay. Of desolation and despair. This place reeked of it. Rodents left alone for too long had left their marks everywhere. The ground was littered with their droppings. Rats, mice, pigeons, and a few other things I refused to guess at. The germs that hung in the air here could give the vampire bacteria a run for it.

Darkness had settled comfortably in for the night, so flashlights were pulled out, mostly for the humans. The vamps didn't need them.

Joe had refused to let me come alone, and for that I would be forever grateful. Not even I was that stupid.

We had also dragged along backup. Two from each team, since we didn't know what we might encounter. Best to cover all the possibilities, both breathing and well, not.

Malcolm had decided to join us and seemed as distracted by the filth as I was. Maybe more so, which I found amusing. He had once lived in times without flushing toilets or running water.

Most of the abandoned warehouses downtown consisted of one large storage space. We couldn't get that lucky here. This place had definitely once been a showplace. The marble was covered in filth but still showed hints of its grandeur. The wood trim, the little that hadn't been torn off and burned for heat by the homeless, was cherry.

Offices divided the space and ran the length of the building. Storage was left in the back, but one glance told us there was nothing hiding in there. That's the good part about big open spaces--they leave nowhere to hide.

Unfortunately, we needed to search the offices, or what was left of them, individually. It would have made more sense to come back during daylight hours, but then we wouldn't have the extra muscle with us. And when it comes to a fight, I want the vampires on my side. Hard to kill, bad attitudes, yep. Just my style.

Everyone paired off, one human and one vampire per team. That way, no matter what we encountered, someone would be able to handle it. When I was automatically paired with Joe, I was both relieved and upset. I wanted to be with him to watch his back, and I knew he would watch mine, but it also meant I was one of the vamps. Okay, I know that to be true, but the reminder gets to me sometimes.

I should have known things were going to go straight down. When the hair on my neck stands, it's a clear warning. I never seem to remember that until it's too late.

I pointed the light at the door, and Joe eased it open. His gun was drawn and ready. Shame I couldn't change on command,

THE CRIMSON FOLD

grow my fangs when I needed them. Then I'd be as armed as he was. As it was, he seemed to have been shorted on the partner deal. I might be a vampire, but if I couldn't change, I was basically worthless.

It all happened in seconds. I saw the two by four coming down on Joe's head just as he was turning toward the guy. He went down hard. I couldn't see the blood, but I smelled it, and for an instant, I thought he was dead. Joe. My one weakness. The only thing I loved in this sorry-ass life. Then I heard him moan. I was ecstatic over that little noise until I saw the man step toward Joe's body to finish the job.

Anger and panic ripped through me, tearing my fangs out and sharpening my nails. I could take anything and not change, mess with Joe and things got ugly.

I grabbed for the board, threw the man against the wall when he didn't relinquish his hold on it. Just when I thought I had contained the threat, I felt the needle slide into my skin. My knees buckled, and I went down hard. I knew I was in big trouble even as I sank into darkness.

* * * *

Never let anyone tell you vampires love dark, damp places. The darkness, well, it's true we are connected to it, which is obvious since we come alive only at night. But damp? No way. Most vampires don't even like water anymore, though I have no clue why. I think it comes from learned behavior.

I mean, I live for my showers, but I lived for them when I was alive. But for most of the older vamps, showers weren't even invented in their time. Most of them bathed in a freezing creek once a month, and the experience doesn't bring back warm fuzzy memories. Since vampires don't sweat and have no way to smell, bathing isn't such a necessity.

But when I opened my eyes and found myself strapped to a steel table in some smelly basement, I could understand their dislike of dampness. It sank beneath my skin, freezing my already icy blood.

For some reason, I had not changed back to human form. Maybe I needed to feed first, but that seemed an unlikely possibility in my current position. More likely, I was going to be the meal.

I wished I could say I was alone. But from the shuffling sound and the tiny moans, I knew there were at least one other, maybe two. I turned my head, but the darkness covered everything.

My arm burned and I knew I had been cut in the scuffle. My luck, I would bleed to death before anyone showed.

I could smell blood, and all of it wasn't mine. That meant somewhere in this room there was blood, and it wasn't still flowing in someone's body.

I squeezed my eyes shut against the sudden bright light that flooded the room. When I eased them open, I was staring up at fluorescent lights. Someone had taken the time and expense to update this smelly place, at least enough so they could actually see the filth.

It seemed it was my lucky day for finding lost humans. Strapped down on the table beside mine was Larry Brown.

There were tubes hooked up to a bag of blood, but it was impossible to tell if it was being filled or emptied. I would bet they weren't filling him up. There was no movement from him, and I wasn't sure if he was already dead.

I heard feet shuffling behind me. I turned my head up and to the right, and saw Peter Caldwell heading toward me. He looked much worse than the last time I had seen him.

His hair was longer, but grimy and limp. His skin was taut against his bones, and he was moonlight pale. He looked like something out of a zombie movie. His eyes were on me, but I swear they looked unfocused and dead inside.

"Peter." He didn't react to my voice. The closer he got to me, the faster my heart raced. He seemed locked on one target, out of his head.

The last time I had seen the kid, he had been sun-kissed and warm to the touch. And breathing. From his appearance, the transformation had been hard on him.

Dying hurts. Don't let anyone tell you different. Mine had been a small taste, but if the sample was accurate, the pain was unthinkable. Luckily, the mind usually shuts down when the experience becomes too much. Looked like Peter's mind had never recovered.

Peter stopped beside the table, his empty eyes looking down at my arm. I saw the needle in his hands but had no time to prepare myself. Not that I could have done much, strapped down like I was.

I had been a nurse. I had slid IV needles in more arms than I could remember and never once had failed to find a vein on my first try. It was something the other nurses had envied me for.

Peter had no experience. It took five tries before he finally hit a vein. It had been nothing more than luck that he found one then.

I watched as my blood began to fill a bag. There is a reality that hits you as you watch your blood drain from your body. A vulnerability, knowing that your life could be drained away so easily.

"What are you doing?" It seemed a stupid question, since draining me was obviously what he was after. I watched as Peter checked the flow, then moved to Larry. Once he determined he had adequately emptied the man, he removed the final bag. He had been drained of blood. I know these things, from more than his translucent skin. I'm a vampire, its means my life to know.

"Peter, can you hear me?" I knew he wasn't simply ignoring me. If I had a prayer, I was going to have to find a way to reach him. "I saw Angel the other day. She misses you. Do you remember Angel?" Recognition flickered in his eyes, then dulled.

"Let me help you, Peter." It seemed I was in more need of help at the moment, but I didn't think mentioning that to him would help me any. "Untie me." He stopped, turned to me, and for a minute, I thought he was going to actually obey me. When I didn't speak, he turned away.

"Peter, look at me!" He did as I commanded. I had the blood of the master in my veins, and the master could command lesser vampires. Could it really be that easy?

"Untie me, Peter." His brows wrinkled as he fought his inner struggles.

"Now! I am your master, and I command that you untie me."

Officially, it wasn't true. I wasn't master over anyone and never would be. Only the vamp that turned you was your master. But the ancients could command lesser vamps and there were only two left, Malcolm and Rena. Hopefully, I had enough of Malcolm's aged blood in me to command the newly turned. It was about time his blood came in handy for something.

I watched Peter approach, watched as he slipped the knife from his pocket, slid out the blade, and pulled it under the bindings.

I grabbed the IV and jerked it from my arm, just as my legs swung off the table. I cursed from the sting and ignored the blood trailing down my arm. It seemed Peter had found a vein and opened it up on the last stick, and now it didn't want to stop. It would take a few minutes to clot.

Peter's eyes fixed on the blood, then glazed over. I knew I was about to be in real trouble.

"Snap out of it, Peter. What the hell's wrong with you?"

"He seems to be suffering from a power high." I hadn't heard anyone approach and spun to face Rena. Why wasn't I surprised?

"It happens on occasion when one ingests the blood of too many vampires." She sighed. "It would appear I need a new test subject." Her eyes moved to Larry. "And another food source."

There really is such a thing as hysterical laughter. I know this from experience. And I was bubbling over with it.

"Okay." I shook my head, trying to process too much information as fast as possible. "Blood research. I understand why Peter would be convenient. But the other humans..."

"He saved me years of work. In fact, all of the men did. Tim was sweet enough to lead me in the right direction. If not for him, I would have taken valuable time finding Peter. Brown was necessary to get me in the lab."

"Why let Dunlund go?"

"You never know when a man of his power might come in handy. His blood served no purpose. Blood is easy to come by. Power, well power is a much more valuable commodity."

"You're searching for a cure." Rena sashayed across the room, her laughter echoing against timeworn stones.

"Oh Lindy, you disappoint me. You cure what is unwanted. What I seek is power.

"You can't imagine what it is to serve a master lifetime after lifetime. Surgis could have released me. For all his claim to care for me, he was too selfish to give me my own life." Rena walked to the table.

"Maybe he was afraid you would leave him."

"Of course I would have left him. He had no right to own me. So I bought my own freedom."

"With Surgis' life. You ended up with a new master anyway."

"Malcolm will never rule me. I am older than him by decades and had I been born male, I would be ruler today." Rena crossed to Peter. He stood statue still, his eyes unseeing. If he was on a power trip, it wasn't one I wanted to take anytime soon. I watched as Rena raked a nail over his cheek. The blood started quickly, and she wasn't about to waste a drop.

Peter was short, and with Rena's heels, she could easily lean into him, running her tongue over the gash to take in every drop.

"You're pissed off. Maybe I can understand that, being controlled by Surgis all those years. But what do you hope to gain by this? Even if you kill Malcolm, the no-female rule still applies."

She licked her blood-red lips slowly, savoring the taste.

"No one would dare challenge one with my powers. But I do not wish to kill Malcolm. Not when I can command him instead."

"You know he would never bow to you." The blood on her lips was looking good to me, and I felt my stomach rumble.

"Ah, but he will if he wishes to save his people."

"You would destroy the vampire?" I was as guilty as the rest of the world. I automatically assumed all vampires would fight to save their own race. Guess not.

"Yes. But it won't come to that. The threat, once proven real, will be all that is necessary for Malcolm to do as I say. It is his one weakness, his need to protect his own."

"He'll fight you, and younger or not, he'll win."

"Possibly. That is why I have no intention of fighting him. Now, while I have enjoyed our little girl talk, I must insist you return to the table. I'm afraid I need to extract more of your blood."

"If you're not after a cure, what good is my blood to you?" I didn't move. No way was I going to climb back up on that table and allow anyone to strap me down. If I was going to die, at least

THE CRIMSON FOLD

I would be swinging when it happened. The vulnerability of being helpless was worse than a quick death.

"Your little cure theory left out one scenario. If Malcolm's dying blood cells will rid you of his mutated virus, then they can kill him as well."

"You have to kill him before the cells will turn on themselves." Which was my problem with the whole cure thing.

"No. I have to kill his cells. Killing you, creates those dying cells. Once the human in you dies, only his cells will remain. Once they begin to die, I can extract his cells and create his killer. All I have to do then is to inject his dying cells into his own body, sit back and wait while they do their job. It will be him that brings on his own death.

Rena smiled. "I really should thank you. Had it not been for the information you gave so freely about your cure, I would still be searching.

"So you see, I really must have your blood."

"Then come and get it. Why send a boy?" I nodded toward Peter, who still hadn't moved. He looked as harmless as a puppy.

Rena looked over at Peter and shook her head. "You know, we share a bond, you and I."

"Bond? Yeah right. Wanting my blood doesn't give us a bond." Okay, drinking it seemed to do the trick as Malcolm can attest to, but that wasn't something I cared to think about.

"Yes. There are few of us, females who do not answer the call of a master. We could rule them all."

Rena held up the syringe that contained the light amber liquid. I stared at it, mesmerized. In that little tube was the answer to my prayers. Doc could analyze it; duplicate the formula to create an antidote.

"It is all here, in this tiny container."

My throat was too dry to swallow. "How did you do it?"

Her laugh was normal, not the laugh of a madman.

"That's the beauty of it, I didn't. I didn't have to do anything except find the right men and they did all of the work. It was simply a matter of removing the disease they were trying to cure and substituting it with our little virus. Your Doc's notes provided the rest."

"If you hurt him--"

"You dare to threaten me, when you hold no power? Really Lindy, that's unwise. I could kill you with so little exertion. But don't worry, I didn't harm your little friend. Oh, I was prepared to take his blood and bend him to my will, but it was not necessary. Your little doctor lives in a world all his own. It was easy to pay him a little attention, a little conversation and he told me everything I needed to know. I removed the memory from him, of course. Very easy to do when the man can hardly remember where he left his glasses."

"I see. And you kept me busy with the rogue."

"There was no rogue, though it would have been handy. Shame I didn't think of it. The boy simply had too much alcohol in his system to remember the event. I could not use his blood, thanks to that alcohol content. Since I had already infected him with the tainted blood, there was nothing I could do but turn him out. I certainly wasn't about to waste valuable serum on him when the alcohol would confuse the results."

Rena's fangs suddenly seemed too large for her mouth. Her eyes glared red, and I knew our chat was about to be over. I also knew there was no way I could match her power.

I had just found something scarier than the roaches. No one knew where I was, and there was no way they were going to find me when I had no idea myself. I wanted Joe. I'd even settle for Malcolm. In fact, I wanted the whole damn task force, vampire and human alike.

Had Malcolm succeeded in finishing what he had started on the muggy dark street in New Orleans, he would have been my master and I would have been able to communicate with him even through the miles. It was because he hadn't done just that that I was even in this mess. In fact, no one would even want my damn blood, had he turned me completely. Again, this was all Malcolm's fault.

Maybe I'd get lucky and Joe would kill him after Rena finished me off. The last time I had seen Joe, he had been knocked out on the floor of some abandoned warehouse. Did he even have a clue that I was missing? I looked down at the cut on my arm, saw the dried blood that had ran down to my finger. Just maybe, I had left a trail behind.

Malcolm's blood was mixed with mine. If there was a trail, no matter how faint, he could follow it. There was hope that they would find me.

"But first, I must tie you to me. My blood is strong, and will bind you as securely as Malcolm would have. Then I will have no need to force you." She reached for the syringe. I knew what the red stuff in it was. Blood. Her blood. If I survived this, I was swearing off the stuff. It had been way too big of a deal in my life lately.

Doc had told me that another vampire's blood wouldn't be enough to defeat Malcolm's blood. That it couldn't harm me. He hadn't said anything about the blood from a vampire more powerful than Malcolm. I had all the foreign little cells swimming in me that I wanted.

Rena couldn't force me to drink her blood. I might be weak, but not that weak. But if she was able to slip that needle into me, she wouldn't have to bite me.

She moved like the wind, one minute standing in front of me, and the next behind me. I tried to turn, but I was just slower.

THE CRIMSON FOLD

Rena grabbed me from behind, pressing the needle against my neck just as the cavalry arrived.

Joe, his gun drawn, was first down the stairs. Malcolm followed him by only seconds. As the room filled with the rest of my team, I sent up a silent thanks to the man above for answering my prayers.

For a second, it seemed everyone just stared at each other. The thought crossed my mind that Rena would just give up now that she was outnumbered. I should have known better.

Joe cursed as the needle slid into my skin. One jerk, and the liquid would be forced into my body. No one moved, I didn't even dare to breath. Lucky for me, I don't do a lot of it when I'm dead. I looked down at the table in front of us, my eyes locked on the antidote. Would it work against whatever this idiot was about to fill me with?

As I felt the cool liquid burn a path through my veins, I realized I was about to find out. Without the threat to me, nothing held Joe back. He shot the bullet straight between the eyes.

Bullets might not kill vampires, but the force and shock knocked Rena back. The arm around my neck drew me down with her when she fell. I knew she would recover long before any of us wanted her to. Kicking just like a girl, I scrambled out of her reach.

There is just something freaky about knowing some creepy little parasite is inside you, finding a home and getting ready to settle in. And from past experience, I know what kind of damage they can do.

Joe was there, lifting me gently and lowering me to the table.

"Grab the other needle."

"You don't know what's in it, Lindy. Wait until Doc has a chance to run tests--"

"By then, no telling what will have happened to my body. Besides, it's the cure. Its what we wanted. Do it now, Joe."

"Not at a risk to you. It could kill you, for all we know. I don't give a damn what you are, I'm not going to watch you die."

I grabbed the needle from his hands and took the choice away from him. I jabbed it into my leg and prayed for the best.

Nothing happened. But then, it had been at least an hour before Malcolm's bite had started killing me.

The shriek from behind me had us all spinning around. Malcolm and Rena were locked in battle and from the sounds, Rena wasn't doing so well.

Ancient or not, it seemed Malcolm had just had more experience with killing his own kind. His nails extended and curled into deadly razors. His face contorted, changed into the monster most humans never witnessed.

Vampires, really old ones, are truly the thing of nightmares. Their ability to grow a second set of fangs, shorter and sharper, had only been a myth. Or so I thought. As I watched Malcolm rip open Rena's neck, I realized there was a lot I didn't know about my new race.

Blood poured down Malcolm's chin, but he didn't seem to notice. Or maybe he liked the proof of his kill. And we all knew Rena was going to die. There was a madness in his eyes that clearly said he would have it no other way.

Rena's eyes searched wildly for a miracle. But Malcolm's nails slashed at her neck, ripping open veins faster than she could heal them. When she was weak, he released his hold on her and she fell to the ground.

I felt the power rising and knew what he was about to do. I wasn't about to stick around this time and watch those damn roaches scatter about.

"Get me out of here." Joe needed no further encouragement. Just as we cleared the top of the stairs, a blood-curdling scream ripped through the air. I knew it would be the last sound Rena ever made.

We stopped by Doc's on my way back to the castle. Doc drew blood. He needed more tests, but apparently the cure had taken care of the nasty little needle that had been let loose inside me. It had done nothing for my other problems. As far as Doc could tell, Malcolm and my blood cells were still waging the battle inside me.

I hugged him, told him I'd stop by next week for my regular donation and returned to the castle.

The only thing left to do was gather my things and go back home to my real life. A life without Joe in it. God, how depressing.

Joe and I filed our reports by phone, promising his chief and the mayor that we'd show up for a meeting come daylight. We showered and met everyone back downstairs. It was too late to worry about going home tonight, and dawn was only hours away.

I had barely sat down on the sofa next to Joe, when Malcolm handed me a glass.

"Brandy. You need it after tonight." See, I told you he was from another era. I turned it up and emptied the glass. I was from another era, too. And in my time, women didn't demurely sip brandy when the world got too rough.

Malcolm raised his brow but said nothing at the empty glass.

"I'm packed. I'll be out of here at dawn," I said.

Malcolm's forehead wrinkled. "I had hoped you would chose to remain."

"The job's done. There's nothing here for me." I hated to admit it felt a little sad leaving. It wasn't the castle or its occupants that made my heart ache. It was leaving the make-believe world I had been living in with Joe.

"We have certain issues that must be dealt with."

Joe spoke up. "No, you don't. All issues between you and Lindy have been settled. We are walking out of here together and no one is going to stop us."

My head snapped around to Joe. "I'm leaving here alone, Joe. There is no reason to drag this out." No way I could take it if he did. The only way I was going to be able to walk away from Joe was to hit the door, run all the way and never look back. One look at his eyes, and I would be a goner.

"You're not walking away from me again, Lindy. Not this time."

I jumped from the sofa to pace. When I turned to look at Malcolm, his eyes were glowing.

"That doesn't work on me, Malcolm. You can't charm another vampire." It was the only thing I had going for me where Malcolm was concerned.

"But you are not a vampire yet, are you? I agreed to leave you alone until this business was complete, and now it is done."

I was locked on his eyes and felt like I was falling. I wanted to look away, to stop the ground from reaching up for me, but I could do neither.

"Come Lucinda, join me. We are one. Let go of your resistance and join me."

I tried to fight it, but his pull was too strong. Like half of me was being ripped apart. I felt the change coming over me and cried out.

"Leave her alone, damn you." Joe jumped up, ready to battle a room full of vamps in order to save me. Not very smart, but sweet just the same.

"No. This must be her decision. You can't interfere."

Strong arms tightened around Joe, holding him back.

There was nothing I could do. I wanted to beg Ian to release him, beg the other cops in the room to take him away so he wouldn't witness this, but they were as helpless as Joe. My feet crossed the room to Malcolm, traitors with a mind of their own. Or instructed by Malcolm's. It seemed Malcolm did hold power over me.

"Join us for eternity, Lucinda. Come, make our union complete." His nail opened a gash in his neck, and I saw the blood flow. My eyes stared at it, mesmerized by the dark red liquid I wanted more than life. I crossed to Malcolm and started to bury my lips for a taste. A moan sounded in his throat as my lips touched the skin of his neck. I wanted to drink from him, wanted to taste him. But something in me revolted, and I took a step back.

"Let me taste you. One bite and we'll be together for eternity."

Malcolm knew where to touch me to ignite the flame. His hand caressed my bare shoulder, lowered to rub against my breast.

I heard Joe's growl, deep in his throat.

Malcolm pulled the hair away from my neck, exposing the dark-blue vein. His tongue glided slowly over my skin. Bloodlust flooded through me.

My head dropped back, offering him what he sought. His mouth opened wide and started to lower.

"No!" The scream tore from Joe's mouth and woke me from my haze. I blinked, wide eyed, and looked back at Joe.

"Come here, Lindy. Come on sweetheart. I love you. I've always loved you. Don't leave me in this life again without you. Please." I stared at those gray eyes, those eyes I could fall into. Joe. He was what I wanted. All I wanted.

I jerked from Malcolm and ran to Joe. Ian released him and he grabbed me. In his arms, I felt safe.

"Welcome home, baby."

I buried my head against his neck, felt life flowing in him. The scent of male, heady and hot, quickened my breath.

"If you ever come near her again, I'll kill you, you bastard." No one in the room doubted that Joe meant it.

Malcolm held up his hand. "There is no need. She has made her decision, and I will honor it. I will not force her will to mine." He turned and walked from the room. I didn't even complain when Joe picked me up and carried me out of the castle. I didn't care where we ended up, now that we had ended up together.

The End

VAMPIRE CLOSE
Susanne Saville

CHAPTER ONE

Scraping sounds stalked Fiona MacPhee down the dark, deserted wynd. She froze once again. Her legs quivered, muscles protesting the repeated restraint. Maybe this time it would be different. Maybe this time the scratching would continue. Simply some dry branch against a window pane. Or a cat out hunting prey. *Hunting me, apparently.* The sounds had stopped when she did. Yet again.

She glanced over her shoulder, down the narrow alley. Just like before. Nothing. Only the bleak brick walls, permanently stained with ancient soot, and the worn cobblestones that comprised the wynd itself. Why hadn't she brought the little canister of CS gas Joan had given her? What did Joan call it? Something medieval ... Mace! Where was it tonight? Protecting the top of the telly, of course, right where she had left it. Fiona mentally kicked herself.

But it was just supposed to be a simple errand. A quick errand. Out and back. No need for a purse. No need for a coat even, despite the crisp October air. *Just my luck.* Out of all of Edinburgh, she would choose the wynd with the serial killer. *Stop imagining things!*

Taking a deep breath, she crept forward. The click of her heels upon the cobblestones sounded unnaturally loud in the strained silence. The scratching had not started. She quickened her step over the uneven surface. It still hadn't started.

Then the scraping sound began again. Fiona laughed. *This canna be happening to me.*

All of a sudden, the hairs on the back of her neck tingled. Something was behind her. As she spun around, disembodied male laughter echoed off the blackened walls and antique buildings. The gloomy wynd was empty. But she was not alone.

Her fingers clenched fistfuls of her skirt's crimson fabric. *He's playing with me.* Cocking her head, she attempted to determine the eerie noise's source but the walls were too close. Imprisoning walls. Enclosing her. Immuring her. *Not now!* She simply couldn't have a bout of her dreaded claustrophobia now.

A smattering of pebbles cascaded down the near wall and clattered upon the cobblestones, jolting Fiona's thoughts back into focus. She peered up into the murky night. Something was crawling on the roofs above. Instinctively seeking light, she ran for the wynd's solitary, quaint street lamp.

"Joan? Are you here?" she shouted, as she reached the pool of lamplight. "Joan!"

Suddenly a man landed on the pavement just a few meters in front of her. Fiona involuntarily jumped back and hit the lamppost. The man straightened from his predatory crouch and sauntered toward her. He entered her circle of lamplight. He had sharp features and tousled chestnut hair that arced in a stray forelock above bottomless black eyes. His stylish, sable clothes accentuated his tall, wiry build, from the winged collar of his long, leather coat all the way down to his pointed boots. He was definitely handsome, in a rakish sort of way. And he was coming closer.

She pressed back against the cold metal post. As if amused by her apprehension, the man gave her an insolent grin. This revealed his exceptionally pointy canine teeth. She guessed that any passerby would think both he and she were somewhere in their mid-twenties, but the presence of his gleaming white fangs made his age irrelevant. He was a vampire. Mace wouldn't have worked anyway.

Then he spoke. His voice possessed remnants of a mellifluous Highland lilt, and the texture of warm honey.

"How would a bonnie lass like ye like to live forever?"

Fiona pushed herself off the lamppost, turning to run. She had taken but one step when her body slammed against the black brick wall. The vampire had pounced on her like a tiger.

She writhed and twisted, trapped between his hard body and the unyielding bricks, expecting to feel the vampire's fangs ripping into her neck at any moment. How close was Joan? Then the vampire surprised her. He stepped back.

Placing his hands against the wall to either side of her head, he pinned her in with his extended arms. There was space between them now. But there was nowhere to go.

She met his gaze defiantly. "Clear off."

The vampire leaned toward her. "Or what?" he replied, chuckling.

"I'll think of something."

He bent even closer to her. "I bet ye would 'n' all." The vampire nuzzled her temple, sniffed her hair.

The contact was fleeting. But the tingling of her skin persisted even after his touch deserted her. Fiona mentally berated her wanton skin. It should be crawling. What was wrong with her?

"Ye should be careful," he continued. "A girl alone on the streets at night. Dinna ye ken there's something dangerous about? And 'tisnae ye or your friend."

"Ye might be surprised," she responded dryly.

She felt him nuzzle her hair again, then nudge her tresses out of the way with his nose, so that his whispered words puffed against the delicate skin of her ear. "Think about my offer."

His head was moving lower. She could feel his hot breath upon her throat.

"Your beauty should be preserved. And embalming isnae half as fun."

Fiona cursed him and tried to duck under his arm. It didn't work. The vampire seized her by the shoulders, but she didn't care. She had caught a glimpse down the wynd. Charging toward them was a swirl of strawberry blonde and steel.

Joan Armstrong, at last.

Joan's sword whacked the sooty brick wall, so close to them that Fiona felt the breeze from the blade.

"That's your only warning. Let Fiona go," Joan commanded. Her American accent complimented the menace her tone of voice expressed.

The vampire turned and casually inspected the lissome newcomer glaring at him with pale gray eyes as hard as flint. Her bright hair was pulled back in a severe ponytail and her utilitarian garb was clearly worn for combat rather than fashion, but she was tall and fit and undeniably feminine. Fiona thought of Joan as a ballet dancer. A ballet dancer in combat boots.

"Quite the wee soldier. I'm guessing ye must be Joan." The vampire released Fiona and stepped back, amusement gleaming in his eyes. "Ye are shorter than I expected. But now that I have your attention..."

"You're going to get more than that, buster." Joan lunged at him.

He dodged the sword. "Leave off! I have a proposition for ye."

"I'll bet." Joan attacked. Her sword reflected the lamplight, sending dazzling flashes piercing through the darkness.

The vampire adroitly ducked and dodged. "I dinna expect ye to feather-bed me, but ye might at least listen!"

"So say something." With a grin, Joan maintained her assault.

"The Fury," he shouted, narrowly avoiding her swinging blade.

The words halted Joan in mid-swivel. "What?"

"Ye want him," the vampire stated. "I can help."

Joan pulled back to a defensive position in front of Fiona. "What do you know about it?"

The vampire rolled his eyes with the air of a recalcitrant schoolboy being forced to recite the patently obvious by a pedantic teacher. "All the signs say that this Samhain eve the

Andromache is going to rise, which gives ye, countin' tonight mind, only five nights to find it before 'tis too late."

"What does the rising of the Andromache mean?" Joan questioned.

The vampire grinned. "Ye tell me. Probably the end of the world. These sorts of prophecies never herald tax cuts or free public transport."

Joan folded her arms. "I don't see what this has to do with the Fury."

"Aye, ye do. The warning's out that the Fury's in town and everyone kens he's trouble. 'Tis for certain he's the one raising the Andromache." The vampire gave them a pitying smile. "Ye shall need all the help ye can get."

"And ye want to help us?" Fiona inquired, peering at him from behind Joan.

The demon touched the tip of his nose with his forefinger, and pointed with his other hand at Fiona. "She's twigged it."

"How do you know all this?" Joan's eyes narrowed with suspicion.

"I listen. I'm a fount of information," the vampire replied smugly.

Fiona snorted. "A shallow fount. The warning the Fury's in town is the biggest gossip goin', I'll wager."

The vampire acknowledged her guess with an indifferent shrug. "The demon community's fair buzzing with it, to be sure. 'Tis much higher priority than the news that Joan Armstrong's over from the States."

Joan's eyebrows arched. "You've heard of me?"

"Aye, but I dinna ken yon dark lassie ye are protecting."

"And you won't know her." She beckoned to Fiona. "Let's get you to safety so I can shish-kabob this guy."

The vampire winked at Fiona. "Ye are turning down an irreplaceable offer."

At first she wasn't certain to which offer he referred, but a sudden flash of memory, his warm breath upon her ear, made Fiona's cheeks begin to burn. She rolled her eyes. "'Tis ridiculous. Why would the likes of ye help humans against the Fury?"

"Ye humans may fear demons, but the Fury is the nightmare demons fear. He is a faceless, relentless destroyer--of demons, vampires, humans, anything. And the tales I've heard of what he does to his prey..." The vampire gave a theatrical shiver. "'Tis horrific even by demon standards. I dinna fancy that sort gettin' the upper hand of anything, let alone control over an enigma like the Andromache. Who kens what powers it might possess? Now if 'twere a friend..."

"Shut up," Joan interrupted tiredly.

Fiona traced the edge of a crooked cobblestone with the tip of her shiny, black shoe. "Mayhap 'tis not such a sketchy idea."

"You *must* be joking," stated Joan.

"He could help with my research."

Joan rounded on her. "You want his help?"

Fiona flinched back. Then, with as much dignity as she could muster, she drew herself up to her full height. "I would rather work with the Undead than the Sassenach."

"That is insane," Joan responded, shaking her head.

The vampire looked about the wynd. "What Sassenach?"

"Nothing." Joan shushed him with a dismissive wave.

"He rang us just after ye left," Fiona continued.

"But that was hours and hours ago--why come out now? I've told you before it isn't safe for you to be out here by yourself."

"What Sassenach?" the vampire repeated.

"Look, is anyone speaking to you?" Joan glared daggers at him.

The vampire smiled. "Ye are dead crabbit for a goodie."

Joan tapped her sword against the cobblestones. Then she spoke, enunciating each word with icy precision. "There's a deacon at St. Giles' with an English accent, and Fiona objects. Satisfied?"

"A Sassenach in the High Kirk." The vampire whistled. "Sacrilege."

Joan turned back to Fiona. "So what did he want?"

"To tell ye he canna meet ye tomorrow." Fiona paused. "I suppose 'tis more accurate to say *today* since 'tis well past..."

Joan interrupted. "But this is an emergency!"

"An' so I told him. Which is why I'm out here now. No sense interrupting your work beforetime."

"What?" Joan snapped.

"He allowed he could see us now, if 'twere that important."

The vampire laughed. "At this hour? What, 'tis last call at the pub and he doesnae wish to get home?"

Fiona ignored him. "He said he'd meet us in front of St. Giles'."

"Are ye certain he's a real deacon? Surely a genuine deacon would be abed by now."

"Enough," Joan snapped at the vampire. She made a threatening twitch with her sword in his direction.

He raised his hands. "What? I'm helping."

"Give me one substantial reason to spare him, Fiona, or I'm running him through right now."

"Well..." She glanced at the vampire. He was a handsome devil. Not that that was a substantial reason. Not that it was *any* reason. Why was she thinking these things? She was going to have to check her protection spell. His vampire magick was obviously affecting her. Yes, that was it. That had to be it. And for his magick to be that powerful, he must know some of the Old Tongue. "I think he could help with the translations."

"The translations." Joan repeated the words slowly, as if proof of their substantiality could be measured by syllable.

"Aye. Some of the ancient languages are dead tricky."

Joan stood silently. It was impossible to tell what she was thinking. Times like these made Fiona nervous.

"Joan?"

She lowered her sword. "Yes, yes, all right, all right."

"So we're all workin' together then?" the vampire queried, rubbing his hands together with exaggerated enthusiasm.

Joan nodded, but her expression was grim. "Everyone to St. Giles'. You--vampire--go in front where I can keep an eye on you."

The vampire led the way out of the wynd and down the Royal Mile, followed by Fiona, with Joan bringing up the rear.

"You won't regret this. I'm good in a fight," he boasted.

"I'm not having you at my back. You're helping Fiona with the research. That's it." The tone in Joan's voice made it clear that this was not up for debate.

In silence the little group walked through the night. The historic street, sparsely populated at this hour, had been invaded by wheelie bins awaiting the morning refuse removal. Fiona sidestepped to avoid one, saw she had veered too near the vampire and overcompensated. She almost lurched into the side of a bus shelter.

The vampire chuckled. "Gone off grace as a virtue, have ye?"

"Belt up," Fiona responded petulantly. She busily smoothed her skirt while she walked, as if there were invisible pleats that needed to be arranged perfectly.

The vampire hung back, attempting to fall in step with her. She ignored him, and continued to obsess about her skirt.

"What do they call ye, lassie?" he asked, affecting a casual air.

She deliberately stared across the street. "Fiona MacPhee. Not that 'tis any of your business."

The opposite side of the street became gradually less interesting as the vampire failed to reply. She shot him a sidelong glance. He was no longer looking at her. Her words tumbled out, almost a challenge. "What's your name, then?"

"I don't want to know his name," Joan called. "He's an evil, undead fiend."

Fiona laughed, and smiled back at Joan. "If we're doin' research together, I can hardly be callin' him Evil Undead Fiend."

"You don't have to call him anything. In fact, I'd shun all contact with him," Joan retorted cheerfully.

The scattered street-lamps keeping vigil over the shrouded pavement seemed more inclined to produce intermittent obscurity than illumination. As they departed one pool of light, the vampire spoke softly.

"Ruaridh." The quality of his accent had changed, thickened, and the word sang with the mystique of an ancient language.

"What?" Fiona glanced at him, but they had crossed the light's periphery and the gloom beyond enveloped them both.

His answer, when it came, seemed to float disembodied in the empty night.

"My name was Ruaridh MacLaren."

Even through the intimate darkness, Fiona could see his profile. It was almost possible to think of him as human.

"I have not been called that for..." His voice trailed off. As they entered lamplight again, she tried to make eye contact, but his eyes were momentarily clouded and he did not see her anymore.

"All right, I'm curious. What did he say?" called Joan.

"My name is Rory," the vampire answered. He glanced at Fiona and shrugged. "She'd never get the accent right."

CHAPTER TWO

St. Giles' Cathedral loomed over the darkened plaza. No city lights obscured the stars glittering high above between the curved hoops of its imperial crown-shaped tower. Fiona paused in her approach and eyed the massive stone structure. It seemed to stare back through its forbidding black windows, a silent predator crouching on a paved savanna. She jumped when a voice spoke at her shoulder.

"I'm not goin' any nearer either."

Fiona glanced back and Rory gave her a quick grin.

"But for entirely different reasons, I dare say," he added.

Joan returned from rattling the iron handles of the two locked wooden doors. "The deacon isn't here yet."

"Are ye certain?" Rory indicated a shifty group of youths clustered upon the wooden benches fencing in the massive stone base of a robed statue nearby. "Dibs he's the punk fellow with the bristly green hair."

"Oh, ha, ha." Joan grimaced.

The vampire ignored her. His attention was still on the gang. He started toward them. Joan grabbed at him but she needn't have bothered. The youths' initial hostility to his approach melted as presumably they caught clearer sight of his countenance and they scattered. Before Joan and Fiona could react further, they were startled by a crisp male voice with a cultured English accent behind them.

"I beg your pardon, but is one of you Miss Armstrong?"

Joan and Fiona both turned around.

The newcomer was tall and very blond, even by starlight. With his build, he should have been riding an armor-clad horse into battle. Or standing in front of a medieval castle's roaring great hearth--perhaps with the leg of some roasted animal in his fist. He was not at all what Fiona had pictured from the word 'deacon'. Joan apparently felt the same.

"I expected a wizened old man, not a big, blond wolf," she whispered to Fiona.

The man stepped closer to them. His expression was wary, but not unfriendly. "I say, pardon me, but are you..."

Joan stepped forward. "I'm Joan Armstrong. You're the deacon?"

He sketched a sharp bow. "Euan St. Clair, at your service."

"A good Scottish name on a Sassenach," Fiona groaned.

Euan looked at her quizzically. "I'm not English. I was born in the Highlands, actually."

"Then ye have sold out," she snapped. "For ye speak as one of 'em."

"Stop it, Fiona," admonished Joan. "We need Mr. St. Clair's help." She smiled warmly at him and held out her hand.

Fiona rolled her eyes. What was in the air tonight? *You would think we never encounter the male of the species, the way we're acting.* An unbidden mental giggle bubbled in her brain. In fairness, they seldom chanced upon such handsome specimens. *Enough of that.* But it had been such a long, long time...

"I'm so glad to meet you," Joan was saying as the deacon shook her hand. "And you can call me Joan, Mr. St. Clair."

"Euan will do," he responded. His eyes raked over Joan appreciatively. "You are most definitely not what I expected."

She lowered her eyes shyly and elbowed Fiona. "Tell him."

Fiona cleared her throat. "We desperately need to have a look at some of the old church records," she began. "When I first rang St. Giles' they said ye were writing a history of the place and were the man to ask."

"I am doing a monograph on the subject, yes." He chuckled politely. "But I fail to see how it merits such urgency..."

"Just lead us to the books, laddie," Rory called with a casual air. He leaned nonchalantly against the base of the statue. "We're almost out of time and the fate of the world's at stake."

Euan stepped around the women and peered at him. "Who are you?"

Rory smiled, but he was too far away and the light too dim for Euan to see that he was abnormally toothy.

"What is going on here?" Euan turned back to the women, frowning. His gaze slid down the arm that Joan previously had been holding behind her back. "Is that a sword?"

"Aye, man Euan, 'tis." The vampire laughed. "But I dare say she's spent too much time on Cockburn Street. Lots of New Age weirdies down there."

Darting around Euan, and skipping a few paces toward Rory, Fiona made shushing motions with her hands. She could hear Joan continuing the conversation behind her.

"Ummm ... yes ... it's for a movie. We're doing research on icons for a movie, y'see. And the production deadline is bearing down on us, and you know what Hollywood's like--it'll be the end of the world if we don't meet this deadline. So we really have to see the records right now. And if you help us, I'll make sure you get a screen credit. It'll be great publicity for your gig here."

Euan's tone was a cross between annoyed and incredulous. "You dragged me from my bed..."

"Ah, c'mon," Joan cajoled. "Everyone wants to be in a movie."

"From where did you say you knew my father?" A clear note of suspicion had crept into Euan's voice.

Joan coughed. "Umm ... What?"

Fiona's spine went stiff. She had forgotten to tell Joan about that bit. From behind Euan's back, Fiona tried to get Joan's attention without being caught in Euan's peripheral vision.

"Your secretary said..." Euan began.

Joan's eyes narrowed slightly as she tried to read Fiona's frantic gestures and silently mouthed words. "School."

"You could not possibly have gone to school with--"

"No, my brother..." *Mother.* "Sorry, my mother. My mother went to school with him."

"I see."

"They're great pals," Joan declared.

"I see." Euan's tone continued to be entirely noncommittal. Joan stepped forward and laid her hand on his arm. "Look. We really need to read these books. It's very important. I have two forms of I.D." She smiled up at him. "Please? You can hold onto my passport."

Fiona walked around to face Euan. He needed to agree. Perhaps she should use a bit of magick? It was wrong to tamper with people's wills. Wrong, wrong, wrong. But they required the books. And what was one person's will when the fate of the world might be at stake?

But Euan had already softened. "All right. I'm currently working through a few books that I think you'll find interesting. They're in my flat. It's quite near here."

Fiona snorted. "Aye. We'll go to your flat straight away. And after that we shall run with scissors. And take sweeties from strangers, an' all."

"I think I'm the one taking the bigger risk here," Euan stated evenly. "After all, there are three of you, and I'm not armed with a sword."

"Three." Joan repeated. She grinned stiffly at Euan. "Would you excuse us for a moment?"

Joan grabbed Fiona and dragged her several feet out of Euan's earshot.

"We can't bring the vampire to Euan's," Joan whispered. "If he invites him in, he could go back at any time…"

Fiona considered their options. "Rory and I could go to my flat and continue the research I've started while ye fetch the books." She paused. "But I dinna feel right leaving ye alone with that Sassenach."

"That's no problem. The problem is how can I feel right about leaving you alone with that vampire?"

Fiona laughed. "I have the bag of goodies ye gave me at home. Stakes, crosses, holy water, the whole caboodle. There is nae problem there."

"You're sure you'll be all right?"

"Whey aye," Fiona assured her with a nonchalant toss of her wrist. "Dinna fret about me."

"Right. Then I'll get the books from Euan's and bring them over to your place."

"Be safe."

Joan gave her a quick hug. "I'm afraid you might need that advice more than I do."

* * * *

Perched at the top of four long flights of stairs was the paneled, wooden door to Fiona's flat. Its white paint was cracked and peeling and, even after her long, antique key finished clanking in the lock, it did not open easily. Fiona shoved impatiently against the edge and, as soon as the door had swung wide enough to admit her, disappeared down the dark foyer.

Rory stopped short at the threshold. "Wearisome rules," he muttered to himself. He could hear Fiona hurriedly puttering about inside. "Howay, lass! Did ye not forget something?"

She dashed back and invited him in. He followed her down the unlit passage to a large open chamber and watched her circle its perimeter, snapping on all the lights in the room as she went, which amounted to two tall, stained glass torchères, a short, porcelain reading lamp, and one overhead chandelier that was attempting to impersonate crystal.

What Fiona's flat lacked in location, it made up for in decor. *Presuming you wanted the Black Prince and Queen Victoria as your interior designers*, Rory thought. The room was full of plush reds and deep velvets. Flamboyant window treatments sent heaps of heavy fabric spilling down ruby walls already adorned with ample, alabaster crown moldings. Hefty furniture prowled upon clawed feet across the thickly carpeted floor. Even the kitchen, tucked away in the back, looked more medieval than modern, with iron skillets and a black cauldron sitting on the counter.

"What is this? Victorian Gothic?" asked Rory, inspecting the carved legs of the nearest dark wood chair. "Where are the puffy-sleeved Romantic poets gettin' sorted in the corner?"

"Ye live in a crypt somewhere, so dinna ye talk," she retorted. "The library's through there. Get reading."

Rory hadn't noticed there was a hallway off the big room until she indicated it. As he came around the corner, he could see three closed doors. The one at the end of the hall should be her bedroom. He guessed that the nearest door to that would be the loo. In which case... He opened the first door on the left. It certainly was a library. Shelves teeming with books consumed every wall from floor to ceiling. And such a collection of books. Ancient, leather-bound tomes sat next to shiny, new paperbacks. Huge, oversized texts dominated some shelves while loose leaves of paper spilled off others.

A long, wooden research table, surrounded by several wheeled chairs with over-stuffed velvet cushions, dominated the center of the room. Its polished surface was peppered with little bronze reading lamps topped by convex shades of green and amber. Rory stepped closer. A book had been left open on the tabletop. He fluttered through its pages of fancy calligraphy and woodcut illustrations and shrugged. *Dreich bit of reading, that.*

Wandering over to one of the shelves that seemed particularly populated by paperbacks, he ran his finger along the dust-free shelf until one exceedingly colorful spine stopped him. He tipped the book to reveal its cover. A man and a woman, apparently victims of a clothing shortage, clasped each other in a passionate embrace. He pulled the paperback off the shelf. *Now this could be worth researching.*

Flopping into one of the chairs at the table, Rory began to read. He was just getting to a good part when he heard Fiona in the hallway. Quickly he removed his booted feet from the table, his chair snapping from its precarious tilt back into an upright position, and tossed the paperback over his shoulder as she entered the room. She had changed her clothes. Sensible shoes and loose-fitting jeans were topped off by a sleek wool sweater upon which bounced a herd of fluffy sheep. She was disguising her natural voluptuousness with sort of a cuddly, virginal outfit. Not actually the way to go if she were trying to repel a vampire. But full marks for effort.

Without a word, she marched to the far wall and knelt to examine its bottom shelf. Head bent sideways, her thick black hair tumbled in waves almost to the floor. With quick, decisive movements, she selected one of the books, nimbly regained her feet, and crossed to him with graceful strides. She wasn't precisely beautiful, Rory persuaded himself. But she was ... vibrant. The mere sight of her sparkling, sapphire-blue eyes and dazzling smile would warm the heart of anyone she favored. Rory had seen her smile so at Joan. She was not smiling at him.

"Right then. Ye take this one." She handed him the musty tome. "And I'll finish this." Fiona scooted the volume lying open on the table toward a chair across from his.

"Why not sit beside me?" Rory patted the seat next to his.

"I dinna think so," Fiona replied. "Across the table will be close enough, thank ye."

She sat and began to study the text in front of her. After a few minutes, she glanced up. "Ye are supposed to be reading, not staring at me."

"I'm thinking."

"About?"

Rory grinned mischievously. "Your breasts."

"Behave!"

"Och, look, they've perked up now that I've mentioned them."

She glowered at him, but did not respond.

He pressed on. "Right now I'm thinking, breasts. Blood. Thighs. Blood."

"That's disgusting."

"We vampires are not so different from living men. We think about food and sex."

She rolled her eyes. "Well, ye can stop now."

He continued to gaze at her. "I canna. I'm mesmerized."

She snorted. "I dinna think much of your chances on the open road, then. Ye must be mesmerized by every shiny object ye see."

"Nae, ye are a right bobbydazzler of a lass."

"Get on wi' ye." She returned to reading.

Rory indicated the book in front of her. "Ye are intelligent. Ye have a quick mind. And your body would drive a vicar wild."

"Stop thinking that way," she demanded irritably, keeping her head down. But he could sense the prickles scurrying over her face. She was going to blush if he kept this up.

"I canna help thinking that way. I'm male." He tried to make his voice as full of innuendo as possible. The rising of her blood sent delicious urges through his frame.

"Look." Fiona raised her head. She put her hands on either side of her book and took a deep breath. "I'm tryin' to make myself as unattractive to ye as possible."

"That could ne'er happen." He started to reach across for her hand. She immediately concealed her hands in her lap.

"Ye won't get 'round me that easily." She leaned forward, a wicked glint in her eye. "Ye are not a real man. So your compliments dinna count."

Unperturbed, Rory languidly bent closer. "I bet a canny bit of fluff like ye has quite a few real men gasping to serve her. I know I would be."

She raised a skeptical eyebrow. She had a good poker face. But she could not mask the scent of her piqued interest. Not from him. Their eyes locked. Rory watched as her bravado melted. Uncertainty flickered in the depths of her eyes. But still she held his gaze. He grinned. She narrowed her eyes defiantly. But he knew he was getting to her. And he aimed to discomfit her further.

"I can smell your blood from here." His voice was smoky.

Her eyes instantly widened in shock, and she quickly glanced down. Then her hands flew from her lap in clenched fists, a jerking motion of chagrin that she had looked away first. Her eyes returned to his face.

"No, you canna," she responded dismissively.

He deliberately licked his lips. "Ye will taste so sweet. Like nectar."

"Read!" she ordered, pointing at the volume in front of him.

"Have ye not wondered what it would be like to be penetrated by a vampire?"

Fiona's expression of exasperated disbelief did not deter him from continuing.

"And afterwards ... we would roam the night together. Sharing the hunt. Sharing secrets mere mortals can ne'er know. Sharing indescribable pleasure. Eternally together."

"Eternally damned, ye mean," she corrected, returning to her book.

Rory contemplated the ceiling. *She's got ye there.* Quiet reigned as he considered another tack.

He leaned toward her. "Have ye e'er made love on the moor at midnight when the heather is in bloom?" His voice was low and seductive.

She continued to read, her reply a study in indifference. "Too cold. Too prickly. Too much trouble."

"I can picture ye naked, with tiny purple petals fluttering across your creamy skin. Ye would be all mist an' smiles. Soft curves amid the bracken." His fingers crept gradually across the smooth tabletop, stalking Fiona's breasts.

She caught the movement and raised her eyes without raising her head. Rory bent so that he could meet her gaze.

"Dinna ye long to ken what 'tis like to misbehave?"

"I've misbehaved plenty. Stay on your side of the table," Fiona directed, glaring at him. She returned to her reading.

His hands paused. Then they resumed their forward prowl.

"I've got holy water," Fiona warned, without looking up from her book.

With a disgruntled snort, Rory slammed his palms on the table and slouched back in his chair. "I'm not bothered," he lied. "I'll have ye gagging for me one day."

She raised her head. "Ye are more confident with less cause than any man I've e'er met."

Rory opened his book and dejectedly paged through it. But he could not keep mum for long. "I like ye. I'm helpin' ye. And I havenae bitten ye nor any of your friends," he mumbled into the pages.

Fiona failed to respond to his melancholy tone. "Your point?" she snapped, continuing to read.

"I dinna ken why ye dinna enjoy my company."

Solemnly she raised her head. "Because that would be wrong on so many levels that it doesnae bear thinking about."

Rory lowered his gaze. Silence cloaked the room for so long that he assumed Fiona had gone back to reading. But when he glanced up at her, she was regarding him with a world-weary cast to her eyes.

"Would ye give me a truthful answer to one question?" she finally asked.

Rory grinned saucily. "Might do."

"Tell me why ye are really helping us."

"Exactly for the reasons I said," he responded, endeavoring to look the picture of wide-eyed innocence.

"Ye must think my mother knitted me," Fiona replied darkly. She returned to her book.

Rory watched her read. She was right. She was nobody's fool. *A pity, that.* He experienced a twinge of emotion long unfamiliar to him and rusty with disuse. She wouldn't be half so much fun to talk to if he had to kill her.

CHAPTER THREE

Euan ushered Joan into his study. "Please do make yourself comfortable, I shan't be a moment."

Joan headed for one of the windows. There had to be some perk to being on the top floor of this elevator-challenged, Georgian building. The windowpanes had those slightly rippled flaws you see in old glass, but the view was first-rate. She could see Princes Street Gardens and the long bridge that spanned the deep valley separating the medieval stone warren of the Old Town from the spacious Georgian architecture of the New. The black void of the valley made the sparkling city lights and illuminated buildings on either side seem that much brighter. Didn't the trains run through that valley? It otherwise might have been a promising vampire lair.

Joan turned her attention to the room. Euan's place could never be called a lair. Like what she had seen of the rest of his apartment, it was totally vogue-a-go-go. Lots of metal, glass and avant-garde furniture. The color scheme was more conventional--mostly a sophisticated hunter green with a bit of plaid for accent.

In the midst of this, his heavy, wooden desk rested in antique splendor. He was currently standing behind it, rifling through a drawer. She decided to mosey over for a closer look.

Euan's desk had a lived-in appearance. A creased leather file stuffed with mail of assorted sizes occupied one corner. A low stack of books grew next to a cube of paperclips and a tall cup of pencils at the other. Several sheets of letterhead notepaper lay scattered over an ink-stained, flat desk calendar. The letterhead bore Euan's full name in large Edwardian script. She noticed two initials following his name--K.C.

Joan indicated the papers. "Are you a knight commander of something?"

He glanced at her, saw where she was looking, and snatched up the sheets of paper. "No, no, it's for Keeper of the Chapel." He stuffed the sheets into the drawer he had been rummaging through and banged it shut. "It's a family joke."

She watched him open another, lower drawer and bend to shuffle through the papers within. "So your middle name's Saint John, huh?"

"Yes," he grumbled. "You might say that's another family joke. It's pronounced *Sinjin*, by the way."

"Really? Wow. *Euan Sinjin Saint Clair.*" She let the name roll off her tongue like a delectable treat. It was a fine name. She had always felt her own name to be kinda plain. This was a name that belonged in Edwardian script. "That's pretty. I mean..."

"Yes, what every boy wants, a *pretty* name," Euan responded dryly.

He glanced at her again, but now his eyes were bright with humor. What dreamy, chocolate brown eyes he had.

"Did you get beaten up a lot at school?" she asked sympathetically.

"No, I learned to fight really rather well." He gave her a pleasant grin and added modestly, "If I do say." Then he went back to rummaging in the drawer. "I have some notes I feel certain you'd like to see, but they seem to have wandered away." After searching a moment more, he straightened up. "I suggest you take the top three books on the desk there for now and I will bring the papers over to your hotel tomorrow night. I should have I located them by then."

She picked up the three books he indicated. They were thick hardbacks, very old and very heavy. She tried to surreptitiously peek at the books that had been beneath them--the ones he had not offered to her. When she looked up, she saw him watching her with an affable smile.

"They're not about the church," he informed her. "The top one's by John Cleland, if you're interested."

Joan could feel her mouth drop open. Not an attractive expression, but she couldn't help herself. She could have sworn she knew that name ... didn't he write a famous erotic novel? Well, an 18th century erotic novel. That would be tame by today's standards. But still.

"You can read that?" she gasped.

"What do you mean?"

Her cheeks were growing hot. She was blushing. He was still looking at her, his expression both amused and puzzled.

"You're a deacon," she finally managed to say.

He chuckled.

"What's so funny?"

"Being a deacon isn't like being a priest. We're commissioned but not ordained. I provide professional support for community outreach programs. And you thought that would restrict my choice in literature?"

"I dunno what I thought," Joan responded, tottering between embarrassment and relief. She took a deep breath. She was not one for prevaricating. Her job had taught her that. If a question needs answering, then you ask it straight out. And she definitely wanted the answer to this next question. "So you could have a girlfriend, then? If you wanted to, I mean?"

Euan gave an idle nod, having returned his attention to the drawer. "In fact, I had a girlfriend, until about six months ago. Yvette. She did all the decorating in here. Except for the desk. The desk is mine."

That explains that. "It's a very nice desk," Joan averred.

"Thanks. Maybe I put them over here." Euan strode away to a bookcase on the other side of the room.

He was utterly engrossed in his task. If only he found her as interesting. Joan gloomily wished that the position of girlfriend was something you could apply for. Hand in a résumé. References. Well, maybe not references. But anything other than having to solely rely on charm. She had many diverse and valuable talents, but unfortunately charm was not one of them.

Leaving him to continue his search, Joan said goodnight, though it should have been good-morning. Euan hurried over to hold the door while she and her armload of books passed through. Then, gently, he closed the door behind her. His flat suddenly seemed hushed and empty. Euan shook his head.

Mad, old Uncle Hamish had said many things before he died. Joan Armstrong had been just one of the names of the eccentrics he had wasted his dying breaths prattling on about. Euan had given his word to the dear old man that he would help Miss

Armstrong if ever she appeared on his doorstep. He had not thought himself likely to be called upon to keep such a promise. Now he was obliged.

For no one else would he have dragged himself out to St. Giles' in the middle of the night. What was decidedly odd was that Miss Armstrong was apparently unaware that she truly was known to his family. He was curious. If she honestly did not know him, why then did she want his help? Who was this girl? This strange, strong and frankly, quite beautiful girl. No, she was definitely not the sort he had expected.

* * * *

Fiona returned from the paperback shelf and, standing, slid a thick paperback across the table to where Rory sat. Its gothic cover was worn and the spine's numerous creases marked it as having been often read.

"*Jane Eyre*," she stated.

Rory nodded thoughtfully as he picked up the book. "I'm not far wrong, I would have guessed *Wuthering Heights* as your favorite."

Astonishment zipped through Fiona's frame. "Ye have read these books?"

"'Course I have, what d'ye take me for? I'll have ye know I read 'em back when they were new."

"So ... back when ye had nothing better to do, then," she responded dryly.

He smiled. "Aye, 'twasnae the telly to watch. Daylight can be dreadful dull oftimes." He flipped through the yellowed pages. "Heathcliff isnae your type?"

She shook her head. "What people forget about Heathcliff is the Puppy Incident."

"Och, aye?" He glanced up at her, his eyebrows raised in mild amusement.

Fiona frowned. He was laughing at her. But she wasn't going to let that deter her. She had a point to make. "Heathcliff may be tall, dark and handsome, but he strung up Isabella's puppy and that makes him a villain any way ye slice it."

Rory gently placed the book back on the table, and then spoke with similar care. "And ye arenae keen on villains?"

She snorted. "Three guesses."

He slid the paperback from one hand to the other on the polished tabletop. "But mayhap he regrets it?"

Fiona's flesh prickled as a flutter of awareness rippled through her. Could he be ... no, of course not. He could not possibly be talking about himself. This was some ruse to gain her sympathy. To trick her into letting down her guard.

"That's not in the book," she snapped.

He never looked up, but continued to slide the book back and forth. "So the fella in *Jane Eyre* is kind to puppies and kittens, is he?"

"Precisely." She deftly seized the paperback from its sliding transit, picked it up and started for its shelf.

"I like puppies and kittens," Rory told her retreating back.

More prickles zinged up her neck at his statement. She tossed her head and tried to ignore them. "Ye also like *Wuthering Heights*, I take it?" She shelved the book and returned to the table.

He shrugged. "From what I remember Catherine's bonnie. Jane's an ugly lass."

She crossed her arms. "She's *not* ugly."

His eyes widened slightly. "I dinna believe it. Ye identify with the ugly one. And ye are such an adorable wee thing."

He was laughing at her again. "*Tall* thing," Fiona corrected him, aware of how petulant she sounded but unable to stop. "I'm tall."

"Joan is tall. Ye are more like average."

That was true enough. Joan was just shy of six feet. And Rory was even taller than Joan. He must be ... Fiona mentally shook herself. Yes, he was tall and handsome. But, *get over it*, as Joan would say. He was a vampire.

"Aye, I'm average," she admitted grumpily. "But I'm not 'wee'."

He smiled at her. "Ye are the perfect size for a cuddle."

"None but ye think so." The words slipped out of Fiona's mouth before she could stop them. She bit her bottom lip. If he knew how inexperienced she really was, he might try to press his advantage with even more vigor. She glanced at him warily. He did not seem to comprehend the full meaning of her words. He was simply staring at her incredulously.

"Lassie, havenae ye ever looked in a mirror?"

She gave him what she hoped was a contemptuous smile. "And what would ye ken about mirrors?"

He grinned. "Nae much lately, I grant ye. But--"

"Mirrors lie. I dinna see what ye see." Fiona flopped into her chair, pulled the closest leather-bound tome over and started to read. "Now we really must get back to work."

* * * *

Spirits not dampened by the climb, Joan knocked briskly on Fiona's door. It was a beautiful day. She had cut through Princes Street Gardens past that gold fountain and it had been shining brilliantly in the sun. You didn't often see that. Edinburgh was a city of rain. It ran the gamut--everything from a light mist to a driving downpour. The citizens probably had a thousand words for rain. She knocked again. No Fiona. Joan gently lowered her armload of books to the floor and proceeded to search her petite leather purse for her copy of Fiona's key. It would be down at the very bottom, of course.

She let herself in to the dark apartment. The living room was empty. All of the heavy curtains were still closed, shutting out any hint of the sunny day outside. But a lone stab of light jutted into the darkness from the hallway to the library. Joan danced over to the library and rounded the doorjamb. Her merry greeting dying on her lips as she froze in the doorway.

Fiona, sitting at the research table, was pointing out something in an oversized book. Rory leaned over her shoulder, his face inches away from hers. But unlike Fiona, his attention was not drawn to the page below. Rory's eyes explored Fiona's face in darting, sidelong glances that would quickly shy away, as if afraid she would meet his gaze, and then just as quickly look back as if equally afraid that Fiona might have looked at him and he had missed it.

Joan could feel her lips pursing into a disapproving scowl. How could Fiona sit so calmly with one of the Undead hovering at her side? Fiona was all about justice. Joan had seen her in action many times. She could deliver impassioned, sometimes interminable, tirades about the historical injustices committed against the Scots and turn right around and use that same zeal to eradicate an unfairly assessed parking ticket. Big injustice, small injustice. It didn't matter. Fiona would rectify it or never let you hear the end of it. So how did a vampire--a murderer by nature--manage to get past her? He must be taking advantage of her scrupulously fair nature somehow. Although what could he possibly have told her? That he was a vegetarian? No, it had to be his vampire magnetism. That Rory thing was in for a surprise, then, because no way would that ever affect her.

"So what's going on here?" Joan asked crossly.

Both Fiona and Rory jumped at the sound of her voice.

Joan strode into the room, dropped her armful of books onto the table with an indignant thud, and flopped into a chair.

"Ye shouldnae use your super-skills on your friends." Fiona fanned her face with her hand, as if she were recovering from a fright. "I dinna expect ye. Would ye like some tea?"

"Yes, please," Joan answered, not taking her eyes off Rory. She deliberately scowled at him but he was completely unaware of it. Rory had perched on the table, watching Fiona trip off to the kitchen.

"I thought vampires had to sleep in their native earth during the day," Joan stated.

Rory glanced at her. "Scotland is my native earth." He shoved the books over and laid back full length on the tabletop. "And the whole sleep thing--it depends on the origin of the vampire that turned ye. Some types are paralyzed during the day, some arenae affected. Some must sleep, some need naught but a wee drop, an' some dinna need any sleep at all. For me, as long as I'm in Scotland, I dinna have to sleep unless I want. I just have to keep out of the sun."

Fiona returned, gracefully carrying a china cup decorated with tasteful pink blossoms by the gold-rimmed edge of its matching saucer. "Here ye are."

"Thanks." Joan sipped the aromatic, pale brown liquid that clearly contained milk. Perfect. Fiona always remembered how she took her tea. "How goes the research?"

Rory propelled himself off the table and onto his feet with one fluid motion. "No joy yet. But 'tis amazin' the arcane knowledge committed to these books. For instance, I've discovered that there are vampire watermelons. I'm thinkin' of gettin' one as a pet."

"I always wanted a pet," Fiona mused, returning to her seat. "I would love to have a pug. But they're so high maintenance."

"Vampire watermelons," Joan repeated slowly.

"Aye, and vampire pumpkins," Rory added.

"I see. Should I be worried?" Joan asked Fiona dryly.

Fiona smiled. "Mostly they just roll around and growl at the living."

"My kind of pet," Rory stated.

Fiona chuckled. "They're more of a nuisance than a threat."

"Still his kind of pet," Joan observed.

Rory's eyes flashed--just for a moment--with the chillingly dangerous aspect Joan had come to expect from vampires. Mentally, she urged him to make a wrong move. She was certain he could use a good pummeling. But almost as quick as it had appeared, the flash was gone. He chuckled. "I come to share the inside knowledge I've gleaned, and here ye are insulting me."

"I'm still surprised you have any inside knowledge to share," Joan replied. "Vampires are notorious loners. I just don't picture them gossiping."

He nodded. "Aye, true enough that we're a loose-knit society. We exist in the verge of civilization's denial. We're that shadow ye catch in the corner of your eye that vanishes when ye turn to look for it. Wouldnae do for us to loiter in coffee shops discussing the latest method to remove bloodstains."

Joan frowned. The vampire was teasing her.

"But we have kin groups," he continued. "And we talk, and word gets 'round."

Joan glanced over at Fiona to see what she thought of the conversation. Fiona was clearly thinking, but apparently not about the conversation. A rueful smile quirked the corners of Fiona's lips while her wistful blue eyes gazed softly upon Rory's countenance, although whether he or inward visions were the focus of her thoughts was difficult to say.

"So has he been helpful, Fiona?"

Joan's question startled her out of her reverie. "Aye, he has been. Very helpful. I can show ye what we've come up with so far."

"And you don't need me to beat him up for you or anything?"

She laughed. "Nae, nothing like that."

Joan looked over at Rory. He was glowering fiercely at her, the dangerous glint back in his eyes. But he was controlling himself. Quite an admirable example of restraint, for a vampire. She mentally shrugged. He seemed to be benign for now. And Fiona wasn't acting enthralled. So if Fiona could put up with him, she guessed she could too. For a while, anyway.

CHAPTER FOUR

Fiona had finished her presentation. Rory watched as she stood at the table's head, her fingertips lightly drumming the tabletop, waiting for Joan's reaction. But Joan remained staring silently at the chaotic heap of loose papers, scribbled notes, and open books covering the research table.

"That's it?" Joan finally responded. "All that ... all *that*." She indicated the heap with a wave of her hand. "And we don't know any more about what's going down on Samhain than we did last night?"

Fiona's brows knit together darkly. "I do the research ye ask of me. Ye are the one who, two nights back, asked for an in-depth report on the Fury's exploits. If ye remember, I said at the time that wouldnae help much."

Joan nodded. "And you were right. I now know more than any one person should about the Fury's killing sprees. And even that's probably incomplete."

"I think ye'll find my research quite thorough..."

"Don't get uppity on me, that's not what I meant," Joan interjected with a smile. "Doubtless the Fury got noticed in the mid-19th century because his victims were the most sparkling aristocrats and the best businessmen. He could have been slaughtering peasants for centuries before that."

Fiona's expression softened slightly. "'Tis true enough. History ne'er records what happens to the mass of us."

Joan was staring at the mound of papers again, shaking her head. "Y'know, that whole report on the Fury could have been summarized as, The Fury--One Big, Bad Dude."

"Exactly," Fiona concurred crossly. "And I've told ye before I dinna think 'tis the Fury we're dealing with. As ye are now well aware, he hasnae any connection with anything called the Andromache."

Rory frowned to himself. Fiona had done quite a bit of work and Joan seemed to be dismissing her efforts. He felt irritated with Joan on Fiona's behalf. And that annoyed him. It was a *good* thing, for him, if they argued amongst themselves. He should be adding petrol to their fire. And yet...

He found himself quite fond of Fiona's company. He relished their verbal sparring. Their conversation was unlike any in which he had ever engaged. Of course, he didn't normally take the time to engage humans in conversation. But Fiona was worth a good deal of anybody's time and it was surprisingly unpleasant to see her upset.

A brief, mental tugging war ensued as he considered his choices. Hinder or help? He was not usually victim to such dilemmas. In fact, not to dilemmas of any sort. The best thing about being a vampire was the hedonistic freedom to do whatever made one feel good--regardless of consequences. If it would give him more pleasure to help, then so be it. That was his nature. No one could blame him if he engaged in what could, in truth, only be described as a minor indulgence.

Rory slid the sheet of notepaper they had been working on earlier over to Fiona and gently tapped her hand with it. "We were saving the best bit for last," he told Joan.

Fiona's mood lightened immediately at the sight of the paper, and she gave him a quick, grateful smile. Odd how such a brief gesture could have such a lingering effect. Fiona was now blithely rabbitting on at Joan, but he could still feel the warmth of her smile in his veins.

"Rory and I have made quite a bit of progress with the Prophecy. As ye ken, the language is ancient and devious in its construction." Fiona picked up the sheet of notepaper. "It's sort of a rhyme. Our translation's a mite rough. But ye can get the general idea. The body deals with the destruction that will be wrought if the Andromache rises."

"Still no clue about what the Andromache is, though?" Joan asked.

"No," Fiona admitted. "But see this phrase here?" She pointed at the sheet. "That says that the rising will trigger the end of reality."

Joan whistled. "Well, that's new."

Rory could see Fiona visibly relax. She was relieved that their efforts were getting some praise at last.

"And we've got an even better piece of news. Together we were able to complete the translation of the final stanza--the one about how to avert the rising." Fiona handed the paper to Joan.

Joan read Fiona's scrawled rendition.

Through mercy at the end of the world,
Redemption's final play unfolds,
While sinful selflessness shall save,

THE CRIMSON FOLD

Solely True Belief forever holds.

Joan handed the paper back. "Interesting. What's it mean?"

"We haven't the foggiest," answered Rory merrily. "Now, would either of ye two lassies like anything from the kitchen? I'd like to avail myself of the premises, if I may."

"What are ye goin' to ... eat?" The apprehension in Fiona's eyes was unmistakable.

"Do ye have any *Twiglets*? I'm in the mood for something crunchy."

Both Joan and Fiona gasped.

"Ye eat *Twiglets*?" Amusement danced in Fiona's eyes.

Meanwhile, shock had sent Joan's voice on a shrill ascent as she simultaneously exclaimed, "You can *eat*?"

"Only a wee bit, or it does me quite a mischief."

Confusion creased Joan's brow. "Then why--"

"I do it for the sensation or for a particular taste. And, foreseeing your next question, nae, it doesnae assuage my hunger in the least. Blood is still essential to my existence." He glanced from Fiona to Joan and back again, savoring the moment. "Nothing for ye lassies then?"

They continued to look at him in silent astonishment.

"I'll take it that ye have declined." Rory spun and was off, a strange warm feeling filling his chest. And he was ready for something even more warming. Rory headed for the kitchen, hoping there were some crunchy, spicy *Twiglets* awaiting him.

* * * *

"I'm sorry about earlier," Joan mumbled after Rory left the room.

Fiona sighed and slumped into a chair, feeling the tension ooze out of her body. "Me, as well."

Joan grinned, plainly happy that the apologies were over with. "Guess the tension's getting to me. Our assignments are usually much simpler. Kill this particular demon. Rid this specific town of vampires. And after that last village, I thought you and I deserved a break. Instead, we're expected to run a last minute defense for some mission that killed the guardian originally assigned to it. What was his name again?"

"Farquharson," Fiona answered. She nodded her head in grim agreement. That poor, isolated hamlet up on the northern coast had contained more than its fair share of ghouls. And now to be plunged into this esoteric crisis the moment they returned... "Why doesnae Evil ever take a day off?"

Joan laughed. "What, like an Evil vacation?"

"Precisely. Evil should take a leaf out of its own book and skive off now an' again."

"And have a cookie or something," Joan suggested.

Fiona put on a mock-serious expression. "Prawn crisps."

"Huh?"

"Evil would like prawn crisps."

Joan screwed up her face and stuck out her tongue. "Ugh. Gotcha. But I still think cookies--"

Fiona shook her head emphatically. "Biscuits arenae evil enough."

"Oh, I don't know. They go straight to my hips."

Fiona let her mouth drop open as if she were appalled. "Hips? What hips? Your hips are so slender ... In fact, your hips are evil."

Joan laughed. "I don't know what you're jealous about. You're the resident sexpot."

Fiona snorted, a derisive sound somewhere between disagreement and disgust. "Pull the other one, it's got bells on."

Joan shook her head, feigning melancholy. "Y'know, there's got to be some rule about having a sidekick who's sexier than you are. It's just not right."

But the timbre of Joan's voice alerted Fiona to the fact that she was only partially joking. Which was nonsense. Joan was tall, slim, and gorgeous. Fiona sighed. In comparison, she was merely average, plump and ... average.

Fiona tapped her fingers on the tabletop. "I'm hardly ... The men ye meet must be daft. I canna believe they dinna climb over each other to get to ye."

"Well, they don't." Joan shrugged one shoulder. "What's to attract them? My ultra-feminine armory? Or the chic bloodstains? Guys expect to compare scars with their buddies, not their girlfriends."

"That dishy Euan might like women with scars," Fiona mused.

Joan gaped at her. "I thought you hated him."

"I do. But I'm just bitter and twisted." Fiona winked. "I think he likes ye."

"Nah. The guys I like never find me attractive." Joan said it flippantly enough, but the tone of her voice betrayed the pain that this knowledge inflicted upon her.

"Well, at least ye dinna have a monster trying to seduce ye," Fiona responded. She huffed a deep sigh. "I dinna ken why he's wasting his time."

"Probably because he thinks you're a sexpot."

Fiona reached for the velvet cushion on the chair beside her and tossed it in Joan's general direction. "Evil hips."

Joan giggled. She threw the cushion on the seat beside her at Fiona. "Sexpot."

Attracted by the high-pitched giggles and thumping emanating from the library, Rory entered the room and swiftly ducked as a cushion sailed past his head. "*Hul*-lo! What's happening here?"

The library was in mild disarray, with seat cushions strewn to all corners and several reading lamps knocked off the research table. The two women, frozen in the midst of their two-fisted pillow fight, burst out laughing.

"Scary how the future of the world could depend on ye two." He gave them a toothy grin.

It did not take long for Rory and Joan to put the library back to rights while Fiona pensively sat at the research table examining the books that Joan had borrowed from Euan.

"So," Rory addressed Joan, in what he trusted was an air of polite disinterest. "How did a nice lassie like ye fall into a gig like this?" After all, she seemed to think that background information on the enemy was a good idea, so he might as well try it.

"It's part of my inheritance," Joan replied tersely. She retrieved the last seat cushion and headed for a seat at the table next to Fiona.

Rory followed her, making encouraging listening noises.

"Ye may as well enlighten him now," Fiona advised, without looking up from her reading. "Trust me, 'tis easier to indulge him than ignore him."

Joan flopped into the chair. Then, with queenly dignity, she swiveled the seat and fixed the full intensity of her gaze upon Rory. "I come from a long line of demon hunters. My father taught me. He was a hunter, as was his mother before him. My family pre-dates the van Helsings."

Rory chortled. "'Tis a family tradition of violence and mayhem."

Joan scowled at him. "It's a family tradition of protecting the weak and innocent. I inherited my father's duty."

Rory leaned against the table with practiced nonchalance. "So how do ye get your assignments?"

But a calculating glint had entered Joan's slate gray eyes. "Why are you asking me this?"

He shrugged. "Just wondering. I'm guessing ye advertise. Though it must be a bit dicey separating serious inquiries from people who are out with the fairies."

Joan made a noncommittal grunt and swiveled to face Fiona. "So are the books helpful?"

"Aye." Fiona flipped to the next page. "There are some fine pieces in the High Kirk's possession, but…"

"Nothing that jumps out and says 'I'm for saving reality'?"

Fiona nodded without looking up from the book.

"Well, Euan's going to bring some more stuff over to my hotel tonight." Joan stood up with a little bounce. "Come over around nine, and make sure you bring these books with you. I want to give 'em back to him immediately if we're not going to need them."

Fiona glanced at Joan. Her eyes flickered with merriment. "Tryin' to create a good impression?"

The two women were sharing some sort of private joke. A pang of jealousy stabbed at Rory's not-so-empty chest. He wished Joan would hurry up and leave.

Which she finally did.

But now Fiona was too engrossed in the hefty book in front of her to talk to him. Rory tried, but she only gave disinterested 'hmmms' in response. He made a theatrical show of his helpfulness, taking one of the other books, sitting across from her, and beginning to write notes from it. But she didn't look up. Exasperation slammed his spine against the back of his chair. And for a blinding instant he was startled by the strength of his own frustration.

Fiona continued to read, head bent, one hand absently twirling a lock of her hair. Why wouldn't she look at him? He just wanted her to look at him. And talk to him. And maybe touch him. More than that. He wanted to know what she'd feel like underneath him. Surrounding him. His fists clenched. If only he could turn her to his side. Then he'd never have to harm her.

"I could save ye."

Fiona looked up at that statement. "What?"

Rory licked his dry lips. "I could save ye."

"How'd ye mean?"

"If I turned ye. Vampirized ye. Ye would be safe then."

Her eyes were an arctic sea. "I dinna want to be saved that way."

"Are ye so certain?"

"Aye. Dead certain." Her voice had an ominous, bitter edge.

But he wasn't ready to admit defeat yet. The pleasurable thought of having her permanently at his side drove him on. He had no qualms about fighting Joan. All he had to do was convince Fiona to join him and the future was jam.

Fiona's other hand rested on the tabletop next to her hardback book. Rory leisurely reached across the table and covered her hand with his own. He was encouraged by the fact that she did not pull away. Her skin felt cool and smooth as marble. He shifted his fingers so his thumb could caress her palm.

"If this all comes to a sticky finish on Samhain, 'twill be a good thing to be a vampire," he said to her in all sincerity.

But her narrow gaze held nothing for him save icy indignation.

"'Tis ne'er a good thing to be a vampire."

"But--"

"Nae." Fiona flipped her wrist and suddenly his hand was now trapped beneath hers. Mildly surprised, Rory's eyes darted from his captured hand back to her face. Fiona's eyes burned with a dark intensity. "There is nae *but*. 'Tis ne'er a good thing to be a vampire." She released his hand with a snap. "Now get back to readin' or get out." She returned to her hardback, dismissing him as surely as if she had slammed a door in his face.

Rory gnashed his teeth. But he went back to his book.

* * * *

Rory tugged at the heavy curtain, skillfully using the thick fabric to shield himself from the sliver of window revealed. The weak light that seeped upon the carpet was hardly worth the precautions. Rory risked a glance at the pink and purple streaked sky. Sunset was only moments away. His skin prickled with anticipation. Soon, very soon, he could go out there. Somewhere supper waited, wandered, with no idea of what was in store. A nice hot supper. His stomach began to growl at the thought of food. It was about time.

He turned to announce the onset of evening but swallowed his words at the sight of Fiona. She was fast asleep, arms resting limp on the table, cheek pillowed on the open pages of the book she had been reading, her hair spilling in a great black halo around her head. She had not slept all day, nor all the night before as far as he knew. She must be exhausted. Humans generally slept ... how long did they sleep these days? He remembered sleeping quite a lot when he was human, but that had been before electricity. There hadn't been much one could do by candlelight. Not without a woman, anyway. And back then he had spent a wee bit of his time--no, truth be told--great heaping bags of his time alone. Rory frowned at the memory. What had he been waiting for? An enchanted princess from one of the fairy stories his grandmother shared when he was too sick to do his chores? He'd been a daft gowk. Still, he hadn't missed much. None of the village girls had looked anything like Fiona.

With unnatural silence, Rory approached Fiona's sleeping form. Her face was so smooth and still. Creamy skin and crimson lips just slightly parted. She might be drooling a tad. But otherwise she resembled a porcelain doll. The contrast between her pale skin and her hair black as a corbie, a raven, was striking.

Rory's hand hovered above her tangled tresses. Cautiously his fingers lowered. Her hair was incredibly soft to the touch. He stroked a cluster of wayward curls, careful not to snag his fingers and awaken her. Her hair felt just as glossy and silken as it looked. With unaccustomed diffidence, he bent over and, gathering a handful of the dark waves, brought them to his lips. The scent of strawberries filled his nostrils. Nice shampoo. But there was something else. A subtle, alluring undertone of...

There was a violent flurry of moment and he inadvertently tightened his grip as her locks flew out of his hand. Fiona had jerked away and was bounding to the other side of the table, in the process leaving behind several strands of her hair in his grasp.

She stood glaring at him across the expanse of wood, with one hand to her smarting scalp. "Too close! What have I told ye? Ye canna get that close to me."

"I didnae mean t'..." He started to hand back the strands of her yanked hair.

She gave him a withering look, and Rory mentally cursed himself. As if giving them back would help. What was he thinking, that she'd glue them back on? What an idiot she must think him.

"Just stay your distance in future," Fiona warned. She hoped her gaze was menacing enough. It seemed to be. Rory was backing toward the window with an almost contrite expression.

"Too right." He nodded. "Ye can sleep in peace now at any rate."

"Why?" She glanced about, irritably wondering what she had missed during her ill-timed nap. Her inability to resist the siren song of sleep irked her, giving her voice a bitter edge. Here she was betraying a weakness to the one individual most likely to exploit it.

Rory pointed at the closed tome on his side of the table and the small pile of his handwritten notes clustered on top of it. "That's me finished. I'm away."

He was leaving. Fiona struggled between relief and distress. At least while he was here she knew the rest of the city was safe. And it had been a pleasant change having someone to talk to, she had to admit. Her work was usually done with only the walls for company. The room seemed emptier already. She stepped toward him. "Wait, where are ye goin'?"

He stretched his arms and lazily indicated the window. "Time for my tea I think."

She gasped. "Ye dinna mean to say..."

He grinned at her. It was such a human expression, containing no malice. Which made his next words all the more shocking. "I mean to say I'm hungry."

She couldn't believe it. She had actually enjoyed his company. And now... "Ye are off to feed ... *on people?*"

"What do ye reckon I do, order pizza for one?" He spoke mildly, as if to a child.

"How can ye even contemplate..." She threw her hands in the air. "I despair of ye."

"I dinna ken why. Ye ken what I am. When ye people are hungry ye eat animals."

She scowled. "'Tis completely different for a person to eat another person."

"Och, not a person, pet. Remember? I'm not people." Rory laughed. "Ye humans are always incredibly annoyed to find out ye arenae the top of the food chain." Then his countenance softened. "Dinna worry, lassie, I'm not going to kill anyone. Just taste, is all."

She raised a caustic eyebrow. "Ye are just off for a bit of neck trauma, then?"

"Not trauma, necessarily." He searched for the appropriate words. "Minor lacerations."

"Neck *lacerations.* Och, that's so much better."

He frowned. "Why do ye fuss so? 'Tis only a sip. I willnae be changin' anyone."

"And ye expect me to just let ye go? When I ken what ye mean to do?"

"I dinna expect ye'll be able to stop me." He winked at her, then turned and threw open the window with one practiced sweep of his arm.

"Ye're leaving by the window?"

"Those stairs of yours are too much of an effort."

She dashed around the corner of the table. "Wait, wait! Why canna ye lick a butcher shop floor? Instead of biting a person?"

Rory paused astride the windowsill. "I'll consider it."

* * * *

Rory's stomach craved blood. It gurgled and twisted and ached emptily. He needed to feed. Yearned for it. Hunger chafed at his brain, pestering his thoughts like an itch just beyond his reach to scratch. So why the delay? He must stop thinking about Fiona and her irrelevant scruples. Concentrate on dinner. There was plenty of blood in the city, all his for the taking.

Distant weeping caught his attention. He sniffed the air, weeding through the scents of the city to detect a pure ribbon of fear, sweet like cinnamon. Not too far off. Moving with preternatural speed, Rory zipped through the medieval alleys and private courtyards, closing in on his victim. The sobbing, imperceptible to those without vampire senses, grew ever louder to his ears, the scent, nonexistent to humans, stronger. Then he arrived.

At the back of a narrow close, in a small, secluded courtyard, Rory found a young girl, her face smudged with dirt and tears. A gangly teenage boy towered over her, holding something high above his head, and dangling it as if he might drop it to the pavement at any moment. The little girl was crying, heartbreaking wails, and waving her arms in a panic-stricken attempt to rescue the object from him. The boy pushed her away, and she fell to the pavement. The bleeding abrasions already marring her chubby knees mutely testified that this was not the first time that the boy had knocked her to the ground. Rory glanced at the dangling item of contention. Legs weakly kicking in the air, the small, hairy animal whimpered piteously. It was a puppy.

Rory crossed the close with the swift, silent bound of a tiger. He grabbed the teenager from behind, one hand on his neck, the other covering the hand that held the puppy, keeping the boy from dropping the dog in his surprise.

"Ye should learn to play nice with others," Rory growled. He forced the boy's arm down to the level of the little girl, who was looking up at Rory with wide, round eyes. "Give the lassie back her dog."

The teenager complied. Anything he might have had to say on the matter was squelched by Rory's vise-like grip upon his throat. He carefully dropped the dog into the girl's waiting embrace.

"Thank you," she said in a tiny voice, hugging the puppy to her chest.

"Now be off home wi' ye," Rory ordered gravely.

She did not have to be told twice. As soon as the fleeing child was out of sight, Rory bared his fangs.

"I'm that chuffed to meet a right bastard like ye," he declared affably. "I'm dead peckish tonight and ye are just the sort no one could object to me havin'."

Rory shifted his grip on the wheezing boy's neck, and buried his fangs in his throat. Hot, spurting blood filled Rory's mouth. He wolfed it down, eyes closed, all his senses focused on his meal. The boy tasted sweet and sour, a mix of fear and cowardice.

"What are ye doing?" shrieked a horrified female voice.

CHAPTER FIVE

Rory looked up. Fiona was dashing toward him. She wore a long red cloak that rippled behind her like a flag in a high wind.

"I'm eating," Rory answered calmly as she approached. "What d'ye think I'm doin'?"

Fiona barreled into his side as if she had no brakes. Rory staggered but held both his ground and his meal. She slapped at his hands and pummeled his side, ineffectually trying to break his grip on his victim.

"Release him," she ordered.

Rory growled, but let go. As he backed away, the teenager slumped to the ground. Fiona bent over him. Rory could see his chest moving. The boy was still breathing. Fiona hoisted the teenager to his feet, gently smacking his face to awaken him until he stood on his own, groggy but aware. Then she shoved him down the close in the direction of the street.

"Ye should go to Casualty directly," she instructed. "There's a call box on the corner. Head for it, and I'll join ye there."

As the teenager stumbled away, Fiona turned on Rory. Her narrowed eyes blazed with anger.

"How dare ye! Ye are supposed to be helping to save the world--not eating the city's inhabitants!" She gesticulated wildly, broad negative motions that matched the outrage in her voice.

"But--"

"Victimizing some poor, innocent bairn," she continued unabated. "Ye truly are a monster."

"But--"

"Not a word!" Fiona deliberately turned her back on him and stormed down the close after the teenager.

THE CRIMSON FOLD

"But he was tormenting the girl! And her puppy!" Rory called plaintively after her. His forlorn voice echoed off the cold stones of the empty courtyard.

Fiona was gone.

With a guttural snarl, Rory threw his hands in the air. "What would ye have me do?" he shouted.

The deserted courtyard did not answer.

* * * *

Darkness sheathed the empty castle esplanade. The ticket windows were shuttered. The buses, cars and tourists had all gone home. The worn cobblestones, alone at last, gradually released the energy of the day to slumber with phantoms from the past. It was the perfect place for quiet contemplation. Which was not something in which Rory generally indulged.

He should be out hunting the crooked streets or lurking in the stately squares, perhaps finding a few female undergraduates to temporarily enthrall and sip from to his heart's content. There had been nights when he had feasted upon eight or ten different quarries, and here he was packing it in after a single, solitary one. And why? Because of Fiona. Her displeasure prowled his thoughts, quelling his blood-spattered imaginings and restraining his urges. And it was annoying the hell out of him.

Why did he care what Fiona thought? Lasses were ten a penny in this city. He could find another. He could find one that understood his cravings. And what was wrong with his cravings anyway? They're perfectly natural. He was a creature of the night. He was supposed to drink human blood. Who was she to disapprove? *Bloody scrubber.*

Snarling to himself, Rory bounded up onto the esplanade's retaining wall. With nimble tread, he hopped across the roofs of the modernized tourist section of the Lower Ward until he reached the sheer, curved face of the castle's half-moon battery. He ran his fingertips over the wall. The stone felt rough and cold to the touch. An impossible vertical climb to humans. But this was something he could do. Because of what he was.

He leapt and landed part way up the wall, continuing his perpendicular ascent like a rampaging spider. The only sound that accompanied him was the muted scuffing of his boots upon the stone. Then he reached the ledge.

One casual flip, and he stood tall atop the battery wall. Rory danced on the perilous corner of the ledge, taunting gravity. From this commanding vantage point, he could survey the whole of the Old Town. He looked out above the peaked roof of the gatehouse, across the flat esplanade, down the Royal Mile and its labyrinthine environs, and away to the giant, humped mountain named Arthur's Seat. This was his dominion.

Rory threw back his head and closed his eyes. The scents of the Old Town wafted over him. Damp stone. Autumn flowers. And

... yes, some poor sod in Patrick Geddes Hall was eating a *Pot Noodle*. Rory sneezed.

What else was there? Stale beer. Greasy, cold, abandoned chips. And ... he couldn't ignore them any longer. Humans. Salty, sweet human blood.

He could hear the lively giggles and careless steps of punters heading in and out of the pubs. Easy prey. Still more snacks stumbled into chugging cabs or wheezing buses. And up from the valley below came the smooth rumble of trains brimming with the promise of savoury new treats. There is so much blood in this city. *'Tis nae fair.*

* * * *

Fiona strolled through Princes Street Gardens on her way to Joan's luxurious little hotel room on the high street of Edinburgh's New Town. Even though Princes Street's shops were closed, the pavement still bustled with life and the busy road was a swirl of headlights and taillights. Which was precisely why Fiona preferred to walk the Gardens, on the opposite side of the wide street, tucked away from the crowds.

The electric lights did not penetrate as far here, and she thought she was alone amongst the elegant flowerbeds and tailored lawn. But as she neared the Scott Monument, with its tier upon tapering tier of notched, black spires ascending to the heavens like a gothic wedding cake, she recognized Rory leaning against one of the arches in its sooty base. She was caught off guard by the sudden, pleasant thrill that tightened her insides at the sight of him.

He was clearly watching her, waiting for her. Fiona stopped. Her tense fingers clutched the books in her arms. They were Euan's, she was returning them as Joan had asked, but now they were a liability. What if Rory were still angry about her interference earlier? What if he tried to hurt her? She should put the books down. Or would that tip her hand, warning him that she was ready to defend herself?

Rory propelled himself off the monument, leapt over a park bench with a floating, animal grace, and halted in front of her.

Fiona tried to shift her armful of Euan's books so that she would have one hand free. It didn't quite work. But Rory wasn't looking at her ungainly posture. His glossy obsidian eyes bore into hers. But he said nothing.

Fiona stared back, determined he would see only her anger. This was, after all, the same monster who had tried to eat a citizen earlier this very night. The charge-nurse had assured her the boy would be fine, but that wasn't the point.

"What d'ye want?" she growled.

"Just to tell ye..." Rory's head tilted to the side, as if he knew he was rebuffed and yet some force was driving him to proceed. "I just want to say ... want ye to ken that..."

"I havenae time for this." She stepped past him.
He grabbed her wrist. "Wait! Listen--"
Clutching the unbalanced stack of books with one arm, Fiona attempted to jerk her wrist free from his grasp. He tightened his grip to keep her. His eyes were surprisingly gentle, in contrast to the harshness of his hold. Fiona's arm shook slightly, muscles rigid, as she continued to pull back and he did not yield.
"Ye are goin' t' hurt yoursel'," he admonished her.
"Not before I hurt ye," she snapped.
"That's it." Rory pulled her sharply to him. The books tumbled to the pavement as she landed up against his solid chest. He gazed down at her, his eyes shining with eerie intensity, and for an instant Fiona wasn't certain what he meant to do with her. His breath hissed through his nostrils and the line of his mouth was grim.
Fiona spun, twisting away, but faster than the wings of a bat Rory's arms wrapped around her in a restraining bear hug and his hands captured both her wrists, forcing them to cross over her breasts. She was imprisoned, her back pressed against his chest. Fiona wriggled in his crushing embrace.
"Get off!" she demanded. She kicked backward at his shins.
"I dinna have a human pain threshold," he replied with a laugh, ignoring her blows.
She could feel his cheek against the side of her head. Then he was nuzzling her hair, her ear, and slowly, deliberately moving lower. She tossed her head back and forth yet his mouth unerringly found its target on the curve of her neck.
Fiona felt two dents prod her skin. Her entire body stiffened. Time and sound seemed to evaporate. She was aware of nothing in the stifling hush save the almost gentle pressure of the indentations upon her throat. She knew they were his fangs and yet, sharp as they were, he never broke her skin. Her spine tingled, ultra-aware of his hot mouth, of the tip of his tongue caressing her defenseless flesh. Still the dents paused upon her neck, provoking torments of delightful anticipation inside her. She heard a tiny sigh and realized it had escaped her own lips. Rory hugged her tighter at the sound.
She was temporarily overwhelmed by his nearness, by the intimate pressure of his unyielding body against her. His unique, musky, male scent filled her nostrils. She was trapped in his powerful embrace, yet his lips felt incredibly tender. A fluttery excitement was rising in her belly and weakening her knees. For a moment, she found herself wondering what his bite would be like. If only he were the one...
Her mind recoiled from the thought with a blinding stab of horror. How could she think such a thing? What was she doing? He was touching her and she was letting him. Joan would think her a traitorous, brazen hussy. *Shameful!*

Self-recrimination lent to her voice a gritty bitterness. "Leave me be or get on wi' it. I havenae got all night."

The prodding dents withdrew. But his arms continued their snug embrace.

"Are ye listening?"

"Your teeth have my attention," she replied tensely.

"I just wanted to tell ye ... I havenae had anything to eat."

"Any*one* ye mean."

"Aye," he agreed, his voice seemed tinged with sorrow. "I mean any*one*. I havenae had anyone's blood at all. And 'tis down to ye."

"Too right, because I prevented ye from--"

"Ye couldnae have stopped me if I dinna let ye. And mark ye, I would let nae other stop me."

"So glad to know I'm special."

Her sarcasm seemed lost on him. Rory persevered, his voice continuing to carry the same soft sincerity. "I'm tryin' to say exactly that. Ye are very special. I have never wanted another lassie, not like I want ye."

Fiona tried to swallow and failed. Her arid mouth gave her nothing to work with. It wasn't fair. How many nights had she gazed into the fire and wished that a man would say those very words to her? And now she must hear such appealing words from lips that lied.

"Ye say that to all your victims," she accused him in a whisper.

"Do I? I dinna ken anymore."

His lips returned to her throat. His lips alone, no teeth. He kissed her tenderly, once, twice, three times, each successive kiss moving further down her neck.

"In future, if ye hate me so much, wear a crucifix. I could never touch ye like this then," he murmured.

Fiona fought the clenched longing his touch kindled deep within her.

"I'll remember the advice," she responded through gritted teeth.

Rory sighed. His lips left her throat. Then she felt him rest his chin on the top of her head. "I dinna ken why ye are so vexed with me. I canna help being what I am. I can only--"

"Aim to lead a blameless life forever more?" Fiona finished for him, with not a little scorn. "That canna make up for your evil past, can it?"

"Mayhap not. But if we canna make up for our past sins, Heaven must be a right empty place."

Fiona ground her teeth, her jaw muscles so tight they hurt. The vampire had a point, an infuriatingly obvious point, and yet ... could such a one ever truly atone? Joan didn't think so, not surprisingly, but the question had bedeviled Fiona in sleepless hours past, and still she had no answer.

Rory's voice was at her ear. "Am I forgiven?"

Realizing she had been holding her breath, Fiona released it in an extended, deflating sigh. "Ye are truly repentant? And ye willnae harm another?"

Rory released her. She turned to scrutinize his face.

He gave her something approximating the Boy Scout salute. "I swear."

He appeared to be so earnest.

"Then I must forgive ye," Fiona admitted grudgingly while her common sense scolded her for being a naïve fool. She bent to collect the fallen books. *'Tis always dangerous when ye hear what ye want to believe.*

* * * *

"Tea's up," announced Fiona, placing two steaming cups on the circular faux-wood table where Joan and Euan sat.

Joan reached for the one closest to her, and pulled it by the saucer across to her place.

"Yours is black," Fiona informed Euan. "If ye want to add anything, 'tis over there." She pointed at the far side of Joan's suite, where the hospitality tray and the electric kettle dwelt.

Euan nodded. "Thank you."

He rose, retrieved a tiny, plastic container of cream and a teaspoon, and returned without comment, without so much as a frown. Fiona felt a tinge of regret for her rude behavior. But he was a Sassenach and someone had to remind them that they had a lot to answer for.

The muted creaking of bedsprings issued from the adjoining room. "This bed is a bit of all right," Rory called.

"Get that dead thing out of my bedroom!" shrieked Joan, jumping up from the table.

Fiona was already at the bedroom door. "Out!" she commanded.

Rory sauntered out of the bedroom. "I was coming out anyway."

"Boy, he is not going to last long," Joan grumbled as she returned to her seat.

"Dead thing?" Euan asked, giving Joan a perplexed stare.

"Oh, ummm..." Joan waved her hand vaguely. "It's a band."

Rory approached the table and pulled out a chair. Fiona followed and waited for him to sit down. He did not. He stood, looking significantly at Fiona. Fiona looked over her shoulder. What was she missing? She turned back to the table. Both Joan and Euan were looking at her now. Joan rolled her eyes in the direction of the seat. Fiona could have smacked herself. *Of course.* Rory was waiting to push in the chair for her.

Shy now that all eyes were upon her, Fiona cautiously complied. Rory seated her as smoothly as a gentleman from centuries past. *Which he well might be.*

Joan, sipping her tea, thoughtfully scrutinized Rory as he continued to stand behind Fiona's chair. Whatever she was thinking, she did not get a chance to say it.

"Thank you for returning my books so quickly," Euan began. "Were they of any use to you?"

"Yeah, some," Joan responded. "Thanks. But we haven't found what we're looking for, exactly. Did you have any luck tracking down those papers?"

Euan bent and opened the satchel that had been sitting next to the books beside his chair and removed a sheaf of loose papers which he placed on the table. The top sheet was covered with sprawling notes handwritten in black ink. "You might find these to be of interest."

"Great! Thanks a bunch." Joan delicately ran her fingertips over the worn corners of the stack. "We'll be very careful with them."

Euan leaned back. An inquisitive smile played upon his lips. "So tell me, how does the High Kirk's history play into your film?"

Joan's mouth froze in a startled 'o' for a moment, but she recovered quickly. "It's a puzzle. There's a puzzle in the movie and we need to find the answer."

"Why don't you simply pick an answer and write the puzzle to fit it?"

"Laddie has a point." Rory chuckled.

Euan tinged his spoon against the edge of his saucer. "Do you want to tell me what is truly going on?"

Joan shot a questioning glance at Fiona. She subtly shook her head and the light in Joan's gray eyes dimmed. Joan wanted to tell him the truth. Whatever for? If he believed, it would darken his world, and if he disbelieved, he would tar them as mad.

"There are some things 'tis better not to ken," Fiona asserted, her voice low.

"None of this will help you to steal any relics the High Kirk might possess," Euan announced. He casually spun his teaspoon, but Fiona had the strong impression that his actions were anything but casual.

"We dinna intend any criminal mischief such as that," she replied, watching him watch the spoon.

"So ... what then? You're writing your own book and this is all a clever ploy to steal my research?"

"We don't want to steal anything, we're not like that," Joan protested.

Euan raised his eyes and gazed intently at Joan. "Then tell me why."

Joan paused, her lips parted. She inhaled.

"Let me have a word with my friend," Fiona interjected. The words were to Euan, but at the same time she tugged on Joan's sleeve and indicated the bedroom with a toss of her chin.

Rory suavely withdrew Fiona's chair as she stood. She gave him a quick smile. He winked, but she was uncertain if he was being encouraging or mocking.

"Please excuse us," Fiona added to the room at large and hustled Joan into the suite's bedroom.

Joan yanked her sleeve free the moment they rounded the doorjamb. "Before you say Sassenachs can't be trusted, just listen," she hissed, with a furtive glance toward the door. "You're listening, right? Okay. He's already seen Rory--you shouldn't have brought him here if you didn't want to tell Euan anything."

Fiona kept her voice hushed as well, trying to preserve their secrecy. "Rory rather brought himself. And he *is* helping..."

"Well, Euan's a deacon. He could help, too. He knows about good and evil. He certainly wouldn't hurt anything. And, as you said, we're taking help from that minion-of-evil-vampire so surely..." Joan let the sentence hang. She moved her palms upward in a sort of urging shrug.

Fiona continued to frown. What was it about that Euan? Joan was normally quite circumspect when meeting strangers. Granted, they had received little notice of this mission and could undoubtedly use aid from any quarter. But to trust an outsider so quickly?

"Aye, I'm taking help from a vampire--but I dinna trust him. And he already accepts the paranormal, being paranormal himself. Do ye realize how much information ye would have to trust Euan with for any of it to make a bit o' sense?"

"I can *so* do an abridged version," Joan objected. "It'll make sense. You wait and see. Then we'll have another brain to pick. Maybe even another fighter--he said he was a good fighter. C'mon, we *are* talking about the fate of the world here."

Fiona shrugged. "Fair enough. Ye're my gaffer, ye say what goes."

With a triumphant grin, Joan led the way back out to the table where Euan and Rory were eying each other suspiciously.

"This looks like a promising place to start," Joan declared.

Euan glanced up at Joan. "Pardon?"

"I'm going to tell you what's truly going on. But you must swear not to tell anyone else. To start with, Rory is a vampire."

"Ye dinna give him time enough to swear," Fiona muttered.

Euan chuckled. "What are you on about?"

"No, it's true. Really. You don't think he looks strange?" Joan asked, pointing at Rory. "Or were you being too polite to mention it?"

Euan smiled. "Courtesy is the foundation of civilization."

"Well, he does look strange," Joan asserted.

"I'd prefer 'roguish' or 'devilish' over 'strange'," Rory interposed.

Joan ignored him. "And he has fangs. Show Euan your fangs."

Rory obliged.

"See? Fangs. He's a vampire."

Euan spoke with kindly solemnity. "I think he's having you on, Joan. I've seen filed teeth before. And special effects makeup. I've even seen some truly incomprehensible piercings--we British perfected punk, you know, and that whole Gothic thing..."

Joan frowned impatiently. "No, you don't understand."

"Think ye might want t' do a bit more expanding and less abridging," suggested Fiona.

"Okay." Joan took a deep breath. "I think the problem is that we're not scared of the vampire. Normally we would be--well, not scared, normally we'd kill it. But we're not killing this one now ... er ... yet..."

"Or ever," Rory supplied affably.

"Because he's helping us with the current mission," Joan continued. "I'm a demon hunter and on Samhain--Halloween--something bad is going down which we can stop if we solve this prophecy--poem."

"A demon hunter," Euan repeated. He shook his head and drawled, "I should have guessed. Why is it that apparently only I live on the sane side of the city?"

Joan laughed and slumped into her chair. "Well, humor the madwoman, okay? Just play along."

"Fine." Euan smiled politely, but there was an impatient edge to his voice. "This had better not be one of those hidden camera programmes, though. So ... you want my help with the poem, is that it? What exactly is the trouble? Bit vague, is it?"

"Prophecies are not known for their clarity," Fiona informed Euan.

Rory chuckled. "Aye, 'tis a prerequisite for the prophecy writers. They must be convoluted or where's the fun?"

"Do you remember the relevant stanza?" Joan asked Fiona.

Fiona repressed the words of protest that were jostling for escape. She recited the prophecy.

"Through mercy at the end of the world,
Redemption's final play unfolds,
While sinful selflessness shall save,
Solely True Belief forever holds."

Euan looked pained. "That poem's not so much vague as terrible."

Fiona glared at him. "'Tisn't supposed to be literary, 'tis supposed to save lives." She moved toward her chair and Rory seated her. "Ta. I dinna doubt that any poetic qualities the prophecy had were lost in our translation. But we did our best."

"In a nutshell," Joan began, steering the conversation back on track. "We're looking for symbols of True Belief. Icons and whatever. We're thinking the 'forever holds' line means the right icon will stop the...bad thing."

"Hence the need for my research?"

"You've got it."

Euan continued to shake his head slightly from side to side, as if in subconscious rejection of everything going on around him.

"You're taking this really well," Joan encouraged him.

Euan rose and went to the window. He moved the curtain to peer outside. "Dawn will be coming in an hour or two."

Rory, meanwhile, reversed Euan's vacated chair and casually threw his leg over to sit astride it, his arms resting on the chair's back.

"Not much time left then. Have ye anything here for an innocently thirsty man?" He winked at Fiona.

Fiona grimaced at him. She hadn't told Joan about Rory's earlier misdeed, and she hoped he wouldn't allude to it again. It would be ... problematic, to say the least. "Ye can have Euan's tea if ye like," she offered. "He dinna touch it."

Rory shook his head. "I ne'er was much of a one for tea."

"I thought everyone in this country was addicted to tea," joked Joan.

Rory smiled. "Well, 'twas long syne, an' I wasnae a laird."

"What were you?" asked Euan. He had turned from the window and was regarding Rory with a speculative air.

Slowly Rory appraised Euan from the designer-stitched tips of his polished shoes to the distinctive tie neatly knotted at his throat. Fiona recognized that the tie demonstrated an affiliation of some sort, but to what school or regiment it meant he belonged, she had no idea.

"A patriot, sir. But little else in your estimation."

Euan's eyebrows rose. "Patriot?"

"I died for my prince and my country," Rory replied.

Joan gave him a scathing glare. "And what battle was that in, the Feeding-Myself-to-a-Vampire Wars of 1878?"

Rory shrugged. "Think what ye like. But I *was* mortally wounded and I would have died. I was lucky. My body was still living when one of the Undead, grazing the aftermath, came upon me on the battlefield."

"When was this?" Fiona inquired, genuinely curious.

"The 'Forty-Five," he replied. A smidgen of pride lurked in his tone.

"Ye are *kidding* me!" she exclaimed, slapping her palms on the table.

"The forty-five what?" asked Joan.

"The Jacobite rising of 1745," answered Fiona enthusiastically, without looking at her. "I grew up on stories of the 'Forty-Five. Which battle?"

"This is a morbid conversation," Joan commented dryly.

Grinning, Rory rode the pause.

Fiona could not stop her legs from shimmying like a hyperactive child. "Well?" she urged. "Well?"

"Culloden," Rory declared grandly.

Fiona gasped. "Och, nae!"

"Aye, 'twas. Culloden."

Fiona's hand flew to her mouth. "Not ... *the Red Barn*?" she whispered, a note of horror in her voice.

"Enough fraternizing with the enemy," ordered Joan, abruptly standing up.

"Sorry. I got carried away," Fiona apologized. She started to follow suit. In an instant, Rory was on his feet, smoothly drawing back her chair.

Joan scooped up Euan's papers. She handed the pile to Fiona. "You go home and get started on these." Joan paused. Her front teeth worried her bottom lip as she glanced at Euan. "We can still borrow your papers, right?"

"Certainly." Euan strode to Joan's side. "I must be going. I hope you don't think me rude." He flashed her a smile that would have melted snow off Ben Nevis.

Joan returned his smile. "No, of course not. As I said, you're taking this really well." She patted his arm. "You go let it all sink in."

"I shall return tomorrow evening, that is, if you wouldn't mind?"

"Course I wouldn't mind. You know where to find me."

"I take my leave of you, then. Goodnight." Euan shook hands first with Rory, then with Fiona. His palm was dry and his skin was surprisingly cool. Lastly, he took Joan's hand. For an instant, it looked as if he would kiss the back of it. Then he seemed to change his mind, and he shook her hand as well. Joan did a poor job of concealing her disappointment. The next moment, the hotel room door closed and Euan was gone.

"I'll be going, too," Fiona mumbled, her arms wrapped around the pile of papers.

"Is that undead thing going with you?" Joan asked, but her eyes were still on the door and her voice was almost disinterested.

Rory snorted. "I wouldnae bide here."

Joan didn't reply to Rory's gibe. Not that Fiona expected her to.

"It shouldnae take me long to read these. I should have something for ye if ye call on me tomorrow afternoon, Joan. Joan?" Joan must be quite deep in thought. She wasn't replying to anyone. Fiona was uncertain how to disturb her, or whether she even should. "Umm ... Joan?"

"What a rippingly delicious pool of blood!" Rory proclaimed in a voice that could have carried the length of the hall.

Joan spun around, fists ready for action. "What?"

Rory sidestepped away. "*Jo*-king." His voice held a playful, sing-song quality.

Fiona stifled a giggle. It was nice to have someone on her side. Immediately she felt a pang of guilt. That was unfair. Joan was her friend. She had weighty issues on her mind. She wasn't ignoring her. She just couldn't be listening all the time. "Call on me tomorrow afternoon. I should have something for ye by then."

"Gotcha." Joan held the door open. Fiona and Rory passed through. "Sure you won't have any trouble with him?" Joan indicated Rory with her thumb.

Fiona nodded. "Certain."

Joan shrugged. "See ya tomorrow, then."

It was only a matter of moments for the lift to carry Fiona and Rory down to the ground floor. They exited the building through the spotless glass doors and stepped into the brisk night air. The once busy pavement was now deserted. Fiona turned and began the journey back to her flat in the Old Town. Then she realized that Rory had turned the other direction.

"My flat's this way," she called.

"Aye, that I ken, but ... I fear I must part wi' ye here for tonight."

Panic clenched Fiona's throat. Was he going to feed again? She skipped closer to him. "Ye are not--"

"Nae, nothing like that," he quickly reassured her as he stepped to her side. "An' I'll be back to help wi' the research, dinna fret on that account." He playfully reached out and tweaked the tip of her nose.

She swatted his hand away, suspicion continuing to gnaw at her heart. "So where..."

He grinned. "Let's just say I have to see a man about a dog."

"Ye may have time for games, but some of us have *work* to do." Fiona spun on her heel and marched off.

Rory called her name three times before she deigned to stop and look back.

"Mind how ye go." His voice was heavy with warning, and his expression was both earnest and solemn.

She rolled her eyes. "Mind that yoursel'--or Joan'll stake ye in the morn an' I willnae stop her."

He just chuckled in response.

* * * *

Fiona was almost home. She had left the electric-bright boulevard of Princes Street, crossed the long bridge, and returned to the medieval neighborhood she knew by heart where tall stone houses clung like stalagmites to the ridge leading up to the castle, and the lamplight shining on the cobblestones made the deserted streets look crackle-glazed.

Normally these sights held a cold, serene beauty that Fiona welcomed. But not tonight. Tonight something was terribly wrong.

It wasn't just the silence, though the wynd was unearthly quiet even for this wee hour of the morning. It was the fog.

There had been no fog until she entered the Old Town, and then it had merely descended in wispy trails that were hardly more than a flossy decoration to wreath the street lamps. But the higher she had trudged up the hill, the denser the fog grew, thickening at an unnatural rate until impenetrable clouds rolled in like silver waves infused with the smell of the sea.

Haar. Sea fog. She felt its unforgiving, damp chill right to the bone. That was familiar enough, but how had it managed to become that thick that fast? And it possessed an odd underlying scent ... faintly ... moldy.

And it creaked.

Fiona froze, papers crushed to her chest, and listened. Something was softly creaking, or was it groaning? Something she had never heard in the street before. And it was getting louder. Gradually louder. As if it were approaching. If only she could see what she was up against. Fiona peered helplessly into the opaque veil of gray.

Rory seemed to coalesce out of the fog in front of her. One moment nothing was there but swirling, gray mists. Then a dark shape gathered, formed, and the fog parted before it and Rory was striding toward her while thin, milky filaments twined around his limbs. His long, black coat billowed out behind him like a giant pair of corbie's wings. He moved swiftly, and yet his tall, black boots made no sound upon the paving stones.

Fiona expected him to slow as he neared, but he did not. He marched right by her, grabbing her closest wrist as he passed and pulling her along behind him without breaking stride.

He spoke only two words, his face grim but composed. "Revvers. Run."

CHAPTER SIX

Fiona tried to peer over her shoulder to see what Rory had seen. "What's coming?"

"Just run." He continued to pull her along by her wrist.

Stumbling on the uneven pavement, she still struggled to look back. Night and fog cloaked the narrow alley, but she could just discern movement behind the mist like vermin squirming underneath a blanket.

Bobbing shapes.

Moving fast.

So many ... *too* many. If only he would pause long enough for her eye to catch more than an erratic swarm of silhouettes.

With her attention upon the specters following them, she almost tripped over a crooked cobblestone.

"Watch where we're going," he ordered. "Ye'll run faster if ye stay on your feet."

There was an edge to his voice that would brook no argument. She clutched Euan's papers tighter and quit trying to look back.

Instead, she concentrated on running, watching the pavement so as to avoid cracks and lifted stones, and let Rory lead her where he would. He seemed to be heading for the most isolated bit of the Old Town. Fiona was relieved. This was obviously not something the general public should witness. Keep casualties to a minimum.

They wound through several alleys, down old stone stairs, past bricked-up windows. They cut back and turned corners, all in an effort to lose their pursuers. To no avail.

"They're gaining," Rory warned.

Fiona snatched a quick look behind them, just in time to see light slash across their leading pursuer as it passed under a street lamp.

'It' had once been a 'he' judging by the suit. He must have been buried in that suit. He was certainly decaying in it.

The pulpy face was unidentifiable. Clumps of flesh had fallen away to reveal startling white bone, while small tufts of hair continued to cling stubbornly to his scalp. Peeling hands grasped the empty air in front of him as he lurched along upon stiffened legs. For all that, he was making incredible speed with each rigorous step.

She glanced up at Rory. "Zombie?"

"Revver. They're much of a muchness."

"Brilliant." Glancing ahead, Fiona searched for something that would give them the advantage. A glimpse of wrought iron snagged the corner of her eye. She recognized that gate.

"This way," she ordered, pulling her wrist free of his grasp.

"Wait--"

Heedless to the caution in his voice, she ducked sideways, banged the gate open with the heel of her hand, and dashed into the narrow mouth of the murky wynd. Then she realized only her footsteps rang upon the flagstones.

Fiona looked back. Rory still hesitated at the entrance. He seemed to shrug. Then, with a burst of supernatural speed, he appeared at her side.

They ran down the alley. A sharp bend loomed ahead.

"This leads back to Greyfriars," she advised as they turned the corner. "A graveyard's the perfect place..."

She was interrupted by the sudden appearance of a brick wall. Too close to stop in time, she twisted so that her shoulder took most of the impact as she slammed into the wall. Rory simply used the momentum to partially scale the barricade. Noticing that she was still on the ground, he dropped to the pavement at her side.

Fiona stepped back and stared at the wall. The wynd was completely sealed off. She had led them down a blind road. They were trapped. She laughed. "I dinna believe it. When did this go up?" She smacked the wall with her palm. "What idiot gave a planning permit for this?"

A soft groaning and tromping heralded the approach of the revvers. Fiona turned to face their advance. Rory was already moving.

He strode out to meet the revvers and halted roughly halfway between the throng and Fiona. He stood ready for action, his legs apart and arms loose at his sides. And he waited as they marched closer and closer.

When they were almost so close that he could have whispered and been heard by them, he spoke. His voice held a dangerous, rough edge that sent thrills down Fiona's spine.

"Whoever touches her gets through me."

The surging throng of revvers paused as if Rory had momentarily kindled a sense of foreboding in their vague consciousness. Then they charged him.

Rory met the horde head on. Fiona winced at the cracking sounds of bone. Despite their precarious appearance, the revvers were a solid, determined mass. They swarmed over him. He swung, kicked, threw them back, slashed at their flesh with his fangs. *Poetry in motion.* Before Fiona had thought the phrase trite, but now she was witnessing it. Rory maintained his fluid onslaught, his long black coat billowing out behind him.

Then a pack of stragglers newly come to the battle tackled him from the side. More piled on. Rory went down. The remaining revvers staggered around the heap and rushed Fiona.

Fiona found herself rooted to the ground, her limbs twitching as conflicting messages whizzed through her mind. *How to--and not--a spell? Which? --och, Rory!* So many thoughts inundated her brain that she could respond to none of them. She was stuck, clutching the papers to her chest and watching the revvers advance.

But the heap they had left behind was still moving. With a furious howl, Rory stumbled to his feet, throwing off his assailants like a mad bear throwing off the baiting dogs. He bounded forward and tackled the group of revvers nearing Fiona.

THE CRIMSON FOLD

He was playing for keeps now, severing limbs, dislocating what he could not rend.

He made short work of the revvers that had come closest to her. But the others had regrouped and now swarmed him. It seemed impossible for Rory to hold them all back.

She dragged her eyes away from the scene, mortified at her earlier inaction. *Ye are nae bairn to be rescued. Do something!* She glanced around for inspiration. Nothing but dirty pavement.

Dirt.

Fiona bent and ran an index finger along the crevice between two paving stones, prying out the dirt lodged between them until she had collected a pinch of it. She jumped to her feet and rotated on one leg, sketching a circle around herself with the toe of her other shoe. Then she threw the pinch of dirt over her left shoulder in what she hoped was a northerly direction as she recited.

"Earth Dragon, stir and rise,
Protect this man before my eyes,
Aid our cause if it be right,
Blessed be our works this night."

Rory seemed to be getting a second wind, his supernatural speed and strength honed to a keener edge. He seemed to be everywhere at once. Tearing, breaking. It was not long before nothing was left of the revvers save jumble of putrid flesh and bone.

Disheveled, blood spattered and triumphant, Rory spun toward Fiona, his coat-tails swirling at the movement. His eyes blazed with a terrible delight. But when his gaze lit upon her, she saw his expression change, almost soften.

His eyes now smoldered with a far more tender passion. She felt that gaze burn to her very core. Her whole body quivered in response.

She hugged Euan's papers to her breast as if they were a shield and tried to think of something witty to say. Nothing. She frantically wracked her brain for anything remotely verbal. Words had deserted her. Her mouth was suddenly so dry. She licked her lips.

As if that were a signal, Rory bounded across the shadowed cobblestones and roughly caught her up in his arms. The papers crinkled in protest as his crushing embrace pinned her laden hands against his hard chest. She was trapped and at his mercy. His mouth came down on hers before she could think to react.

And he was kissing her.

Kissing her if he were human. Hot, tender kisses that pulled at her insides and made her melt like warm honey.

Whatever else he was, he was devilishly handsome and he had just come to her rescue like a knight in shining armor. For this moment, he was her hero. For this brief moment...

Abandoning the papers, she wriggled her hands free. Her fingers sought then clung to his broad shoulders as she ardently returned his kiss. He moaned and clutched her closer.

She pressed herself full-length against him. She could feel the demand growing within his body. The fierce pressure of his mouth upon hers increased, insisting on deeper access, and she complied. He tasted of blood and battle and she didn't mind.

It was Rory who broke the kiss. He nipped at her jaw line and then nuzzled her neck, his breath coming in hectic chuffs as he whispered endearments to her. Lyrical endearments in Gaelic that caressed her ears while his lips caressed her throat. She hugged him tight and felt his willing muscles twitch and jerk in response.

One of his hands stroked her side as if itching to access her more intimate parts. She shifted, yielding to his insistent touch, and his hand claimed her breast. First his palm, then his keen fingers incited a tempest of pleasurable jolts within her. She could not keep still. He groaned as she wriggled against him and his lips recaptured hers.

But her movement released a few of the papers that had been sandwiched between them. The rustle of their escape brought Fiona back to her senses. She must not loose Euan's papers.

She must not kiss a vampire.

Dropping her arms, she started to pull away. She was half afraid he would not let her go, but in that, she misjudged him.

The moment he felt her resistance, Rory tore his lips from hers with a groan full of pain and yearning, and stepped back. She noticed that he was panting, his breath coming in quick, jagged gasps. Her own breathing was not any calmer.

"We've..." She coughed and started again. "We've got to collect the papers."

"Aye," he agreed.

But neither of them moved. Fiona finally broke the spell, bending to scoop up several nearby pieces. Rory immediately began to chase down the farther roving papers that an evening breeze was aiding to escape.

"Do we have t' collect them, too?" Fiona attempted to indicate the revvers without actually looking at what was left of them.

"Nae, dinna fret about them. Once they're destroyed they melt away like the broken spell that animated them. Someone'll find a right lot of compost here come the morn."

She rolled her eyes. "Lovely."

* * * *

Swearing several colorful oaths, Fiona pushed herself violently away from the research table. Her wheeled chair skated back several feet before she lowered her heels to halt it. Abandoning the chair where it stopped, she stomped off to the kitchen and banged the cupboards and drawers in a pointless search for

THE CRIMSON FOLD

nothing in particular. Then she twisted the outmoded sink's ornate cold water tap and splashed the icy water on her face. While patting her skin dry with a clean tea towel, she took several deep breaths. Between being chased through the streets by murderous corpses and trying to identify correct verb tenses, it was fast becoming a rather taxing night.

Rory had been surprisingly solicitous after the attack. He had insisted on carrying every single one of the papers, once they had been collected, and he had escorted her all the way to her front door. But did he come in? Did he share the tedious burden of translation and research? Not at all. He was out gallivanting about while she was stuck at home with irregular adjective declensions.

'Twas a pity Euan's papers had not been more illuminating. They were at least in English. The tortuous language of the ancient volume to which she had switched her attention was enough to drive one mad. So much work and precious little new information. The only useful bits she had gleaned were references to the rending of a veil. Doubtless the veil between the worlds. It was thinnest at Samhain. It probably meant the Andromache's rising was in actual fact a crossing from the opposite side. Joan would be unimpressed by such trivia, however. Fiona sighed. Perhaps she should abandon herself to sleep. She folded the tea towel into a neat square and replaced it on the countertop.

Then the floor creaked.

Prickles shivered up the back of Fiona's neck. It was an old building, she told herself. It could just be--

The floor creaked again.

Someone is here.

Fiona crept out of the kitchen. There was something ... She stood and listened. It was like the whispered movement of a breeze.

It came from the library.

Returning to scan the kitchen for a weapon, her eyes lit upon a wooden spoon. She snatched it and began to inch down the hall, gripping the spoon by the bowl so that it became an impromptu stake. It wasn't sharp, but didn't necessarily have to be.

Her stealthy steps serpentined across the floorboards. She had learned long ago which ones creaked. Almost there. Fiona held her breath and paused, listening, just before the library's doorway. Nothing.

She crouched and peered around the corner.

Empty.

The room was completely deserted. But her things had been rearranged.

Fiona stood. With cautious steps, she approached the research table. One of her thick, leather-bound books now commanded the center of it, directly in front of her neatly pushed-in chair. On top of this book's worn cover perched a small figurine she had never seen before.

It was a plain piece, simple white porcelain embellished solely with a few decorative gold curlicues. An aura of times past lingered about the delicate, hand-formed statuette. However, for Fiona the charm of the object lay not with its age or appearance, but in its subject matter. Joyful recognition replaced her initial surprise at her discovery. The figurine was of a pug dog lolling upon a plump cushion.

Delighted, she glanced around the room, searching in vain for the giver of this precious ornament. Her room slumbered silent and empty, and kept its secrets. She carefully lifted the figurine and cradled it in the palm of her hand.

"Such a bonnie puggie," she whispered, and made gentle pug snorting sounds at it.

* * * *

Fiona was awakened by the slamming of her front door.

"Breakfast's here!" Joan's merry voice resounded in the hall, followed by the metallic banging of pots in the kitchen.

"Do none of ye believe in knocking?" grumbled Fiona.

She opened her eyes. She had passed out at the research table again. One of these days she was going to use that bed. She pushed herself into a sitting position and ran a hand over her face. Then she patted the papers that had pillowed her head, hoping she had not drooled. It was a curse not to sleep prettily. The papers seemed fine. She stood and hobbled out to the kitchen.

Joan was frying eggs. "It's about time you were up."

"Do I look presentable?" Fiona brushed her fingers through her hair.

"Weren't you wearing that last night?"

"Besides that. My face."

"Yeah, you always look fine." She returned to the eggs.

Fiona stretched and shook out her limbs. Mornings were hard. Pity Joan hadn't waited until afternoon to call, like she'd been asked.

"So what were you up to all hours doing?" Joan looked over her shoulder and winked. "Don't tell me Euan's papers are *that* riveting."

"They well might be, but I wasnae looking at them. Nae, nae eggs for me."

Joan slid the eggs onto a small china plate with the dexterity of a professional chef. Fiona waited until Joan had finished pouring herself orange juice before she spoke again.

"We were attacked last night."

"What?" Joan slammed the juice carton on the counter.

"On my way home with Euan's papers, a horde of revvers ... I believe they tried to kill me."

"No way! What'd'ya do?"

Fiona shrugged. "Not much. Rory appeared and foiled them."

Joan made a noncommittal grunt. She turned and rummaged through the silverware drawer until she found a fork. "What are revvers, anyway?"

"A type of zombie peculiar to Edinburgh." Fiona hoisted herself onto the kitchen counter and swung her legs back and forth while she watched Joan eat. "I looked them up last night. They're rare, but their existence isnae surprising. Many of the graveyards 'round about have dark histories. D'ye ken the story of Burke..."

"I don't need their backstory. They're zombies. I get it. How do we destroy them?"

"Eliminate the source. According to my research, revvers are unique to Greyfriars cemetery. 'Tis a huge place with untold thousands buried there. Tonight we must bind the corpses to their graves so that nae future batches can be made."

"Sounds like a plan to me," Joan said through a mouthful of eggs.

Fiona picked up the neatly folded tea towel and refolded it. This next bit was going to be tricky. She took a deep breath. "Do ye not wonder why they attacked me?"

Joan shrugged. "Because you're with me, obviously."

"Aye, but why then? And how did they ken where I'd be?"

"You ask that like you already know the answer. What's your theory, Sherlock?"

"Have ye considered ... what if Euan is a vampire?"

Joan snorted derisively. "I won't even dignify that with an answer."

Fiona jumped down from the counter. "Nae, really. Have ye e'er seen him eat? Or seen him by daylight? He doesnae drink his tea, an' that's a fact. And I've only seen him after sundown."

Joan set down her plate with an angry clatter and strode off to the library. Fiona followed her inside.

"Are these his papers?" Joan voice quavered slightly as she waved her hand at a stack on the research table. "Are they any good?"

Fiona shrugged. "I havenae found anything pertinent yet..."

"They're worthless?"

"No, no I wouldnae say that..."

Joan cut Fiona off again. "Then why would he give them to us if he wasn't on our side?"

"Why mind giving if ye are planning in a few minutes time to take 'em back? He gains our trust and loses naught."

Joan paced around the table, hands clasped behind her head. "What about that Rory-thing? He knew where you'd be. He could want the papers."

"And he'd see them when he helps with the research," Fiona answered, keeping her voice as neutral as possible. "He has nae need to attack me for them. Besides the fact that he rescued me..."

"That could've been a setup--to gain our trust, like you said."

Fiona sighed. "It takes powerful magick to raise revvers from their graves."

"So?"

"I dinna smell that sort of power on Rory."

Joan stopped her pacing and glanced at Fiona. "Whatcha mean, *smell*?"

"I should have said *sense*. Ye ken I dabble with magick."

Joan nodded.

"Well, those who use magick can sense it in another."

"Sort of 'takes one to know one'," Joan observed.

"Precisely."

Joan resumed her pacing, shaking her head all the while. "So you think Euan's the Fury?"

A sharp groan of impatience escaped Fiona's lips. "Nae, as I have said before, I dinna think the Fury's involved. But Euan could be. Especially if he's a vampire."

"But he can't be," Joan protested. "No. He just can't be."

"Why? Because ye think he's dishy?" Fiona regretted the remark the moment she said it. Joan could just as easily use those same words to reprimand her about Rory. Luckily, Joan didn't seem to have heard her.

"Euan's a deacon at St. Giles', for Pete's sake," Joan proclaimed.

Fiona played her last card. "What better way to survive than going undercover in the very last place anyone would ever look?"

Joan's face slowly turned white. "That would be very deep cover indeed."

CHAPTER SEVEN

Joan's hand froze inches away from the doorknob. Something was wrong. Had she left the *Do Not Disturb* sign that askew? She shrugged off her coat as her eager fingers sought the wooden stake strapped to her side.

It was probably nothing. Someone had most likely knocked the flimsy sign by accident. The hotel's hallways were surprisingly narrow by American standards. She took a deep breath. It was probably a completely innocent incident. Probably ... for anyone else but her.

She kicked open the door, flipped across the room and landed crouched in the center with her upraised stake clutched in one hand.

Rory lounged in one of her chairs, his booted feet crossed and resting upon her suite's circular faux-wood table.

"They'll make ye pay for that," he drawled, indicating the door with a casual nod of his head.

Joan straightened, rising with deliberate dignity to her full height.

"You are *so* about to be dust." She did not bother to disguise the annoyance in her voice. "What are you doing here?"

"Dinna fret, I'm not stopping." He swung his feet to the floor and stood.

Moving with an air of lethal grace that she found both fascinating and repellent, he approached a mound of outerwear piled on a nearby chair. He had obviously used the jumble of coat, hat and scarves to protect him from the light of the sun.

"I came merely to ask a question, one ally to another," he explained as he began to don the garments.

Joan toyed with her stake. "You came out in the noonday sun to ask me a question?"

"That I did."

"Do you have a bridge to sell me as well?"

"Sorry?" An affable confusion clouded his eyes and he smiled at her more like a bemused puppy than a wolf.

Curiosity tugged at her mind. What could this vampire possibly want to ask that was important enough to risk sunlight? She was intrigued ... and how annoying was that? She shouldn't care about his thoughts, or that he even had thoughts at all.

"All right. What's the question?"

He picked up his hat, revealing some pretty cool sunglasses that had been buried beneath the pile of clothes. "Do ye read romance novels?"

"What?" The word carried the tone of a flat statement rather than a question. Of all the things she might have imagined his question to be about, that was so completely off her radar ... it was like down the stairs and three blocks over from where the radar even was. "Say that again."

He pulled the hat firmly into place. "Romance novels. Do ye read them?

Fiona reads them."

Joan crossed her arms. "And how would you know?"

A smile quirked his lips. "I've been in her library and--just a wee clue here--it contains books."

"Ha, ha, very funny." She was not amused.

The Undead thing continued to prepare for the outdoors. "Well then?"

"Well then what? Just what is it you're asking me?"

She could have sworn some sort of soft emotion flickered in the vampire's eyes. But that was impossible.

"Nothing," he muttered, turning away.

Joan walked to the window and poked at the closed curtains with her stake. She should just open the curtains and let the sunlight slash across the room. Of course, he was almost fully covered by now, so it probably wouldn't work. What was he up to? Some sort of mind game? Had to be. And it was aimed at Fiona no doubt. Rory's voice intruded upon Joan's troubled thoughts.

"Those books..."

She turned on him with an exasperated groan. "Are you still here?"

"If I tried something--"

"If you tried *anything* with Fiona I'd have to kill you."

"Nae, that's not what I mean."

Joan watched him carefully wrap his final scarf in place. What *did* he mean? The glimmer of an idea rose in her brain, only to be ruthlessly shot down. Impossible. Vampires don't do romance.

Rory continued to fiddle with his scarf and avoided her probing gaze.

"Do ye ken ... Do lassies like..." He rolled his eyes and picked up the sunglasses. "Biting people is bags easier."

Joan shook her head and her grip on her stake tightened. "You're sick."

Rory snarled at her, put on the sunglasses, and left through the broken door.

* * * *

Fiona wasn't in her library. Rory swung his legs inside and attempted to shut the window behind him with one hand. This time the antiquated wooden frame stuck, forcing him to place the purple carrier bag on the floor and use both hands to gently overcome its resistance. The window capitulated with a bang.

"Ye startled me," Fiona declared from behind him. She did not sound startled in the least.

He turned.

Fiona leant against the doorjamb, arms folded and ankles crossed. "Is that how ye got in to leave me the pug figurine?"

He nodded as he began to divest himself of his protective outerwear. "Ye sussed 'twere me?"

She smiled, but her expression was unexpectedly wistful. "None other would be leaving me pressies."

"So did ye like it?" He placed his sunglasses on top of his piled up garments.

"Aye, 'twas grand." The sincere warmth in her voice evaporated as she asked, "Why are ye here now?"

He gave her his least wolfish smile. "I've come to rescue ye."

"Och aye?" she chuckled. "And from what? The tedious grip of research?"

Rory shrugged. "If that's what's goin'."

In one smooth motion, he seized the handles of the purple bag and stepped toward her. Her eyes flicked from his face to the bag as he approached.

"Dinna come any closer," she warned, although she did not alter the nonchalant angle of her body. "What have ye there?"

He pulled a rectangular box out of the bag and thrust it toward her. Her eyes lit up at the sight of the scrawled logo.

"Chocolates! And ye got me the large one, too!" Her words were yelps of pleasure.

She lunged toward him, snatched the box out of his hands and dashed over to the research table with it.

He sauntered after her. "I dinna have any chocolate experience mysel', but the shop girl said that was the one to get."

Fiona slit the cellophane with her fingernails, freed the box from its wrapper and lifted the top. The aroma of rich milk chocolate escaped. She closed her eyes and inhaled deeply.

"Perhaps I should leave ye two alone?" Rory teased.

She turned to him with a sheepish smile. "Sorry. Would ye like to try one?" She started to hand him the tray of assorted bonbons.

He backed away. "Nae, 'tis all for ye, pet."

She popped an oblong chocolate into her mouth and closed her eyes. She made little yummy noises. Her expression ... the sounds... Erotic images of Fiona flashed through Rory's brain and he realized that his excitement in her pleasure was getting out of control. He gripped the back of the nearest chair with both hands.

Fiona replaced the box top.

"Ye dinna want any more?"

"I can only handle a little at a time," she answered, beaming at him. Her eyes were so bright when she smiled. "'Tis another dead brilliant gift. Ta."

"An' that's nae all." He took a deep breath while ordering his body to remain calm. "Go 'n' put on a crucifix 'n' anoint y'self with holy water while I arrange your bed."

Her jaw dropped. "What?"

"I want ye to feel perfectly safe wi' me."

"I'm not going to bed with ye." Fiona's voice was suddenly as wintry as her glittering eyes.

"Of course not." He held up his hands in a protestation of innocence. "Nae bodily fluids will be exchanged. Of any sort."

She raised a disbelieving eyebrow. "None?"

"None," he replied solemnly.

"Then what're ye going to do to my bed?"

"Nothing permanent. Now away wi' ye."

She hesitated.

"Ye canna think I mean to kill ye." Rory kept all but the slightest tinge of exasperation from his voice. "I brought chocolates."

Fiona laughed. "And that makes all the difference."

But she acquiesced.

Rory left to prepare her bed. Fiona walked out to the big lounge. She stared at the crowded shelf upon which Joan's multitudinous gifts of holy water and crucifixes sat collecting dust. She kept telling Joan she didn't need any more, but Joan seemed of the opinion that you could never have too much--of anything.

Leaving the shelf undisturbed, Fiona turned to her drawer of stakes and idly flipped the pendant drawer-pulls. It would be a giant leap of trust to be in close proximity to a vampire without a handy stake. A foolish, reckless leap. Even if it were a handsome, chocolate-bearing vampire.

She smiled to herself and shook her head. Why did she keep hoping Rory was truly interested in her? He must have ulterior motives. He had to want something beyond her. He couldn't possibly ... like her.

She took a deep breath. Not that his true intentions mattered now. She had the perfect excuse to go along with whatever he was planning--she would never find out what he was up to if she didn't play his game. She flipped the drawer-pulls once more. She should take a stake with her.

Fiona turned and headed toward the bedroom. She did not take a stake.

* * * *

Fiona's duvet had been removed from the bed and the pillows had been rearranged. She recognized the configuration.

"Ye are goin' to give me a massage," she gasped.

"Aye." Rory looked inordinately pleased with himself.

She crossed her arms. It was certainly tempting. She didn't often pamper herself, and a massage would be such a treat. But she shouldn't be letting him touch her so intimately.

As if he sensed her reservations, his expression softened. "I can do only a certain area of your body, if ye have a mind to limit my access."

That was about as safe as such an offer was likely to get. She exhaled. "I shouldn't mind a scalp massage."

"As ye please." In a few moments, he had reorganized the pillows so that she would be lying slightly diagonally. This positioned her head better for access from the bedside.

Fiona eased herself onto the bed, throwing her knees over one set of pillows and leaning back to let her neck be supported by the remaining one. Her spine seemed to relax immediately as it rested flat against her mattress.

"Are ye quite comfortable?"

"Aye, as much as I could be with ye in the room."

She could sense him standing behind her. Then she felt his fingers lightly touch her temples. He started with small circles, gently rotating, round and round, and then slowly enlarged the orbit to creep down, swoop by swoop, to her jaw muscles.

"Ye are quite tense," he said as his fingertips softly pressed into her skin.

"That isnae my scalp. Ye havenae any idea what ye're doing, do ye?"

"Whisht, lassie, hush and be still. I've read a book, I have."

He continued to work. She could feel her muscles unlocking, her jaw releasing. There were many things she had imagined his long fingers doing, but this was certainly not one of them. He was fair talented for an amateur.

"So ye are wearin' just the holy water, then."

Her jaw set immediately. "What?"

"Since there's nary a crucifix to be seen on your bonnie bare neck."

After a long pause, words reluctantly crossed Fiona's lips. "Nae. I'm not wearing holy water either."

Rory whistled. "Do ye trust me so?"

"That would be one answer. Or I simply want the massage to extend to my neck."

"Aye, m'lady." His dexterous fingers moved to stroke the sides of her neck.

She had half a mind to purr. This was lovely. His fingers trailed back up to the top of her head. Using his fingertips, he made tiny, circular motions at pressure points along her scalp. It was both pleasurable and energizing. She felt tingly all across her scalp and down her spine.

"I've been thinking about the prophecy," Rory began. "Which belief system do you think is the True one?"

Her body involuntarily tensed. Whatever game he was playing might be beginning now.

"With vampires it's usually Christianity," she answered in what she hoped was a casual manner.

"What if the Fury pre-dates Christianity?"

"What if it isnae the Fury?"

"Ye ken what I mean," he responded, amused. "If whatever it is pre-dates Christianity, ye canna use a cross against it. That sort of thing isnae retroactive."

"Then what do ye suggest we do? Collect icons from every belief system we can identify?" she asked derisively.

"Mayhap ye should find out precisely how old he is. We could be talking the Greek or Roman pantheon."

"But how do we find his age when we dinna even ken who 'tis we're looking for?"

"The age of the prophecy, then? Could be the belief of the writer bein' referred to."

She frowned. Not a bad suggestion. "Ta, I'll get right on that."

"Nae, lassie, ye'll bide here a wee while longer. I must finish your massage."

Fiona did not argue. In fact, she was glad of an excuse to remain. His pressing, stroking fingers were magical. "I still canna believe ye are helpin' us."

"I'm not," he replied brightly. "I'm only helping ye."

After a few minutes of silence, relaxation crept back into her body. She closed her eyes. His touch was so soothing. She could sense his focused intention to give her pleasure. Though he had no body heat to transfer, Fiona felt warmer than she had in ages. Everything was so cozy and toasty. She was going to just dissolve into the bed, imagining that everything was perfect.

"Hmmm?" Rory said in answer to her blissful sigh.

"Nothing. Just thinking."

"About?"

"I'm pretending we both have souls," Fiona replied.

* * * *

What would a barrier spell be doing here? Rory stepped back from the golden glow that barred the way in front of him. It stretched from the vault's rocky ceiling to its stone floor. He would have to pass through it if he wanted to continue deeper into the catacombs.

He gritted his teeth. The spell would not harm him. It merely protected those within its bounds from hexes and the like. But passing through it would cause all sorts of dreadful sensations, and he naturally objected to experiencing pain without good reason. And there was no good reason for this that he could see. It wasn't like this section of underground Edinburgh was ever visited by tourists.

If only he could have stayed with Fiona. The massage had sent her straight to sleep and she had looked so ... angelic. But duty called. A disagreeable duty. And this barricade was just another bit of unpleasantness.

Rory plunged through the glowing barrier and kept going, down one tunnel and then the next, each one burrowing ever deeper under the city. This dank, pitch-black warren of clammy stone would have been a deathtrap to anyone else, but Rory knew where he was going. And not only because of his vampiric sight. He had been here before.

THE CRIMSON FOLD

At last he saw a phosphorescent yellow light gleaming ahead. The sort of light that only came from an illumination spell. This was it.

The crumbling passageway opened into a long, illuminated cave. At its end was an imposing altar chiseled out of the rugged rock of the cave itself. The altar was ancient, the stone worn and scored by the ages. The noxious monster standing facing the altar was even older, though he was all sharp angles and long claws, and his sallow flesh seemed untouched by time.

Rory paused at the threshold and filled his nostrils with the delectable smells of evil and power infusing the air of the cave. This was precisely what Fiona and Joan were looking for. If only they knew.

He sauntered inside. The monster turned and his eyes burned an eerie green as he watched his approach.

Stopping just an arm's length away from the altar, Rory slouched against the wall and grinned. "Ay up, big man."

He waited for the monster to deliver his expected reprimand, waited for his familiar rumbling voice and precise, measured speech.

"It is about time you returned to report," the monster growled.

CHAPTER EIGHT

The sallow monster tapped one of his long claws on the rock altar. It was a relentless, impatient sound. He shook his head and eyed Rory with dissatisfaction. "You have not learnt much."

"They dinna ken much." Rory grinned, immune to the other's disapproval. "Might level the playing field a bit, Miklos, if I gave 'em a clue. Give ye more of a challenge."

Miklos ignored him. "Is Armstrong's associate in your thrall yet?"

Rory turned and walked the width of the cave.

"Well?" Miklos called after him.

"Not exactly." Rory leaned up against the cave's far wall. "She's..." He searched for the precise adjective to describe Fiona's resistance to his charms. Independent? Tenacious? Bloody-minded?

"You are losing your touch," Miklos interjected.

"Nae, she likes me, I'm certain. But she's very committed to the cause--just as much as Armstrong is." Rory tapped the heel of his boot against the wall, affecting a nonchalance that was rapidly slipping from his grasp. He found it impossible to speak of Fiona with indifference. He was well aware of this weakness. But he didn't want Miklos to be aware of it, too. His brain buzzed with different word combinations, trying to come up with the most neutral phrase possible. The moment he began to speak, he knew he had made the wrong choice. "Fiona isnae the weak link ye thought she'd be."

Miklos grinned. Double rows of little triangular teeth sprung from his olive gums both on top and bottom, almost eclipsing his unusual, needle-like vampiric fangs. "*Fiona*, is it? And how you speak the word. I believe you are soft on the chit."

Rory snorted. "Dinna be daft."

Miklos raised his scaly hand, palm toward Rory, and scanned the air. "Yes, your killer instincts seem ... blunted." He smiled again. "You wish to be this maiden's lapdog."

Rory launched himself off the wall, swearing vociferously. He strode toward Miklos. "There's nothing wrong with my instincts. I'd just as soon rip out her throat as look at her. She's nothing to me."

"Calm yourself, child," Miklos replied with a patronizing air. "Perhaps I misread."

"Damn straight ye did. I've waded in blood up to my ankles and corpses above my knees. I've cut a swathe through--"

"I remember, I remember." Miklos laughed.

"Aye, well, see that ye keep that memory handy."

Miklos turned to the altar and stroked the coarse stone as if it were the most delicate lace. "Soon I will not need memories. Soon she will live again, and we shall soak this world in gore."

Rory could read that gargoyle-like face better than most. While others might not have noticed the softening of Miklos' twisted countenance, Rory saw the tragic love brimming there.

"It's been a long time..." Rory began, but words failed him. Miklos was an old vampire--roughly a couple thousand years old. He had left the last of his humanity back in the early days of Christianity, though it might as well have been the rosy-fingered dawn of the ancient Greeks. So many centuries had passed that by now he had more in common with ogres born than he had with ex-human vampires. Except for his ability to feel love. And she had been lost long before Rory had met him.

"Yes," Miklos agreed. "It has been an epoch that this emptiness has plagued me. Still, it gnaws on my stomach and chokes my throat. In this world, there is no more bitter curse than loneliness." He groaned. "Your brain can not conceive of the pain through which I have been."

Rory thoughtfully scuffed the ground. *Little do ye ken.* He shrugged one shoulder. "Mayhap I dinna--"

"No, you do not!" Miklos replied with unexpected vehemence. "She is mine. She belongs to me. By what right was she taken from me?" He laid his head upon the altar. "But she will rise again. The Blood Moon was in Scorpio. The planets are correctly aligned. Extreme power flows to the cross quarter, and the veil will be at its thinnest... Soon I will have her at my side, and the world will suffer for its indifference."

Rory waited silently for Miklos to compose himself. After a few moments, Miklos stood and addressed Rory in his normal, cold voice, as if his emotional outburst had never happened.

"Kill the girl."

Rory coughed. "Sorry?"

"Armstrong's associate. Kill her. She is unlikely to be replaced. Make it look as though the Fury did it. That should keep Armstrong off-balance long enough."

Rory turned and walked the length of the cave. "I dinna like the idea of impersonating the Fury. Might bring me to his attention."

"I would not waste your talents on an *easy* assignment."

Rory reached the other end and turned. "Ye havenae seen hide nor hair of the Fury yet?"

"No. I am beginning to think that rumor groundless."

"I'd prefer it if ye were definite. Ye canna find him out, even with all your magicks?"

"A locating spell will only succeed if you have something of the one for whom you search. If I had anything of the Fury's, you could safely wager that I would be doing more to him than simply finding his location."

Rory made a sweeping gesture with his arm. "And the barrier spell?" He gave Miklos a teasing grin. "Better safe than sorry?"

"Nothing must interrupt my plans." Miklos' eyes narrowed. "I believe you are deliberately attempting to distract me. Do you have a problem with my order?"

"Nae, not at all."

Miklos strode over to Rory. His cloven feet clacked hollowly on the stone floor, but he moved with a grace one would not have assumed possible. "This Samhain a new realm, a new reality shall form. As its creators we shall wield supreme power. Anything you have ever imagined can be yours for the taking." Miklos gripped Rory's shoulders and stared deep into Rory's eyes. "Anything."

Rory nodded. He had somewhat forgotten how overpowering Miklos was up close. His gruesome jaws were twice the size of Rory's head, and his breath smelt of sulfur. Miklos' bulging muscles made his enormity even more intimidating. He could probably crush a human with his bare hands. Even in this loose embrace, Miklos' claws were perforating Rory's flesh.

"What care you for one girl when you can have thousands?" Miklos continued.

"Aye, ye are right, of course," Rory answered, forcing an amiability he did not feel.

Miklos released him. Abruptly and without a word, Rory wheeled about and headed for the cave's entrance. Thousands were certainly better than one. Undoubtedly. So why did he feel as if he had just traded his best claymore for a carton of milk past its sell-by date?

"Do not turn your back on me, MacLaren."

Rory froze at the hostility in Miklos' rasping voice. He turned his head slightly. Enough to speak over his shoulder, but not enough to see. And he did not turn around. "Ye must reposition your door if ye dinna wish a view of my back."

He could hear Miklos laugh low in his throat. "You were ever a bold one. But my natural fondness for you is not unlimited. Remember that. Now go and accomplish the service you owe me."

Rory stiffly started forward. But Miklos' voice called him to a halt again.

"Mind me well. If you do not kill that Fiona of yours, I will. And I shall be most displeased with you."

Rory looked down at his boots and sighed. His whole body felt weighted with lead. It was like the night he had learned the rebellion was forever lost, that the Highlands were doomed to years of government sanctioned brutality and subjugation, and that he and his friends had died in vain. That had pierced even the shell of his vampire's heart, and he would have cried had he the tears to shed. But he didn't. And he never would. And time would roll on now as it did then, and he would continue without this girl as he did before he met her.

Rory turned to face Miklos. "Have ye e'er been displeased with my work before?"

"No," Miklos answered gravely. "But I will be watching."

* * * *

"You awake?" Joan asked, impatiently shaking Fiona's shoulder.

A much rumpled Fiona rolled over on her back and opened bleary eyes. "Aye, now I am."

"You're always napping in your clothes."

Fiona gingerly raised herself into a sitting position and straightened her blouse. "I was ... umm ...where is... Are we alone?"

"You are so not awake."

Fiona grunted and rubbed her eyes. "'Tis sunset?"

"Almost." Joan turned and headed out the bedroom door. "Meet me in the kitchen, we've got issues."

Joan was on her second cup of coffee by the time a less disheveled Fiona entered the kitchen.

"Of what issues do ye speak?" Fiona asked as she inspected the contents of the nearest cupboard.

"Vampires." Joan banged her mug on the countertop for emphasis.

Fiona stopped fiddling with the cupboards and stepped to Joan's side. "Are vampires not always an issue?"

THE CRIMSON FOLD

She hopped up to sit on the countertop beside Joan's mug. Joan could hear Fiona's stomach gurgling.

"D'ya want some coffee?"

"Not on an empty stomach. What about vampires?"

Joan took another swig of coffee. Why did she feel so uncomfortable? She wasn't meddling in Fiona's private life. This was for her own good.

"I want you to dis-invite that Rory-thing of yours."

"He isnae mine," Fiona protested before adding, "I thought we had resolved this."

"Yeah, well ... I think he's getting ideas about you."

"Ideas?"

"Has he touched you at all?"

Fiona's eyes widened. "Sorry?"

"Earlier today he came to see me..."

Fiona raised her eyebrows. "Whyever for?"

"He had some fool thought ... He asked ... You're sure he hasn't touched you? Wait, are you blushing?"

Fiona's normally pale cheeks had perceptibly reddened. She crossed her arms and attempted a defiance that her mortified eyes belied. "I have come to nae harm."

"He *has* touched you!" Joan swore under her breath. This was worse than she had imagined. Fiona was generally so strong against the demon world. "Lemme check your neck."

"Ye shall find nothing," Fiona warned, but she compliantly tilted her head one way and then the other as Joan gently inspected her throat.

True enough, nothing there. Joan stepped back. "Well, you're lucky you're clear. Don't let him near you again."

Fiona saluted. "Any other orders?" Her merry expression slowly slid into seriousness. "I expect ye wish me to do the binding spell on the revvers now."

"Ummm, actually, no. They're just a nuisance in the big scale of things. But it's vital for me to know who's at my back." Joan took a deep breath. "You know how you said ... about Euan..."

"That he might be a vampire?"

"Yeah. Well, I stopped by Euan's place before I came here and he's not home. I need you to find him."

Fiona winked. "My, we are desperate."

"I'm not kidding." Joan looked down at her feet. "Time is getting short and I need to know if you're right."

Fiona nodded solemnly. "Fetch me one of his handwritten papers from the library."

When Joan returned with a page simply covered in Euan's handwriting, she found that Fiona had moved to the carpeted great room or lounge or whatever she called it. Fiona knelt upon the carpet, directly beneath the dimmed chandelier. She had just finished casting a circle and was gazing into a peculiar crystal ball.

Joan held out the page. "Like this?"

"Precisely." Fiona took the paper and placed it beneath the large, spherical crystal. It was not what Joan pictured a traditional crystal ball should be. It was a deep, dark blue in color, but it was clear as glass within.

Fiona's hands floated just slightly above the surface of the ball, gliding in effortless circles. A mist started to form in the crystal's blue depths. Fiona froze. Then her hands swiped across the ball a few more times. She froze again.

"What is it?" Joan whispered.

Fiona's hands moved as if she were drawing invisible curtains across the ball, then dropped to her sides.

"I ken where ye shall meet Euan. Ye are going to have to bring your sword."

CHAPTER NINE

It had not taken Rory long to locate Fiona. Her unique scent was entwined with the smell of blood. Two of his favorite aromas. But it surprised him where he located her. She was staggering out of the broken door of a darkened butcher shop, clearly closed for business, bearing two clear plastic containers of looted liquid. She was hunched over, shielding them from the nearby lamplight, but Rory guessed the liquid they contained was red.

"What have we here?" he asked lightly.

Her head flew up like a startled doe at the sound of his voice. Eyes wide, she stumbled sideways, then steadied herself.

"I was just ... just..." She attempted some sort of gesture which her full hands prevented.

Rory advanced. "Finding me a floor to lick, were ye?"

She backed up almost to the lamppost. But she was not afraid. Her lips twitched as if caught between indignation and amusement. Amusement won out.

"How did ye guess?" She smiled. "I was taking these home, but as ye are here..."

Fiona offered the two squat, plastic containers to him. He could smell their contents even through their tightly sealed lids. *Blood.*

"Ta, luv." He accepted one of the little vessels and popped off the lid. Unmistakably red liquid sloshed inside, gleaming in the lamplight. It was animal blood, and not warm. Truly unappetizing. But it would nevertheless assuage his vampiric hunger.

He raised the container to his mouth, gulped down the contents, and grimaced. "Would ye like a taste?"

She rolled her eyes. "Och, I had some earlier." She handed him the other container and he drained it, too.

"There's a bin over there." She was pointing across the road.

"Ye think I dinna do my part to keep Edinburgh clean?" he teased, crossing the road to pitch the two empty containers into the trash bin. "So where is your protector?" he asked as he returned to her side.

"Joan? She had business elsewhere in town."

Rory moved closer to her. "D'ye ne'er get tired of doing the errands while she gets the glory?"

"Not especially."

"She shouldnae leave ye alone."

"I can take care of myself." Fiona sounded surprisingly sure of herself despite his proximity.

Generally his nearness would have provoked some sort of fear response by now. He was close enough to easily kiss her. *Kiss her?* Perhaps that was the problem. He was only thinking of kissing her.

Where had his predatory instincts gone? Maybe Miklos was right. Maybe he was being domesticated, his instincts blunted by this lass. He should kill her.

She was nothing to him. Or she *should* be nothing to him. The life of one solitary female was not worth compromising his long-standing loyalty to Miklos. Though, wasn't Miklos ready to destroy reality for one female? He would say his situation was different, of course.

This woman Fiona was not meant to be a partner for his kind. She was dinner. One did not court the main course.

But then why did every cell in his body call out for him to take her in his arms? A rash act that would be. She would never allow such intimacy without a fight. She was gazing at him now with a wary look to her eyes. She was wondering at his strange silence. But she did not seek to back away from him. She would kiss him if he were human.

If only he were human.

Rory moved closer, blocking out the lamplight. He bent forward. Fiona felt his cold lips gingerly kiss her forehead. She shivered at the touch. Rory continued, creating a trail of tender kisses down her temple to her cheek. Prickles climbed Fiona's spine and tingled in her scalp. No one had ever made her feel this way, so excited, so alive.

His kisses continued down to her throat. Sudden fear made Fiona flinch as his lips touched her vulnerable skin. She braced herself to fight. But he merely kissed her. A quick, light kiss, as far away from a vampire's embrace as possible. Then he pulled back and looked into her eyes.

"Am I so very unpleasant?" he asked. His voice was husky, as if he were trying to restrain himself.

Fiona's lips parted, but no words issued. What was she doing? She should punch him and go home. Why wasn't she revolted by his touch? There was no fault in her protection spell. The defect was in her.

Rory took her silence for consent. He bent his head, lowering his lips to hers. His kiss was earnest and not demanding but it swept away the last of Fiona's resistance. She closed her eyes and yielded to him, admitting him greater access, a deeper kiss ... which she eagerly returned.

Rory's knuckles turned white as his fingers gripped the wall, and he kissed her with a new urgency. If he were still possessed of a pulse, it would have been racing. Her response was more than he had dared to hope. He pressed up against her, pinning her to the wall with his body. His hands moved to caress her breasts. She was scented with sandalwood and promise. He needed to feel her skin against his.

Quickly he tore off his shirt, revealing his wiry, toned muscles. The moonlight shone on his dead-pale skin. Clumsy in his excitement, he attempted to release the buttons of her shirt. One button defied him. Impatiently, his hand tore the fabric away from the resistant button and plunged inside her blouse. Fiona gasped at his icy touch upon the naked skin of her breast. His fingers went unerringly for her already erect nipple.

Pulling aside her shirt, Rory ducked his head and captured her shell-pink nipple in his mouth. His tongue caressed her. She moaned softly, arching her back. He needed no further urging to suckle. Then he delicately grazed the hardened nub with his teeth. She moaned again, and impulsively reached out for him.

He quivered as she ran her fingers through his hair. Then her hands lowered, massaging his shoulders. He could scarcely believe it was real. He had dreamt of this for so long. Standing to look into her eyes, he took hold of one of her hands and deliberately placed it upon the front of his trousers. His desire for her was obvious. Shyly, she glanced away. But she began to fondle him.

His eyes rolled back, and with a long groan he leaned heavily against the wall for support. Her acceptance of him meant everything. They could have said the Fury was coming for him right now and he would not have moved. It was not merely the contact, but the fact that it was she who touched him. It was the nearest he had ever come to bliss.

Rory roughly grabbed Fiona and pulled her close. With a quick swirl of material, his hand darted beneath her skirt. His fingers brushed across her leg to the tender skin of her inner thigh.

THE CRIMSON FOLD

She found herself wishing his hand would explore just a little higher. She ached for his touch. Her tight muscles longed for release. Just a little higher.

"Do you wish it?" he whispered. His fingers lightly stroked their target, sending what seemed like a lightning bolt through her body. She convulsed, and her head smacked the brick wall.

"Careful, pet." Rory protectively cradled the back of her skull with his other hand, shielding her from the bricks. "Do you wish it?" he repeated, his voice breathless.

She had never wanted anything so much. She gazed up at him. His eerie eyes blazed, and yet his expression was so compassionate. She longed to surrender to him. Hungered to melt into his arms and permit him have his way with her.

He saw the passion in her eyes and beamed delightedly, but she never saw the love in his face. Fiona saw only his sharp fangs glinting in the lamplight. Instantly her brain was back in control. She would despise herself forever if she gave in.

"No," she responded. "I canna." She crossed her arms defensively. "I canna."

"Then I will wait until I am asked." Rory backed away from her, hands upraised. He gave her a mournful smile. "And I never even tried to bite ye. Remember that."

He turned, retrieved his shirt, and the shadows swallowed him as he disappeared up the close.

* * * *

Cobblestones sucked. Joan grimaced as she recovered her balance. Sidewalks you could creep along no problem. Even the most uneven sidewalk didn't have round edges to slide off of and even the most broken concrete couldn't compare to this mess of uneven stones. Sneaking shouldn't be this much effort. At least the moon was cooperating. In its silvery light, she could see clearly that Euan was heading toward Greyfriars cemetery. Joan's heart quickened its beat.

Please don't tell me he's returning to his grave.

Fiona had said she would need her sword. If she needed it to lop Euan's head off, Joan was going to be sick for a week. She'd do it. She had to do it. But it totally wasn't fair.

She followed Euan through the gate, past the huge, gloomy church, and out among the grassy graves and what seemed like miles and miles of tombstones of all shapes and ages. An unaccustomed shiver darted up her spine. The air tonight felt even more clammy and cold than usual for Scotland. Why was she never assigned to Florida or southern California or somewhere warm?

Euan's steps were slowing. He was looking for a grave all right. Joan's grip upon her trusty sword's hilt tightened. She steeled herself for the inevitable. Then an odd noise caught her trained ear.

She could hear ... munching? Or staggering? What the...
That was earth moving.
And Euan was still walking. It wasn't him. She scanned the graveyard, but it was too dark to see much. Hadn't Fiona said something about Greyfriars cemetery? She really should pay more attention. Wait, were those shapes, there, way at the back?

Yes, those were shapes. Silhouettes. And they were moving closer. Not even using the monuments as cover. Just staggering closer.

This was not good.

Joan glanced at Euan, torn between springing into action or delaying to watch how he would react. The dark shapes were only a couple rows of tombstones away from him. She silently willed him to look up, to notice them. It seemed like ice ages before he finally raised his head.

He did a small double-take and stepped back. Whatever the shapes looked like close-up, they were not something he was familiar with. She hurried forward, swiftly gliding between the gravestones. As she approached she could smell rotting flesh.

Zombies. That was what Fiona had spoken of, some zombies native to Edinburgh. And as the moonlight revealed the horrible nature of the shapes, Joan knew they were definitely zombies. She charged.

Once during the fight she caught sight of Euan from the corner of her eye. He was standing unnaturally still, arms upraised, as if he had been frozen in place. His mouth might even have been slightly open. You could have looked him up in the dictionary under 'shocked'.

Joan made short work of the zombies, despite the fact that they had been five determined little devils. She twirled her sword as the last one fell to the ground. She felt energized. If there had been more of them she would not have been able to defeat them so easily. And that was a funny point, because zombies usually attacked in larger packs. Fiona would fret about it when she told her of tonight's adventure, but Joan was not about to let a mere inconsistency dampen her triumph.

She turned and saw Euan still in his frozen position. *Oh, dear.* Taking a deep breath, she approached him with slow, careful steps. When someone was first confronted by the paranormal, it was never a good idea to rush up on them.

"Are you okay?"

Euan swore several times before he was able to form a coherent sentence. "What *are* those things?"

"Zombies. Fiona called them something else though. But they're zombies." She paused to catch her breath. "Lucky whoever's controlling them didn't allot more to you. We might have been in trouble."

He shook his head. "This is not happening." He spun away from her with violent energy. "This is not my life." He threw back his head and yelled up at the sky, "I have said it before, this is *not* my life."

Joan sympathized. "It's normal to go all wiggy at this point."

He turned to look at her. "I am not at all ... *wiggy*." He took a deep breath. Then he chuckled and ran a hand through his hair. "Quite a suspicious character, you are." His eyes swept down to her bloody sword. "Continue to run about with a sharp object like that and the police are bound to take you in eventually."

"*I'm* suspicious?" She scowled at him. "Don't you think this is a funny time to go to a graveyard?"

"Not awfully, no." But the grin Euan gave her was sheepish. "I was going to have words with my uncle. He's buried in there."

Joan's heart skipped with suspicion. "Have words?"

"Just a wee, one-sided argument, nothing more," he quickly explained. A long pause followed, during which she could tell he wished to speak but the words were hiding.

"Do you want to come over to my hotel and talk about it?"

He cocked his head. "Which part?"

"What?"

"Nevermind. Let's have a coffee."

"Yeah, like that's a normal reaction. Are you about to go hysterical? 'Cause I could slap you if you want."

Euan smiled. "No, I am not hysterical. But I would appreciate some company. Would you mind terribly coming over to my place for a coffee?"

* * * *

It was a soft day. Wet fog hung like gauze about the housetops, accompanied by the soothing hiss of rain sheeting mistily from the obscured sky. The thwarted sunlight shed only a muted glow upon the cliff-top Castle car park where Fiona stood, her face to the sky, eyes closed and arms outstretched. Raindrops pattered on the slick, dark pavement around her. They prickled as they fell upon her skin. The ends of her drenched bangs dripped on her eyelids. Water trickled off her face, down her neck. Fiona wiggled her fingertips, imagining the drops spraying off them as tiny fractures in the smooth sheet of falling water. She inhaled through her nose. Everything smelled new and clean. This was what they had to save. Days when simply the air was enough. Exhilarating.

"Ye are wet," commented a familiar voice. "Did ye forget your plastic mac?"

Fiona snapped to attention. Rory stood in front of her. There was a strange light to his eyes which made her suddenly highly aware of her saturated skirt and blouse. The wet fabric clung to her skin. She felt dreadfully revealed. She lowered her arms and folded them in front of her chest.

"What are ye doin' out?"

"No sun," he replied cheerfully. "'Tis refreshing to come out early."

She nodded. "I know what ye mean. The air is so..."

He grinned and raised one eyebrow. "Stimulating?" His gaze raked over her body.

Involuntarily, she shivered. And she wasn't cold.

"Here, take my coat." Rory swung out of his long, black overcoat and draped it around her shoulders before she had time to protest. "I dinna mind gettin' wet 'n' all."

His face was very close to hers as he adjusted the collar, pulling it up to shield her neck. She felt his fingertips brush the side of her throat. She swallowed. His fingers returned. Lingered. Her overly sensitive skin tingled where he touched. They were so close. She caught a faint whiff of his pleasantly musky scent. His thumb continued to stroke her throat.

She forced herself to meet his gaze. His black eyes showed no reflection of her, and yet they were not empty. Embers in their depths glowed with something more than passion. She could not stop the excited response that tugged at her insides. Her body wanted him to touch her like he did last night. Why did she have to feel this way about a vampire? But he was so sweet and solicitous and brave. Fate was so cruel. If only they both had souls.

Fiona reached out and tenderly brushed his dripping forelock out of his eyes. Rory chuckled. It was a deep, pleasant sound. He caught her slippery hand and brought it to his lips. But his salute was interrupted by the abrupt blare of a car horn.

She jerked away, startled. "What the--"

An engine revved irritably behind Rory. His height prevented her from seeing over his shoulder, so she peered around his side. Despite the relative emptiness of the enormous car park, and their remote location in it, a large, shiny motorcar wished to drive directly through them. The impatient driver aimed several vulgar gestures at her between the rapid swipes of his windscreen wipers.

Fiona emitted an embarrassed squeak and started to step out of the vehicle's path. Then she realized that Rory was also emitting a sound. A low growl resounded in his chest. Before she could stop him, he whirled on the car, eyes blazing, teeth bared in a fierce snarl. He leapt toward the driver.

Alarmed, she darted forward and grabbed his arm. "Not here! Dinna give yoursel' away."

He hesitated, glaring balefully at the car and gnashing his fangs.

"*Please*. Come away." She tugged his wet sleeve.

Rory obeyed. He allowed her to pull him over to stand by one of the statues along the perimeter of the car park.

She looked back at the driver. The windscreen wipers dutifully kept his shocked expression visible through the rain. He sat stiffly, face blanched, eyes staring at the now empty space in front of him. He rubbed his eyes, then gazed doubtfully over at Fiona and Rory. Rory grinned at him and waved. Shaking his head repeatedly, the driver rammed his car into gear and zoomed away.

"What was that in aid of?" Fiona brushed dripping tendrils of her breeze-blown hair back from her face. "Ye must ken that ye canna go about with your fangs out like that. What if he had a stake or something?"

He shrugged. "He did something ye dinna like."

"But ... but ... ye dinna even see what he did."

"So? Ye were displeased. I was going to teach him a lesson," Rory countered simply.

Fiona felt weirdly flattered, and quickly tried to suppress the emotion. "Well, ye canna be doin' that."

She brushed her hair back from her face again, only to have her sodden tresses instantly whipped back in her eyes. The breeze that had quickened during their conversation was rapidly gaining force. The rain had intensified as well. It lashed at them sideways, blown horizontal by the wind.

Rory's eyes sparkled. He stood straight and tense, every nerve alert. "Something's coming."

Sudden, preternatural gusts howled up the car park, skewing the few parked cars into each other with shrieks of protesting metal. One gust knocked Fiona to the drowning pavement. Another blew her up against the stone wall that guarded the edge of the cliff. Buffeted by the blasts, Rory hoisted Fiona to her feet. Together they struggled to the center of the parking lot, as far as possible from the cliffs on either side.

"Look!" shouted Fiona, pointing down the Royal Mile.

A malevolent black mass with the thick, cauliflower texture of smoke from a giant tire fire surged up the street toward them. It smelled powerfully of rotten eggs and curdled milk. Frantic pedestrians, coughing and falling in the deepening puddles, attempted to scatter out of its way as it advanced. It paid them no heed. The black cloud crushed everything in its path, whether flesh or the metal of parked cars, with the careless indifference of a tank.

Rory's skin prickled. The street was electric with all the swirling, delicious fear. He could taste it in the back of his mouth. It flooded his senses. Almost drowning out ... something familiar. He tried to pull that other emotion apart from the maelstrom. It vibrated in his bones as the dark cloud inexorably approached. Lust? Hatred? Cloaked somewhere within that choking chaos was something with an overpowering appetite for evil.

And he knew who it was.

"We've got to get out of here," Fiona wailed against the wind.

"Aye," he agreed grimly. "We'll split up. Tell Joan this is what she's been lookin' for. Go!"

Rory shoved Fiona. She hobbled away, splashing through the puddles, cuffed from side to side by the gale. He watched her go. And watched the cloud. It rotated, tracking her. Then the cloud surged after Fiona. *So it has come to this.*

Rory stood dead still in his tracks. He had known the cloud would follow her. She was edible. Crushable. Perhaps even negotiable. It was only to be expected.

The threatening mass closed in on Fiona, driving her to the wall. Swirls of smog snaked out of the cloud, grabbing at her legs and arms and only narrowly missing as Fiona serpentined gamely. Rory caught himself rocking from side to side, as if dodging with her. What was he doing? He turned away from the scene. He was getting soft. Evil could have anyone in the city, as far as he was concerned.

Bracing himself against the wind, Rory trudged across the streaming pavement. He was glad of his tall, black boots. He tried to focus on the deepening water. But thoughts of Fiona kept getting in the way. How she had looked so cute with her hair dripping... So kissable... What sort of vampire was he? Chaos was taking place all around him. He could probably attack anyone he wanted, right now, in the street. Anyone at all. No one would notice. Here was a chance to go on the feeding frenzy of a lifetime. So why didn't he care?

The urge to look back gnawed the corners of his mind. How was Fiona doing? Was she still fighting? She'd go down fighting. But she couldn't win.

He had gone down fighting once, as well, and that had also been for a hopeless cause. Such a long time ago. She probably would have fought with him if she had been there. And he would have told her not to. But she wouldn't have let him stand alone. *She* wouldn't have stayed standing in a puddle.

Rory stomped the water beneath his heel. He felt the cobblestone under the water crack. He wasn't betraying Fiona. He had never truly been on her side to begin with. She should never have trusted him. She would get what she deserved for being so soft. He didn't care what happened to her. To her intense eyes. To her inviting laugh. To her lovely body.

She was so enchanting. But hundreds of women could be enchanting. Thousands. Not that he had ever met any ... until her. If Fiona were dead...

An image of her body, ravaged and motionless on the pavement, thrust itself unbidden into his brain. He pictured her broken, with a glassy countenance that would never again light up when she smiled. And he felt his panicked breath catch in his throat.

What was wrong with him? He couldn't be in love with her--he simply liked it when she smiled. That was it. She was a nice person with a nice smile, and sometimes she'd smile at him. Sometimes she'd look at him in that one particular way. And it would stir him all the way to his toes. She had even touched him, once. Touched him, with her eyes smoldering like nothing he'd ever seen. He had wanted her so desperately. Even beyond carnal desires. To have her devotion ... to share with her... Rory swore every vile oath he could think of, but he knew it wouldn't change anything. He had already decided.

Rory spun back around. Evil could have anyone in the city--except her. He charged, fangs and talons ready for battle.

Fiona was running out of space to maneuver. Her eyes widened as she saw Rory rushing toward them.

"Nae!" she yelled. "Warn Joan!"

But Rory ignored her.

CHAPTER TEN

With a ferocious howl, Rory tackled the cloud like a blind rugby player, talons flailing in the mist, desperate to connect with something solid. He found it.

The snapping tendrils abruptly coiled back on themselves. The cloud knotted and writhed. Screeches, more piercing than fingernails on a blackboard, issued from the cloud. Fiona covered her ears against the unholy sound. She shouted Rory's name. Her squinting eyes vainly searched for him within the thick black mass. For a moment she spotted him, battling something she could not make out, as the snaking swirls attacked him. Then, before the swarming tendrils enveloped him completely, she saw him gather himself for a leap. In horror, she realized there was only one place a jump would take him. She yelled a warning, but her voice was swallowed by the storm. It wouldn't have mattered anyhow.

Using all of his supernatural strength, Rory launched himself over the stone wall. Fiona screamed as Rory and the imprisoning black mass plummeted over the side of the cliff. In an instant the wind was gone. The rain was gone. There was no storm, no noise whatsoever. Even the puddles were swiftly draining away. All was calm. Stars twinkled in the suddenly clear twilight sky.

Fiona ran to the wall and looked over the edge. Both the sheer side of the cliff and the gloomy ground below were empty. Rory and the monstrous mass of smoke and shadow had dissipated into the night.

* * * *

Whose bed is this? Joan's waking thought sent her bolt upright upon the softly yielding mattress. Her right hand automatically fluttered along her side, searching for her sword, but it was not there. She shoved aside the cream-colored comforter and glanced down at herself. She was still dressed in her clothes from last night, although her feet were bare. Swinging her legs over the side of the large bed, Joan stepped out onto the lushly carpeted floor. Lots of creams and tans in this bedroom. And a bit of plaid for accent. It had to be Euan's bedroom.

That's right. They had been drinking coffee while she tried to convince him that being a demon hunter was a real job. He must have served decaf. And she had fallen asleep. Joan shook her head. Some people just don't get it. The whole point of coffee is the caffeine. And now ... she walked across to the window, her toes enjoying the feel of curling into the luxurious carpet. Lifting the blind revealed no sunlight at all, just developing dusk. Her heart sank. She had overslept big time.

Quickly she tiptoed out of the bedroom, down the hall, and found Euan wearing adorable plaid pajamas, asleep on his avant-garde, hunter green couch. The couch looked very uncomfortable. She smiled to herself. What a gentleman. She wouldn't have minded sharing the bed. In fact, she had half a mind to be offended that he hadn't tried to share the bed. What was wrong with her, for Pete's sake?

She turned and marched down the short passage to the kitchen. It was a sparkly, modern kitchen. It simply begged to be cooked in, but she didn't have time. She opened what she thought was the pantry only to disturb a jumble of metal pans.

"Joan?" Euan's voice was thick with sleep.

She winced. "Yeah, just me." She hated to wake him, but she needed to eat. You can't fight evil without fuel.

She could hear Euan padding down the carpeted passageway. "What time is it?"

"We slept through the day. It's past sunset." she continued rummaging through his cabinets. Where was this man's food? "I can't believe we slept all day."

Euan appeared in the kitchen doorway and yawned. "We must have needed it."

"Yeah, well, we can't waste time like that. Don't you have cereal bars or anything?"

He staggered over to one of the as yet unexplored kitchen cupboards. "Waste time?"

"We only have tonight and tomorrow."

"And then what?"

"You don't want to know."

He pulled a packet of cereal down from the shelf. "I see." He turned and nonchalantly opened the next cupboard and retrieved a bowl. He was way too calm.

"I'm serious," she added.

"Of course you are."

"Don't you take that patronizing tone with me. You saw the zombies last night."

"I am uncertain of what I saw. Science can explain..." His voice trailed off.

"Rotting corpses tried to kill you. Go ahead and explain that."

Euan was silent as he placed the packet of cereal and the bowl on the spotless counter beside her, then went to fetch milk from the small fridge.

When he returned he suggested, "It might have been a delusion. Sometimes a delusion can be shared."

"You're telling me you think I'm crazy?"

"Well, not in the psychotic sense obviously."

"You are *so* in denial." She rolled her eyes.

He chuckled. "Steady on."

Joan dumped a mound of cereal into her bowl then sloshed on some milk. "What you saw is inexplicable unless you acknowledge the paranormal. Admit it. Just suck it up and move on. Now where's the spoon?"

Euan got her a spoon. "It's not inexplicable, we simply have not thought of the correct rational explanation for it yet."

She attempted a biting retort but it was lost in a mouthful of crunchy cereal.

He smiled. "So what is your plan for tonight?"

"I dunno. I hate pre-emptive stuff." She spooned up another mouthful of cereal. "I'd almost rather wait for the Andromache to do whatever it does..." she continued between bites, "...and then deal with it. It gets born, I kill it. It makes the Fury super-powerful, I destroy the Fury."

"It paints the castle pink, you get some builders in."

Joan grinned and pointed her spoon at him. "Exactly."

"Still, an ounce of prevention and all that."

"That's what Fiona says." Joan took another spoonful and crunched thoughtfully. "Okay, first, we need to bind the zombies to their graves so they can't be used against us anymore. We'll need Fiona for that. Get dressed and we'll bop on over to her place. Oh, and could you find my boots? And my sword?"

* * * *

She had to find him.

He had protected her. How could she not return the favor? It was unthinkable. The thing had come for her, after all. Fiona was not about to let anyone suffer in her place. She must find Rory.

Fiona unfolded an ancient map of the city across her large research table, the dry parchment crackling loudly in the silence of the library. The huge map engulfed the table such that only a small border of cherry wood peeped out. Ornate calligraphy labeled every inch of the page, in detail so explicit that it must have taken the cartographer half his lifetime to complete.

Next she opened the mahogany chest she had dragged in from her bedroom. Inside were her very best, her very strongest magick accoutrements. That cloud had felt extremely powerful which meant she needed to work magick of equal potency. Selecting her paraphernalia with a meticulous eye, she situated them upon the table. She had everything she needed for a locating spell ... except something belonging to Rory.

Twinges of panic rose in her heart. This must work. She would find something and make it work. Her eyes scanned the library. Vampires did not shed, so there would be no hair. But Rory had spent most of his time in here. There had to be something he had held for a long enough period of time.

She crouched beside the pile of research books that she had moved from the table to the floor. Which of those books had he handed to her? Wait--something *given*. She leapt to her feet. *That porcelain pug!*

Swiftly she fetched the little figurine from where it sat upon the mantelpiece. It had not exactly belonged to him, of that she was certain, but Rory had given it to her and in so doing it should have had contact enough with him for the spell to work.

She placed the porcelain pug next to the small, black velvet pouch she had positioned at one corner of the table. No, better to be sure. Opening the velvet pouch, she deposited the figurine inside. Rory's connection with the object was not optimal and the magick powders within would need all the help they could get.

Next she lit a match and touched the sizzling flame to each of three indigo candles she had arranged in a triangle over the map. Then she turned out the lights. Scents of magnolia and tuberose gradually filled the air. By the flickering light, she proceeded to cast a circle.

The graceful twist of her hands and sinuous motions of her arms made the ensuing ritual seem like an exotic dance. Keeping her voice soft and entreating, she began to chant. The language was ancient and not her own. Finishing her incantations, Fiona reached for the velvet pouch and, holding it such that the figurine stayed within, she poured the rest of its contents into her hand.

An arc of glittering pink dust cascaded into her palm. Gently she placed the pouch back on the table. Clutching the dust in her closed fist, she bowed her head over it and whispered an invocation.

With one abrupt motion she raised her head, her arm shot straight up and she tossed the dust mixture high into the air. It seemed to float and pause as it fell, as if immune to gravity.

THE CRIMSON FOLD

Gradually it coalesced into a small ball of neon pink. Descending in tighter and tighter circles, the glowing pink sphere spun lower and lower over the map until it landed and burned upon a single point.

She had found Rory.

Exultation bloomed within Fiona, then froze and withered as she recognized Rory's location. He was to be found precisely where she swore she would never, ever again be.

Apprehension constricted her throat as she reached into the chest for her juniper oil, juniper candles, and cache of juniper berries. Rescuing Rory would require as strong a protection spell as she could muster. Her hands shook slightly as she arranged the candles. Taking a deep breath, she tried to push her fears to the back of her racing mind. It was down to her. She had to save him. She couldn't lose Rory now.

* * * *

"Funny. You'd think she'd be home." Joan stopped knocking her sword hilt against Fiona's old, crackly-white door. This was a pain. She didn't want to go all the way back to her hotel. Especially with the police convention the Old Town had become tonight. Something significant had gone down, and she was pretty sure it was supernatural because the authorities were in full denial mode. She was sorry she missed it, but it seemed to have been pretty localized and it wasn't there now so there was no sense wasting time on it. Joan stepped back. Maybe Fiona wouldn't mind if she just kicked the door in.

"What do you reckon happened up by the castle?" Euan inquired from behind her.

"Weather balloons."

"Sorry?"

"Trust me, anything that smells of bizarreness they always blame on weather balloons."

Euan chuckled while Joan continued to contemplate the door.

"What are you thinking?" he asked.

"That we should have stopped at my room and picked up my purse. I have her key in it." She raised her right foot.

Euan quickly grabbed her shoulder, turning her slightly sideways as he stepped around to face her. "Tell me you are not about to kick in Fiona's front door."

She shrugged his hand off. "Why not? She won't mind. It's an emergency. I can manage a rudimentary binding spell, but I'll need some of her magick supplies to do it."

She tried to line up on the door again but Euan shifted so he was standing directly in her way.

He crossed his arms in front of his chest. "I am not entering anyone's house without their express permission."

Joan's breath caught in her throat. Her heart pounded an alarm. She narrowed her eyes. "Just what do you mean by that?"

He paused, and immediately Joan leapt back while simultaneously raising her sword so that its point was aimed at his neck.

"Talk fast, buster, or your head is going down that flight of stairs without you."

She had assumed when the zombies attacked him that he wasn't a vampire. She had never checked him for a pulse. He had slept all day. She still had never seen him eat. And now he needed an invitation to enter a residence. Joan swore ferociously to herself. She had liked him, so she had let down her guard. Of all the amateur mistakes to make.

"You're thinking I'm a vampire, aren't you?" Euan stated, eyeing the point of her sword. He cautiously unfolded his arms. "I'm not."

"Yeah, right. Keep still."

He offered her the inside of his wrist. "I don't suppose you would be willing to come close enough to me to take my pulse."

"Nope."

He shook his head and sighed heavily. "I just meant that it's not right to force entry into Fiona's flat. Not when I know of an alternative."

"An alternative?"

"I know where you can obtain magick supplies. No breaking and entering necessary."

Joan raised a disparaging eyebrow. "I thought you weren't a believer."

"I'm not." Euan hesitated, then continued in a low voice as if the words were imposed upon him, "But I knew someone who was."

"Keep talking." She did not bother to hide her impatience.

He frowned in response. "We are at rather an impasse. Might I suggest you extend me an iota of trust?"

"I'd like to trust you," Joan replied. "I really would. But who exactly are you?"

* * * *

Fiona's shoulders brushed against the cold, damp walls. She had to shrug them together and pivot with each step as she descended the coiled stone staircase. Anything could pop out at her from behind the blind curve and she had no room to defend herself. *No room.*

The walls and the dark were closing in around her, the blackness dwarfing the thin beam from her torch. She was being engulfed. A knot squirmed in the pit of her stomach. Her instincts frantically chanted to get out, get out now. Fiona swiped at a cluster of cobwebs that sprang to sudden illumination in front of her. *Not fun. Not fun.*

She stumbled and grazed her palm on a bit of rough stone in the wall as the steps came to an abrupt end at the mouth of a low

THE CRIMSON FOLD

archway that forced her to duck to enter. The tunnel itself was no taller. The hair atop her head skimmed along the ceiling. She tried to duck lower.

But then she couldn't breathe.

No, that was ridiculous. There was nothing to worry about. Granted, she was bent double, squeezing through a cramped passageway, deep below the city's streets. And there were insects. But not to worry. She might be crawling into her own grave, and those were undoubtedly some muckle-big creepy-crawlies skittering in the darkness beyond her torch's shaft of light, but not to worry.

Just breathe.

Ignore the walls.

And whatever you do, keep moving.

She wiped her palm on her trousers as she crept forward. She had known this place would be unbearable. Seeking strength in the familiar, Fiona tightened her grip on her torch and focused on the click, click of her spiked boot heels upon the stone floor. One never knew when one might need an extra spike. Fiona's breath came shallow and quick. When would this tunnel end? And isn't that wall moving inward?

Attempting not to panic, she braced her hand against the wall. No, it was simply curving. She followed the curve of the tunnel. And then she saw the light.

Fiona scrambled out into a large stone room, airy by comparison, with high ceilings and low arched doorways leading off to other portions of the catacombs. Lit by a bare safety bulb hanging incongruously from the antiquated ceiling, the room was clearly part of the underground Edinburgh shown to tourists. Why tourists should want to visit the built-over remains of ancient streets Fiona often wondered.

Over the centuries, these subterranean vaults had witnessed unbearable desolation and they reeked of it. Medieval Edinburgh's protective battlement, the Flodden Wall, effectively shut in the populace--the Netherbow gate became known as the World's End because it was considered unsafe to live beyond it. So over the centuries, as teeming Edinburgh grew to fair bursting behind the wall, there had been nowhere else for the people to go but down. Cellars had been built upon cellars. Later, streets were built on top of streets. And always it was the most vulnerable, the most destitute who were forced to seek this plutonic shelter. Plague victims once had been quarantined here, most never to leave alive.

Fiona shivered. Enough dark thoughts. *Pull your socks up, lassie.* There was much to do.

She crossed to the third doorway and ducked through. The floor of the hall beyond was smooth, its paving stones dipped and warped with age. She stole down the hallway. At the sound of a distant drip of water she bowed through the nearest opposite arch and descended a slanting passage away from the sound. Her destination wouldn't be near running water.

Something solid thumped into her ankle, almost tripping her. She staggered, recovered, and quickly shone her torch on the ground at her feet.

Nothing.

But she could feel... Fiona reached down, fingers outstretched, feeling for ... a hairy back. An invisible, shaggy back. A welcoming whine issued from thin air.

Fiona relaxed. "Aye up, wee ghost doggie," she whispered.

The phantom dog cheerfully snuffled her leg and wiggled beneath her hand as she petted its back.

"Ye havenae seen an ancient Evil wandering about, have ye? Such a good dog. Somewhere down there, mayhap?"

Fiona stood and wandered forward until she ran into a stone wall. Rory should be in this direction, yet the passage was completely walled up. She touched the bumpy surface. The rocks felt surprisingly warm.

The spirit dog was bouncing against her legs as if it wanted her attention. She glanced down and it began scratching at one of the rectangular base stones. Lowering herself to the cold, damp floor, she placed her torch on the ground so that the beam hit the hefty stone at which the dog had scratched.

"This is the way forward, is it?"

Pulling at the stone's edges, she murmured an empowerment chant. The mortar around the stone cracked, crumbled, and the stone came away from the wall. Unfortunately, the black hole left behind was barely wide enough for an adult to squirm through.

"Och, ye are havin' me on," she moaned, leaning back on her palms and kicking at the wall with her spiked heels. "I hate, hate, *hate* small spaces."

With a heavy sigh, she thumped her heels back to the floor. The spectral dog brushed past her leg and scampered down the gap.

"Aye, ye do that, but then nae harm can touch ye," she grumbled.

Harm. Who knew what harm Rory was enduring? Fiona's breath caught sharply in her throat. She had delayed too long already. Some rescue mission. She gazed into the pitch-black aperture and swallowed. There was nothing else for it.

Rotating onto her stomach, and rolling the torch in front of her, she inched headfirst through the hole. The rugged edges of the entrance were harsh to the touch. They scraped at the fabric of her cotton shirt, snagging along her shoulders and back. She closed her eyes and wriggled forward, pulling with her fingers and pushing with her toes.

*I willnae get stuck. I willnae get stuck.
Ye owe me greatly, Ruaridh MacLaren.
I willnae get stuck.*

* * * *

The creature had reneged on their deal. Miklos still could hardly fathom it. He stomped the width of his illuminated cave and returned. To be betrayed like this--and with Andromache's time so close. Miklos fingered the blade of his ancient, ceremonial dagger and regarded Rory MacLaren's battered body lying on the stone floor at his feet. His one good deed. For over two hundred years he had never regretted it. And how was he repaid? With disloyalty. Treachery.

He reached down and casually stabbed Rory in the side.

Rory coughed and spit blood, but his unrepentant eyes glared up at Miklos. "May ye die alone. And may ye lie unburied, far from your native land."

Miklos laughed. "A curse! How quaint. How very 'Highland' of you."

Rory continued to glare at him and Miklos had to admit there was an undaunted quality to the vampire even now. How did he manage it? It had been that ... that *spark* which had drawn him to the dying MacLaren human in the first place. His aura had blazed with such menacing valor, such dark promise--a promise fulfilled, for as a vampire he had possessed a true talent for bloodshed. Miklos smiled at the memories. He had been very proud of his creation. But that was all in the past. He had the future to think of. And he had been betrayed.

"Perhaps I won't kill you. Perhaps I shall torture you to the brink of madness." Miklos continued to grin as he warmed to his subject. "Then I could force you to turn on that brunette harlot of yours. I could force you to--"

"Force me to die," Rory growled. "'Twill be the sole thing ye can force me to do."

* * * *

Finally.

The tunnel, an ordeal direct from her nightmares, ended. Fiona crawled out and collapsed, panting and shaking, on the open vault floor. It was a big chamber, coated with the dust of centuries, and empty except for some chalky bones strewn in a corner that glimmered in the golden light.

Golden light that should not have been there. She hadn't turned on her torch yet.

Still shuddering, she glanced about her. The whole room was dimly illuminated by a golden glow. Warily, she stood. The glow seemed to form a sheet, dispersed across the room like a drawn curtain. She stepped up, raised her palm, and swept the wall of light. It prickled like static electricity. Some sort of barrier. Tentatively, she touched it, then slowly inserted her fingers through it. And suddenly it felt like her insides were being sucked out of her chest. She yanked her hand back. A dampening field. No hexes or battle spells would work beyond this.

The dog whined at her feet.

"Go home now, doggie. Go on home." She shooed the ghost dog back to the mouth of the narrow passageway. "This is nae place for ye. Home!"

She heard the dog scurrying into the tunnel.

Fiona turned, took a deep breath, and strode through the barrier. At least this horror was fleeting. A pounding moment of panic as her entrails seemed about to be sucked out of her, and then it was over and she was out, coughing, on the other side. There was another doorway ahead, and more catacombs beyond.

But now she knew she was close.

* * * *

Shirtless, Rory lay broken on the floor. For a fraction of a second, Fiona saw the beauty of his chest and arms, his sculpted and toned muscles, before the agonizing bruises and bloody slashes disfiguring his milky skin registered. His body tremored with pain. But his face held nothing save weary defiance.

He must have heard her involuntary gasp for he looked toward the sound. His eyes had difficulty focusing, but when he recognized her, his resolute expression changed. Fiona recognized fear. Fear for *her* safety. She felt a rush of tenderness toward him that brought hot prickles to the back of her eyes. That he cared so for her, even now, just about broke her heart.

"I see we have a guest."

Fiona turned toward the grating, new voice. A vampire with the face of a gargoyle stood appraising her with insolent eyes. He was primevally demonic. His body was pale gray and scaly and he wore no clothes to cover it. His feet were cloven and his hands were clawed. He must have been one of the Undead for an impossibly long time. Which meant that he was either very lucky or very powerful. From his talent with the magick shield, Fiona knew it was unlikely that luck had anything to do with it.

"Dinna touch her," Rory commanded. Bracing himself against the wall, he struggled to his feet. "This is between us."

The demon laughed. It was an ugly sound.

"Run, lassie!" Rory urged.

Fiona stepped into the cave.

"She dinna ken anything. Let her go," Rory pleaded.

"Your sentimentality is becoming annoying," responded the demon. He raised a clawed hand. His gnarled fingers clutched an antique-looking, ritual dagger.

"Leave him alone," Fiona ordered. She stamped her spiked heel on the stone floor. The sound rang across the room like a warning shot.

"Why should I? I do not need him. You I will keep. You shall make a fine hostage. Armstrong values you. He, on the other hand, is taking up space. Space he no longer deserves."

The demon threw the dagger at Rory's chest.

Fiona crossed the room in the blink of an eye, catching the dagger in mid-air.

"I told ye to leave him alone," she growled.

As if an invisible veil fell from her face, for the first time her features appeared unmistakably feral. Rory blinked.

Fiona was smiling viciously at the ancient demon. Her pointed teeth glistened. "Clearly ye dinna ken what's good for ye."

Flipping the dagger in her hand like a gunfighter twirling his six-gun, she sauntered toward the demon. Her eyes glowed an unearthly red.

"Do you know with whom you are dealing?" Rory had rarely heard Miklos sound so outraged.

Fiona laughed. It was an eerie sound coming from a human throat, resembling the silvery chime of a crystal water goblet when tapped by a spoon. "More to the point, do ye?"

She stopped in front of him, the dagger gripped in her right hand, and shifted her weight from the ball of one foot to the other.

"I am Miklos." It was meant to be a grand statement, but the sentence ended in a howl of pain. Fiona, rolling low, had sliced the side of his knee as she went past.

Miklos lashed after her using both of his clawed hands. She dodged but he followed, still striking. She dived. He caught her flesh, but only a glancing blow. Just enough to knock the dagger from her grip and send it skittering across the floor.

She tossed her hair back, revealing a grin that was somewhere between manic and merry. "As if that'll stop me."

A flicker of uncertainty crossed Miklos' craggy features. Fiona charged. He met her blow for blow. A dreadful dance of smashing forearms and elbows. She kept coming.

"Who are you?" he asked, the words spat out to the rhythm of his fists.

In a clever feint, she drew him out and spun under his guard.

"I am Fionnseach the Fury." Her hand whipped out and seized his throat. Yanking him toward her face, she whispered, *"Fear me."*

CHAPTER ELEVEN

With a deft slash, Fiona laid open Miklos' cheek with of one of her fangs, and then whirled away before he could touch her.

Miklos wiped the viscous green ooze that seeped from his wounded face. "I heard the warnings you were in town," he muttered.

"Ye should have heeded them."

Fiona leapt with the grace of a tiger, but Miklos dodged her lunge. He snatched at her arm, caught her shoulder and rammed her into the wall. She staggered back, and he slammed her up against the wall again. A second splatter of her blood decorated the rocks.

Reeling, she punched at him and missed. With a grating laugh, he struck her--a vicious backhand that knocked her to the ground. She landed heavily next to the dropped dagger. Scooping up the dagger in one fluid movement, she threw herself at Miklos.

He contained her charge, trying to crush her between his arms. She twisted, used his own strength against him, and flipped him onto the floor. His eyes widened, but whether from surprise, fear, or the impact of the floor was hard to tell. She plunged the dagger down. With a panicked swipe, he deflected the blow. The dagger penetrated his chest, but not his heart. Fiona snarled. Unable to dislodge the dagger, she left it where it stuck and bounded backward as he rose, slicing at her shins.

The pair faced each other across the narrow cavern stained with blood and slime.

"This is tiresome. You are not even edible," Miklos grumbled. "I have more productive ways to spend my time."

A violent gust of wind sprang up from nowhere. Great plumes of smoke swirled around him, braiding together and obscuring him from view. Then suddenly all was clear and still. Miklos had vanished.

Fiona staggered over to Rory.

"Ye defeated him," murmured Rory. His own voice sounded strange to him, its tone revealing something akin to awe.

"Nae, laddie. I'm good, but I'm nae that good." She crouched beside him. "He just didnae wish to bother with me. Can ye stand?"

He reached out a shaky hand and tenderly stroked her cheek. Her skin was cold, dry and unyielding, as if some alchemist had formed her through mixing bone china with steel. How could this be possible? He glanced at her throat and now saw the pair of little, jagged scars. How had he failed to perceive the truth?

"I was right. T'was something different about ye," he whispered. "Ye are like me."

"Aye," she replied, lowering her eyes.

"But ye said ye hated vampires."

With a sudden upward glance, Fiona met his gaze. Her eyes burned with an eerie inner fire. "I do."

Somehow she managed to get a world's worth of loathing and despair into those two little words. But he could not quite process her emotions. His brain was still dealing with the surprise. "Why dinna ye tell me?"

"Ye have to ask?" she mumbled.

The air rippled in front of her features. Suddenly her face was purely human again. No longer were her teeth canine and her skin cold. Even her bite scar had disappeared.

Rory whistled appreciatively at the transformation. "How do ye do that?"

She shrugged. "Glamour magick."

He continued to gaze inquiringly at her.

"A sorceress taught it me a long, long time ago, so?"

"Then ye are a witch as well."

"Aye, I'm all sorts of evil," she replied with a melancholy grin. "But as ye are in desperate need of a witch right now, 'tis for the best. Let's get ye home so I can mend ye."

She helped him to stand. He groaned at the painful effort it cost him.

"Och, laddie," she sighed and kissed him lightly on the cheek. "Ye were a bonnie brave lad."

He felt an effervescence at the touch of her lips that practically made him forget the pain. "Ye kissed me."

"That I did. I must be punch-drunk for sure."

* * * *

Euan sighed and leaned back against the hallway wall. "I could define myself in many ways, but what's probably of greatest importance to you is ... I am Hamish Farquharson's nephew."

Joan lowered her sword. "Farquharson. I know that name. He was..."

"The poor idiot assigned to the same, strange reenactment troupe with which you carry on."

"Y'know, there's a point where denial crosses into stupidity," Joan snapped before the facts of what he was telling her fully entered her brain. There was something... "Wait. Wait a minute." The man who had this assignment before them... "He died."

"Yes, he did."

There was a significant pause during which neither of them spoke before Joan quietly said, "I'm sorry."

He nodded his acknowledgement of her words. "It was a fire."

She shook her head. "It was whatever is trying to raise the Andromache."

"You people." He snorted derisively. "You can't live in this fantasy world forever. If you would just focus on practical things, like not smoking in bed..."

She could feel her impatience rising. "Why didn't you tell us before that you were Hamish Farquharson's nephew?" she interrupted, then held up her hand. "No, don't answer that.

Because then you'd have to discuss all this with me as if it were real, is that it? I wasted some valuable time wondering about you, y'know."

"Then don't waste any more time about it now. We need to be binding those things back to their graves at Greyfriars, don't we? Not mucking about in Fiona's hallway."

"I don't know about '*we*'," she grumbled.

"If you know how to do the spell, I know where to get the supplies."

"And that would be where?"

"Uncle Hamish stored his surplus magick ingredients at my flat. I didn't see what harm it could do, so I let him." He shrugged. "Perhaps I shouldn't have indulged his delusion, but he was my uncle. I'm sure we can find what we need to do your zombie binding ceremony."

"I dunno. I didn't see any magick stuff."

He smiled. "I'm surprised. You were in the kitchen. They're in the spice rack."

"You keep magick stuff in your spice rack?"

"Many spell ingredients are spices. You would be amazed at what one can do with a bit of cinnamon and clove."

* * * *

"Your skin needs to be cleaned before I can begin," Fiona explained as she helped Rory into the bathroom. "Can ye manage?"

"Of course." Rory tottered toward the gleaming, navy-blue tiled shower, then paused in his approach to lean heavily against the wall.

"Are ye all right?"

"Aye, just overdressed for the occasion." He fumbled with the buttons of his trousers.

"Right then," she blurted, snatching for the doorknob. "I'll be out here." She almost hit herself with the door as she rushed out.

Rolling her eyes heavenward, Fiona softly banged her forehead on the hallway wall. *How embarrassing--Champion of Justice afraid of a naked man.* She retreated to her bedroom.

The bedsprings creaked as she threw herself on the mattress. He must think her a glaky, callow, naïve ... virgin. Why did he distress her so? Naked men weren't completely unknown to her. She had a television. She had art books. She'd seen statues--the ones without the fig leaves.

Muted sounds of rushing water issued from down the hall. Fiona rolled off the bed and started to gather her accouterments. He would wonder what she'd been up to if he were ready before she was. A resounding, hollow bang made her jump. It was closely followed by a torrent of muffled swearing.

She dropped the bottles on her bed and dashed to the bathroom door. "Rory?"

Through the door she heard him laugh. "Turns out I canna manage."

She stared down at the brass doorknob. A big glinting apple of wicked enticement. She should walk away.

"Are ye still there?" Concern tinged his voice.

Fiona twisted the doorknob and opened the door. The sound of rushing water intensified. She peered around the corner. A light mist clouded the room. Her eyes gravitated to the shower. Rory's pale body was blurred by the beveled glass and fog on the long shower door. But he was definitely in there. His barely concealed figure seemed both mysterious and vulnerable.

She lowered her eyes. "Do ye need help, then?"

"Aye. Ye are going to have to wash me." He said that so matter-of-factly.

She could feel her cheeks growing hot. "Ye mean, go in there ... with ye?"

"That's the most obvious interpretation."

Now he was laughing at her. She clenched her fists. His blurry form moved and the shower door opened with a tiny, metallic pop. Quickly she looked away.

"Dinna tell me ye have ne'er seen a naked man before."

"'Tis not like they go wandering the fields," she snapped. Her eyes returned to the shower door. Only his top half was visible. She relaxed.

Rory's expression held a mixture of inquisitiveness and disbelief. "How old *are* ye?"

"Belt up!" she responded with more venom than she actually felt.

"Nae, really. 'Tis a serious inquiry."

"Old enough." He was still looking at her, oddly earnest, and she softened. "In my century ... I was a good girl. An *unmarried* good girl."

He nodded slowly. "So ye died a virgin."

"Aye."

He frowned, as if commiserating with her. "Ye were hard done by."

She snorted. "Now ye are takin' the mickey."

"Nae, lass. I find your maidenly blushes endearing."

"Piffle. And ye are gettin' water all over the floor. Get back to washing."

"I told ye, I need your assistance. Think of it this way, the faster ye get in here, the quicker the door gets closed and the less water goes on the floor."

"I dinna..."

He placed his hand symbolically over his heart. "I willnae touch ye. I promise."

"Well..."

"Ye'd be helping a creature in pain."

She stepped forward, then hesitated. "This is strictly for therapeutic purposes, ye understand."

He smiled. "Aye, strictly for therapeutic purposes."

Still she hesitated, but now from astonishment at herself. Was that actually excitement quivering in her belly? The modesty she had been trying to preserve had apparently already left her. "All right. But I'm keeping my underthings on." Balancing first on one leg, then the other, she pulled off her boots.

"Nae problem."

Fiona took a deep breath, trying to overcome the discomfiture she knew was pending, and let her trousers drop to the floor. She tried to extricate herself from the bundle of fabric gracefully--and was unsuccessful. *Charming.* She despaired of herself twice more before she was finally divested of all her outer clothing.

She crossed her arms, suddenly cold in the steamy room. "I'm probably not going to be any good at this. I've never washed a man before."

"Pretend I'm a pony," he suggested.

She chuckled and shook her head. "I canna believe I'm doing this. Shove over, I'm coming in. I'll do your back first."

The water was hot against her skin. There was a moment of awkward positioning, during which she tried to keep from looking down, then she grabbed her waiting bar of oatmeal soap.

"Ready, steady, go," she whispered to herself.

Rory stood, head bent, arms raised, with both hands clasping the pipe behind the showerhead. Delicately she scrubbed his back. His skin was slithery with soap and water.

"So your real name is Fionnseach?"

Fiona almost giggled. Having such a mundane conversation in this exotic situation was a relief. "Aye. Fiona dinna become popular 'til long after I died. But I like it. I think 'tis very me."

"And ye are the Fury." He shook his head. There was wonder in his voice.

"Dinna speak of that."

"Why? Ye should be proud of your record of destruction."

She scrubbed the soap across his back more vigorously. "I was dispensing justice. I destroyed evil where I found it, human or demon."

He grunted. "Have a care, lass."

"Och, sorry." She resumed her gentler strokes.

"So how did ye get involved with our Joan?"

"'Tis a long tale. But I felt I could do everyone more good, myself included, if I played on her team. Right, that's your back finished." With small steps and averted eyes, she moved to his front.

"I'm over here," he jested.

Cheeks burning even under the cascade of hot water, Fiona raised her eyes to his injured chest. "Tell me if I hurt ye," she said, indicating his wounds.

"Dinna fret. Ye'll know."

She washed his torso with hesitant strokes. Her soapy fingers glided over his sculptured muscles.

He grinned. "I'm gettin' the idea that I should have threatened ye naked."

She tensed with alarm. "What?"

"Well, ye were never as afraid of my bite as ye are of my body."

"I'm not afraid," she lied. But she had to admit that other emotions were beginning to surface, making her belly flutter and her nerves dance.

He leaned toward her.

She jerked her head back and glanced up at his face. "Are ye sniffing my hair?"

"Aye. Why is it ye dinna smell dead?"

"'Tis part of the spell that makes me seem living. And also a product of many scented wares."

As she watched, he closed his eyes in concentration. She could see his mind working, evaluating the scents filling his nostrils, painstakingly identifying and casting aside the false ones meant to deceive him until all that was left was the raw essence of her. Her individual scent, by which he could identify her even in a city of teeming millions.

He bent his head toward her again. This time she stayed motionless. He continued to lower his head until she felt his lips at her ear.

"Ye still dinna smell dead so much. Just a little bitter. Like plain chocolate. Ye smell like plain chocolate and dark earth."

"Well, ta for that," she answered, wiping water out of her eyes. "Now let me get on."

"I am at your mercy."

She snorted, but drowned by the falling water, the sound didn't have quite the disdainful emphasis she had been hoping for. She concentrated on finishing his chest. And then ... on to the next bits.

Gradually, her hands swabbed lower. And lower. Descending past his navel. A deep rumble resonated low in Rory's throat.

She quickly looked up, halting in mid-stroke. "Sorry. That hurt?"

"Nae," he growled. "That wasnae pain."

Suddenly she felt his iron grip upon her shoulders. He pulled her up into his arms, kissing her ferociously as the water gushed down upon them.

Fiona broke the kiss, gasping convulsively though she had no need of breath. "I thought ye said ye wouldnae touch me."

He nuzzled her cheek. "I'm not touchin' ye. I'm kissing ye."

"Och, no." She pushed him away. Her hands slid on his skin. "I must be going. Ye are clean enough to be going on with. I have things to prepare."

He chuckled as he let her go. "Ye are leaving me at a time like this?"

"I'm thinking ye can carry on without me."

* * * *

Rory wrapped the fluffy white towel around his waist. Its soft nubbiny texture felt decidedly decadent next to his skin. As he opened the bathroom door, its hinges squeaked in protest.

"I'm in here," Fiona's voice called.

He stepped out into the cool, dark apartment. A flickering glow emanated from the direction of the lounge. He limped toward the light and found Fiona kneeling on the carpeted lounge floor with a fuzzy, plaid blanket spread before her. She wore a blue, silky nightdress and a matching ribbon holding her hair back from her face. A tingling thrill surged through Rory despite his injuries. She did not seem to be wearing anything under the nightdress. It clung to her breasts in a most revealing fashion.

On the low coffee table nearby, nine candles quietly burned. Three white, three black, and three green. They cast a subtle blend of scents into the air. Rory could distinguish apples, blackberries and ... something very subtle ... cucumber.

"Lie down here. On your back," Fiona instructed, patting the blanket.

He eased his aching body down. "Not as easy as it sounds," he murmured as his towel slipped precariously. Fiona tugged it back into place with averted eyes. He finished lowering himself to the floor. "Can ye hear my joints creak? I sound like a fleet of rusty door hinges."

She giggled. "Aye, 'tis always a racket when door hinges get together."

"Damn partying door hinges." With a final groan, he lay back.

"'Right now. Think about your breathing," she instructed as she reached across his body. She seemed to be placing things in a pattern about him. Probably crystals. "I know 'tis difficult to remember, but I need ye to inhale. The scents are part of the magic. So if ye could try to breathe continuously it will help heal ye quicker."

He grunted and took a deep breath.

"That's it. Now just relax."

With great care, she positioned her hands, palms down, one above his forehead and the other low on his abdomen. She did not make contact. Instead, her hands hovered barely above his skin. He could sense their presence and his skin prickled in acute anticipation of her touch. But she did not touch him.

Slowly she brought her lower hand up from his abdomen, over his chest, across his face, so both hands were together above his forehead. Her fingers swirled the air, creating ever increasing circles, first encompassing his head and then along the entire length of his body. After she passed his feet, she shook her hands, several quick snaps, as if shaking invisible water from her fingers. Then her hands went back up his body, gently combing the air surrounding him. She swept past the top of his head and shook her fingers again. With each pass, his pain lessened.

Next, she lowered her hands to rest on either side of his chest. It was a soft, lingering touch. Her palms felt hot upon his skin. Then her hands were moving, her fingertips tracing their way across his torso, scrupulously stroking every inch, floating over the angry wounds. Her fingertips left tingling trails in their wake as if she were finger-painting on his chest using prickles and sparks instead of thick, creamy paints.

He gazed up at her. The candlelight threw dancing shadows over her face. Her deceptively human face. Skin smooth as porcelain. Ruby lips. Which were moving. Yes, she was chanting. He could hear the faint melody as her hands moved. Brows knitted in concentration, she was a portrait of compassionate humanity. Except that her half-closed eyes glimmered with their own unnatural flame.

Fiona's hands, sweeping low over his abdomen, brushed against the edge of his towel. A delicious shiver scurried all the way from the base of his spine to his scalp. His arm tensed. He had the sudden urge to untie the blue ribbon that swept back her damp hair and let her tresses cascade down upon her shoulders, and maybe, if she were close enough, tumble onto him. Suddenly her nimble fingers were massaging his arm muscle.

"Try to relax," she directed quietly. "Let your body go limp. Think about how each of your limbs is becoming grounded with the earth." She ran her fingers up his arm and went back to stroking his chest. "Just let your body melt."

"I hate to disappoint ye, but your touch does not promote melting," he responded jovially. "And absolutely nothing about me can be described as limp."

"Whisht, be still," she murmured. But he could see the color rising in her cheeks.

Her hands left his torso. She edged around to kneel behind his head. Rory felt her fingers slide beneath his neck and lightly press what must be special places, for subtle pulses of energy resonated within his body in response. Then her hands smoothly swept up and rested on either side of his face, her palms cupped over his cheekbones. Again, he felt the heat emanating from her palms. It warmed his face, awakening distant memories of the noonday sun and how it used to feel, back when its bright rays could bake his skin in a non-lethal way. When she removed her hands, an involuntarily gasp of protest escaped his lips at the abandonment.

Fiona was scooting back to her original place by his side. She twisted to reach behind her. He could hear quiet rustling, like stiff tissue paper, and then a muffled snap. She turned back to him. She held an open ampoule from which she poured a dollop of fluid the color and consistency of treacle into her palm. Once empty, she flipped the ampoule over her shoulder.

Rubbing her hands together, she charged her fingers with the syrupy liquid. "This is one of my favorites. 'Tis good for all sorts of healing. Including breaking hexes. And ye'll love the scent. 'Tis a blend of lavender and rosemary, with a hint of sandalwood."

With stately grace, she anointed him. First his forehead. Next the spot on his throat where his pulse would have been. Then she drew an ancient sign directly over his heart.

He caught her wrist and brought the back of her hand to his mouth. Despite the elixir coating her skin, he could still catch her own distinctive scent.

"I think ye smell even better." He kissed the back of her hand and heard her breath catch in her throat.

Shifting his grip, he rotated her hand to expose the vulnerable inside of her wrist. He brushed his lips back and forth against the ultra-sensitive skin. Then lingered upon her defenseless pale blue veins.

She quivered. But she did not move away. And she did not make a sound except for her sharp, irregular breathing. Little ragged breaths that betrayed her excitement.

He kissed her wrist, keeping his teeth as far as he could from her tender skin, trying to be as human as possible. He was rewarded by another soft gasp.

Without letting her go, Rory sat up. She gazed at him with wide eyes.

"I'm not done," she whispered.

"I'm feeling much better."

Using her captive wrist, he pulled her toward him until her mouth hovered millimeters away from his.

"I canna," she protested, but the words were more a breath than even a whisper.

He touched his lips to hers. A brief, grazing caress that teased and did not linger. As he drew back, she leaned toward him, instinctively seeking to continue the contact.

He did not need any more encouragement. His other hand plunged into her wavy mane and, by a fistful of her hair, pulled her to him. His lips captured hers, kissing her fiercely. Surrendering to his possession, her lips parted. Then gradually her lips began making demands of their own.

Her soft curves pressed against his chest, inflaming his need as she returned his kisses with growing fervor. He felt a primal growl rising in his throat and attempted to stifle it into a more human moan. His body ached. He needed her touch. Only she could grant him the release he craved.

With an effortless maneuver, he had her with her back to the blanket and gently laid her down. As if her recumbent position had triggered an alarm within her, her hands flew to his chest, pushing to hold him at arm's length. He looked down into her panicked eyes.

"Ye ken what I am." Her lip quivered ever so slightly.

"Aye," he replied. "Ye are wonderful."

His mouth stifled any protest. Without breaking the kiss, he lowered himself full length upon to her, his weight imprisoning her against the blanket and the floor.

The last of her reserve crumbled, no proof against an onslaught of so many new, exhilarating sensations. This was what she had yearned for, for all those empty decades. To love and be loved. But not by just anyone. She had waited for someone special, someone who could inspire love in the vestiges of her absent soul and yet accept her for the fiend she was. Someone who was Rory. She wanted to be loved by this man alone. The depth of her desire almost frightened her.

Her arms wound around him, clinging to his muscular back as his lips left hers and blazed a searing trail down her throat. Every nerve she had hummed with restless delight as he nipped at her sensitive skin. His gentle love-bites ignited tempestuous cravings within her. She arched her spine, savoring the weight of his body upon hers.

Rory possessively stroked her left side, from the curve of her breast to her hip. Then he shifted to afford himself full access to her left breast. She could feel his cold fingertips even through the thin fabric of her nightdress. He brushed her taut nipple, each caress sending uncontrollable jolts through her body. She ached to surrender herself to him.

But what if she wasn't any good at this? She knew, roughly, what the mechanics were. But, according to all those articles she had skimmed in the flashy women's magazines, it took skill to keep a man satisfied. What if she hadn't any skill?

He seemed to sense her sudden confusion.

"Have I hurt ye?" Concern filled Rory's eyes.

"Nae," she breathlessly assured him. "I was but thinking."

"Am I so poor a lover that your mind wanders?"

"Och, nae!" She didn't want him to think that for an instant. "Ye are perfection itself. 'Tis just that ... I am greatly afraid that I shall be the poor lover."

He shifted to lie on his side next to her. She could have sworn his eyes were alight with laughter. With a casual tug, he pulled away the towel that was still loosely wrapping his lower half, revealing himself in all his naked splendor.

"Does it look like ye are a poor lover?"

She tried to look away, a voice from the past echoing in her mind, scolding her for her lack of modesty. But she couldn't tear her eyes from the magnificent sight. He was clearly very happy with her indeed.

His hungry eyes blazed and she sensed what he wanted, what he was hoping for. Her keenness overrode her shy uncertainty. She reached over and started to caress the smooth shaft. It twitched willingly at the touch of her fingertips, accompanied by his sharp intake of breath.

"Enough of that, sorceress, or I shall come undone here and now." His voice held an edge of desperation.

She giggled. But she didn't stop until he firmly took hold of her wrist. He used the captured arm to force her back down on the blanket.

"May I dispense with this?" He indicated her nightdress.

She nodded and helped him pull the gown over her head. As it came off, it carried her ribbon away with it and her hair cascaded free.

He gazed down at her, the admiration in his eyes obvious even in the flickering candlelight. With great tenderness, he kissed her shell-pink nipples, teasing each of them with his tongue until she moaned and squirmed beneath him.

His kisses trailed down her belly. Lower. Apprehension stiffened her legs. Her knees clamped together. He raised his head, his expression kind and questioning.

She swallowed. "I canna ... I canna..."

"What, my pet?"

"I canna ... I dinna ken what will happen if..."

"If?"

She took a deep breath and avoided his eyes. "If I lose control."

He smiled. "Ye forget, what harm ye could do me has already been done--and long afore I met ye. Vampires need have no fear of one another."

"Are ye certain?"

"Believe me." His fingers gently massaged her knees, and then carefully started to part them. Grudgingly, she yielded. He kissed the inside of one knee, then blazed a line of kisses up the inside of her thigh, very aware that her body virtually was humming with tension. Looking up at her face, at her squeezed shut eyes, he called her name. Her smoldering, deep blue eyes opened and he could feel her ardent gaze all the way down to his toes.

"Ye are wonderful," he repeated. And he lowered his mouth to her tight curls and kissed her. Reverently.

Her whole body surrendered to him at that moment.

He continued kissing her, licking her. Slowly. Enjoying her. When his tongue found its main objective, she yelped. An involuntary cry of delight.

Then he let his fingers explore her, venturing inside with gentle pushes as she moaned and thrust against his hand. He felt her twitch and spasm around him. It was almost too much for him to endure. She was moaning, deep sensual moans. Desire burned through his frame. He glanced up, his pleasure intensifying at the sight of the arousal clear upon her face. Eyes squeezed shut, her head tossed back and forth, while her bright teeth bit into her ruby bottom lip.

Suddenly her eyes snapped open and she pulled him full length upon her. He felt her legs stiffen and her whole body started to convulse. He rode her trembling form as she shrieked with joy. Her body curled toward him, her fingernails raked the skin of his back, and then her cries were muffled as she buried her fangs in his neck.

Rory gasped. The sensation was exquisite. He groaned, drawing ragged breath after ragged breath through gritted teeth. He wasn't going to last. But he had given her pleasure. It was the zenith of his existence.

Just when he thought he could restrain himself no longer, she released him and lay back, still emitting little giggles and squeals. Savagely his mouth pressed down on hers, devouring her jubilant cries, as if he could feed on the essence of her rapture.

He did not release her until she lay still. Her eyes glowed as she looked up at him and she wore a beatific smile.

"Your turn," she said simply.

She pushed him down on his back. Gracefully, she lowered her head, past his chin, past his neck. Her hair swept down his chest, down his abdomen, tickling his skin and tormenting his beleaguered willpower.

His body was straining at the edge. The soft touch of her lips upon him was almost more than he could stand. Then he felt her tongue. And her mouth.

He couldn't believe what she was doing to him. And he was so damn grateful. His groans came faster, more urgently. She met his pace. He ached for the release that only she could give him. She was brilliant. She was spectacular. She was...

Suddenly, all thought was eclipsed. His face contorted in agonized ecstasy as pleasure slammed through his groin and radiated out through his body, gritting his teeth and clenching his toes. He screamed.

As his torrents and spasms subsided, he realized she was gazing lovingly at him. Exhausted, he gave her a weak smile and held out his hand. She moved so that they could cuddle, she cradling his bowed head upon her breasts. He sighed and nuzzled deeper, eyes closed. This was where he had dreamed of being. She shifted and a small animal sound of protest escaped his lips at her movement. He wrapped an arm about her possessively, holding her to him.

"Please. Stay." His voice was muffled, and the words half-formed, but he trusted she would understand him nonetheless.

"Ye want us to stay like this for the night?" she asked, stroking his hair.

With great effort he raised his head. "Forever."

CHAPTER TWELVE

"It says here that your zombies are more correctly called revvers." Euan looked up from the sizeable, leather-bound book he was holding open in front of him. "Did you know that?"

"Keep chanting!" Joan ordered as she sprinkled her dry concoction of charms and spices upon the earth in the center of Greyfriars cemetery.

Euan awkwardly shifted the book in his arms as he resumed the Latin chant. Holding the book with one hand and his flashlight in the other was clearly a tricky situation.

"That's my father's book so don't drop it." It was one of the few books she owned, one of the few non-weaponry items her father had handed down to her.

He nodded and kept chanting. When they had begun the spell the cemetery had been dark and empty. It was still dark. But it was no longer empty.

Joan had expected some zombies, or revvers, or whatever, to be sent to stop them. But so many! It was hard to distinguish in the starlight, but the eerie, shuffling mob approaching them seemed to be a hundred deep and so very, very wide. She kept casting the dust of her charm. Her wooden bowl was almost empty. The binding spell had better get effective soon.

"It's working," he called.

She glanced at the shadowy horde. The revvers were slowing down. They were definitely slowing down.

"Keep chanting," she repeated, "or it won't be soon enough."

The revvers were slow but they were only a few feet away now. She released the last of the magick powders with a flourish just as one of the revvers reached for Euan's face. He swatted at the decaying hand with his flashlight.

The revver seemed stuck in place, yet it was so close to its target that it refused to give up. The beam of light darted violently as the revver and Euan struggled for control of the flashlight. The light fell to the ground as the flashlight was knocked from Euan's hand.

Joan couldn't quite see the struggle, but it looked like the revver tried again to grasp at Euan's face. He grabbed its hand. Their fingers momentarily intertwined and she heard one of the revvers' skeletal digits break off with a snap.

In almost the same instant, a sudden gale whipped through the cemetery. It wildly swirled the fallen leaves in its path and cut through the revvers like a hot knife through softened butter. The revvers were disintegrating before them, becoming pillars of dirt that poured into the wind. In seconds, the revvers were gone.

Joan wiped her watering eyes and groaned. "I think I have zombie dust in my eyes. *So* totally gross."

When her vision cleared, she glanced at Euan's dark shape. He was standing very still. She retrieved the still shining flashlight.

"Euan?" She approached him slowly. "Are you all right?"

She shone the flashlight on him, revealing that he was standing staring down at the bony, decomposing finger that the now departed revver had left in his hand.

"It's okay," she assured him. "They're bound now. They can't come after us or anyone else anymore."

Euan turned and hurled the finger into the night. Then he shuddered.

"You believe now, don't you," she stated quietly.

"Yes." His voice sounded dour and weary. "I believe."

* * * *

"Joan just rang from that Sassenach's place. She's coming over directly. Dinna tell her. About me, I mean." Fiona adjusted her thick curtains against the morning light.

Rory chuckled. "Ye dinna think your friend will approve of ye now?"

"Aye." She smiled ruefully as she cleaned, arranged and otherwise made her flat presentable for Joan's impending visit. "For one thing, people automatically assume they've been downgraded from friend to snack. Ye just dinna feel the love."

He sidled over to her. "Ye dinna have to go back to being her sidekick. The end of the world willnae be so bad for us. We can go to the Highlands. Or Wales--there'll probably be dragons there again. Dinna go back. Come bide wi' me." He wrapped his arms around her waist. "I shall willingly be your slave."

She did not look at him. "Ye ken well that I canna. Justice isnae merely what I do, 'tis what I am. Its pursuit is my only hope of redemption."

"Ye realize that when Joan twigs what ye are, she willnae just send ye to Coventry. She'll kill ye."

"She will not," Fiona declared, enunciating each word with more conviction that she felt. Dread was a cold, iron fist in the pit of her stomach. She had been daft to think this day would never come. Sooner or later she was bound to reveal suspicious experience or knowledge that Joan would notice and she would be unable to explain away. Perhaps it was better to have done with the lying now. Joan knew her. They were chums. Joan would recognize that she was good. Wouldn't she?

It felt like eons, although the clock said they had not waited long, before Joan arrived in a flurry of excitement.

"*So* glad you're home! You shoulda been here last night," Joan called as she headed for the kitchen. "You missed Euan and me binding the revver-zombie-things to their graves. Euan was really good about it, too. I stayed with him overnight in case he had, like, nightmares or anything. He's still sleeping. Apparently belief takes a lot out of you."

Fiona arrived at the kitchen doorway to see Joan peering into the little refrigerator.

"Still no orange juice? Never mind. I see yogurt." Joan straightened, a tub of yogurt in each hand, and closed the refrigerator door with a bump from her hip. "So what were you up to last night?"

Behind her, Fiona could hear Rory chuckling. She unsuccessfully attempted to control her blushes as she contemplated her answer. Luckily, Joan was too busy fetching a spoon and then peeling off the foil tops to notice.

"I discovered what is trying to raise the Andromache."

Joan stopped in mid-peel and gasped in surprise. "Well, don't just stand there, tell me!"

"'Tis a very old vampire named Miklos."

Joan frowned as she continued to open the second yogurt container. "Have we heard of him before?"

Fiona shook her head. "Nae. He's located in the old Underground City. Or he was."

"Any relation to the Fury?"

"None whatsoever," declared Rory.

"I didn't ask you." Joan stuffed a heaped spoonful of creamy, white yogurt into her mouth and swallowed. She looked at Fiona. "So how'd you find this out? How'd you do a location spell without something of his?"

"I ... I ... Let me do ye a nice fry-up. Ye shall need your strength for tonight." It was the least she could do to help Joan. Especially as she might never again have the chance to do anything for her. Fiona skipped over to her little refrigerator and collected one brown paper wrapped packet of sausages and one of bacon from inside.

"Do beans," Rory urged. "I could do with a spot of nice, tomato-y beans."

Fiona pulled a tall, green and white tin of baked beans from the cupboard.

Joan ate another spoonful of yogurt and shook her head. "Why you British like baked beans for breakfast I'll never know." She waited until Fiona had the beans in a pot and the meat frying before asking again, "So how did you find out about this Miklos?"

Fiona fiddled with the sausage, listening to the crackle and hiss of the frying meat and wrestling with her answer.

"Miklos kidnapped me," Rory volunteered. He stepped across to stand close to Fiona's side. Fiona stirred the beans and resisted the urge to lean on Rory for support.

"And you got away? Bizarreness." Joan swallowed some more yogurt. "Why didn't Miklos kill you? There's something we're missing. Coffee."

"What?" asked Rory, clearly confused.

Joan finished one of the yogurts. "I need coffee."

Fiona turned to Rory. "Might ye put the kettle on?"

"No, no, I can do it," Joan insisted. She grabbed the kettle and took it to the sink.

Fiona's attention returned to the sizzling meat. She could hear Joan puttering with the taps, followed by a gush of water hitting the heating element inside the kettle.

"What are we missing?" Joan murmured to herself distractedly.

Rory poked Fiona in the arm.

Fiona waved him off.

"Surely an old, powerful vampire wouldn't just let Mr. Undead over there wander away from him," Joan reasoned as she turned off the taps.

Rory poked Fiona again.

No, Fiona mouthed at him.

"She'll be on the wrong track," he warned.

"I ken why ye are so helpful," she whispered irritably. "Ye think if she rejects me I'll gang w' ye."

Rory gave her a toothy grin.

"What are you two hissing about over there?" asked Joan. She snapped the kettle on. "We should research this, right?"

Fiona sighed and looked over her shoulder. "We dinna need to research it."

Joan gazed at her quizzically.

"I ken why Miklos didnae kill Rory," Fiona admitted. She started to serve the sausage, bacon, and beans. Even though she did not hunger for any of it, there was something reassuringly domestic about the smell of fried bacon.

"Well?" Joan urged her to continue.

Fiona handed Joan a full plate. "Eat."

"But I still have yogurt."

Fiona smiled. "Eat."

Joan genially stuck her tongue out, and then went for a fork. "Do you want a fork, too?"

"Aye, please."

Joan tossed Fiona a fork. She caught it and handed it to Rory along with a saucer bearing a small portion of beans.

Joan frowned. "That wasn't for you." She shoveled a forkful of beans into her mouth.

Rory grinned and slouched back against the counter. "Cheers, hen." He scooped up some beans on his fork and saluted Joan with them before beginning to eat.

Beside him, Fiona hoisted herself up on the countertop and sat, letting her legs dangle. She took a deep breath. It was time for the truth. "Miklos didnae kill Rory..."

Still standing, mouth full, Joan gestured with the piece of bacon in her hand for Fiona to hurry up. Then, ignoring her fork submerged in her beans, Joan continued to eat her bacon with her fingers.

"Because I rescued Rory before Miklos could kill him," Fiona finished.

"*You* rescued..." Joan trailed off.

"I'm nae a bad fighter," Fiona explained. She could not look at Joan.

"Now you tell me," Joan responded dryly.

"I ask ye to believe that had ye truly needed my help, I would have given it."

Tentatively, she made eye contact with Joan.

"Never mind." Joan munched on a link of sausage. "So why didn't you tell me?"

"Truthfully? I was ashamed."

"Why?"

Fiona sighed. Rory had stopped eating his beans and was watching her closely.

Joan finished her sausage and licked her fingers. "Well?"

"A long time ago I came to Edinburgh to find work. Many in my situation had followed the same plan, and we found there wasnae work for us all. Unemployment was high. Money was scarce. We homeless made our homes in the Underground City. But it wasnae half so nice then as now. 'Twere an underground maze of cellars and vaults, with too many people crammed into each dank, cramped cubbyhole. People stored like wine bottles in a cellar, just ... just rats sheltering in caves. No light. No room. Putrid air. Crime became the only way out." Fiona paused.

"And what happened?" prompted Joan.

"The streets are not kind to the meek," Fiona observed. She glanced away quickly, but failed to prevent Joan from seeing her pooling tears.

"So you did things you're not proud of, and survived any way you could," Joan continued grimly.

Fiona chuckled, and faced Joan again.

"Actually, no. I died."

THE CRIMSON FOLD

CHAPTER THIRTEEN
South Uist, Outer Hebrides
August 1851

"What are you about, Fionnseach nighean Dubh-sìthe?"

Fionnseach recognized the teasing voice. Donnachadh. She did not bother to look up.

"Feeding your fairy kin?" Donnachadh continued. He clicked his tongue in feigned reproach. "Maighstir Fearghas wouldn't approve of this."

Fionnseach finished pouring her libation of milk at the foot of the standing stone and rocked back on her heels. "It does no harm to remember the old ways."

She reached out and brushed her fingertips against the rough surface of the stone as if parting with a sentient being, then stood.

Donnachadh chuckled. "And to remember the old stories?"

She spun to face him and saw his brown eyes were alight with laughter. He was deliberately baiting her. She inhaled deeply. She was not going to let him anger her. Or at least she was not going to show it.

"This is why you and I shall never wed," she said with as much disdain as she could muster. "You know I can not abide teasing and yet you persist."

Fionnseach stepped past Donnachadh and, cautious of the slick grass, began to gingerly descend the steep hill. Her heart pounded madly within her chest. She wanted to punch Donnachadh. But only heathens and whores engaged in such behavior and she was a good girl. She shouldn't even be thinking about punching him. Repeatedly. No, no, such behavior would only substantiate those wild rumors about her mother.

Many times as a young girl, she had come out to this standing stone with her mother, watched her perform the ancient ceremony and listened to her tales of the sìthe. It was one of her favorite memories. Her mother had known the tale of every fairy that dwelt in the islands, and as she was so skilled in the healing arts and old ways, some whispered that she must consort with the fairies personally.

Yes, her mother could heal most any malady ... until the childbed illness that carried her off following Muirgheal's birth eight years ago. It was only then that the whispers began to be spoken aloud. Salacious stories circulated quickly, stories about the desires of the sìthe, and about what her mother might have got up to when she wandered abroad at night. Admittedly, brunette Fionnseach did not look much like her blond kinfolk. But her skin had worn thin with the scourge of bearing a shame that was not of her own making.

"Your eyes flame so brightly when you're angry, my darling." Nimble Donnachadh had caught up with her.

"I am not your darling."

"No? No other man wishes to call you so." He spoke lightly, as if he were oblivious to the pain it caused her. "Scorn me and you shall remain an old maid forever."

"Even so," she answered through gritted teeth. "Now be off with you. I have chores to do once I am home, and Muirgheal will be wanting her breakfast."

"So you haven't heard the news, then?" He sounded surprised.

"What news?"

"Everyone must assemble in Lochboisdale."

She sighed. "What drivel do you speak now?"

"A tall ship docked in Lochboisdale harbor early this morn. Can you see it?" He pointed out to the harbor in the distance below them.

"You know I can not." Nevertheless, Fionnseach glanced in the direction he indicated. The sea and sky were a fuzzy mix of blue and white. There could have been a ship down there amongst the blur. But for all she knew there could be a dancing water-monster. Her eyes did not see the distance that others' did.

She resumed concentrating on the grass beneath her feet. "What care I for ships in the harbor? Fishing boats come and go."

"This one isn't fishing. Iain Oig says it is come to take us to Canada."

Fionnseach laughed. "And what would Iain Oig know about it?"

"He heard the English talking when he was on the pier." Donnachadh was serious.

She snorted. "I understand the sheep better than Iain Oig understands the English."

Donnachadh chuckled. "With your witchy ways, you probably do. They don't call you Fionnseach nighean Dubh-sìthe for nothing."

Fionnseach, Daughter of a Dark Fairy. She clenched her fists and struggled to remain calm. "You know very well what I meant."

"True. But something is definitely afoot. I have never seen so much activity on the pier. Iain Oig said the landlord's agent is here and has called a meeting. And that's certainly what it looks like."

"I don't believe it," she replied, nevertheless she quickened her step.

They soon reached the bottom of the hill. Her family's little thatched cottage snuggled in the glen but a few yards distant. A stone structure with heather in its thatch, it looked as if it had grown out of the land rather than having been constructed upon

THE CRIMSON FOLD

it. Peat smoke drifted in lazy spirals from the chimney. On the hillside beyond she could discern the fuzzy forms she knew were her flock of little sheep, and somewhere back there would be her black milk cow. It seemed such a normal day.

"I'll say good morning to you now, if you don't mind," she began, but Donnachadh was not to be dismissed.

"I should speak with your father."

"Please yourself."

She hurried toward the peaceful cottage. Surely this morning was no different from any other morning. Surely the Clearances had not come here.

A little girl dashed from around the corner of the house, her yellow plaits streaming behind her. Fionnseach halted just shy of the painted door, propped open to let in light and air, as the girl careened past her and inside.

"Muirgheal?" Fionnseach followed her in.

"A great, white-sailed ship!" Muirgheal proclaimed, running in reckless circles around the room. "It is *so* big, sister! You should see! A great, white-sailed ship!"

She knocked into their wooden table and Fionnseach had to lunge to catch the loaf of bread tottering too close to the edge.

"Careful, Muirgheal, or you'll be eating your breakfast off the floor," she scolded.

"But the ship! Come see!" Muirgheal tugged at Fionnseach's cotton skirts.

"Eat first." Fionnseach extricated herself from her sister's grasp and crossed to the large, black cauldron suspended over the smoldering peat from a hefty hook embedded in the fireplace. Using a long wooden spoon, she stirred the porridge bubbling within.

"Donnachadh, Donnachadh, have you seen the ship?" Muirgheal asked breathlessly.

"That I have, little one."

Fionnseach could hear him moving around behind her, and then the muffled sawing of a knife against crust as Donnachadh helped himself to a slice of bread. She turned to scold him, and saw her father standing in the doorway. His face was in shadow, but his whole body seemed to be sagging, as if its weight was too much to be borne. He had looked that way the day the pony died.

"I come bearing news, sir," Donnachadh began, "But I fear you have already heard it."

Her father crossed the floor with heavy steps to a wooden chair that creaked loudly as he collapsed into it. "We have been doomed since the Bonnie Prince left us. This is yet one more cross we must bear."

Fionnseach watched as Muirgheal looked from one gloomy male face to the other, the child's own expression becoming more and more anxious.

"Come and sit, Muirgheal." The girl skipped over to the stool Fionnseach patted and sat. Fionnseach ladled porridge into a little wooden bowl and served her the bowl and a spoon.

"Are you certain of what Iain Oig said?" Fionnseach asked Donnachadh.

He nodded. An oppressive silence descended upon the room. The smacking sounds of Muirgheal happily eating her porridge seemed to grow in volume as the silence lengthened. Fionnseach could bear it no longer.

"What nonsense. This is all a misunderstanding. You'll see."

Her father shook his head. "We are a doomed race, nighean. We have been ever since Culloden. It is our tragedy, and we must bear it with dignity."

From far off came waves of yelling. Donnachadh strode outside. The clamor grew. Coming nearer. Fionnseach started for the doorway and almost ran into Donnachadh as he ducked back inside.

"Constables are combing the hillsides," he said. "They're ordering everyone down to the shore."

She gasped. "What, they think to drive us like cattle?"

Just then a stranger poked his head around the doorway. "Get a move on, you lot!" He brandished a police truncheon in their general direction.

"For what reason? You can't order us out of our own house," Fionnseach snapped, but Donnachadh and her father were already moving to the door.

"Not yours for much longer, girl." The constable pushed past the men and grabbed Fionnseach by the arm. "Get the child and get moving."

"I shall not." She planted her feet solidly on the floor and pulled in the opposite direction.

"You'd rather be fined forty shillings?" The constable's tone was as brusque as his grip. "Don't see anything here worth half that much. Not even what you've got beneath your skirts."

"Of all the impudence..." Fionnseach jerked her arm out of his grasp and held out her hand to Muirgheal. The girl dropped her bowl and ran to her, burying her face in the folds of Fionnseach's skirt.

"Sir, you can not so abuse me in my own home." Fionnseach looked to Donnachadh, waiting for him to come to her aid. He would set this lout straight. Or her father. One of them would say something. Her shoulders slumped as she realized no rescue was forthcoming. The men were not looking at her. They were leaving. They were skulking out of the house like shamefaced trespassers caught on someone else's private property. The sight shook her more than she cared to admit. How could this be happening?

Her eyes returned to the constable's smug face, and anger flared within her once again. Someone should put up some sort of resistance. This was their *home*. Her hands clenched into fists. Then a muffled whimper brought her thoughts crashing back to the girl at her side. Behaving like a hoyden would hardly help calm Muirgheal.

"We like the shore, do we not?" she said, stroking the child's hair. "Let us take a stroll down to the shore."

Fionnseach strode past the constable with her shoulders straight and her head high. Holding her sister's tiny hand firmly, she walked out the door and began the trek down the long, winding path to Lochboisdale.

* * * *

Hundreds and hundreds of people crowded the pier and spilled into the nearby streets. Fionnseach had never seen so many people all in one place. It was as if the entire island had turned out. The land must be empty for miles around.

On a platform at the head of this sea of humanity, a well-dressed man spoke loudly and with great animation. She was too far in the rear of the crowd to discern much beyond an occasional syllable, and it took her several moments to realize she would never understand him anyway. He spoke in English. His words would be lost to the Gaelic-speaking populace, even those close enough to hear him.

"What's happening?" asked Muirgheal plaintively.

"I do not know." Fionnseach stood on tiptoe, searching for Donnachadh in the crowd. She spotted him conversing with Iain Oig. Fionnseach pushed her way through the crowd, pulling Muirgheal behind her.

Iain Oig had attracted his own audience, being one of the few able to translate the stranger's tongue. Fionnseach and Muirgheal arrived at Donnachadh's side in time to hear Iain Oig's translation.

"He's saying that we are all to be evicted," Iain Oig announced in a voice laden with doom.

The crowd groaned in horror.

"Evicted? They can't do that," Fionnseach protested. "We're not a penny in debt."

Murmurs of outraged agreement emanated from the crowd.

"Wait, there's more," warned Iain Oig. "Since ... since this is no longer our home ... we will be taken to a new one."

The crowd waited breathlessly as he listened for what seemed ages to the incoherent speech.

"This very ship in the harbor will transport us to Canada forthwith," Iain Oig finished.

Fionnseach turned to Donnachadh, trying to ignore the panic breaking out around her. "But ... but ... Clanranald would never allow such a monstrous thing to be done to his people."

"The island has not belonged Clanranald for years. What does he care?"

"He sold it to a man who does not want us," Iain Oig said sadly.

"But surely the new landlord can't just transport us like chattel? Not if we don't wish to go?"

Iain Oig nodded. "Apparently he can. That man on the stage is the landlord's agent. He has papers with government seals and constables to do his work for him."

She gasped, still grappling with disbelief. "But what is the land without people to work it?"

"They want to put caoraich mhor on the land," answered a new voice, Seumas Buidhe's voice, from behind her. "The Great Sheep are worth more than tenants."

Fionnseach turned around. Seumas Buidhe's usually cheerful blue eyes were dark and sad.

"Great Sheep?"

"Yes, they are an odd breed, much bigger than our little ones. These sheep need more land."

Muirgheal pulled on Fionnseach's skirts. "What is Canada?"

"A land on the far side of the ocean," Seumas Buidhe answered.

Screams issued from the front of the crowd.

"Now what is happening?" Fionnseach struggled to see the blurry action at the front while the crowd around her started to press and shove and attempt to retreat.

"The constables are tossing people onto the ship and chaining those who resist," Seumas Buidhe replied. "It would go better for us if we board willingly."

The crowd surged and jostled around them like an animal uncertain of where to flee.

"I want to go home!" Muirgheal wailed.

"Of course we're going home," Fionnseach assured the girl, pulling her close. She turned to lead her back to their cottage and saw what could only be smoke blackening the sky. Far too much smoke, and in areas where it had no right to be. Panic rose in her throat. There was only one explanation. "They're burning the cottages!"

Fionnseach stumbled up the hill, struggling with her skirts and pulling Muirgheal. She had to get home. Perhaps she could drag clear what few possessions they had before the constables consigned their little cottage to the flames.

Frantic screams caught her attention. That was Afraig's voice. Fionnseach veered off the path and headed toward her friend's cottage.

"I want to go home!" Muirgheal cried.

"I know, we shall be there soon." She tried to sound comforting but her jaw was too tightly clenched.

THE CRIMSON FOLD

As they approached Afraig's cottage, Fionnseach could see a blurry group of men carrying torches and hear their laughter. Afraig was pleading with their leader. She headed to Afraig's side.

"They will not listen, Fionnseach." Afraig's eyes were red, puffy and streaming with tears.

Suddenly the men started chanting, "Domhnal Sgrios."

Fionnseach turned and saw a fuzzy, bay pony approaching the cottage. It did not bode well that his rider was apparently nicknamed Donald Destruction.

The pony halted in front of them. His rider was a stocky man, with dark hair and doughy features. So this was Domhnal Sgrios. Fionnseach was not impressed. She had rather expected him to have cloven hooves.

"Why is this cottage not alight?" he snapped.

"The woman says she needs more time," answered the leader of the torch-bearers.

Domhnal Sgrios waved his arm. "Time? There isn't any time. Burn it down."

"You dare! You have no right to burn her things," Fionnseach declared. "You have no right to burn her house, either. Afraig has always paid her rent. She is a good tenant. We're all good tenants. No one is in arrears here."

"As if that matters." Domhnal Sgrios gave her a withering glance. "A landlord has a right to do whatever he wishes with his property. Burn the cottage!" His men moved forward.

"You can't! Marsailidh Bhinneach is still inside," Afraig wailed.

"Hurry up and bring her out."

Palms up, hands pleading, Afraig knelt at his pony's feet. "She's on her sickbed. She can't be moved. Just give her time to recover. Then we'll go. We'll even burn the house when we leave."

"You're leaving now."

"But, sir." She wept. "Marsailidh is old, and frail, and gravely ill."

"Then she has lived too long." Domhnal Sgrios grabbed a burning brand from the closest man and threw it onto the roof. The thatch was ablaze in seconds.

Afraig dived inside the burning cottage, closely followed by Fionnseach. The smoke was terrible, thick and choking. Together they bundled Marsailidh in her bedclothes and dragged her outside. Sparks burned through her blankets and Marsailidh, feverish and dazed, screamed in uncomprehending terror.

Once they had lugged the sick woman to a safe distance, they collapsed, coughing and gasping.

"Is anyone else inside?" Fionnseach asked. She had to yell to be heard over Marsailidh's shrieks. Afraig, hunched over, could only cough.

Fionnseach turned back to the cottage in time to see a terrified cat jump from a blazing window. Somehow Domhnal Sgrios caught it and threw the poor animal back into the flames. He was a monster, first trying to kill a defenseless old woman, and now a harmless little cat. Again the cat leapt for its life, and again the man snatched at it. Fionnseach's seething anger boiled over into unstoppable fury.

With a bloodcurdling howl of rage, she sprang to her feet and charged for his pony, flailing her arms. The successfully startled pony reared and his rider crashed to the ground. The cat sprinted to its freedom in the hills.

Pouncing, knees first, onto fallen Domhnal Sgrios' stomach, Fionnseach hauled back and punched him in the nose. There was blood and screaming, but she was beyond noticing such details. She hit him again and again.

He waved his fists about in blind self-defense. One blow connected square upon her jaw, knocking her backward. She crouched, momentarily stunned by the pain, while he struggled to his feet on unsteady legs. She crawled toward him, ready to pull him down, but by now three of his stunned men had reacted.

Out of the corner of her eye, Fionnseach caught movement. She ducked and suddenly her shoulder shattered with pain as something hard crashed into her back. She collapsed like a felled tree. Domhnal Sgrios' men had truncheons. She writhed, crawled, tried to get away. But the constables continued to cudgel her. Pain hammered her ribs, her back, her arms. Hands grabbed at her. Her dress ripped. She kicked and kicked, and caught several of her attackers with glancing blows, until her bashed legs hurt unbearably and all she could do was curl into a defensive ball. Then her head exploded in a searing burst of agony.

Dazed, she closed her eyes and wished for unconsciousness.

"Think you did for her with that one."

It was one of the men. He sounded uneasy. She held her breath. Maybe they would think her dead and leave.

"Can't have," came the coarse response. "She's just willing to be more friendly now."

She felt a brutish pair of hands fumble through what remained of her skirts and grope her thigh.

"Leave her be. She's dead."

"They'll have you up for unnatural acts," cautioned another voice.

The hands disappeared. It sounded like the men were moving away. Or maybe she was moving away. Everything became silent, which was just as well for she was incredibly tired.

THE CRIMSON FOLD

The next thing Fionnseach knew she was alone. When she raised her head, she could make out the burning wreck of Afraig's cottage and nothing else. No shrieking Marsailidh. No Afraig. No Muirgheal.
No Muirgheal.
Alarm seized Fionnseach's heart. Anything could have happened to the girl. This was her fault. If only she had behaved with more dignity. Her body would not now be racked with pain and poor Muirgheal would not have been left alone.

Perhaps she had tried to get home. Fionnseach looked up the glen in the direction of their cottage. Thick black smoke hung menacingly in the distant air. She struggled to her feet. With any luck, her sister would be at what remained of their cottage. Maybe her cow or one of her little sheep might have escaped as well. There was still hope.

CHAPTER FOURTEEN

Fionnseach turned away from the pile of burning rubble which was all that remained of the only home she had ever known. Nothing was left. All of her animals were gone. And though she repeatedly called out for her, Muirgheal did not answer. She was not there.

It seemed to take ages to drag herself down the hill to the shelter of the village church. It was the center of their community. Her sister might have gone there. Even if she had not, surely there would be others there who could aid her hunt. There had to be people somewhere. But the village already seemed unnaturally empty. Fionnseach tried the church door.

It was locked.

She collapsed on the front step. Her pounding head felt several sizes too large. Fighting back waves of nausea, she tentatively touched her scalp. Her hair was matted and sticky, and she realized it was clotted with her own blood. She laughed. The world had clearly gone mad today.

From her sitting position, she pounded on the church door. It felt good to pound on something. She was not expecting the door to open, but eventually it did. Unfortunately, the man who opened the door was a stranger and his solemn clothing was not that of a priest. This was not right. Fionnseach wanted the village priest.

"Where is Maighstir Fearghas?"

"He is not here. What do you want, child?"

"Where is everyone?"

"Down at the pier, I expect, as they should be." The man frowned at her. "They are behaving as good Christians, not disloyal hussies."

Fionnseach felt her mouth drop open. It took her a stunned moment before she could gasp, "Disloyal?"

"You owe your landlord your obedience. You owe your country your obedience. You have been told the law requires you to evacuate, yet you have the impudence to resist."

"But..."

"Those who fly against the natural order of things tempt the vengeance of Heaven."

"But it can not be right--"

"You presume *you* know what is right?" The man drew himself up to his full height. His glittering eyes glared down his beaked nose at her. "This is being done not only for the betterment of the Highlands, but for the betterment of the people. You should be thankful. The colonel is giving your people a new life in a new country. And you meet his charity with rebellion." He shook his head gravely from side to side and his tone became reproachful. "You are an ungrateful, contrary girl."

"I see no 'betterment', I see destruction, and this charity of yours smells mightily of greed. Something is contrary here, sir, but I do not think it me." The words had left her mouth before she could stop them. Even as Fionnseach heard her voice speaking, she knew it was a mistake.

She raised a defensive arm and cringed back, eyes closed, waiting for a blow. But none came. She snatched a furtive glance at his face. His bulging eyes glared daggers at her from a face that had turned an apoplectic crimson. He made little sputtering noises, and when words finally returned to his tongue, his voice was hoarse with indignation.

"You are perverse, girl, a blight to your own deliverance. Eternal damnation awaits you."

He slammed the door shut. Fionnseach stared at the closed door, wishing she had thought of a clever riposte. But the icy, sick feeling in her stomach was smothering her wits. What if he were right? And where was Muirgheal?

She clambered to her feet and hobbled away, hoping she could make it to the pier.

"Not so pretty now, are you?"

Fionnseach slowly and stiffly turned her head. Domhnal Sgrios stood behind her. A cruel smile twisted his bruised lips.

"You do not look much better." Fionnseach tried to continue her shambling progress but he seized her arm. She glared at him. "You have no honor. May you die unknown and may no one weep for you."

"A true witch's curse. I might have known." He chuckled. "I hear they call you Fionnseach nighean Dubh-sithe. Your mother consorted with the sìthe, did she? Let one get her in the family way?"

Fionnseach looked straight through him and ignored his words. She had heard the jibes before.

He was still talking. "I should have burned you along with your cottage, my sweet witch. I probably could burn you still."

Tiredly she focused her eyes on his. "I do not fear you, Domhnal Sgrios. It is your luck that I am not a man, or I would kill you with my bare fists here and now."

"You're right that it's your bad luck to be a woman. The frontier needs women. Did you know that? They can't wait to get their hands on a woman out there. You'll be mated to some thick-lipped, thick-booted clod."

"A relative of yours, no doubt."

He smacked her across the face.

Blood trickled from the corner of her mouth, but she grinned nonetheless. "I may be going to Hell, but if there is any justice in the world, I shall have company."

Domhnal Sgrios smacked her again, this time knocking her down. "First you're going to the pier."

* * * *

"I heard Aonghas tell Ealasaid that this Canada is a wonderful land," whispered Catrìona Ruadh. "A tree grows there that can supply you with fuel, soap and sugar."

"A single tree can do all that?" Iseabail shook her head in wonder. "Could it be true?" She looked at Fionnseach hopefully.

Fionnseach reached over and gave Iseabail's arm a quick squeeze. "Foreign foods are a constant amazement. Remember the stories of how we of South Uist resisted the potato? And then it turned out to be just as good a food as Clanranald had said."

Catrìona Ruadh clasped her hands together. "Then life truly might be better there."

"Of course it shall." Fionnseach smiled at Catrìona Ruadh and Iseabail and tried to believe her own lie.

Sighing, she shifted her hips. Her legs were going numb with all this sitting, waiting on the pier in the lengthening shadows, waiting to be loaded aboard ship like cargo. And she still had not found Muirgheal. Would she ever see her sister again? She would never see her animals again, nor her home, nor her beloved island. It was too much for her mind to comprehend. She wanted to cry but the tears would not come. She just felt empty and dead.

Murmuring and movement drew her attention further down the pier. That blur was dressed in familiar colors.

"Is ... is that Afraig?" she asked Iseabail.

"Yes."

Fionnseach swallowed. "Where is Muirgheal? Do you see Muirgheal? I last saw her with Afraig."

Iseabail shook her head. "No, Afraig is alone."

A constable shoved Afraig to the back of the queue. Fionnseach waited for him to move away before she painfully, slowly crept on her hands and knees down the queue to Afraig's side.

"You're alive," Afraig gasped. "The saints be praised."

"No, do not hug me, bits of me might break off." Fionnseach tried to sound light. "Have you seen Muirgheal?"

Afraig's eyes filled with tears. "Marsailidh and Muirgheal..." She stifled a sob. "Marsailidh and Muirgheal... Some of Domhnal Sgrios' men..." Afraig looked up as Iseabail joined them. "I survived, but what those brutes did to ... to..." Afraig broke down and wept.

Fionnseach sat and watched her and felt an utter absence of anything. Iseabail put her arm around her shoulders.

"They are dead?" Iseabail asked.

Afraig nodded, still sobbing. "There was nothing ... I could do. I am so ... terribly ... sorry."

"It isn't your fault, Afraig. It's mine," Fionnseach replied quietly.

"Nonsense. Those men are at fault, not anyone here." Iseabail took a deep breath. "Let us be glad for Marsailidh and Muirgheal. They have gone to a better place. And one day we shall all meet again."

Fionnseach felt hot tears streaming down her face. There was such a tightness in her throat, in her chest. But she had to maintain her control. She would never get off the pier if she didn't. She started to crawl away.

"Where are you going?" Iseabail whispered.

"I don't know. But I'm not going to Canada. At least I can thwart Domhnal Sgrios in that."

Iseabail attempted to catch her by the arm. "But what about your father? And Donnachadh? They must be already onboard."

"They can take care of themselves. They certainly don't need my help. They capitulate well enough on their own."

"But where will you go?" asked Afraig between sniffles and hiccupping gasps.

"Edinburgh perhaps. It doesn't really matter."

"You don't expect to get off the island," Iseabail stated.

"Not particularly."

Iseabail frowned disapprovingly. "Suicide won't get you where you want to go."

"True. I'll aim for the mainland then."

Afraig gave Fionnseach a weak smile. "Good luck, Nighean Dubh-sithe. If anyone can get free from here, you can."

* * * *

"So the caoraich mhor has come to the islands at last." The captain nodded grimly, his eyes as doleful as his voice.

THE CRIMSON FOLD

Fionnseach hugged her knees and edgily waited to see what he would do. It had taken her hours of inching farther and farther away down the pier before she was able take advantage of the night to slip over the side and down the rock steps to one of the fishing boats out from Oban that had been temporarily moored at Lochboisdale. She had thought herself well hidden, but she had been mistaken. She had been found at first light.

"Don't worry, girl. I shan't turn you out. I remember the Year of the Burnings, when they came for my village." The captain ran a hand through his gray hair. "I can carry you to the mainland. Beyond that I have no aid to give you."

Fionnseach did not come out on deck until after the boat had sailed clear of the harbor. Then, with great effort, she made her way to the stern. Laboriously avoiding the crew, avoiding the boat's gear, avoiding losing her footing, she finally reached her objective.

She stood while the deck pitched and tossed in the rough water. Steep waves slapped at the hull, sprayed the deck, and saturated the air with the smell of salt. But still she stood in the stern, her feet as steadily planted as her beloved standing stone, and her white-knuckled hands gripping the side such that the wood bit into her palms. Wind whipped her damp hair in thick tangles across her face, obscuring her view of South Uist. But it didn't really matter.

Her weak eyes could not make out the cluster of buildings comprising Lochboisdale, nor the track that led to her cottage, nor the individual hill that she walked every day. It was all one blurred hump, a long, bleary mound rising out of the water and quickly becoming part of the sea and sky in the early morning light. Soon the island would disappear entirely from the reach of her sight.

A sympathetic hand gently pressed her shoulder. "Come away, girl, there's nothing there for anyone anymore." The captain's voice was gravelly but kind.

"No, it's still there," Fionnseach replied. "I just can't see it."

CHAPTER FIFTEEN

Dùn Eideann. Edinburgh. A city of smoke and stone.

Fionnseach huddled in the dank corner that was her bit of the cavernous cellar she shared with three separate families. Like many of the destitute and dispossessed, they had come to Edinburgh in search of work, and unable to make a living wage, were trapped in the poorest of rooming places--the maze of cellars and caves that practically formed a city underground.

A disturbance amongst the prostitutes down the aisle drew her half-hearted attention. The male voices were speaking a foreign language, probably English. She tensed as a hazy but obviously trouser-clad man approached her carrying a small lantern. Yet another Sassenach looking for sport.

"A fine evening to you, daughter of the islands."

He spoke in Gaelic. Fionnseach's heart leapt. He could not be a Sassenach after all. She fought her aching joints to struggle to her feet.

"And to you, sir."

The man held the lantern higher as if he were trying to inspect her by the candlelight. "How much?"

Her insides congealed like cold porridge. Of course. She was such a fool. Men hardly came underground looking to chat.

"You mistake yourself, sir."

She turned away but he caught her by the shoulder before she could leave. His grip hurt. "Leave me be," she ordered, trying to jerk away from him but he held on to her like grim death itself.

"Let us go somewhere more private," he whispered in her ear.

She snorted. As if there were any need. No one down here would prevent him from molesting a perceived prostitute.

"There are plenty of women a great deal more desperate than I." She spat the words out. "Go find one of them and leave an honest girl be."

He laughed. It was an odd, almost tinny, sound. "Still an honest girl, are you? And what brings an honest girl underground?"

"Caoraich mhor."

With what seemed to be one action, he released her shoulder and held his lantern up to illuminate her face. He stared intently into her eyes. She raised her chin and met his gaze with defiance.

"Your village was cleared?" he stated more than asked.

She nodded.

"Tell me."

His expression seemed sympathetic, but Fionnseach continued to glare at him. "Why should a Sassenach care?"

He smiled then. "Even an Englishman can recognize injustice."

Gently he slipped his other hand around her arm, as a gentleman might do to escort a lady to the theatre. He was still looking into her eyes, but now his gaze seemed ... deeper. As if he could stare directly into her brain.

"Come." It was a quiet command yet somehow it was impossible not to obey.

Feeling an unnatural sense of calm, she let him lead her down first one little passage and then another. Perhaps she had finally found a friend. At last, someone who cared enough to give her aid. They were moving away from the more populated areas. He seemed to be looking for a specific place. It was not long before they wandered into one of the lowest arches, damp and long deserted due to the persistent leak of water from above, and the gentleman stopped. Then he opened the lantern and blew out the candle.

Pitch black.

"Neither people nor candlelight shall intrude here." The man's voice seemed to float out of the darkness.

Panic surged through her chest. She *knew* with icy clarity that there was danger in this dark void. But she was unable to make her limbs move. It was as if she were no longer attached to her body.

"I have a gift for you." His voice was closer.

She tried to run, wanted to run, but her body refused.

"This will be the best thing ever to happen to you." He whispered into her ear.

She felt his teeth on her throat. Then there was only blood and suffering, and a slow draining into unconsciousness.

* * * *

There was no pain.

She had been dreaming about something ... she couldn't quite remember what. But it was gone, melted away, and she was floating toward consciousness. Just as her eyelids started to flutter a wave of realization rippled through her. There was no pain.

The constant pounding in her temples was gone. Her back no longer ached. Her fingers were no longer cramped, her legs no longer sore. She inhaled deeply without a stitch in her side, elation filling her heart as the air filled her chest. At long last, *relief*. There was no pain. *How wondrous!* She opened her eyes.

And there was nothing.

Pitch-black nothing.

The breath froze in her throat.

Where was she? Fionnseach began to sit up. Her head whacked into rough stone. She crumpled back and lay still for a moment, stunned not from the pain in her head but at the lack of it. That should have hurt.

Taking a deep breath, she attempted to extend her arms. Her questing fingertips collided with stone everywhere. She lay on stone, with stone directly above her, and on either side of her. Such a wee space. She squeezed a hand over her face, beyond her scalp, and hit stone. She was surrounded by stone. Stones joined with mortar. Not unlike a wall.

Terror gashed her mind. She'd been walled in somewhere. Immured. Buried alive.

How could this be? What had happened? Had Domhnal Sgrios found her? A lump formed in her constricted throat. Her aching chest no longer seemed able to expand properly. She just needed a little more air. Why couldn't she breathe?

Fionnseach clenched her jaw, choking back the frantic screams that ricocheted through her brain. She must not scream. Whoever did this to her could be waiting to hear just that. No screaming. *Do* something. *Think!*

She pointed her toes. Nothing. No wall. She pushed on the stones above her, scrunched her back and dug with her heels, and was rewarded with a few inches of movement.

And still no contact with stone.

She writhed and scrunched. A snail could have gone faster. But she was moving. And there was no impediment. Her body had to have got in here somehow--and if this were the way in, it would also be the way out.

Finally she slid out of her stone grave onto a cold, damp floor. She sat and tried to catch her breath. Where was she now? The room was pitch black. It was impossible to tell its size. She gathered her feet under her and cautiously stood. Then, arms straight out in front of her, she started forward. There must be a door somewhere. Her foot hit an uneven stone and she stumbled in the dark.

"Stop thinking of yourself as human."

Fionnseach froze. She recognized the male voice, but could not place it. Her eyes desperately scanned the blackness. The speaker was out there somewhere. She had to find him before he found her.

Gradually the void started to gain depth. Shapes emerged. What had been nothing but black was now an infinite variety of gray. She could see in the dark. No, more than that, she could see *details.* Details her weak eyes had never before shown her. She could see the thin lines where mortar joined each stone in the wall. She could see the variation in color, the shiny glints or the tiny black specks, in each individual rock. Everything was in sharp focus, and the clarity thrilled her even though what she was looking at was far from thrilling.

"I can see," she whispered in awe.

Bits of memory came trickling back. She was in the underground warren, not too far from the dreary corner she called home. Her body had apparently been stuffed in a fissure behind one of the arches. Her *body.*

That Sassenach had bitten her...

"Of course you can see." The Sassenach's voice was patient, as to a child. "You can see better than anything living could ever imagine."

"What do you mean ... anything living?"

"I have made you a vampire."

"A what?"

"You are undead. Pain can not ravage you. Time can not touch you. You possess superior senses, strength and beauty. Be

THE CRIMSON FOLD

happy--you have won at last. You have triumphed over everything, including death."

"I don't understand..."

And then Fionnseach realized she could not feel her heart.

All this time, and before when she was trapped, her heart should have been pounding. Instead there was a numb void within her chest. She clutched her bodice just beneath her left breast. The thin cloth was cold, as if there were not a trace of difference between her body and the chilly air. She had never felt so comfortable and yet her body was dreadfully still and she was cold to the touch. How could this be?

She backed away, shaking her head. "I'm not dead."

"Correct. You are not dead," he agreed with a smile. "As I said, you are undead. But perhaps I should put it in a context you understand..."

"Have I joined the ranks of the sìthe? Am I part of the Otherworld?"

"No. To be precise, you are closer to the demon realm. You have heard of demons, yes?"

"Are they not minions of the Devil?" Fionnseach gasped. "You are saying... No, no, that can not be."

A demon would never meet Muirgheal in Heaven. A demon would never meet anyone in Heaven. *Never*.

"You have destroyed me." Tears burned her eyes. Her chest hurt. It was a tight cage inside of which a desperate hatred squeezed and raged and tried to escape. "The one thing, the *only* thing I had left ... and now even that's gone. You took the hope of Heaven away from me."

She tried to continue but words abandoned her. Only harsh breath escaped her lips. Bile rose in her throat. Her stomach tightened and twisted. Though her heart could not pound, anger writhed inside her chest like a mad wolf seeking any escape. She hugged herself as if her tightly wrapped arms could prevent her emotions from exploding through her ribcage. This was too much. Too much. The *hatred*. Her brain pounded with it. Her ears buzzed. Darkness swelled within her ... and she knew ... *Wrath*.

It was unbearable.

He was saying something about avoiding stakes and decapitation now. She watched him talk, watched his lips twist in front of his pointed teeth. The teeth that had ... she was tottering on the brink. It would be so easy to give in.

Vengeance. The word resonated in her mind, a frisson so sweet she could almost taste it. It had been too long since she had tasted anything sweet. Life had been so cruel. So unjust. Her murderer spoke more, but the meaning was lost to her. She had been victimized for the last time.

Fionnseach flew across the floor before she even realized she was moving. Her fangs pierced his unsuspecting throat, sinking all the way to her gums. He struggled but to no avail. She sawed through his neck like a guillotine. He exploded and his blood spattered her face.

Stepping back, she blinked and wiped her eyes. His dust and blood covered her, evidence of his destruction. Evidence of her sin. She threw back her head, and did not immediately recognize that the anguished scream echoing endlessly down the stone corridors was her own.

CHAPTER SIXTEEN

Edinburgh, Present Day

Fiona's fists were clenched so tightly she could feel her nails biting into her palms. Joan was standing very still, her mouth ever so slightly open. She blinked several times, then she just stared at Fiona with hard and distant eyes. Fiona swallowed. This was not a good sign.

Finally, her eyes still drilling into Fiona, Joan spoke. "You're telling me you're a vampire."

"Aye, she is at that," Rory interjected cheerfully.

Both women told him to shut up.

Joan shook her head. "This is *so* not happening." The hand that held the mug of coffee she had prepared while Fiona told her story began to tremble. She thrust the mug onto the counter beside Fiona and backed away. "I *trusted* you."

"But nothing's changed," Fiona whispered.

Joan glared at her. It was a frightening, baleful glare. Fiona had the sudden, icy realization that she was now what Joan considered a viable target.

"But I've done naught but helped ye. And I havenae ... I have tried to be as human as possible since I met ye."

"That's certainly true," Rory commented.

Joan spun on him. "You knew?" she asked accusingly.

"Nae," he protested with a grin. "Do ye think I'd've been wasting my time tryin' to convince her to like vampires if I kenned she was one?"

Joan snorted. "Good point."

"There's more," he added.

She raised an eyebrow. "Oh?"

Fiona swore softly and jumped down from the counter. Joan took a step back. She did so to have both vampires in her field of view, Fiona knew. She smiled sadly to herself, for she had got down from the counter for better self-defense, knowing precisely what Rory was about to say and Joan's probable reaction. How quickly trust evaporates.

"She's not just any vampire," Rory continued.

Fiona braced herself.

"She is the Fury."

Joan's lips remained pressed in a tight, thin frown as her gaze shifted from Rory to Fiona.

"I never meant to be," Fiona said softly.

"When does this suck-fest stop?" Joan's voice was flat.

"I lost everything in the Clearances. And 'twasnae me alone." Fiona's words tumbled out in a rush. "Go ye to the Highlands today and be amazed at the emptiness. This vast, untouched wilderness isnae empty because 'twas never settled. 'Tis empty because the people who lived here were taken away. The land is a ghost ship, waiting for its people to return. But the people will never come back. And the land sits, forlornly waiting. Many recognize the mournful beauty of the Highlands--few understand 'tis the majesty of a tomb. Surely ye can appreciate my desire for revenge."

"Revenge?"

"I hunted down Domhnal Sgrios and his men, one by one. Later, I set out to be the bane of every murderer, abuser, usurer, and extortionist in existence, be they human or demon. I hunted them and I destroyed them. And when they were human, I fed on them. I dinna ken who came up with the name. It wasnae me. I think 'twere five years before I realized the stories of the Fury were tales of my deeds."

Joan slowly shook her head. "You totally deceived me. This is ... this is ... I can't believe this. I thought you were human. I thought you were my friend." Her voice bristled with a strident edge of anger.

"Dinna get your knickers in a twist. 'Tis not like she enjoys herself being a vampire," Rory remarked.

"So she should have destroyed herself and done us all a favor," snapped Joan.

Fiona rolled her eyes. "Och, aye, like suicide would get me into Heaven."

"What're you smoking?" Joan exclaimed incredulously. "You're a demon. You're never going to Heaven."

"But are ye certain? 'Tis quite a tormenting conundrum," Fiona replied. "By definition, I'm soulless. So that begs the question, where is my soul? Is it trapped until I am destroyed? Or is it already in Heaven? Philosophically, my murderer shouldnae control the fate of my soul. My actions in life should determine its final destination. Therefore my soul shouldnae be trapped. So then, say that my soul is in Heaven by now. Where does that leave me--the me that I am currently? If I am destroyed, does this consciousness join my soul in Heaven? Or do I--the me talking to ye right now--go to Hell? 'Twould be some consolation to think that there is probably another me enjoying Heaven, but 'twill be small comfort if I am enduring the tortures of Hell. Unless Hell really is being trapped in a room with some Frenchmen, in which case, as ye would say, 'been there, done that'."

Everyone stared at Fiona in silence.

"I've had a lot of time to think about this," she added.

"Apparently," commented Joan.

There was a long pause, during which Fiona watched Joan clench and unclench her fists.

"So ... what am I supposed to do now? Accept that you are an okay sort of vampire?" Joan's voice dripped with ice. "I have a sacred duty to kill your kind. What part of that sounds negotiable?"

Fiona took a deep breath. "Right now, ye need me. Samhain is tonight. Ye mayn't want my help, but ye need it just the same."

Joan scowled and shook her head. "Out of my way," she ordered.

Fiona and Rory made room for her and Joan strode out of the kitchen.

"You two will stay here," Joan continued. "Do research on ... you know what? I don't even care. Whatever. Just stay here. Because if I see you on the street..." Joan veered for the nearest wall and punched it, leaving a fist-sized, crumpled dent with little cracks radiating away from it.

Rory whistled. "No need to fall out with the walls."

Joan swore viciously at him.

"Joan," Fiona began but she interrupted her.

"Don't even! Don't even try." Joan headed for the door. "You're *undead* to me now."

* * * *

Euan's chairs were chic and modern and all, but they were not quite squashy enough for a good, dramatic throwing-yourself-into, Joan reflected as she winced and shifted position.

"You will *so* not believe what happened," she called to Euan.

Euan returned from the kitchen carrying two glasses full of an unrecognizable liquid. "Snake bite?"

"Excuse me?"

"Equal parts cider and lager with a spot of raspberry cordial. You looked like you needed it." He smiled as he handed her a glass. "And if *you* need it, I'll wager I need it, too. Now..." He sat down opposite her and took a swig before asking, "What happened?"

"Fiona is a vampire." Joan downed several gulps of her drink. It wasn't near the disgust-a-thon she thought it would be. She glanced at Euan.

THE CRIMSON FOLD

He was looking genuinely shocked. "I say ... Your friend Fiona?"

"My ex-friend Fiona, yeah. She's a vampire. And get this, she even told me how she became one--like it would matter to me or something..." Joan broke off.

She felt like she was standing on top of a skyscraper, peering over the edge, watching the giant, black, gooey blob of her swirling emotions boil and inexorably rise up the sides of the building. Joan took a deep breath. She had to keep it down, stay in control.

Euan shook his head. He frowned sympathetically. "What will you do?"

Playing for time, she emptied her glass. Her tongue squirmed back in her mouth at the peculiar mix of flavors and she grimaced. She glanced at Euan. He was watching her, expecting an answer. She sighed. There was only one answer she could give. "I should slay her."

"I meant, how does this affect your mission? Didn't you tell me something big is happening tonight?"

"I should still slay her."

He sipped his drink. "You can not be feeling as nonchalant as you sound."

She shrugged. "Why not?"

"The two of you seemed close."

"Yeah, well..."

Carefully he rolled his glass between his palms. "You must be rather cut-up..."

"You don't say?" she snarled. "My brain is like some wacked Möbius strip, just over and over, stuff we've been through, stuff we've done together, and all of it meant nothing. *Nothing*! It was nothing but lies. I thought she was my best friend, and here she was one of my mortal enemies. I actually *liked* her. A foul, heinous, demonic murderer. It makes me sick..." Joan paused, the physical revulsion too much for her to continue.

She had valued her friendship with that fiend. Actually enjoyed her company. How could she not have realized? Shouldn't she have a sixth sense about this sort of thing? And Fiona was probably snickering behind her back the whole time, the deceitful little bitch.

"Joan?"

"Yes?" she snapped, her attention jerking back to Euan. His eyebrows were crooked with concern. "I'm fine. No big. It's all *mucho* irrelevant, anyway." Joan placed her empty glass on the end table with a decided thunk. "She's a vampire. I slay her."

Euan theatrically rolled his eyes. "Discriminate much?"

"What?"

"I am attempting to communicate in your vernacular."

"No, I meant, what's up with that? I don't discriminate. I treat all vampires equally. I destroy them all."

"And what if what's equal is not the same as what's fair?"

She groaned. "Don't give me this."

"Your Fiona--"

"She's not *my* Fiona."

"She's spent a fair bit of time fighting the forces of evil at your side, hasn't she? Perhaps she truly is..."

"Is what? One of the white hats? So what? She's a vampire. It's my duty to terminate her with extreme prejudice."

"And you have no difficulty with that?"

"Where would the world be if my family just abandoned their duty whenever it got tough?"

"That's not what I'm saying..."

She interrupted him. "I don't remember my grandmother. My father lasted longer than most, I'm told, but he died for the cause just the same. What do their sacrifices mean if I don't..." She stood and paced back and forth in front of her chair. "Look, we protect humanity. That's what we do. We *protect*. Bottom line is that we don't have to be fair or just or whatever. We must do what we have to, to keep the world safe."

"If you sacrifice justice, what exactly is the world safe from?"

She snorted. "Don't go all English on me."

Euan smiled. "Yes, well, let us leave aside the slaying your friend. Tell me what happens tonight."

"Right. Okay." Joan sat and took a deep breath. "Basically, there's this totally old vampire named Miklos and he's got this thing called the Andromache and it's supposed to rise at Samhain."

"What is going to rise?"

"Good question. We don't actually know what it *is*, we only know it's called the Andromache. Okay, so since Samhain doesn't even begin until sunset, and it usually takes a bit for a good hex to get rolling, I'm assuming this 'rising' deal will occur at midnight. Especially because, hey, isn't midnight always the time? So theoretically we must locate and stop Miklos before midnight."

"Or..."

"Or this Andromache rising will trigger the end of reality."

"The end of reality." Euan stated each word very slowly.

"Yup."

"The 'something bad' you alluded to when you borrowed my papers is in actual fact the end of reality?"

"Yup."

"You might have mentioned this to me a bit sooner." He sounded slightly irritated.

"Yeah, well, evidently I am totally lame in the knowing-who-to-trust department."

THE CRIMSON FOLD

Euan stood. For a moment, he looked like he was going to speak then instead he turned and strode the length of the room, his hands stuffed into his trouser pockets.

"You were searching for icons of True Belief, as I recall." His back was toward her and he did not turn around as he spoke.

"Yeah, Fiona had ... we had some idea that such a thingie might stop the Andromache from rising. Guess now I could just go ahead and let it rise and kick its ass."

"Not necessarily." Euan turned around. "I know where one of the most powerful icons in the world is said to be located."

"Oh yeah?"

"Yes."

"And you didn't tell us this before now because...?"

He folded his arms. "Because it is a deeply private, well-guarded family secret, never to be mentioned unless in the most dire emergency--which you never said this was. And..." He sighed. "...Because I did not honestly believe in its existence. Not its literal existence."

"What do you mean? What icon are we talking about here?"

"You must understand. My following in Uncle Hamish's footsteps was never on the cards. Mad uncle Hamish was...well...*mad* as far as I was concerned. His stories were just fairy stories. But if vampires and revvers are real ... then I reckon this must be real in the literal sense as well."

"What icon?" Joan repeated impatiently.

"When you first came to my flat, do you recall the initials you saw following my name?"

"On your letterhead, yeah. K.C. You said it was for Keeper of the Chapel."

"The chapel in question is Rosslyn Chapel." He waited, eyes bright, an expectant look on his face.

She shook her head. "That means absolutely zilch to me. Why does Rosslyn Chapel need a keeper?"

"Because the Holy Grail is hidden there."

Joan's mouth opened but her mind went blank. She finally gasped, "The Holy Grail. As in the actual Holy Grail?"

"No, as in the counterfeit one I made a fortnight ago. Yes, the actual one, what do you take me for?"

She frowned. "Wait, so you didn't believe in the Holy Grail? You're a deacon, why wouldn't you believe?"

"Of course I believe in what Holy Grail *represents*," he answered impatiently. "I just never truly believed the tangible object was in my family's chapel!"

"You're shocked."

"I should say. This is rather like telling me that not only does Nessie exist, but she's in the back garden."

* * * *

Rory picked up a book from the library table, then tossed it down with a thump. "Joan so much as told ye to get your cards, why are ye still working for her?"

An exasperated moan escaped Fiona lips. "Are we forgetting the end of reality or are we just getting up my nose?"

She continued to flip through the oversize pages of one of her larger, leather-bound tomes.

"What are ye looking for?"

"It suddenly struck me ... do ye remember the Flodden Wall?"

He grinned. "Little before my time, pet."

"Well, obviously, but ye ken how it contained Edinburgh and led to the Underground City. I was thinking on it when I had to journey underground to rescue ye. The Netherbow gate..."

"Was called the World's End," Rory finished for her, his words quick and his tone keen. "Where's that prophecy?" He shuffled through the pile of papers on the table.

"Over here." She picked up the sheet and quoted the first line, "Through mercy at the end of the world."

He nodded. "So ye are thinking the 'end of the world' bit refers to more than just the result of Miklos' plan to rend the veil between the worlds?"

"I am thinking the phrase is meant as geographical location as well as a temporal condition. I am thinking the ceremony Miklos is planning may have to be held at that particular point. Because..." She went back to flipping through the oversized book. "Here!"

"And that is?"

"A map of mystical convergences. There is a doorway on World's End Close."

He chuckled. "If ever there were a more apt name..."

But a little shiver of warning was wriggling at the back of Fiona's brain. "Did I tell ye about the veil?"

"Hmmm?" Rory sounded indifferent but he had frozen in place.

"I canna remember ... did I tell ye about the rending of the veil?"

He shrugged. "Ye must have done."

Fiona tried to calm herself. Just because she did not recall telling him did not mean it had not happened. So much had happened of late. She must have told him. Or perhaps he had seen one of her translations. That was the answer. That had to be it. "Of course."

She stared down at the map in front of her. Everything was silence.

Fiona swallowed. "Aye ... ummm ... the prophecy's 'Belief' line is still troublesome." Despite her best effort, her voice sounded stilted and unnatural. "And I still canna find the date for..."

Rory interrupted her, his voice flat. "I kenned that bit about the veil before I met ye."

Fiona clasped her hands together. An icy, sick feeling was spreading through her stomach. "Did ye?"

"Aye. And ye dinna need to search for the prophecy's age anymore. I can tell ye Miklos' age."

"Can ye now," she remarked, still staring down at the map. "Might I take it then that ye are on the other side?" It was not really a question.

"Not anymore."

She risked glancing at him. Rory's expression seemed decidedly troubled.

"I owed him my allegiance." He laughed, but it was a caustic sound. "I reckon Miklos feels as betrayed by me as your Joan feels betrayed by ye."

"Why did ye owe him?" she asked quietly.

Rory raised his hand. His long fingers paused on his throat, then he dismissively ran his hand through his hair. "Miklos created me."

CHAPTER SEVENTEEN

"Drummossie Moor was nae place to be that morn. Sleet pelted our faces. We were tired from a night march, hadnae eaten in two days, and the wind from the North Sea felt bitter cold." Rory slowly pushed one of the amber table lamps into line with the oversized book in front of Fiona. "The MacLarens fought alongside the Stewarts of Appin." A ghost of a smile appeared on his lips at the memory. "We were aye fearsome. When we charged the government troops--straight into their muskets and smoking cannons..." His eyes darkened. "The Highland charge hadnae changed in a thousand years for good reason. We were undefeated in battle. But this moor by Culloden House was flat-- and deceptive. 'Twas completely unsuited for us and perfect for them. We had a long way to charge across ground that wasnae as level as ye'd think. A ridge put paid to our line, splitting our charge. And the red-coated devils had loaded their cannon with grapeshot. Great numbers of us were cut to pieces in that hail of metal bits before we had got anywhere near the government lines."

Rory shook his head. "The din from the guns was enough to drive ye mad and the smoke that thick ye could choke on it. Grapeshot fractured my left thigh. Still I advanced. I was lucky-- my sword engaged the enemy. I broke through the infantry to the second line before a bayonet opened my scalp and I was blinded by my own blood. More bayonets stabbed my arm and my stomach…eventually I dropped but didnae die straight away. I lay in agony in the heather and listened to what became the tumult of our brave laddies' retreat." He swallowed before continuing, "The red-coats combed the moor for rebel injured after the battle."

"Aye," Fiona said grimly. She well knew the stories of Culloden's aftermath. Any wounded person they found upon the battlefield--man or boy--the government soldiers bayoneted or shot or beat to death where they lay. Where a group of wounded had taken refuge in a nearby byre at Old Leanach, the government troops had deliberately blocked the door and burned the Red Barn down with the wounded trapped inside. Soldiers had told injured prisoners they were being taken to a surgeon and instead took them to a firing squad. And when the dragoons had chased retreating clansmen, they indiscriminately slaughtered neighboring civilians, women, and little children as well.

"Not far from me, I heard men's voices asking '*Are you Jacobite?*', and then the faint answer, '*Aye*', followed by hideous … *hideous* cries." Rory closed his eyes tightly. When he opened them again, his gaze possessed thoughtful cast. "The red-coats who butchered us that day had souls. I dinna see how souls can be the only access to righteousness. But ye will be wanting my story, not philosophy. Where was I?"

"Incapacitated and forced to listen to the slaughter of our bonnie laddies."

"Aye. Presently a deep voice spoke above and behind my head, where I could not see my executioner--*the coward*, I thought. He asked me the question, '*Are you Jacobite?*' I proudly answered, '*Aye*', and waited with gritted teeth for the final bayonet. I was determined not to scream if I could at all help it. I didnae wish to give them the satisfaction. But there was nae bayonet. Instead the voice asked, '*Do you wish to die this day?*' I think I swore at him." Rory chuckled. "Ye must recollect, I was falling murky from loss of blood. The deep voice asked if I would like to keep on killing. And I could only think of the battle and how it all shouldnae have ended this way when we had almost taken London, and through my gritted teeth I declared, '*Aye*'. I raised my arm, reaching for the disembodied voice, and the last thing I remember clearly was something with talons clasping my upraised hand." He shook his head and sighed. "As ye ken, the Pacification of Scotland followed Culloden. But I nae longer cared. I was a vampire."

"Ye didnae care what happened to your clan?"

"Miklos was my clan now, and I was his fearsome warrior."

"Which entailed…"

"Quite a bit of mayhem, aye." He frowned sadly. "Shall this be a problem between us?"

Fiona sighed. "'Twould be a bit pot-and-kettle of me. According to Joan, we are equally black." She sighed again. "So ye were against Joan and me--"

"Only at the beginning," He hastily interrupted. "And as I recall ye never believed me about being on your side, did ye?"

Her lips quirked in a small smile. "Not particularly."

"And I'm a goodie now. So ... all's well that end's well?" He smiled hopefully at her.

"Aye." She returned his grin. "Returning to Miklos, then... He fed off the battlefield before nightfall?"

Rory nodded. "Miklos can walk in daylight, though his powers are much reduced. However, he doesnae get out much at all anymore. For the past five years he has preferred to keep to Andromache's side, or as close as he can be to her on this side of the veil, her time being so near."

"*Her* time?"

"Aye, Andromache is a she, not a what. An ancient vampire."

"Rather like Miklos, then."

"She is Miklos' mate."

Fiona raised her eyebrows. "Miklos had a mate? What happened to her?"

Rory shook his head. "I never met her. I dinna ken how she was trapped on the other side of the veil. I always reckoned she attempted an apocalyptic spell and it went pear-shaped."

Fiona nodded. "Aye, that isnae unlikely when conjuring with dark forces and negative magick."

"It happened long ago, when they were young and inexperienced. We willnae have that benefit today. Miklos is powerful and determined. He has been awaiting the proper conjunction of stars and forces--all those magick bits and bobs--to occur at Samhain for a very long time now."

"Speaking of time... His age?"

"Miklos harks back to early Christianity. A significant Christian icon should work against him. But it must be right significant, for he's dead powerful."

"One of the older icons from the High Kirk should do it, then, if it can be done." Fiona sighed. "We shall need all our strength for tonight. I reckon 'tis time to break out my emergency blood ration."

"Emergency blood ration?" Rory smiled, amused. "Why dinna ye share this with me earlier?"

"Because 'tis only to be used in the most dire emergency."

"And because it means admitting your vampire nature?"

"Insightful bastard. Get to the kitchen and get pouring."

He stood. "In the refrigerator, is it?"

"Aye. 'Tis the dark brown bottle in the far back labeled 'Haggis'."

Rory crooked his eyebrows in confusion. "Haggis doesnae come in bottles."

Fiona grinned. "Aye, but Joan didnae ken that. She simply believes in leaving sheep innards well enough alone."

* * * *

"Excellent!" Joan clapped her hands together. Finally they were getting somewhere. "How far away is Rosslyn?"

"The village is Roslin," Euan corrected her. He was slouching against the wall next to the window and did not look anywhere near as excited as she felt. "The chapel is Rosslyn."

"I don't hear a difference."

"Nevermind. It's a mere jaunt south from Edinburgh. Depending on traffic."

"So we just zip down to the chapel, grab the grail, and we're golden." Joan stood and briskly started for the door.

"It is not quite that simple," he called after her.

"What, you think the traffic's that bad?" She turned.

He had not moved. "No, it isn't that."

"Don't tell me you don't have a car."

"In point of fact, I don't..."

"Of all the ... How can you not have a car?"

"Have you seen the price of petrol here?" he retorted lightly. "But that's not the reason either."

"Well, fast forward and get to the reason."

Euan walked over to one of his bookshelves and pulled out a colorful, coffee-table-sized hardback. He found the page he wanted and held out the volume toward her. "It's not like the Holy Grail is kept out on a shelf."

Joan strode over and took the book. It was open to two full-page, black and white photographs. On the left was a photo of an ornate stone column with flowers or leaves or some such design running up and down it. On the right was a photo of an even more elaborate column. On this one, flower and leaf vines looped in diagonal swirls up and down the column like ribbons. It didn't seem possible that such flowing, delicate garlands could be made of stone.

"They're both nice, but that one on the right's just incredible." Joan shifted her hold on the book so she could trace the path of one of the twisting vines with her fingertip.

Euan nodded. "Notice how the vines are issuing from the mouths of eight dragons coiled around the base of the pillar? Those are the eight dragons of Neifelheim. They guard Yggdrasil, the tree that binds together heaven, earth, and hell in Norse mythology."

"Okay, binding reality together, that's what we want. What's the problem?"

"The grail is hidden inside that pillar."

"Inside as in really *inside* the column?"

"Inside as in we shall have to destroy the pillar to get it," Euan answered gravely.

"I suppose the pillar is like five hundred years old or something."

"Tad older than that, actually."

"And it's a national treasure."

"It is certainly a family treasure."

"Ah, but if reality is destroyed chances are no one's going to care about art." Joan closed the book and handed it back to him. "When you're saving the world you've got to expect casualties."

"Such an endearingly bloodthirsty attitude." Euan tucked the book under his arm. "Or, alternatively, we could find a spell to remove it without damage."

"Fiona..." Joan cut herself off. Fiona might know a special transportation spell but what of it? She wasn't part of the team anymore.

"Are we going to ask Fiona about a spell?" Euan's voice sounded clear and completely unruffled. Joan wondered how he did it. Her stomach was tightening in knots.

She crossed her arms. "No."

He raised his eyebrows. "Why not?"

"What d'ya mean? Why would we?"

"I think we owe it..."

"To posterity?" she interrupted, her voice sharp with scorn. "Just to save some artsy column?"

"No, to Fiona. I would have thought that you at least owed it to Fiona to give her a chance to prove she's not evil."

Joan wanted to haul off and punch something. Anything. The man was deliberately not listening. Fiona was a vampire. She didn't ever want to see Fiona again. That sounded childish. Joan released an aggravated growl. She couldn't allow her feelings, for or against Fiona, to interfere with her work. They were trying to save reality. They must take advantage of all the resources they had.

"Okay. *For you*, we'll go ask about a spell. Maybe we can get her to zap the Grail straight over here, no harm to the pillar, no need to drive. We'll go and we'll do that." Joan uncrossed her arms. Her fists were clenched so tightly they hurt. Gingerly, she stretched her fingers. "But I'm not making any promises about not slaying her afterward."

* * * *

Rory spun one of the smaller hardback books on the smooth tabletop. It twirled very nicely. "We've got '*the end of the world*' as the place as well as the action. We're thinking a Christian icon, the older the better, should work for the '*True Belief*' to '*forever hold*' Miklos. What are we hanging about for?"

Fiona closed her eyes and massaged her temples with her fingertips. "The two middle lines. '*Redemption's final play unfolds*' and '*while sinful selflessness shall save*'. They mean something important or they wouldnae be part of the prophecy."

She heard a slight scuffing as he spun the book around again.

"Perhaps ye should fetch Joan," she suggested, her eyes still closed. "We shall need her or the Sassenach to handle the icon." She opened her eyes and gazed across at Rory. "I fancy Euan kens which pieces in the High Kirk's collection are the oldest."

"I'm nae fetching Joan." He crossed his arms. "She's as like to slay me as look at me."

Fiona sighed. He wasn't wrong. And she was bleakly aware that Joan would have much the same attitude toward her.

"Never mind. Help me with this. It might better our chances of success."

Rory leaned forward and looked at the paper in front of her.

"Right then. What is both sinful and selfless?" He frowned thoughtfully. "Sounds mutually exclusive. A sinful, selfless act."

Fiona felt like first light had caught her unawares. Shock and excitement surged through her tense frame and she sucked in a quick breath. "I have it!"

"What?"

"Suicide. 'Tis a sin and by committing it ye are self-less. Ye lack your self."

"Due to being dead. I follow." He smiled. "All we need to do is find a suicidal bugger and relocate him to the ritual site."

Fiona's mind was racing. Her eyes repeatedly scanned the little paragraph of the prophecy. There was more. Her initial exhilaration was turning into icy cold lumps within her stomach.

She swallowed. "Nae, wait, 'tisnae just any suicide. Suicide by one who needs '*redemption*'. From the line above. '*Redemption's final play unfolds*'." She glanced at Rory.

He was staring at her quietly. Then he stood. His body had an unnatural quality of stillness about it and his black eyes were unreadable. "Nae, lassie."

"Nae, what?" She widened her eyes and tried to sound ingenuous.

"I ken what ye are thinking."

Fiona shifted in her chair. She had the uncomfortable feeling that he was right. "What am I thinking?"

"Who is more need of redemption than a vampire?" he answered darkly. "Ye are thinking it needs a vampire to commit suicide."

She nodded with grim determination.

"Ye shan't be doing that." There was a dangerous edge of warning to Rory's statement.

She rose from the table. "How can I not?"

"Fionnseach..."

"I am the Fury. If I can kill to protect the innocent, I can die to protect the innocent."

"*Ye* need do nothing. Even I ken enough of strategy to realize ye never sacrifice the queen when ye can sacrifice a pawn. *I* shall go."

A stab of horror pierced her heart. "Nae, ye canna ... I couldnae live with myself if ye were destroyed."

"D'ye think I've not got the same feelings?"

He sounded exceedingly earnest. Why was he making this so difficult for her? Fiona felt tears rising in her eyes. She concentrated on staring at her rows and rows of books along the library walls. No, wasn't making the problem, he was the problem. She had trusted no one, not even Joan, with her confidences and her true nature until him. He knew precisely what she was and he loved her regardless. Until him, she had had nothing to lose.

She swiped at her eyes. "This is a pointless argument. Redemption has always been my goal, not yours. Ye ken quite well that I must do this."

"I willnae let ye."

"Ye canna stop me."

"If needs must, I will."

"Och, aye?" Fiona started to step forward, but hesitated as Rory continued to block her way. "Let me pass. I dinna wish to harm ye."

"We're vampires, pet." He chuckled. "We're not opposed to a bit of violence."

In one swift movement, Fiona ducked past Rory but he caught her by the wrist. She swung at his face. He dodged and did not release her.

"Ye must let me go," she growled, kicking at his shins, an attack which Rory ignored with an irritating excess of nonchalance.

"Never. We'll stand here 'til reality ends," he replied, his eyes blazing into hers. "Ye arenae falling on your sword, not for toffee."

Fiona's skin began to tingle with the approach of sunset. Samhain was beginning. She could linger no longer. Violently she jerked her imprisoned arm and when he again did not release her, she looked down at his long fingers crushing her captured wrist.

"Och, that hurts," she whimpered.

For a mere second, Rory's grip loosened. It was an involuntary reaction to her sound of pain. She knew he would react so--she was relying on it. Awareness of her trick dawned in his eyes even as his fingers relaxed but it was too late. In the instant before he could restore his grip, she had twisted away.

She leapt on top of the table. With a string of words more like a shriek than a sentence, she flung her hands out to him, fingers straight and stiff. The air seemed to ripple and shimmer and suddenly his legs collapsed beneath him. He crashed to the floor, joints loose, limbs unable to move.

"What have ye done?"

Fiona landed beside him with feline grace.

"Cheated." Her eyes glinted with wry mirth, but her husky voice almost broke upon the word.

CHAPTER EIGHTEEN

Her image vanished as the world faded to black. It was some sort of paralyzing spell. He was being sucked into unconsciousness. Rory struggled against the void that threatened to overwhelm his senses. Epithets of protest swarmed through his brain, to no avail. He felt Fiona caress his cheek, but he could not see her. His heavy eyelids refused to open.

"I must be off now."

Dinna leave me. Not like this.

Not like this.

"For what 'tis worth…ye are the one thing in my god-forsaken life that makes me wish this duty wasnae mine." She sighed. The sound was edged with both resignation and anger. "And that wish shall undoubtedly render me unworthy of redemption. As always I am a blight to my own deliverance."

In the following silence, he felt her soft lips alight upon his mouth. It was a chaste kiss, reverential. Like at the end of a fairy story. Only he would not awaken. There was to be no 'happily ever after'. This was nothing but a dismal nightmare. His mind screamed at the injustice.

Her breath caressed his ear. "Mind how ye go."

The whisper held just a hint of a smile. He could imagine her valiantly attempting a grin.

Then Rory could no longer sense her presence. She was gone. It was like one of his own limbs had torn itself off and left him. Wretched waves of despair began to drown what consciousness he had left. The words *I love ye* died on his soundless lips. There was only oblivion.

* * * *

Joan had brought her key this time. But Fiona's flat was dark and eerily quiet.

"I don't believe Fiona is home," Euan commented as he followed Joan across the threshold.

"Thank you, Mister Obvious." Joan snapped on the nearest light switch. The Gothic living room was empty. So was the

THE CRIMSON FOLD

kitchen, apart from the dirty pans and plates from this morning. That seemed ages ago.

A quick search revealed an unconscious Rory in the library but no Fiona anywhere.

Joan stood, her hands resting on her hips, and surveyed the vampire. "He doesn't seem to be injured." She gave him a swift kick in the ribs.

"What, so you're trying to give him an injury?" Euan sounded appalled.

Joan shrugged. "We need him awake." She drew back her foot again.

"Hold off, let's think about this logically. Vampires don't faint and it's just after sunset, so if he's unconscious it must be a spell, correct?"

She shrugged again. "Your point?"

"With all these books here I am certain we can find a counter spell to awaken him. It should be far more effective than kicking him."

Rory groaned and rolled on his side.

"Or we can just wait for the spell to wear off," Euan finished evenly.

The vampire sat up like he was a rusted metal folding chair. One hand went to his forehead, then he squinted up first at Euan then at Joan. "Fiona?" His voice was hoarse.

"She's gone," Joan replied.

Rory's face grew gray at the news. Joan was mildly surprised that that was even possible.

He hefted himself to his feet with another groan. "We must go after her."

She raised her eyebrows. "Why?"

"What d'ye mean, why? She's gone t' off herself."

"Good riddance."

She started to turn away but Rory deliberately stepped into her line of sight.

"We have t' gang after the lass," he demanded, his voice like steel.

"Hardly. If she wants to run off, that's her business. We have to save reality."

He snorted impatiently. "She's away to defeat the baddie. Isnae that your job? Ye should be there."

Joan clenched her fists. She had had just about enough from this undead thing. Why she was even still listening when she should be slaying…

"Does no one believe in details anymore?" Euan sounded annoyed. "I thought we needed an icon to defeat this Miklos person."

"Vampire," corrected Joan.

"So why is Fiona killing herself?" Euan finished, looking at Rory.

"She believes the prophecy calls for a vampire to commit suicide in order to stop Andromache's rising."

"And Andromache is--"

"Miklos' mate."

Euan smiled. "Well, I must say, there's hope for everyone, isn't there?"

"To get to where Miklos is performing the ceremony we must pass through a mystical doorway, a vortex, on World's End Close," Rory continued. "We dinna have time to hang about."

"That's what I say. Let's go watch."

"Solidarity, Joan." Euan looked again at Rory. "And do we still need an icon?"

"Aye. Fiona thought we could stop Miklos with an icon from the High Kirk, until she came up with this daft suicide idea. Fetch one and meet me at World's End Close."

"It is the fetching that might be a bit sticky. We came to inform Fiona of a very special icon that should resoundingly solve our Miklos problem, but it is sited some little distance away."

Rory nodded. "Tell me. Speed and distance arenae difficulties for a vampire."

"Combusting on the doorstep is," Joan commented.

Rory looked questioningly at Euan.

"The icon is inside Rosslyn Chapel," Euan explained. "It's the Holy Grail. And before you ask, the answer is yes, I am speaking of the actual Holy Grail."

The vampire grinned. "I wasnae going to question ye."

"So you see how you have no hope in Hell of getting anywhere near it," declared Joan.

"We shall see." Rory turned to Euan. "With the Grail, we shall be able to defeat Miklos without Fiona sacrificing herself. Give me the chance to fetch it--I'll need but thirty minutes. Ye will still have enough time, if I dinna return, to fetch it y'selves."

Joan rolled her eyes. "Waste-ola. He's just going to disintegrate."

"If I canna save Fiona, then I *should* cease to exist," growled Rory. He turned to face Joan. She was almost nonplussed by the intensity of his unwavering gaze. Little red flecks burned deep within his eyes. "And I tell ye now, with Euan to witness, that if in our battle with Miklos Fiona is destroyed and I am not, then I will come to ye unarmed and ye must slay me. I ask here and now for your pledge that ye will."

"Of all the…" Joan began.

"Why?" asked Euan quietly.

Rory glanced at him. "If Fiona is destroyed, then Joan must slay me. For I willnae let Fiona suffer Hell alone."

* * * *

In the gloom of the close one might almost have missed it. The tall, red brick walls of the buildings confining the narrow path, despite being marred by periodic cracks and blackened windows, nevertheless presented a continuous, nondescript front that seemed to go on forever as well as up to shut out the sky. But Fiona knew what she was looking for.

Halfway down the close, above the lintel of a boarded-up door and recessed from the bricks surrounding it, lurked a stone beam. Carved letters undulated across it. Time had worn their curves, but they were still legible. *Lord Be Merciful To Us*.

Mercy at World's End Close. This would be it, the vortex she was looking for. Once she passed through, she would find Miklos on the other side, performing his ceremony to raise Andromache.

Fiona's nervous fingers fidgeted upon the thick, wooden stake clasped in her fist. It was the first time she had availed herself of one of the many defensive gifts Joan had pressed upon her. The first time, and it would be the last as well. The smooth feel of the wood was rather disconcerting. Or perhaps it was simply the use to which she knew it would be put. Could she really stake herself? She hoped the adrenaline of the moment would strengthen her strike. She would get only the one chance. Miklos was unlikely to give her another go. One chance to get past Miklos, get within the circle of his ceremony, and stake herself. She was Fionnseach the Fury. She could do this.

Fiona glanced toward the open, street end of the close. The pedestrians were taking no notice of her. She was too far down the unlit close to be seen by them, most likely. Of course, they had been no more interested in her when she had been strolling through the medieval streets with a stake scarcely concealed between her inner forearm and side. Edinburgh was a city accustomed to eccentrics.

Quietly, Fiona began to chant in Latin. It took several stanzas before a breeze formed. As her voice gradually grew louder, so did the breeze strengthen, ruffling her hair and forcing her to squint. Then a weak, blue glow started at the corners of the stone beam. It rapidly spread across the beam, growing brighter and brighter, the lettering standing out brightest of all.

Now!

Fiona strode forward. The boarded-up door felt like warm treacle as she passed through it. Then suddenly she was inside a smoky, candlelit room and her nostrils were assailed by an overpowering scent of mint. It was the same cavern in which she had fought Miklos, and yet it wasn't. Gone was the cave interior illuminated by magick. Instead, the walls were plaster-smooth and covered with classical wall frescoes and a large mosaic decorated the now tessellated floor. Her eyes were drawn to

Miklos, glaring at her from beside his candle-crowded, rock altar.

"You!" He snarled, and the sound echoed slightly. His grip upon his glinting, ceremonial dagger tightened but he had yet to move.

Exploiting his delay, Fiona swiftly assessed her situation. There was now a mural depicting an arched, marble-looking gateway directly above the rock altar. That painted gateway would be where the rend would open. She must get herself onto the altar to complete her mission.

A crescendoing growl warned her that she had no more time to prepare. Miklos was already charging toward her.

* * * *

The haunting, stone splendor of Rosslyn Chapel appeared like an organic part of the surrounding Pentland Hills. Masonry curves echoed the hardy, rolling ground. Tall trees flourished like the plentiful spires. The chapel was isolated only from humanity, not from nature.

Rory vaulted the stone wall enclosing the chapel yard and crossed the tidy bit of lawn to the gravel pathway which circled the building. The pebbles crunched beneath his boots as he strode along the building's side. It was so dark and silent. He glanced up at the arched, stained glass windows. This edifice smelled of secrets and wore its quiet like a shroud.

At last he found a door, a rounded wooden door with black metal trappings. Rory started to reach out...and hesitated. Every nerve he had quivered. It was a perfectly normal old church door. He had seen doors like these before. But he had never tried to go through one. His stomach determinedly tried to twist its way out of his body. It was an unpleasant and unfamiliar feeling, and he hated it. He was used to being the predator, not the prey. His dark powers could not avail him in this place, and he knew it. Here he was not dangerous, he was in danger.

His instincts bellowed at him to retreat. Sanctity. He could smell it. Not just incense and candles. This was a blessed space. With crucifixes. It was not for the likes of him. His unclean flesh shrank from entering. So many things in this chapel could destroy him. What if he didn't even survive the threshold? Rory took a deep breath and steadied his mind. His fate might be uncertain, but Fiona's was sealed unless he entered this building.

Tentatively he touched the wood. It did not burn his fingers. Which made sense. A chapel is open to everyone. He could go in. He must go in. There was some sort of security, but he could pass under the door as vapor and never trigger the alarms. Rory closed his eyes. Combustion was quick. He'd heard it said it happened so fast you never felt a thing. So if this didn't work, he would never know. His only regret was that Fiona wouldn't know either. She wouldn't know of how he'd tried. Of how he had risked anything to save her. Rory tilted his head back. He felt lightheaded, then dizzy, then suddenly he had no weight at all and was floating toward the unknown.

* * * *

She had been doing so well.

Fiona swiped the blood from her cut lip as she rolled her bruised and aching body away from Miklos' charge. He was too close and she knew it. He was going to catch her trailing leg and there was nothing she could do. She felt his talons close around her ankle.

Suddenly she was on her back and being dragged across the blood and slime splattered floor. Miklos was hauling her away from the altar, outside the ceremonial circle. Fiona curled forward and struck at Miklos, embedding her stake in his scaly arm. With a grunt of pain, he released her ankle.

Fiona scrambled to her feet as Miklos wrenched her stake from his arm.

"Nothing is interfering with my ceremony," he growled.

Fiona heard cracking and splintering as the pressure of Miklos' fist crushed her stake. Then he abruptly tossed the wooden bits into his mouth.

"Ye *ate* my stake!" Fiona could not believe it. She also felt strangely insulted by the gesture.

Miklos smiled. "Now you do not possess the tools with which to complete your purpose."

Hands on her hips, Fiona stood and glared at him. This was ridiculous. There must be something else here made of wood. She raked her gaze over the altar with its dozens of red candles in sturdy, clear quartz holders. No wood. She glanced at Miklos. No joy there either. All he held was the polished, ceremonial dagger. The same dagger with which he had tortured Rory.

A dagger which injured vampires.

Which meant that in all likelihood it could be used kill vampires. She was in with a chance.

"I mayn't have the tools to complete my mission, but ye do."

The slightest hint of uncertainty briefly zipped across Miklos' countenance. "What?"

Fiona smiled. "I'll just be borrowing your magick dagger."

CHAPTER NINETEEN

He did not combust.

Rory crouched on the chapel's stone floor as he readjusted to solid form. His clothes had come across with him, so he had performed the shift correctly. But nonetheless, something was wrong. The stone floor was cool under his fingertips. Yet the air enveloping him felt thick, hot and cloying to the exposed skin of his face and hands. Was the chapel's atmosphere always so oppressive or was it him? He stood and stretched. It was like stretching into candy floss. He shook his head and a nauseating pain shot through his temples. It was undoubtedly him. His polluted flesh was unwelcome here. But there was no time to dwell upon that.

Rory crept up the south aisle, ignoring the air that seemed to cling and weigh him down. Even in this stifling environment, he could not fail to notice the splendor of the chapel's decoration. Its lofty, vaulted ceiling, flights of arches, stained glass, and intricate stonework were magnificent even in the dark.

The main altar was ahead on his left. He felt as if it were glowering at him, dissecting him as he approached. Such a simple, elegant thing. Nothing but a swathe of white cloth embroidered with gold thread, a pair of taper candles in slim, gold candlesticks, and a tall, gold cross. But it filled him with a sense of overpowering dread.

Pressing himself to the outer wall, Rory crept past the altar. It was terribly humid in here. The gold cross was too close, too close. His agitated instincts screamed at him to run. He focused on the flagstones beneath his feet. Squares. Rectangles. All sorts of odd sizes. Just a few more…a few more…and he was past. Rory took a deep breath, straightened and moved to the center of the aisle. The altar was behind him.

Ahead on the left, he could see his vine-bound target. Its beauty grew the closer he got. Rory paused in front of the pillar. Such a shame. He had never seen anything like the complex carving on this column. Hopefully the Holy Grail was in the center. Then he could preserve the dragons on the bottom and even perhaps the foliage on the top.

From the top of the pillar, Rory's eyes followed an attached stone beam as it crossed over the aisle and connected the pillar to the outer wall. His gaze continued on to the adjoining stained glass window, which was framed by a stonework arch of maize. *Maize?* He glanced again at the window. How did Indian corn come to be in a medieval chapel? Fiona would know. He would have plenty of time to ask her. She was going to live. The pillar had to be destroyed.

He turned back to the pillar but the stone beam once again caught his eye, as if part of the design were begging for closer inspection. Those lines were actually letters. There was writing carved into the beam. He struggled with the elongated script before recognizing it was Latin.

Hadaway, ye daftie. How could he ever suss its meaning? Latin had not crossed his thoughts in centuries--and his tutor had been of the mind that he hadn't thought much about it then either. But

THE CRIMSON FOLD

even as he turned away, part of his brain was attempting a translation. He glanced back.

Perhaps because the air did not seem so cloying, he could think better. Vocabulary he would have assumed long forgotten bubbled to the surface. The first line was *'Wine is strong'*.

Wine is strong. The king is stronger. Women are stronger still. Rory chuckled to himself. Fiona would like that line. But the translation was not complete.

Wine is strong. The king is stronger. Women are stronger still, but truth conquers all.

And the truth was that he must destroy a work of art to save the world. He shook his head. Truth was such an odd, subjective word. Such a shame that the crux of the prophecy involved it. *'True Belief'* could mean anything and nothing. For most vampires, the phrase would refer to Christianity. Yet Christian symbols could not destroy a vampire who predated the religion.

Why was that? He had never actually thought about it before. Never cared, to be honest. A belief's mere existence did not make it 'True,' did it? So why must the icon needed to crush a vampire depend upon the belief system in force at the time the vampire was created?

Rory's mind raced. He was on to something. The air felt almost sweet now. He had been afraid of this place but now it seemed...

He had been afraid.

He had feared this place because it was holy and he was its antithesis. Because he *believed* it was holy and he was its antithesis.

A surge of exhilaration spread through his frame. Belief exists in the minds of its followers. Crosses worked against post-Christian vampires because the vampires themselves believed. They recognized Christianity was their adversary and they believed the crosses would work. So...perhaps the *'True Belief'* they needed was simply a literal, absolute belief in something-- something that Miklos would also recognize.

Rory paced back and forth in front of the pillar, too excited to be still and not bothered about stealth any longer. His boot heels rang against the stone with a bell-like echo. It was a clarifying, almost encouraging, sound.

What did Miklos believe in? Power, of course. Revenge. Destruction. Although, the destruction was a side effect in this case. Acceptable collateral damage as part of raising his beloved Andromache.

Rory stopped pacing. Miklos was doing all this for love of Andromache. Miklos believed in love.

In which case, the pillar was safe. He did not need the Holy Grail. He did not need any icon. He had what they needed within him.

And Miklos would recognize it.

* * * *

Forehead resting on the cold stone floor, Fiona swore under her breath. Miklos just would not give up his dagger. Neither would he slay her, the contrary bastard. She started to push herself off the floor once again. It was getting more painful each time. She could taste her own blood in her mouth. It tasted bitter. She felt bitter.

Miklos was saying something, his arm upraised, the dagger pointed to the ceiling. He was continuing with his ceremony, despite having to fend her off between verses. Why did he not kill her? Perhaps he, too, reasoned her death at his hands might qualify as suicide, since this was to all intents and purposes a suicide mission. Or perhaps he just did not care enough to finish her off. His focus never shifted from the ceremony. She felt like a single biting midge, no more than an irritation to be swatted.

Just then a jaunty whistle sliced the air and echoed merrily about the stone chamber. Fiona's whole body twitched. That tune was unmistakable. It was the chorus of *Scotland the Brave*. The stirring notes sent shivers down her spine. Surely only one person would be whistling that here.

Fiona regained her feet. A human figure was approaching. A tall male. His face was shrouded in shadow, but that raffish swing to his stride was instantly recognizable.

Rory.

Miklos had frozen at the sound of the whistle. Slowly he turned his head to watch Rory's approach.

"Why are you here?" Miklos seemed to snarl each individual word.

Rory shrugged. "I'm here for high endeavors, like the song says."

"Nothing but destruction awaits you."

"I see we're of similar minds."

"What do you mean by that?" Miklos snapped.

Rory grinned. "I've come to witness your destruction." He dodged around Miklos and ran to Fiona's side. "Ye are hurt." He reached out to touch her cheek.

She stepped away. "Only a wee bit."

He caught her arm, preventing her from moving further away from him. "Ye dinna have to lose, pet."

"Dinna do this. Nothing's changed."

"Aye, it has. I solved it." Rory beamed.

"What are ye on about?" She glanced over at Miklos who was taking advantage of her distraction to complete the next step in his ceremony. "Ye are jeopardizing the world with this delay."

"That bit about True Belief. I solved it. I ken we dinna have the time now, but I'll explain it to ye later." Rory placed his hands upon her shoulders. His grip was gentle yet the gesture was enough to command her full attention. He stared directly into her eyes with such intensity she felt disconcerted. "Just focus on the fact that I believe in ye. I love ye."

"But what…"

"And I believe I love ye more than Miklos loves his Andromache." Rory released her. "Now go kick his head in."

A gasp of painful laughter escaped Fiona's lips. "Bless ye, but I canna--"

"Aye, ye can. I believe."

* * * *

Was there a non-smoking section of the ceremony? Joan pressed her hand over her mouth and nose. The vortex had been exactly where the undead thing said it would be, but he hadn't mentioned the whole secondhand smoke issue. And what was up with the minty freshness? Not to mention the vibrating ground.

Joan steadied herself against Euan's side as her eyes adjusted to the candlelight. Plaster, or whatever the walls were made of, was falling off in chunks and shattering on the tiled floor, which was beginning to show little, zipping cracks itself. And the noise! All the shattering and splintering was gradually growing into a reverberation that sounded like thunder on steroids. Apparently they had skipped the previews and passed straight into the apocalypse.

Yet the dead thing ... Rory ... never moved.

There was an aura around him, as if he had been colored over with blue highlighter pen. He stood, his legs braced slightly apart, his arms at his sides and his fists clenched, watching Fiona fight. No, more like staring at the battle, as if by sheer strength of mind alone he could will Fiona to win. The room was tearing itself apart. Everything was falling down around him. But he never wavered.

A deep bellow yanked Joan's attention back to the fight. Fiona must have gotten a piece of that giant fiend Miklos. She pressed her advantage but Miklos backhanded her. Fiona's head swung from the force of the blow, her hair flew back and Joan caught a glimpse of blood oozing out from her ear.

Miklos returned to his altar, attempting to continue his ritual. Joan could not allow that to happen. *Showtime.*

Lurching across the fracturing floor, Joan flung herself at Miklos' back. The force of her strike would have driven her stake clean through a normal vampire, but not this scaly skin. It hardly even dented him. Miklos swiveled like a crazy bull, throwing Joan off with humiliating ease. She crashed into the floor, barely managing to keep her grip on her stake and losing her breath entirely. As her lungs thrashed for air, Miklos turned, his arm upraised to slash her out of existence.

Suddenly Fiona was standing above her, parrying his blow, defending Joan from the fearsome demon. What was she doing? Joan hadn't asked for this. She didn't want this. She didn't want aid from a vampire. On her elbows and knees, Joan squirmed clear of Fiona's legs. She was behind Fiona now. She stood.

Fiona was still intently deflecting Miklos' blows. Her undefended back was so close. And Joan had a sacred duty.

It would only take one swing.

Joan swiped at Fiona with her stake. Fiona whirled as if she had heard the stake cutting through the air and caught Joan's stake hand by the wrist.

"Not here." Her voice was deep with anger and her fingers bit into Joan's flesh.

A terse, frustrated shriek escaped Joan's lips. "You're a *vampire*, remember? Get with the evil bloodlust!"

"Havenae the time. Saving the world, me. What are ye doing?"

With her free hand, Joan chopped Fiona's wrist, breaking her grip. Joan whirled away, noticing as she did that Miklos was standing like he was stuck on pause. Had he been human she would have said he was confused. *Join the club.*

Fiona smacked the demon a good one across the nose and the fight was on again. Joan started to launch herself back into the fray but Euan grabbed her arm.

"Fiona's not your enemy," Euan shouted over the rumbling.

Fiona's body sailed past them, hit the wall, and slid down with a shower of broken plaster. It looked bad, but Fiona was already moving, shaking her head and climbing laboriously to her feet. For an instant, she looked in Joan's direction and their eyes met.

Joan still expected to see a stranger there, a vampire. But somehow it was just Fiona. Research girl. The one who remembered how she liked her tea. The one who always had her back--even today, even now.

As she watched, Fiona charged toward Miklos once more. She was very determined. Joan could be just as determined. When she had to be. But maybe Euan was right. Maybe defeating the Miklos portion of evil was enough for now. She'd take the Miklos path in the wood and leave the other path to do some other time. She would fulfill her duty, all right. But just maybe not today.

Joan glared at Euan as she jerked her arm away from him. "Fine. Whatever."

Then a flicker of white light caught her attention. Over by the wall with the painted gateway, a glowing fissure was gradually forming as if there were an invisible curtain in front of the mural and it was slowly being parted.

Joan swore. "She's just delaying the ceremony, not stopping it."

"Is that the rend?" Euan asked.

"What do you think?"

"Wait …wait ... Rory said Andromache was going to pass through the rend in the veil…"

THE CRIMSON FOLD

"What am I waiting for?"

Euan's eyes were tightly shut. "I'm trying to remember what Uncle Hamish said about matter transference, if you'll have a little patience."

"Take your time. I'm sure the apocalypse will wait just for you."

"It's not like I thought this would ever be useful." Euan held his fingertips to his forehead. "The rend is already open, which means that transference is irrevocable. Something must pass through. Ah! But it can pass through either way." His head jerked up. "All we need do is shove Miklos through the veil."

"That's all, huh?"

"Yes. Once he passes through, the rend will seal and reality will be safe." He smiled. "And he'll be with his Andromache so it will be a good thing all around, really."

"You're totally dewy-eyed puppies and Christmas ever after, aren't you," Joan commented, shaking her head.

"Speak to me when you learn proper English. Now go tell Fiona to shove him through." He gave her a little push.

"I'm going, I'm going."

Joan staggered as quickly as she could across the heaving floor. Both Miklos and Fiona had also seen the growing split in front of the painted gateway, and their struggle had taken on a new kind of desperation as Miklos tried to complete his ceremony and Fiona tried to stop him. Miklos connected a ferocious punch and Joan dodged Fiona's body as it skated across the broken tiles of the floor.

She jumped to Fiona's side and offered her a hand up. Fiona met her eyes like she had never doubted her and clasped her hand.

"We must push him through the rend," Joan said as she pulled Fiona to her feet.

"Sorry?"

The room was thundering way too loud.

"Push him through," Joan yelled. She pointed at the radiant tear.

Fiona gave her a quick nod, turned and charged Miklos. She tackled him around his knees and took him down. As they wrestled on the floor, Joan realized Fiona was gradually moving the demon closer to the gateway. Miklos broke away. He struggled to stand on the shaking floor, but Joan rushed forward and pushed him over. He rolled on the cracked tiles. His body slid up against the altar, beneath the glowing rend. His head jerked in Rory's direction and his eyes widened. Perhaps he hadn't noticed the whole blue scene Rory had going.

"MacLaren!" Miklos roared. "Do not dare--"

Fiona pounced on Miklos. She was glowing now, too--the same blue aura that coated Rory. Miklos writhed and sliced at her, but

Fiona grasped his neck. Even though her two hands could not encompass his thick throat, somehow she was lifting him up by his neck. He was taller than her, yet he could not get his feet under him. Fiona was unstoppable. She raised Miklos before the gleaming rip and then whirled and heaved him into it like a sack of potatoes. Miklos disappeared into the white light.

For an instant Joan thought the momentum of her toss would carry Fiona through the rend as well, but Rory bounded across. His arms wrapped around Fiona's waist, catching her, anchoring her to this side of the veil. The glowing rip sealed upon itself, disappeared, and the destruction stopped. For one excruciating moment the room was cloaked in an eerie, utter silence, broken only by the hushed hiss of a few guttering candles. Then the entire room lurched wildly on its side, plunging into pitch darkness with a thundering boom.

Joan tumbled into someone, probably Euan. All tangled legs and arms, they slid painfully into the wall that was currently occupying the space where the floor should be. But even in this chaos, Joan never lost hold of her stake. Not when there were still vampires around.

Using the palm of one hand and the closed fist of her other, Joan extricated herself from the other person. She couldn't see anything. There was no way to tell who was near her or what was happening. She was helpless. Her heart pounded in her ears. Suddenly the room was moving again, listing like sinking ship. Joan scrabbled at the wall with her free hand but there was no purchase.

Iron fingers clamped around her wrist. Joan twisted in the direction of the interloper but even as she moved, her body was being raised by her wrist as if she were weightless. Then she was staring straight into a pair of red, glowing coals.

Vampire eyes.

Joan's stomach coiled on reflex.

"Time to go!" The voice was Fiona's, shouting to be heard as the room rumbled and tilted again. Somehow she was managing to maintain her footing and hold Joan upright as well.

"Euan's through!" That was Rory, his words just barely intelligible over the rolling thunder. "Hoy her o'er!"

"Don't you dare," Joan began, but Fiona tossed her like a rag doll before she could get any more words out.

Her flight was stopped by hands roughly catching her around the midriff. Instinctively Joan squirmed and swung her stake. "Let me go!"

"Ye dinna want to stop here, hen." Rory's voice again.

Rory pushed her away and for the second time that night she had the unexpected sensation of falling through warm syrup. Then she was suddenly tumbling across hard stones and into the

THE CRIMSON FOLD

middle of a cold, moonlit puddle on drizzly, deserted World's End Close.

CHAPTER TWENTY

Fiona rolled out onto the wet cobblestones, sprang to her feet and anxiously looked back for Rory. Through the misty rain, the air shimmered and then Rory appeared in mid-leap, landing effortlessly beside her. The air shimmered behind him and then went still as the vortex closed. All was silent except the peaceful patter of the rain. Just a common or garden night on World's End Close.

Rory seized Fiona's shoulders and pulled her tightly against his chest. "Are ye all right?" he mumbled into her hair.

Fiona nestled against him. The truth was her whole body ached, some bits sharper than others. Yet when he held her, everything seemed less painful. She felt so warm and protected in his embrace. This was where she belonged.

"Whey aye," she sighed.

He chuckled. "Give us a cuddle, then."

She hugged him. The back of his leather coat was just beginning to feel slick from the beaded, cool raindrops. Rory was kissing her damp hair. She raised her face to his. His lips captured hers before she could speak. The kiss was long and deep and she could taste what was probably her own blood but it didn't matter. Everything tasted delicious.

"Very romantic." Joan's tone was cold.

Warily, Fiona disengaged herself from Rory. Joan and Euan were standing a little way down the close. They were damp and their clothes a little mucky, but they seemed unhurt. Euan was actually smiling. Unfortunately, Joan was not. And she was brandishing her stake in a very unfriendly manner.

"What d'ye intend to do now?" asked Fiona.

Joan shrugged. "Well, I was thinking of a wicked ice-cream pig-out, but then I remembered, hey, you're a vampire."

Rory protectively stepped in front of Fiona, his very stance menacing, primed to attack. Joan twirled her stake and tensed, set for Rory's charge. Fiona grabbed his arm.

"We arenae fighting her," Fiona commanded, moving to block his progress. "Not even in self-defense."

He grinned toothily, eager for action. "Och, but if she's *asking...*"

"Still think you can be friends with monsters?" Joan asked Euan, emphasizing the last word by pointing her stake in Rory's general direction.

Fiona glanced at Euan. He was still smiling gently.

"I don't see monsters," Euan calmly replied.

Joan shook her head. "Calling Euan's brain--come back, all is forgiven."

He raised one eyebrow. "Forgiven, precisely."

"Is that supposed to be irony or sarcasm?" retorted Joan, fists resting on her hips. "Because I get those two mixed up."

"It's meant to be sardonic, if anything."

Joan glared at him.

"But more to the point, it means I believe in the forgiveness of sins."

Joan rolled her eyes. "Oh, yeah, I was forgetting. Deacon alert."

"Dinna be rude to the man," Fiona chastised her.

"Me?" Joan was outraged. "You're the one always calling him a Sassenach."

"And I was wrong," Fiona answered quietly. "I see that now. I shouldnae have allowed my past experiences with a few Sassenachs to prejudice me for all time against all Sassenachs…er…Englishmen."

Joan scowled. "You're just saying that because he wants me to spare you."

"If you were listening to what she said, there is a rather piquant parallel…" Euan began, but Joan turned on him.

"No, there is no parallel. No paralleling," she snapped.

Euan sighed impatiently. "Then might I at least suggest an armistice? I'm wet and I could quite do with a spot of tea."

"I don't see how I can walk away. They're still standing and I still have a stake."

With startling swiftness, Euan reached out and snatched Joan's stake from her hand. "Now you don't."

"I…I…give that back!"

"Stuff that for a game of soldiers."

"Huh?"

"The answer is no. You shan't be playing Kilkenny cats while I'm about. I've better things to do than watch your mutual destruction." Euan folded his arms across his chest. "I helped save the world and I deserve dry clothes, a nice fire, and scones heaped with enough clotted cream to surpass the recommended caloric intake of the entire village of Ullapool."

Joan's face seemed caught between glowering and giggling. "Seriously, give me back my stake."

"Seriously, I will not. Now let's have a go at the armistice idea."

The rain spattered on the cobblestones through a long, dark silence as everyone tensely watched each other and waited for someone to make the next move. But a guarded feeling of hope was rising within Fiona. It wasn't like Joan to wait if she were going to attack. The rain continued to patter, cool and refreshing.

"I can disarm you, you realize," Joan finally stated.

"I wouldn't if I were you," Euan replied. "Nessie could very well be in my back garden and I shan't invite you if you're naughty."

"I'm not laughing. You're trying to give me a graceful way out of doing my duty and it's very condescending of you."

"Perhaps. But only a fool ignores a graceful way out."

The rain pattered a moment more before Joan nodded slowly. "All right. We'll truce it. But you keep him in line," Joan ordered Fiona, pointing at Rory.

"Aye, of course."

Rory stepped behind Fiona and wrapped his arms around her midriff, holding her close. "Now we're all mates again, let's gang 'round to Fiona's. Some of us are gasping for a drop of haggis."

Fiona sighed. Keeping Rory in line might be a full-time situation. "Ye are dead irrepressible, ye are."

"Haggis? Wicked gross." Joan stuck her tongue out, clasped her throat and made exaggerated gagging noises.

Euan laughed. "I'll thank you not to insult my national dish." He paused. "A *drop* of...?"

Fiona made hushing motions at Euan, which Joan luckily did not notice as she was still being mock sick. Euan took the hint.

"Shall we be walking, then?" he asked, quickly changing the subject. "I reckon Fiona's is the closest."

Joan shrugged. "You're the one with my stake." She fell into step beside Euan. Rory and Fiona followed them down the close and out onto the street.

Joan glanced over her shoulder at Fiona as she walked. "So why did the room self-destruct?"

"Andromache probably created that room when she was conjuring her original spell," Euan answered. "Then when her spell went wrong, the space was stuck, if you will. Waiting for a resolution. Which tonight it finally got and thus the need for it to exist ceased."

Joan smiled at Euan. "Is there anything you don't know?"

"Yes." Euan looked back at Rory. "What was your blue aura about, then?"

"Whisht," Rory hissed at Euan. He glanced uncomfortably, almost shyly, at Fiona, then swiftly looked away.

Euan was enjoying Rory's embarrassment. "It was the power of your belief in--or your love for--Fiona, wasn't it? Go on, tell us about it."

"Ye mingin nyaff..."

"While I'm not admitting that demons can feel love," Joan interrupted. "How did you know that your whatever-passes-for-vampire-true-love was stronger than Miklos' same deal for Andromache?"

"No," Euan corrected. "Based on what Rory told us when he returned from Rosslyn…"

"Yeah, I didn't listen to that part. Too philo-boring," commented Joan before Euan could finish.

Fiona turned to Rory. "Ye went to Rosslyn Chapel?"

He nodded.

Fiona's breath caught in her throat. To have entered such a sacred place--had he hazarded that for her? Love brimmed from her throat right the way down to her toes and threatened to overwhelm her. She wanted to bask in the sheer joy of it. Rory was magnificent. If only she could have seen the chapel with him. It was widely held to be a marvel.

"Was the chapel pure canny gorgeous?" she asked, breathless.

He smiled at her tenderly. "Aye, it was that an' all."

"The real question," Euan announced, raising his voice to be heard over the general chatter. "Is how did *Miklos* recognize that Rory's love was stronger?"

Everyone gazed at Rory.

He ducked his head. His pale skin seemed to ever so slightly blush. "I can only say…I knew Miklos was willing to kill for Andromache. But Miklos knew I was willing to die for Fiona."

* * * *

Their victory celebration had been quite the success. Comfortably full of tea, scones and clotted cream, Joan had fallen asleep on Fiona's claw-footed sofa, slouched against Euan's shoulder. Euan's head was tilted toward hers and he was snoring softly.

Rory looked up from where he lay sprawled on the carpeted lounge floor. "Bonnie couple," he commented, indicating the slumbering pair.

"Aye." Fiona shifted her position so she could pillow her head on Rory's chest.

"Not so bonnie as us, though," Rory added with jocular seriousness, as if he had been studying them for appraisal.

Fiona giggled. This had turned out to be a champion day. She felt Rory tousle her hair.

"So shall we be married, then?"

Her breath caught in her throat. Was he sincere? Marriage was not a state commonly entered into by their sort. But then, they had convinced Joan they were uncommon vampires. And she loved him terribly. Perhaps it was not such a dodgy undertaking after all.

If he were in earnest.

Fiona stretched, attempting a nonchalance she did not feel. "That's nae way to ask a lass."

"Right." He gently shook her shoulder. "Up, up."

She groaned in protest but stood nevertheless. Before she even realized what he meant to do, Rory had swiftly moved into a kneeling position at her feet. Tenderly he took her hands in his and kissed the palm of first one, then the other. Prickles zipped up Fiona's arms at the touch of his lips on her skin. Slowly he raised his eyes to hers.

"*Cha toigh leam neach ach thusa. Am pòs thu mi?*" His eyes shone--not with a vampiric red glow but with very human love.

"What'd he say?" Joan murmured sleepily from the sofa.

"He said--"

"I'm willing to repeat it," Rory interrupted, smiling. "I love nobody but ye. Will ye marry me?"

"Ding, ding--last stop, Crazy-town. Everybody out." Joan yawned and snuggled closer to Euan.

Fiona grinned. "She may think I'm mad, and mayhap I am, but…yes. I will marry ye."

Rory jumped to his feet and swept her into his arms. He lowered his head to kiss her but she stopped him.

"Ye will be promising to love none but me for a very long time," she warned. "Do ye truly wish to be held to such a promise?"

"*A Fhionnseach, mo ghaol.*" Rory chuckled. "Did I not already say I love none but ye? In truth, ye are my only love in nigh three hundred years, give or take a decade or two. I fancy ye shall be my only love for at least three hundred more." He playfully kissed the tip of her nose. "Can ye make me the same promise?"

Fiona grinned. "What, to love ye for three hundred years? Aye, I reckon I could, if pressed."

"Cheeky lass." Rory's hands flew to her sides and he started tickling her. Fiona tried to squirm away, caught in a fit of giggles. Her laughing shrieks awakened Euan.

"Might you take that outside, please?" Euan mumbled, good-naturedly but not fully awake. "Civilized people sleep at this hour."

Joan grunted in agreement.

"We're away." Rory took hold of Fiona's hand and with eager speed pulled her toward the front door.

"Where are we going?" she asked between puffs and giggles.

"Top of Arthur's Seat. I wish to share the impressive view…among other things."

Fiona could not have felt happier as she followed Rory out to greet the magickal, Samhain night.

The End

WITHDRAWN FROM
BEEBE LIBRARY
WAKEFIELD, MA

WITHDRAWN FROM
BEEBE LIBRARY
WAKEFIELD, MA